HAMMOND INNES

Hammond Innes was born in Sussex in 1913. He has now written twenty-nine international bestsellers, including most recently *Isvik* and *Target Antarctica*, both available in Pan. He has also written a superb history of the Conquistadors, two books of his world travels and sailing, and an evocative illustrated book on East Anglia. It was in the early fifties, with books like *The Lonely Skier*, *Campbell's Kingdom*, *The White South* and *The Mary Deare*, all of them filmed, that he achieved international fame. Hammond Innes' knowledge of the sea, so evident in his books, comes from his very considerable experience of ocean racing and cruising.

Antarctica – explorers, sealers, whalers – it was a world that Hammond Innes could not resist. In Norway, at Blombaag Hval, he boarded a catcher and went north into the Arctic with Captain Schulstok to see how the whale skippers kept their hands in while waiting for the next expedition to the White South of Antarctica. 'It was all there,' he says, 'the characters, the ships, the techniques, the language – everything I needed.'

Also by Hammond Innes

FICTION

Wreckers Must Breathe
The Trojan Horse
Attack Alarm
Dead and Alive
The Lonely Skier
Maddon's Rock
Killer Mine
The Blue Ice
The Angry Mountain
Air Bridge
Campbell's Kingdom
The Strange Land
The Mary Deare
The Land God Gave to Cain
The Doomed Oasis
Atlantic Fury
The Strode Venturer

Levkas Man
Golden Soak
North Star
The Big Footprints
The Last Voyage
Solomon's Seal
The Black Tide
High Stand
Medusa
Isvik
Target Antarctica

TRAVEL

Harvest of Journeys
Sea and Islands

HISTORY

The Conquistadors

HAMMOND INNES

THE WHITE SOUTH

PAN BOOKS

First published 1949 by Collins

This edition published 1996 by Pan Books
an imprint of Macmillan General Books
Cavaye Place London SW10 9PG
and Basingstoke

Associated companies throughout the world

ISBN 0–330–34219–3

1 3 5 7 9 8 6 4 2

A CIP catalogue record for this book is available from
the British Library

Phototypeset by Intype, London
Printed and bound in Great Britain

CONTENTS

1   DISASTER IN THE ANTARCTIC   1

2   DUNCAN CRAIG'S STORY OF   13
THE LOSS OF THE 'SOUTHERN
CROSS', THE CAMP ON THE
ICEBERG, AND THE TREK
THAT FOLLOWED

3   THE SURVIVORS   368

CHAPTER ONE

DISASTER IN THE ANTARCTIC

Dawn was breaking as the first news of the disaster reached London. It was 10th February and the rattle of milk bottles was the only sound in the black, frost-bound streets. Up in the City, Covent Garden and Billingsgate were halfway through the day's work and the pubs were open. In nearby Fleet Street a Reuter's operator was handed a news flash and his fingers ran automatically over the keys of his machine as he transmitted the message to subscribers. Two blocks away, in the office of a big London daily, a sleepy subeditor heard the clack of the message as it came through on the teleprinter. He watched it as the carriage of the machine jerked back and forth. Then the yellow tongue of paper was thrust through the slit in the glass top. He tore it off and stood there reading it:

CAPETOWN FEB 10 REUTER: SOS RECEIVED FROM FACTORY SHIP SOUTHERN CROSS. SHIP IS CAUGHT IN ICE IN WEDDELL SEA

1

AND IN DANGER OF BEING CRUSHED.
NORWEGIAN FACTORY SHIP HAAKON 400
MILES FROM POSITION OF SOUTHERN
CROSS GOING TO RESCUE.

REUTER 0713

The sub-editor yawned, tossed the sheet of paper into the news basket and returned to the work of subbing a feature page article. In a big office block in Fenchurch Street, the telephone rang incessantly on the third floor. These were the offices of the South Antarctic Whaling Company and only the cleaners were there. The telephone went unanswered. In Whitehall, at the Admiralty, a messenger hurried along the empty, echoing corridors. He handed a message to the duty officer. The duty officer rubbed the sleep out of his eyes, read the message through, placed it in a basket marked 'for immediate attention' and inquired about tea. High up above Queen Victoria Street an operator at one of the switchboards in Faraday Buildings noted the urgency of an incoming call from Capetown and searched the telephone directory. Then she switched the call from the offices of the South Antarctic Whaling Company to the flat of Albert Jenssen in South Kensington.

Albert Jenssen was still in bed. The telephone woke him and he was half asleep as he groped for the receiver and lifted it to his ear. A moment later and he was sitting up in bed, wide awake and speaking rapidly into the phone. When he had finished, he replaced the receiver automatically and sat there for a moment,

2

regardless of the cold air that blew in through the open windows, a dazed expression on his face. Then he fell upon the telephone and call after call went out from the flat in South Kensington: cables to Durban, the Falkland Islands and the whaling stations of South Georgia; calls to Sandefjord and Tönsberg in Norway, to Leith in Scotland, to the BBC, to a Cabinet Minister and finally to the Admiralty. The duty officer at the Admiralty was forced to abandon his second cup of tea and interrupt an admiral in the midst of shaving.

And by eight o'clock messages were pouring over the ether: Admiralty to C.-in-C. American West Indies; Admiralty to H.M. Sloop *Walrus*, at Port Stanley in the Falklands; Director South African Naval Forces, Capetown, to Admiralty, London; British Broadcasting Corporation to Australian Broadcasting Commission. And as the official messages increased in a desperate effort to avert disaster, the news agencies joined in and the tempo grew – Reuter's Correspondent, Capetown, to Reuter's London; U.P. to New York; Tass to Moscow; Havas to –

By midday more than 150 million people knew that a ship of 22,000 tons belonging to a British whaling company was locked in the grip of the Antarctic ice and was being slowly crushed. As they sat at their desks or worked in their factories they were secretly thrilled at the thought of over 400 men face to face with death in the pitiless, frozen wastes of the Antarctic.

The Admiralty ordered the sloop, *Walrus*, to

proceed to South Georgia, refuel and then make an attempt to reach the *Southern Cross*. A South African naval corvette was dispatched from Capetown, also with orders to refuel at South Georgia. The Board of Trade diverted a tanker, unloading in Durban, to South Georgia to fuel search vessels. *Det Norske Hvalselskab* of Sandefjord, Norway, announced that their factory ship, *Haakon*, which had steered for the *Southern Cross* within half an hour of receiving the first SOS at 03.18 hours, was now within 200 miles of the ship's last position. The United States government offered the services of the aircraft carrier *Ohio* then cruising off the River Plate.

Meanwhile events moved fast in the Antarctic. An early report that the *Southern Cross* had dynamited an area of clear water and was being warped round, was followed by the news that the way out of the ice was blocked by several icebergs which were charging into the pack. The tanker, *Josephine*, and the refrigerator ship, *South*, were standing by on the edge of the pack, together with the rest of the South Antarctic Company's fleet, unable to do anything. By midday the whole of the starboard side of the *Southern Cross* was buckling under the pressure of the ice, and at 14.17 hours Captain Eide, the master, gave the order to abandon ship. In a final message before unloading the radio equipment on to the ice, Eide warned the *Haakon* not to enter the ice beyond the line of the icebergs. That was the last message received from the *Southern Cross*.

All that night the lights blazed in the South Antarctic Whaling Company's offices in Fenchurch Street. But no message came through from the survivors. Utter silence had closed down on the abandoned ship and it was clear that this was the worst sea disaster in peacetime since the *Titanic* went down in 1912.

The most detailed picture of the events leading up to the disaster available on the morning of the 11th was contained in a feature article in London's largest daily. The writer's main sources of information were Jenssen, London manager of the South Antarctic Whaling Company, the company's agent in Capetown, the Admiralty, *Det Norske Hvalselskab* and the files of his office library. The article gave the full story of the South Antarctic Company's whaling expedition. It was headed – DISASTER IN THE ANTARCTIC – and read:

'The *Southern Cross* left the Clyde on 16th October last with a total of 411 men and boys. In charge of the expedition was Bernt Nordahl, factory manager. Hans Eide was master and as assistant manager was Erik Bland, son of the chairman of the South Antarctic Whaling Company. About 78 per cent of those on board were Norwegians, mainly from Sandefjord and Tönsberg. The rest were British. With her sailed an ex-Admiralty corvette, converted to act as a whale-towing vessel, and the refrigerator ship, *South*.

'The *Southern Cross* arrived at Capetown on 14th November where her catchers and a tanker were waiting for her. The expedition sailed on 23rd November. The fleet then consisted of the factory ship, a vessel of 22,160 tons, 10 whale catchers, each of under 300 tons, two buoy boats (catchers used for towing), three ex-naval corvettes for towing whales, one refrigerator ship. One of the towing vessels was later sent back to Capetown to pick up electric harpoon equipment. The company intended to experiment during the season with the electrocution of whales, a method of killing that was in its infancy prior to the war.

'The whaling season in the Antarctic is of four months' duration – December, January, February, March. These are the summer months and whaling expeditions are limited to a certain period by inter-national agreement in an attempt to preserve the whale and allow uninterrupted breeding. Unrestricted killing during the last century in the Arctic resulted in the complete extermination of whale in the Northern Hemisphere for many years. The present season for fin whale opened on 9th December. But prior to that, operations are permitted against the sperm whale. Most expeditions avail themselves of this in order to test equipment. This season, apart from the South Ant-arctic Company's expedition, there were eighteen others – ten Norwegian, four British, one Dutch, one Russian and two Japanese.

'On 29th November the *Southern Cross* sighted South Georgia and was in radio-telephone communi-cation with the shore-based whaling stations on this island. They reported unprecedentedly bad conditions. Temperatures were much lower than normal with pack ice still piled against the western and southern shores of the island. Their catchers, operating in a 200-mile radius, spoke of heavy drift ice with bergs much more frequent and much bigger than usual. On 2nd

December the *Southern Cross* commenced operations, her catchers killing 36 sperm whale in seven days, despite low temperatures and severe gales. On 9th December she began full-scale operations. She was then about 200 miles west of South Thule, the most southerly of the Sandwich Group, and steaming south-west. Reports of both Nordahl, the factory manager, and Captain Eide, the master, to the London office all spoke of violent and incessant gales, low temperatures, loose pack ice and an unusually large number of gigantic icebergs.

'Whale seemed very scarce by comparison with the previous bumper season and on Boxing Day Nordahl reported trouble with the men. This is almost unheard of in Norwegian or British whaling fleets where the men have a financial interest in the catch. But when Jenssen was pressed for further details he said he had no statement to make on the matter.

'The matter must have been serious, however, for Colonel Bland, chairman of the company, left London Airport on 2nd of January for Capetown in a privately chartered plane. He undertook the journey against the advice of his doctors. He had been seriously ill for some time with heart trouble. With him went his daughter-in-law, a German technical adviser on the electrical harpoon and Aldo Bonomi, the well-known photographer. His daughter-in-law, Mrs Judie Bland, is the daughter of Bernt Nordahl. On 3rd January news was received at the London office that Nordahl, the leader of the expedition, had disappeared the previous night, presumed lost overboard.

'Colonel Bland arrived at Capetown early on the 6th and left the same night, together with Nordahl's daughter, in the towing boat which had been dispatched to collect the new harpoon equipment. On reaching the *Southern Cross* on the 17th Colonel Bland assumed control of the expedition. Only 127 whale had been caught at that time against a previous season's total of 214. In a week of bad gales the ten catchers had only brought in 6 whale. Bland sent his catchers out in a wide search. They found heavy pack ice to the south and south-east and one of the catchers had difficulty in extricating itself from the ice. All catchers reported few whale. Meanwhile radio contact had been established with the *Haakon*, 600 miles to the south-west. The Norwegian ship reported whale in plenty. Colonel Bland decided on the 18th to steam south. A great deal of loose pack was encountered, but on the 23rd the vessels were in open sea in Lat. 66.01 S., Long 35.62 W. with an abundance of whale.

'Operations from the 23rd January to 5th February produced 167 whale. On the 6th and 7th there was a bad storm and on the night of the 7th one of the catchers, which had run into the ice for shelter, damaged its rudder on a floe. When the wind had died down a catcher and a corvette were sent to its assistance. But in the early hours of the 8th these two vessels were in collision in the ice, one of them being sunk and the other set on fire. The mishap occurred about 120 miles south-east of the *Southern Cross* and within sight of the catcher they had come to rescue. Both crews were reported safe on the ice with the loss of two men.

'Another corvette was sent to the assistance of the three vessels. Meanwhile, the *Southern Cross*, which had already refuelled from the tanker, completed the transfer of whale oil to this ship. On the night of the 8th the corvette reported that heavy pack ice was preventing her from approaching nearer than 20 miles to the damaged catchers. No further news had been received from these vessels.

'The wind had risen again to gale force. But despite this the *Southern Cross* herself went to the assistance of the catchers. At 6.30 p.m. on the 9th she sighted the corvette, which had run into loose pack in order to shelter from the heavy seas. The whole fleet was then together with the exception of the three missing catchers, for owing to the bad conditions no catchers had been sent out after whale. A conference was held on the *Southern Cross* and it was decided to steam into the pack ice, following leads which ran east and west in the direction of the damaged vessels.

'It is not difficult to picture the scene. The *Southern Cross*, big and squat like an enormous tanker with her fat funnels aft, steaming into the ice, the sea slopping about in the stern hole through which the whales are drawn up on to the after-plan. There is a gale blowing and the *Southern Cross* is steaming into it, steaming against the whole weight of the pack ice thrust westwards by the howling fury of the wind. All round her is loose pack – a flat, broken plain of white, glimmering in that peculiar twilight that is night in a region where the sun never sets. The loose pack draws closer together until it is solid pack ice. There are icebergs now and they are smashing into the pack. And the great ship steams steadily on along a lead of black water that winds deeper and deeper into the ice, past the icebergs, right into the heart of the danger area.

'Was it madness to go on, risking all for a handful of lives? That factory ship represented nearly £3,000,000 of money and on board were over 400 lives. What drove Colonel Bland on? What made him take the risk? What about his officers – didn't they warn him? A ship like that, of 22,000 tons, with specially strengthened bows, can smash through ice 12 feet thick. But if those jagged edges once grip her thin steel plates, they can smash her in no time. Didn't he realize the danger? Or was the lead so narrow that once they were in it they couldn't turn back, but had to go on?

'The truth of the matter we may never know. All we know at the moment is that at 03.18 hours on 10th February the *Southern Cross* was firmly beset by the ice and she was sending out an SOS. Sometime during the night that lead must have come to an end. The westward-driven pack ice closed round her and in a matter of hours she was gone.

'That a ship of 22,000 tons should be crushed so easily may seem strange to those who remember that Filchner and Shackleton, beset in much smaller vessels in this same Weddell Sea, existed for months in the ice and saved themselves in the end. But these men were explorers. Their ships were specially built for the ice.

The sheer sides of the *Southern Cross* were never designed to withstand the huge lateral thrust of ice piled up into pressure ridges by the battering force of giant icebergs.

'For the full story of what happened we must await the reports of survivors. In the meantime, it is to be hoped that the Government and other whaling companies will do all in their power to speed the rescue of these men. They probably have good stores of whale-meat and blubber on the ice with them. But their equipment is unlikely to be very good and they clearly cannot survive a winter in the Antarctic.'

So much for the story of the *Southern Cross* disaster, as the public knew it then. It was a nine days' wonder that ousted everything else from the headlines of the world's newspapers. Then, as the rescue attempts dragged on without success, it quietly faded out. Interest revived momentarily when the United States aircraft carrier, *Ohio*, arrived on the scene and flew its first sorties. But bad weather hindered the search. And since the failure of protracted rescue attempts is not news and public interest wanes rapidly in the face of negative results, the fact that well over 400 men were marooned somewhere in the Weddell Sea was forgotten.

By the middle of March winter was setting in. Conditions became very cold with new ice beginning to form. By the 22nd all search vessels had turned back. They refuelled at Grytviken in South Georgia and proceeded to their bases. By 15th April Jan Eriksen, factory manager of the *Nord Hvalstasjon*, Grytviken, reported to his company: *All search vessels have now left Gryrviken.* Haakon *and rest of Det Norske Hvalselskab fleet passed within 100 miles South Georgia yesterday on their way back to Capetown. There are now no vessels in the area of the tragedy. Winter is closing in. If any survivors are still alive, God help them – for no man can until summer. I am preparing to close down the station.*

That report wrote *finis* to all attempts to rescue any possible survivors of the *Southern Cross*. It was dispatched to the offices of the *Nord Syd Georgia Hvalselskab* in Oslo and Eriksen began the work of closing the whaling station at Grytviken as the Antarctic winter closed in on the ice-capped island of South Georgia.

But the story doesn't end there, for on 21st April, two days before he sailed with his men for Capetown, Eriksen radioed a message that set linotypes and presses the world over rolling out the name *Southern Cross* in great, flaring headlines. For, on the 21st April –

But this is Duncan Craig's story. Let him tell it.

CHAPTER TWO

DUNCAN CRAIG'S STORY

OF THE LOSS OF THE 'SOUTHERN CROSS', THE CAMP ON THE ICEBERG, AND THE TREK THAT FOLLOWED

ONE

I did not actually join the *Southern Cross* until 17 January, only three weeks before the disaster occurred. Indeed, a month before that date, I was unaware of the existence of the ship or of the South Antarctic Whaling Company. I am not a whaler, and apart from a season's work in Greenland with a university exploration club, I had never before been in high latitudes. I wish to make this point clear at the outset so that those who have long experience of Antarctic conditions and of whaling in particular will understand that what is familiar to them came to me with the impact of complete novelty. The reason I have been asked to set down a full account of all that occurred is due to the fact that, through circumstances largely outside my control, I was in close association with the personalities concerned in the disaster and know probably more about the real cause of what happened than anyone now living.

My connection with the events that led up to the loss of the *Southern Cross* began with the New Year. I was emigrating to South Africa and on the night of 1st January I was waiting in the offices of a private charter company at London Airport in the hopes of hitching a ride to Capetown. The decision to emigrate had been made on the spur of the moment. And if I'd known then where it was going to lead me, I'd have turned right back, pocketed my pride and resumed the routine of a clerk's life in the offices of Messrs. Bridewell & Faber, tobacco importers of Mark Lane.

The flight was scheduled for 01.00 hours. The plane had been chartered by the South Antarctic Whaling Company for a Colonel Bland. There were five seats available and Bland's party numbered three. That was all I knew. Tim Bartlett, the pilot of the aircraft, had tipped me off at a New Year's Eve party the night before. As far as he was concerned it was okay. He'd take me. But it was up to me to talk my way into one of the two spare seats.

Bland arrived at twelve-thirty. He came into the terminal offices, stamping and blowing through his cheeks. 'Is the plane ready?' he asked the clerk. His manner was peremptory. He had the air of a man always in a hurry. There were three other people with him – two men and a girl. A blast of cold air blew in through the open door and outside I saw a big limousine, its lights glistening on the wet tarmac. A uniformed chauffeur brought in their baggage. 'The pilot's waiting,' the clerk said. 'If you'll just sign these forms, Colonel Bland. And here's a cable – arrived about half an hour ago.'

I watched his thick fingers rip at the envelope. He pushed his horn-rimmed glasses up on to his forehead and held the cable closer to the light. His eyes were hard under the tufty brows and his bluish jowls quivered slightly as he read. Then he swung round abruptly. 'Here, read this,' he said to the girl. He held the flimsy cable sheet out and it shook slightly in his thick, hairy hand.

The girl came forward and took it. She was dressed in a pair of old slacks and a green woollen jersey. A lovely mink coat was draped carelessly over her shoulders. She looked tired and her face was pale under its make-up. She read it through and then looked at Bland, her lips compressed into a thin line, her eyes blank.

'Well?' Bland's voice was almost violent. She didn't say anything. She just looked at him and I saw she was trembling slightly. 'Well?' he barked again. And then the violence inside him seemed to explode. 'First you and now your father. What have you got against the boy?' His fist suddenly crashed down on the desk top. 'I'll not recall him. Do you hear? Your father had better learn to get along with him. Any more ultimatums like that and I'll accept your father's resignation. He's not the only leader available.'

'He's the only one that can get you the results

you've been accustomed to,' she answered defiantly, a flush of anger colouring her cheeks.

Bland was about to reply, but then he saw me and stopped. He turned abruptly and seized the forms that the clerk had thrust towards him. His hand shook as he signed them. And as I watched him Capetown seemed to recede. I'd met his type before. He was the aggressive, self-made business man, even to the black hat and black overcoat with astrakhan collar. He was as hard as a lump of granite. And he looked as though he were on the verge of a nervous breakdown. To ask him for a lift in his plane would be like asking for the loan of a gold brick from the Bank of England. And the hell of it was that I'd burned my boats. I'd given up my rooms, requested my bank to transfer what little money I possessed to Capetown and the letter throwing up my job had been posted that afternoon.

As though he sensed that I was watching him, he suddenly turned and stared at me. His small blue eyes were distorted by the thick lenses of his glasses. 'Are you just waiting for a plane, sir – or do you want to speak to me?' he demanded aggressively.

'I'm waiting for a plane,' I said.

He grunted, but didn't take his eyes off me.

'Whether I get it depends on you,' I went on. 'My name's Craig – Duncan Craig. The pilot of your plane is a friend of mine. He told me there might be a spare seat and I was wondering whether you'd be –'

'You're trying to scrounge a lift?'

The way he put it made me curl. But I kept a tight

hold on my temper and said, 'I'd very much like to come with you to Capetown.'

'Well, you can't.'

And suddenly I didn't care. Perhaps it was his manner – perhaps it was the way he'd spoken to the girl. 'There's no need to be offensive, Colonel Bland,' I said angrily. 'All I asked for was a lift.' And I reached down for my bags.

'Just a minute,' he said. The violence seemed to have died out of him. As I looked up, he was leaning against the desk, his thick fingers tugging at the lobe of his left ear. 'There are some two hundred thousand people waiting to get to South Africa. Why should I take you more than any of the others?'

'It happens that I'm the one that asked you. They didn't.' I had picked up my bags now. 'Forget it,' I said and moved towards the door.

'All right, Craig,' he said. 'As it happens there is a spare seat. If the pilot vouches for you and you're through the formalities in time, you can have it.'

He seemed to mean it. 'Thanks,' I said and made for the door to the airfield.

'Check you bags and sign the papers,' he said. The abruptness was back in his voice.

'I've done all that,' I said. 'I did it in advance – just in case.' I didn't want him to think that I'd taken it for granted I'd get the lift.

His thick brows dragged down over his eyes and his jowls quivered. Then he suddenly laughed. 'Where did you learn efficiency – in business or in the services?'

'In the services,' I replied.

'Which – the Army?'

'No. The Navy.'

That seemed to exhaust his interest in me. He turned and watched the baggage being weighed. Tim Bartlett came through from the flight office with his co-pilot, a man called Fenton. He glanced at me with a lift to his eyebrows. I nodded and he grinned. He introduced himself and Fenton to Bland and asked the clerk for the passenger details. As he glanced through the papers he said to Bland, 'I see you've increased your party from three to four?'

'Yes. Mrs Bland wanted to come.' He nodded in the direction of the girl.

Tim Bartlett's brows lifted and he nodded. 'Which is Weiner?' he asked. One of the two men standing in the shadows by the door came forward slowly into the light. 'I am Weiner,' he said. His voice was a guttural whisper and he moved like a marionet, as though jerked along against his will by invisible strings. He was a Jew and his clothes were several sizes too large for his shrunken body. He had a bald head, thin, emaciated features, and a tubercular cough. 'Do you wish to see my papers?' he asked in that same wretched whisper.

'No, that's all right,' Tim said.

'And I am Bonomi – Aldo Bonomi.' It was the fourth member of the party. He stepped out of the shadows into the light with the swagger and bounce of an opera singer. He wore a camel-hair coat with padded shoulders and tie-on belt and round his neck was a silk scarf of peacock blue with little yellow designs. Gold rings flashed as he seized Tim's hand and pumped it up and down. 'I am so pleased to know that we shall be in such good hands. You are an artist. I can see that. I, too, am an artist. I go to take pictures for *El Colonnello*.' He paused for breath and peered anxiously up into Tim's face. 'But I hope you are a careful driver. Last time I fly the driver he make play with the airplane and I am very seek.'

Tim got his hand back from the Italian and said, 'It's all right. You needn't worry, Mr Bonomi. It will all be very dull, I hope.' And he went out to the airfield.

The rest of us followed as soon as Bland's party had had their passports checked and been through the customs. We piled into the plane. The luggage was strapped down, the doors closed. Fenton came through from the cockpit and told us to fix our safety belts. The engines roared into life and the plane taxied out on to the tarmac. The lights of the airport glittered frostily. We made the end of the runway and waited there for the okay from the control tower. My stomach suddenly felt hollow. It always does before a take-off. That uninsurable half minute! I don't know anyone who's really got over it.

I looked round at the others. Their bodies were self-consciously relaxed, the muscles under the surface rigid against the possibility of a crash. Nobody spoke. Bland had closed his eyes. The girl had her hands thrust deep in the pockets of her fur coat. Her grey eyes were wide and stared straight in front of her. Little curls of fair hair had escaped from beneath the silk scarf that covered her head. Bonomi wriggled in his seat. He couldn't keep still. He was like a rubber ball, his head darting about, one moment peering forward out of the window, the next twisted round to examine the inside of the plane. Only Weiner seemed completely relaxed. He lay slumped in his seat like a bundle of old clothes. A nerve twitched at the side of his mouth, but his expression was one of complete apathy. His hands were held against his stomach, the long, nervous fingers plucking at the locking device of his safety belt.

The engines suddenly roared. The plane rocked and vibrated. Then the brakes were off and we were gathering speed down the runway. I braced myself automatically and peered out of the window, where the lights of the plane showed the concrete streaming by. The rear end of the fuselage bumped twice and then lifted. The lights of the control tower showed through the darkness moving slowly away from us. Then suddenly we were riding air, smooth and steady, the note of the engines changing to a solid drone, the seat pressing my body upwards. The control tower was a rapidly receding pinpoint of light now. Headlights cut swathes along the narrow ribbon of the road bordering the airport. Then we banked and the lights of London stretched away to the darkness of the horizon. Clear in my mind, like a montage, was the notice I'd pasted on my office desk – *Gone to South Africa*. Was it only yesterday evening I'd put it there? I thought of Mr Bridewell standing there, staring at it, uneasy, suspecting a leg-pull, completely unable to comprehend why I had left. Even my letter wouldn't explain that to him.

I undid my safety belt. Now I was actually on my way, I wanted to sing, shout, do something to show how I felt. Across the gangway, the little Jew was still twining his fingers round the lock of his belt. Behind me Bland suddenly said, 'Judie. Change places with Franz. I want to discuss this electrical killing gear with him.'

I half turned in my seat. Nobody seemed to notice my surprise. The girl said, 'Don't you think you ought to rest?'

'I'm all right,' Bland replied gruffly.

'Doctor Wilber said – '

'Damn Doctor Wilber!'

'If you're not careful you'll kill yourself.'

'I'll take a lot of killing.' He stared at her for a second. 'Where's that cable? I gave it to you.'

The girl felt in the pocket of her fur coat and brought out the crumpled flimsy cable. I heard him smoothing it out on his brief-case. Then he snorted. 'Bernt's no right to cable me like this.' Anger was catching hold of him again. 'He's not giving the boy a chance.' I heard the cable crushed in the sudden clenching of his fist. Then: 'The trouble is that only Erik stands between him and full control of the company when I'm gone.' His voice was a deep, angry rumble.

'That's not fair.' The girl's voice blazed.

'Not fair, eh? What the hell am I to think? They weren't a week out of Capetown before there was trouble between them.'

'And whose fault do you suppose that was?' the girl demanded angrily.

'Bernt was playing on his lack of experience.'

'That's Erik's story.'

'What of that? Do you expect me not to believe my own son?'

'Yes, but you don't know him very well, do you? You were in London all through the war and since then – '

'I know when a boy's being victimized,' Bland snapped back. 'Why, Bernt even had the nerve to cable that he was causing trouble among the Tönsberg men. There's never any trouble with whalers. They're far too interested in the success of the expedition.'

'If Bernt said he was causing trouble among the Tönsberg men, then he was.' The girl's voice steadied. 'He's never thought of anything but the interests of the company. You know that.'

'Then why does he send me this ultimatum? Why does he demand Erik's recall?'

'Because he's seen through him.'

'Seen through him? That's a fine way to talk of your husband.'

'I don't care. You may as well know the truth about him.'

'Shut up!' Bland's voice vibrated like a plucked string.

'I won't shut up,' the girl rushed on. 'It's time you knew the truth. Erik's – '

'Shut up!' Bland's voice was thunderous. 'Don't talk like that. I can see what's happening to him now.

You undermining him at home and your father undermining him out there. His confidence in himself is being sapped by the pair of you. No wonder he needs – '

'His confidence!' The girl's tone was half contemptuous, half hysterical. 'You don't know him at all, do you? You still think of him as the gay, reckless boy of ten years ago – sailing his boat, winning ski jump championships. You think that's all he wants. Well, it isn't. He likes to control things – men, machines, an organization. He wants power. Power, I tell you. He wants control of the company. And he's got his mother – '

'How dare you talk like that!'

'God! Do you think I don't know Erik by now?' She was leaning forward across the gangway, her body rigid, her face a white mask. 'I've been meaning to tell you this for some time – ever since that first cable. But you were too ill. Now, if you're well enough to travel, you're well enough to know what – '

'I refuse to listen.' Bland was trying to keep down his anger. 'You're hysterical.'

'You've got to listen. I'm not hysterical. I'm telling you what I should have told you – '

'I tell you I won't listen. Damn it – the boy's your husband.'

'Do you think I don't know that?' Her voice sounded frighteningly bitter. 'Do you think he hasn't made me aware of that every hour of the day we've been married?'

Bland was peering at her through his thick glasses. 'Don't you still love him?' he asked.

'Love him!' she cried. 'I hate him. I hate him, I tell you.' She was crying wildly now. 'Oh, why did you agree to send him out as second-in-command?'

'You seem to forget he's my son.' Bland's voice was ominously quiet.

'I haven't forgotten that. But it's time you knew the truth.'

'Then wait till we're alone.'

The girl glanced at me and saw that I was watching her. 'All right,' she said in a low voice.

'Franz!' The man next to me jerked in his seat. 'Come and sit back here. Change places with Franz,' he ordered the girl. 'And try to calm down.'

She got up heavily and changed places with the German. I watched her as she settled in the seat across the gangway from me. Her face was tense, her small hands clenched so tight the knuckles showed white. She sat there, quite still and rigid, as though frozen.

I sat back and stared out of my window at the red glow of the port navigation light. The Kent coast was sliding from under us. Ahead, the corrugated surface of the Channel was lit by a crescent moon. And above the drone of the engines I caught snatches of Bland's conversation.

'The equipment has arrived . . . cable two days ago from the Cape . . . *Tauer III* is picking it up . . . I've ordered Sudmann to wait for us . . . all prepared for test.'

I think I was too excited to sleep. In the end I got

up and went through into the pilot's cockpit. Fenton was at the controls. Tim was pouring coffee from a thermos. 'Well, there's the last you'll see of England for a bit,' he said, nodding through the side window. 'Should begin to get warmer tomorrow. Getting on all right with Bland's party?'

'I've hardly spoken to them,' I said. 'Bland and the girl have just had a hell of a row. Now he's talking to Weiner about some new equipment or something. Weiner's German, isn't he?'

'That's right. He's an expert on electrical harpoons. He's on loan to Bland from one of the big Ruhr companies. Poor devil! Think of it. Four months in the Antarctic. Flying over the Alps is quite cold enough for me.'

'Is Bland going out to the Antarctic, too?'

'Yes, they're all going as far as I know. There's a boat waiting for them at the Cape to take them out to the factory ship. I gather there's some sort of trouble on board the *Southern Cross*. Anyway, Bland sounded as though he were in a hell of a hurry to get out there.'

'Do you mean to say the girl's going, as well?' I asked. He shrugged his shoulders. 'Don't know about her,' he answered. 'She only joined the party at the last moment. According to her papers, she's Norwegian by birth and South African by marriage. Looks rather a poppet.'

'She doesn't behave like one,' I answered. 'More like a wild cat. And she's all tensed up over something. It's an odd set-up.'

'You should worry. You got your ride, didn't you?

If you want company, go and talk to Aldo Bonomi. There must be something behind the bounce, for he's one of the world's best photographers. Like some coffee?'

'No, thanks,' I said. 'I'll sleep better without it.'

He set down the flask. 'That reminds me. I'd better hand out some blankets. You might give me a hand, will you, Duncan?'

Back in the main body of the plane everything was just as I'd left it. Bland and Weiner were poring over sheets of figures. The girl sat staring out of the window. She didn't look up as we came through. It seemed as though she hadn't moved since I went through into the cockpit. Bonomi, however, had fallen asleep, his mouth slightly open, his snores lost in the sound of the engines. We handed round the blankets. 'Breakfast at Treviso,' Tim said as he went for'ard. I settled in my seat across the gangway from the girl. She had wrapped her blankets round her, but she still sat tense and wide-eyed. My thoughts drifted to South Africa and the new world that lay ahead. I still had a sense of excitement about it. It wasn't real yet. I thought of Table Mountain as I'd seen it once before in a vivid dawn from the bridge of my corvette as I convoyed reinforcements for Egypt and the Sicilian campaign. What sort of a job would Kramer find me when I got there? The drone of the engines gradually lulled me to sleep.

A frozen dawn showed us the Alps as a wild barrier of snow-capped peaks with the crevassed glacier ice tumbling down through giant clefts. Then we were over the flat expanse of the Lombardy plain and setting down at Treviso for breakfast.

I was right behind Bonomi as we went into the canteen. I was curious about Bland and I thought Bonomi the most likely of the four to gratify my curiosity. He picked a table away from the others and I seated myself opposite him. 'I gather you're a photographer, Mr Bonomi,' I said.

'But, of course. You have heard of Aldo Bonomi, no?'

'Er – yes, of course,' I murmured quickly.

The corners of his mouth dragged down and he spread his hands in a little gesture of despair. 'You do not fool me. You have not heard of Aldo Bonomi. Where do you leev, Mistair Craig?' His brown eyes gazed at me pityingly.

I thought of the people I met at the office and at my rooms. I was right out of this world. 'And you're going to take pictures of whaling in the Antarctic?' I said.

'Si, si.' The waiter came and he ordered, speaking fast in Italian. 'May I order for you, Mistair Craig? I think I get you something good.'

'Thanks,' I said. And when the waiter had gone I asked him whether he liked the idea of going to the Antarctic.

He gave a little shrug to his shoulders. 'It is business, you understand.'

'But it's a rather unusual assignment, isn't it?'

'Unusual? Per'aps. But my business is often unusual. One day I take pictures of a zoo, another day

I am photographing the Rand mines. Then again I am with the Canadian Railways.'

'You travel quite a bit then?'

'But, of course. Oh, you do not understand. I am Aldo Bonomi. Everyone wish for my photographs. One week I am in America, next I am in Paris. Travel, travel, travel – I am always in trains or aeroplanes.'

'And now you're going to the Antarctic with Colonel Bland. Tell me – what do you think of him? You heard the row he had with his daughter-in-law? Is there something wrong on board the factory ship?'

His hand fingered his little green and red bow tie. 'Mistair Craig – I never talk about my clients. It is not good for business, you understand.' The flash of white teeth in his swarthy face was half ingratiating, half apologetic. He smoothed his hand over the shining surface of his black hair. 'Let us talk about you,' he said. The waiter came with our breakfast. As he poured the coffee, Bonomi said, 'You emigrate to South Africa, yes?'

I nodded.

'That is very exciting. You throw up everything. You go to another country and you start again. That is the big adventure. You have no job, but you go all the same. That needs guts, eh? You are a man with guts. I like men with guts. You like a drink with your coffee?' And as I half shook my head, he said, 'Just a leetle one, so I can drink your health. Besides, I like to drink with my breakfast.' He turned to the waiter. '*Due cognaci.*'

'What makes you think I haven't got a job?' I asked as the waiter disappeared.

'If you have a job, then you do not need to ask for a ride. It is all fixed by your company. I know because I am always working for some company. But tell me – what makes you leave England?'

I shrugged my shoulders. 'I don't know,' I said. 'I just got fed up.'

'But something make you decide very quick, eh? Oh, I do not mean something serious, you understand. Life, she is not like that. Always it is the little things that make up our minds for us.'

I laughed at that. 'You're right there.' And suddenly I was talking to him, telling him the whole thing. He was conceited, effeminate-looking and full of his own importance, but he was easy to talk to. 'I suppose I've been feeling a sense of frustration ever since the war ended,' I explained. 'I went straight from Oxford into the Navy. When I came out I had a queer idea that my country owed me a living. Then I found that commanding a corvette didn't qualify me to run a business. I finished up as a clerk with a firm of tobacco importers.'

'That is not so much after commanding a ship, eh?' he nodded sympathetically. The waiter came with the cognac. '*Salute!*' he said as he raised his glass. 'I wish you *buona ventura*, Mistair Craig. And what is the little thing that brings your frustration to a head, eh?'

'A fiver,' I said. 'Mr Bridewell, the man who ran the business, gave us each a fiver on New Year's Eve. But the fool had to make a speech about it.'

'And you do not like this Mistair Bridewell?'

'No. It wasn't that. He's a decent little man. And it was a decent gesture. But I couldn't stomach the lecture. I thought it was a hard way to earn a fiver. I went out and got drunk with it. And during the course of the evening I ran into Bartlett, the pilot of our plane. He told me he was flying to South Africa with two spare seats and I decided to chance it.'

'I understand. But do you know what conditions are like now in South Africa?'

'Oh, I know the post-war boom is over, the same as it is in England. But a fellow I met during the war said he could always find me a job if I came out.'

'Ah, yes – a fellow you meet during the war.' He shrugged his shoulders and stared at his drink. At length he gave a little sigh and said, 'Well, I wish you luck. I hope the job he have for you is a very good one.'

Tim Bartlett came in then and said it was time to leave. We finished our drinks and walked out to the plane. But as we roared down the runway and swung into the blue of the Italian skies, South Africa seemed suddenly less exciting. I should have contacted Kramer about that job first. I'd known it all along. But I'd pushed the thought into the back of my mind. Now, as South Africa became a reality – and a rapidly nearing reality – the problem of that job loomed more and more important.

The trip over the Med was bumpy; the sea very blue, but flecked with white. The Western Desert looked cold and drab. Cairo came up at us marked by the geometrical square of the pyramid at Giza. An icy wind blew dust across the airport. Tim told us there'd be a six-hour stop there. We'd start again at ten. Bonomi went off with a journalist friend who'd arrived in a B.O.A.C. plane. Bland decided to rest. His big face was pale and sweaty. He looked ill and exhausted. Weiner was suffering from air sickness. I stood around, wondering what to do with the time on my hands. Cairo was one of the places I'd got to during the war. I'd just made up my mind to go and find some place to get a drink when a voice behind me said, 'Mr Craig.'

I turned. It was the girl. She looked cold and pale. 'Could you – would you mind taking me into Cairo – for a drink or something?' Her grey eyes were wide and her mouth trembled slightly. I think she was on the verge of tears. She was all wound up like something that's tied too tight and ready to burst.

'Come on,' I said, and took her arm. I could feel the tightness inside her. She wasn't trembling, but it was there like a charge of electricity. We found a taxi and I ordered the driver to take us to Shepheard's Hotel.

There was a long silence as the taxi rattled out through the airport gates. I didn't hurry her. I knew it would come. She suddenly said, 'I'm sorry.'

'Why?' I asked.

'Inflicting myself on you like this. I – I don't think I'll be very good company.'

'Don't worry,' I said. 'Just relax.'

'I'll try,' she said and closed her eyes.

At Shepheard's I took her to a table in the corner. 'What'll you have?' I asked.

'Whisky,' she said.

I ordered doubles. We tried a little small talk. It didn't work. When the drinks came, she drank in silence. I gave her a cigarette. She dragged at it as though her nerves were screaming out for a sedative. 'Wouldn't it help to tell me about it?' I suggested.

'Perhaps,' she said.

'It'll help spread the load,' I added. 'It always does. And it's not likely we'll meet again.'

She didn't say anything. It was as though she hadn't heard. She was gazing at a noisy group at a nearby table. But she didn't see them. God knows what she saw. For a girl who couldn't be more than twenty-five, her face looked almost haggard. Suddenly she said, 'I'm scared about my father. I don't know why I'm scared, but I am. It came over me last night in the plane. It was as though – ' She put her elbows on the table and rested her head in her hands. 'Oh, God!' she said in a choking voice. 'It all seems such a mess.'

I wanted to do something to comfort her. But there was nothing I could do. I lit another cigarette and waited.

At length she raised her head. 'All last night,' she said, 'I was thinking about my father and Erik – down there in the Antarctic.'

'Erik is your husband, is he?' I asked.

'Erik Bland. Yes.' She nodded.

'And your father's there, too?'

'Yes. He's the manager of the factory. He's also

32

leader of the expedition.' Her fingers were clutching her glass so hard that the knuckles showed white. 'If only Erik weren't there,' she whispered. And then with sudden violence, 'If only he'd been killed during the war.' She looked at me sadly. 'But it's always the wrong ones that get killed, isn't it?' And I wondered whether there was somebody she'd been fond of. She looked down at her glass again.

'I'm frightened,' she said. 'Erik's been working for this for two years. Through his mother, who's Norwegian, he's got a lot of Sandefjord men of his own choosing into the crew. And now, this season, he's persuaded Colonel Bland to let him go out as assistant manager. They weren't a fortnight out of Capetown before he was cabling that my father was turning the Tönsberg men against him. There were other cables and then finally one which said: *Nordahl openly saying he will have control of the company soon.* My father would never say a thing like that – not in front of the men. I know he wouldn't. It's all part of a plan to drive a wedge between him and Colonel Bland.'

'Is Nordahl your father?' I asked.

'Bernt Nordahl – yes. He's a wonderful person.' Her eyes came alive for the first time since I'd met her. 'Nineteen seasons he's been out in the Antarctic. He's as tough and – ' She checked herself and her tone flattened as she said, 'You see, Bland's just had a stroke. It's heart trouble. He knows he hasn't got long to live. That's why he finally agreed to Erik going out this season. Normally he wouldn't. He knows he hasn't sufficient experience. But he wants Erik to follow him in the company. It's natural. Any father would. But he doesn't know him. He doesn't know what he's like.'

'And your father does?' I suggested.

She nodded. 'Yes.' She hesitated and then said, 'That cable Bland received at the airport last night – it was from my father. It said either Erik must be recalled or he would resign.'

I looked at her, trying to understand why she had married Erik Bland. She wasn't beautiful. She was a little too stockily built for that, and that ridiculous little up-tilted nose gave her face a snubbed appearance. But she had grace. She had strength, too, and a bubbling vitality that showed even through the blank misery of her present mood. She'd been brought up on skis and long treks through the mountains. I'd been at the landings at Aandalsnes in 1940. I knew the country and to me she was all Norway with that lovely golden hair, creamy skin and wide, generous mouth. She was the sort of girl that's born to fight for the right to live alongside her man. And from what I'd heard on the plane it was clear she'd made a wrong choice.

'Mind if I ask you a personal question?' I said.

Her grey eyes were suddenly defensive. 'Go ahead,' she said.

'Why did you marry Erik Bland?'

She shrugged her shoulders. 'Why does any girl marry the man she does?' she answered slowly. 'It was in 1938. Erik was very attractive. He's tall and fair and very boyish. He's a fine skier, dances beautifully and keeps a lovely little yacht at the Dronningen. Everybody thought I was very lucky.'

'And he was a sham?'

'Yes.'

'When did you discover that?'

'During the war. We grew up during the war, didn't we? Before, all I thought about was having a good time. I studied in England and in Paris. But it was the parties and the ski-ing and the sailing that I lived for. Then the Germans came.' Her eyes, which had sparkled for a moment, clouded now. 'All the boys I knew disappeared from Oslo. They went north to join the fighting. And when that was over, they were back, some of them, for a little time. But one by one they drifted away, some across the North Sea to join the Norwegian forces, some through Finland and Russia, others up into the mountains to continue the fight.' She stopped then, her lips pressed tight together.

'But Erik didn't go,' I finished for her.

'No.' There was sudden violence in her tone. 'You see, he liked the Germans. He liked the Nazi way of life. It fascinated him. It satisfied a sort of – it's difficult to put into words – a craving for self-expression. Do you understand?'

I thought of the mother who adored him and the father whose personality and achievement had dominated his whole life, leaving him nothing to strive for. I could understand. I nodded.

'It meant nothing to him that Norway was fighting for her existence,' she went on. 'He didn't seem to understand – ' Her voice trailed away. When she spoke again it was in a softer tone. 'Perhaps it wasn't altogether his fault. Life had been made too easy for him.'

'But why wasn't he interned?' I asked. 'He's English, isn't he?'

'Well – South African. He claimed Boer descent on his father's side, and of course his mother's Norwegian. Their police checked on him periodically, that was all.'

'Was Colonel Bland over in Norway during the war?'

'No. London. But Erik's mother remained at Sandefjord. She'd plenty of money, so it didn't make much difference to him.' She hesitated, and then said, 'We began to have rows. I refused to go out with him. There were Germans at most of the parties he went to. He took them ski-ing, even out in his yacht. He just couldn't see my point of view. Then the Resistance got going. I tried to make him join. I thought if I could only get him to mix with the boys who were going on with the fight he'd wake up to understanding what it was all about. I kept at him until at last he agreed to join. They thought he might be useful because of his German contacts. We forgot that the Germans might think him useful because of his Norwegian contacts. He went up into the hills for one of the drops. A week later the same dropping ground was used. The Resistance Group collecting on that drop was practically wiped out. Nobody suspected.'

'Except you,' I said as she stopped, her teeth biting into her lip.

She nodded slowly. 'Yes. I got it out of him one night when he was drunk. He actually – he actually boasted about it. Said it served them right, that they were on the wrong side anyway. It was horrible. I hadn't the nerve to tell the Resistance. He knew that and he – ' She glanced up at me quickly. 'Nobody knows what I have just told you,' she said. 'So please – ' She tossed the request aside as unnecessary. 'It doesn't matter though.' Her tone was suddenly bitter. 'No one would believe it. He's so devilishly charming. That's the hell of it – to know what he is and see him keeping up his front of popularity. His father – ' She spread her hands helplessly and sighed.

'You've never told him about the Resistance business, of course?' I said.

'No,' she said. 'I wouldn't want to tell any father that about his son – not unless I had to.'

There was a long silence after that. There was nothing I could say. She stared past me, her mind far away, out there in the white wastes of the Antarctic where she was going. Suddenly she finished her drink. It was a quick, decisive movement, like the ringing down of the curtain. 'I can hear dance music,' she said with a sudden hard brightness. 'Let's go and dance.' As I rose, she put her hand on mine. 'Thank you,' she said, 'for being – so nice.'

I don't know how she managed it, but we had a lovely evening. Perhaps it was reaction. Maybe it was a sheer effort of will. But her gaiety, which was forced and brittle as we went on to the floor became quite natural as we danced. She danced with her body very close to mine. She seemed to want to dance with complete abandon, and she danced divinely. Once she murmured, 'You said we'd never meet again.' Her lips were almost touching my ear. In the taxi going back to the airport, she snuggled close to me and let me kiss her.

But when the taxi swung in through the gates of the airport she straightened up. As she made up her face, I saw the worried look was back in her eyes. She caught my glance and made a wry face. 'Cinderella's home again,' she said, and her voice was flat. Then with a sudden rush of warmth she took my hand in hers. 'It's been a wonderful evening,' she said softly. 'Perhaps if I'd met somebody like you –' She stopped there. 'But there'd have to have been a war first, wouldn't there? You see, I was a spoilt little bitch myself.'

It was just on eleven. The others were waiting for us. We went straight out to the plane. Ten minutes later the lights of Cairo were vanishing below us and the black of the desert night stretched ahead. We settled down to sleep.

It must have been about four in the morning that Tim came through from the cockpit. The sound of the door sliding back woke me up. He had a slip of paper in his hand. He went past me and stopped at Bland, shaking him awake. 'Urgent message for you, Colonel Bland,' he said, speaking softly. Bland grunted and there was a rustle of paper.

I turned in my seat. Bland's face was white and puffy. He was staring down at the slip of paper that trembled in his hand. He swallowed twice and then glanced across at Judie, who was fast asleep.

'Is there any message to be sent?' Tim asked him.

'No. No, there's no reply.' Bland's voice was barely audible. It was as though he'd been belted in the stomach and all the breath had been knocked out of him.

'Sorry to bring you bad news at this time of the morning.' Tim went back to the cockpit. I tried to get back to sleep. But I couldn't. I kept on wondering what was in that message. Somehow I was certain it had some connection with Judie. Twice I turned round. Each time Bland failed to notice my movement. He wasn't asleep. He was sitting there, slumped in his seat, his eyes open and staring at the message.

Dawn came and with it a glimpse of Mount Elgon on the starboard beam. Shortly afterwards the snow-covered peak of Kilimanjaro was above the horizon and we were landing at Nairobi for breakfast. We all sat at the same table. Bland didn't eat anything. I thought at first that he was suffering from air sickness. The last part of the flight had been pretty bumpy. But then I saw he kept on glancing at Judie. He looked almost scared.

Bonomi, who was sitting next to me, suddenly leaned closer and said, 'What is the trouble with Colonel Bland? He looks as though he is very seek about somethings.'

'I don't know,' I said. 'But he got a message during the night.'

When we got up from the meal I saw Bland motion for Judie to join him outside. He wasn't gone long, and when he came back he was alone. 'Where's Mrs Bland?' I asked. 'Is anything wrong?'

'No,' he answered. 'Nothing.' His tone made it clear it was none of my business.

I lit a cigarette and went outside. I thought maybe Judie had gone to powder her nose. But as I turned the corner of the building I saw her walking alone across the airfield. She was walking aimlessly, as though she'd no idea where she was going and didn't care anyway. I called to her. But she didn't answer. She just kept on walking, following her feet, changing her course like a ship without a rudder.

I ran after her then. 'Judie!' I called. 'Judie!' She stopped then and half turned, waiting for me to come up with her. Her face was quite blank. 'What's happened?' I asked. Her eyes were empty, her whole being withdrawn inside itself. She didn't answer. I caught hold of her hand. It was as cold as ice. 'Come on,' I said. 'Tell me. It's the message your father-in-law received during the night, isn't it?' She nodded bleakly. 'What did it say?' For answer she opened her other hand. I took the crumpled ball of paper and spread it out.

It was from the South Antarctic Company, dispatched at 21.30 hours. It read: *Eide reports Manager Nordahl lost overboard from factory ship stop further information later signed Jenssen.*

Her father dead! I read the message through again, wondering what I could possibly say to her. She'd worshipped him. I knew that from the way she had talked about him in Cairo. *He's a wonderful person.* I remembered the way her eyes had lit up when she had said that. The message didn't say how it had happened; didn't even say if there'd been a storm. It just said – *lost overboard*. 'Who is Eide?' I asked.

'The captain of the *Southern Cross*.' Her voice sounded numbed.

I took her arm and we walked on slowly for a while in silence. Then suddenly the pent-up emotion inside her broke out. 'How did it happen?' she cried wildly. 'He couldn't have just fallen overboard. He's been on ships all his life. Something's wrong down there. Something's wrong. I know it is.' She began to cry then, her whole body shaking, her head buried against me like a puppy that's lost its mother. I remember thinking then that if Erik Bland had had any decency he'd have cabled her himself.

TWO

It was summer in Capetown. As we swung down towards the airport the scene was like a colour plate – the houses all white and Table Mountain a mass of brown rock against the brilliant blue of the sky. My stomach felt hollow inside me. Somewhere down there my future was waiting for me – if I could find it. I was excited and nervous all in one. It was the start of a new life. The very fact that the sun was shining in a clear sky gave me a wonderful sense of freedom. I'd left winter behind. As we touched down on the long ribbon of the runway I wanted to sing. Then I glanced across at Judie and the mood was gone. She was slumped in her seat, staring tensely out of the window the way she had been all the way from Mombassa. I remembered the ride in the taxi at Cairo. And then I remembered that moment on the airfield at Nairobi when she had broken down with her grief. I wished there was something I could do. But there wasn't.

At the airport buildings I thanked Bland for the trip. He shook my hand. His grip was like iron, but his face was white. 'Glad we could give you a lift.' He mumbled conventional good wishes automatically and then went out with Weiner at his heels. I said good-bye to Tim Bartlett and then Bonomi popped up like a jack-in-the-box, smiling and shaking my hand. 'If South Africa is no good, Mistair Craig, you go to Australia,' he said. 'Here is the name of a man in Sydney who is useful. Tell him Aldo Bonomi send you.' He handed me a piece of paper on which he had scribbled an address. I thanked him and wished him luck in the frozen south. He pulled a face. 'I prefer to stay here, I think.' Then he shrugged his shoulders and grinned. 'But I sacrifice everyt'ing for my art – even my comfort.'

Then Judie was coming towards me. 'Well, this is good-bye, Duncan,' she said, and held out her hand. She even managed a little smile. Her fingers were warm and firm in my hand. 'Just two ships . . .' she said. 'Are you going to a hotel?'

'Yes,' I said. 'I'll go to the Splendide. I'll probably end up in some dingy boarding house, but just for a few days I'm going to pretend I'm important.' She nodded and smiled. 'Where are you staying?' I asked her.

But she shook her head. 'We part here,' she said. 'We shall probably go straight on board. Everything is arranged. In an hour's time we'll be sailing out of Table Bay.'

I hesitated. I didn't know quite what to say. But I had to say something. 'I hope you – you – ' I just couldn't put it into words.

She smiled. 'I know. And thanks.' Then suddenly on a higher pitch: 'If only I knew what had happened. If only Eide or Erik had cabled details. But there's nothing at the airport – nothing.' Her fingers squeezed my hand. 'I'm sorry. You've got problems of your own. Good luck. And thank you for being so sweet.' She reached up then and kissed me on the lips. And before I could say anything she had turned and her heels were tap-tapping across the concrete floor as she went out to the car that was waiting for her. She didn't look back.

That should have been the end of it. I should have got myself a job and they should have sailed for the Antarctic. But it didn't work out that way.

I got myself fixed up at the Splendide and then rang Kramer. He was down in the book as a mining consultant. His secretary told me he wouldn't be in till after lunch. In the end I didn't get him till almost tea time. He sounded pleased to hear from me until I mentioned why I was in Capetown. 'You should have written me, old man,' he said. 'Then I could have warned you. This isn't the moment to come out here looking for a job, not when you haven't any technical qualifications.'

'But you said you could get me a job any time,' I reminded.

'Good God!' he said. 'That was during the war. Things have changed since then. They've changed a lot in the past year. And you couldn't have picked a worse moment than this. It's sticky – very sticky, old man. Right now there's a scare on and everyone's got cold feet.'

'What's the trouble?'

'One of these West Rand outfits – a company known as "Words" – has turned out a stumer. It's only a small company, but everyone's panicky – afraid the whole field may turn out the same way. But I'm throwing a little party out at my place to-night. Come along. May be able to fix you up with something.' He gave me the address and rang off.

I put the phone down and sat staring out of the window. The sunshine suddenly seemed a brittle sham. I went and had a bath. And whilst I was lying there thinking it out the phone bell rang. I flung a towel round me and went through into the bedroom. 'Is that Craig?' It was a man's voice, abrupt and solid.

'Craig speaking,' I said.

'Oh, Bland here,' said the voice and my spirits sagged again. 'My daughter-in-law tells me you commanded a corvette during the war.'

'That's right,' I said.

'Where and how long for?'

I didn't see what he was driving at, but I said,

'Pretty well everywhere. I took command of her in '44 and had her for the rest of the war.'

'Good.' There was a slight pause and then he said, 'I'd like to have a word with you. Can you come down to Room 23?'

'You mean here – in the hotel?'

'Yes.'

'I thought you were sailing right away?'

'I'm staying here the night.' The tone was suddenly abrupt. 'When can you come down?'

'I'm just having a bath,' I told him. 'But I'll be down as soon as I've dressed.'

'Fine.' And he rang off.

I didn't hurry over my dressing. I needed time to think it out. I'd got a damn-fool idea in my mind that I couldn't shake off. It was that question of Bland's about my being in command of a corvette during the war.

But at last I was dressed and couldn't put it off any longer. I went out and took the lift down to the second floor. I knocked at the door of Number 23. Bland answered himself. 'Come in, Craig,' he said. He took me into a big room facing Adderley Street. 'What would you like? A whisky?'

'That'll do fine,' I said.

I watched him as he poured it. His hands shook slightly. His movements were heavy and slow. He gave me a cigar with the drink. 'Sit down,' he said. 'Now then, suppose you face facts, young man. You haven't got a job and you've found that the prospects here aren't too good.'

'Oh, I don't know,' I said defensively, 'I haven't started to look – '

'I said, let's face facts,' he cut in with the imperturbability of a man accustomed to being listened to. 'I know a lot of people here. I've interests in South Africa, too. There's a gold scare on and things aren't going to be easy for a newcomer.'

He settled his big bulk carefully into a chair. I waited. He sat for a moment staring at me impersonally. Suddenly he heaved himself farther back into the chair. 'I'm prepared to offer you a job with the South Antarctic Whaling Company,' he said.

'What sort of a job?' I asked.

'I want you to take command of *Tauer III* – that's the towing ship that's waiting to take me out to the *Southern Cross*. Sudmann, her skipper, and the second mate were involved in a car crash last night. They're both in hospital.'

'What about his first mate?' I asked.

'He's not on board. He was taken ill before *Tauer III* left the factory ship. I gather you know that Nordahl, the manager of the *Southern Cross*, is dead. It's essential that I get out there as soon as possible. I've spent all day looking for a man to take command of *Tauer III*. But I can't find anyone suitable. Those that are suitable don't want to spend four months out in the Antarctic. It was only this evening that my daughter-in-law told me you had commanded a corvette during the war. These towing boats are ex-Naval corvettes, converted. I rang you straight away.'

'But I haven't the necessary papers,' I said. 'I

couldn't just walk on to the bridge of – '

He waved his thick hand. 'I'll fix that. You can leave that to me. I take it there's no technical problem? You can remember how to handle them, eh? You haven't forgotten your navigation?'

'No. But I've never taken a ship into the Antarctic. I don't know that – '

'That doesn't matter. Now then, as regards terms. You'll get the same pay as Sudmann – that's £50 a month plus bonus. You'll sign on for the season with the option of being landed at the Cape or taken back to England. You understand that your command of *Tauer III* will be a temporary one covering the trip from here to the factory ship. You'll hand over to the senior mate in the catcher fleet. I can't engage you over their heads. But we'll find you something interesting to do. And you'll have the same pay as if you were in command of the boat. Now what do you say?'

'I don't know,' I said. 'I'd like to think it over.'

'There isn't time.' His voice had sharpened. 'I want to know now. I must get out there and find out what's happened.'

'Have you no further news about how Nordahl met his death?' I asked.

'Yes,' he answered. 'A message came through just after lunch. Nordahl disappeared. That's all. There wasn't any storm. No reason for it at all. He just vanished. That's why I want to get out there.'

In the silence that followed I tried to shake my thoughts into some sort of order. I'd be away nearly four months. And then the search for a job would start again. Whilst, who knows, Kramer might have talked to somebody so that I'd get the offer of a job at this party. 'I'll need to think this over,' I said. 'I'm seeing a friend this evening. I'll let you know after that.'

His cheeks quivered slightly. 'I want your answer now,' he said.

I got to my feet. 'I'm sorry, sir. I appreciate your making me this offer. But you must give me a few hours.'

He was about to make some violent retort. But then he thought better of it. For a moment he sat, regarding the end of his cigar. Then he gave a grunt and levered himself up out of the chair. 'All right,' he said. 'Ring me when you've made up your mind. I'll wait up for your call.'

I had a drink or two at the bar downstairs, hoping to see something of Judie. In the end I got the hall porter to call me a cab. All the way out to Kramer's place the thought of Judie and her father's mysterious death occupied my thoughts. I felt as though I were destined to be mixed up in the business. I'd felt like that ever since Bland had phoned me. And something inside of me had kept saying: *Give yourself this one chance to get clear of it. Give yourself this one chance.* But as soon as I reached the party I knew that it wasn't going to be any good. I was destined for the Antarctic.

Kramer's house was built on the lines of a Dutch farm. A lot of money had been spent on it. A good deal more had been spent on the interior. The party was in full swing. There was plenty of liquor about. The males were mostly business men. There were a lot of young women. Kramer greeted me with warmth, but the way he talked I might have come out there just to get an introduction to one or two of 'the gurls' as he called them. He left me in the clutches of a pretty little thing who proved a salacious gossip. I passed her on to a man in the hardware industry and went to the bar.

A group of men were discussing the latest mining gossip. One of them said, 'But suppose the mine wasn't salted?'

'Of course it was salted,' another replied. 'If it weren't absolutely certain, they'd never have dared go as far as arresting Vynberg. I thought all along the assays were too good to be true.'

'Sure it was salted,' said the third, a stout American with a lot of gold fillings. 'But Vynberg's only the front, poor devil. There's others behind him.'

'Who?'

'I've heard three names mentioned. Vynberg's and two guys I never heard of before – Bland and Fisher. They were unloading for all they were worth twenty-four hours before the thing broke.'

'Excuse me.' I was bored, standing there by myself – or perhaps it was the association of the name Bland. 'Everybody I meet talks about the effect of the "Words" crash on the financial situation out here. Just exactly what is "Words"?' The three pairs of eyes fastened on me and were instantly hostile. 'I only arrived out here from England this morning,' I explained quickly.

'You mean to say you don't know what "Words" is?' the American asked me.

'I know nothing about finance,' I said.

I sensed their instant relief. 'Well, I'll be damned!' said the American. 'It's a real pleasure to meet somebody who hasn't got his fingers burned. "Words" is the market name for Wyks Odensdaal Rust Development Securities. The abbreviation has turned out remarkably apt. The ten shilling shares have risen from nineteen shillings to just over five pounds in the last four months on development reports showing high values at comparatively low depths. Now the whole game's bust wide open. The managing director's been arrested. They've stopped dealing in the shares on the stock exchange. I don't reckon you could give 'em away right now. And they're too thick to be used for bumph,' he added crudely. 'I've had some myself.'

'Who's this man Bland?' I asked almost without thinking. 'You mentioned – '

'Young fellow, I mentioned nobody of the name of Bland. And if I had it's a common enough name. And I don't like people listening to what I'm saying.' His fishlike eyes were staring at me coldly. I glanced at the others. The hostility was back in their eyes, too.

I turned away and picked up my drink. When I had finished it I slipped quietly out and strolled down through the velvet-soft shadows to the lights of Capetown. It was beautiful. The air smelt of blossom and the cool of evening after hot sun.

Down where the lights began I got a taxi back to the hotel. As I went towards the desk to get my key, a girl got up from a corner of the entrance hall and came towards me. It was Judie. I scarcely recognized her. She had on an off-the-shoulder evening gown and she was wearing little high-heeled slippers. She looked much taller and more graceful. A fur cape was flung round her shoulders. 'I've been waiting for you,' she said. Her face was very pale in the gold frame of her hair.

'For me?' I said. 'Why?'

'Have you made up your mind yet? Will you take command of *Tauer III*?' Her eyes pleaded as they stared at me.

'Yes,' I said.

'Thank God!' she breathed. 'If you hadn't it would have meant waiting for them to fly a man out from England. I couldn't have waited that long.'

'I'm sorry,' I said, realizing what a wait of even a few hours had meant to her.

She took me straight up to Bland's room. He nodded when he heard my decision. 'Everything's fixed,' he said. 'I guessed what your decision would be.' He picked up the phone, ordered a taxi to stand by and arranged for our luggage to be brought down. 'Yes, Mr Bonomi and Mr Weiner will be leaving, too. Also Mr Craig, Room 404.' He turned to me as he replaced the receiver. 'Get yourself packed up, Craig,' he said. 'We're leaving to-night.'

Tauer III lay in the inner basin of the harbour. Picked out in the dock lights as she chafed the concrete, she didn't look much like a corvette. She was dressed in black and grey paint, the bows had been built up for smashing through the ice and all the armament that gives the jagged look to a warship's profile had been cleared out of her. Her line was quite smooth now, though still basically the corvette line with the low after-deck. She looked what she was, a narrow-built, very fast, very powerful tug. Two seamen came down the gangway for our bags. They were big, bearded men. They said, '*God dag,*' as they passed us.

The deck hands were all Norwegian. But by the grace of God the chief engineer was a Scot. There was a knock at the door of my cabin and there he was. 'Me name's McPhee,' he said. He was a little man with thin, sandy hair. He held out an oily hand.

'I'm Craig. I'm taking over from Sudmann.'

His face lighted up and he seized hold of my hand. 'God-Christ, mon,' he cried. 'Anither Scot. There's no anither Scot walking his ane bridge in the whole fleet. Ye're the one and only. The rest of 'em is all Norwegians.'

'The appointment's temporary,' I said. But I couldn't help smiling at his excitement. 'I hope you've got some Scotch on board to celebrate with?'

'Och, aye, Ah've got a wee drap tucked away.' He peered up at me quickly. 'Tell me, mon, do ye know anything aboot these tin cans? I hope to Christ ye do, for she's an ex-corvette and a mean cow in a big sea when she's got some ice on her.'

'You needn't worry, McPhee,' I said. 'I was brought up in corvettes.'

'Och now, that's a relief, sur. Me, Ah was on the big ships.'

'Then we'll have plenty to talk about,' I said. 'Now, what about fuel and water?'

'Tanks all full.'

'Steam up?'

'Aye, we've been standing by, ready to sail, since this morning.'

'Fine,' I said. 'As soon as we get the okay from Colonel Bland, we'll be moving out. Any of the Norwegian hands speak English?'

'Most of them speak a word or two.'

'Then send the brightest linguist up to the bridge, will you?'

'Aye, aye, sur.'

As he turned to go, I stopped him. 'McPhee. When was this ship last cleaned down. She smells dirty.'

He grinned. 'Och, that's whale,' he said. 'Ye'll no worry aboot it once you get alongside o' the factory ship.'

'It's not very pleasant,' I said.

'Wait till ye've got four rotten carcases alongside. Ye'll remember what ye're smelling noo as the pure odour of carbolic.'

When he'd gone I went up on to the bridge. It had been rebuilt together with the accommodation. I looked aft along the slim length of the ship. The paint was beginning to show rust marks and she was dirty. Over everything hung the indefinable, sickly smell of whale – like a mixture of oil and death on a light breeze. But warps were neatly coiled and everything was greased and cared for. It might not be Navy fashion, but it was workmanlike.

One of the crew tapped me on the arm. 'The *hr direktör*,' he said. Bland was coming up the gangway.

I watched him lumber for'ard along the deck and then he was heaving himself up on to the bridge. 'Find your way about all right?' he inquired.

'Yes, thanks,' I answered.

'Come into the chartroom then and I'll give you the position of the *Southern Cross*.' He found the chart he wanted. 'She's about there,' he said, stabbing his finger at a point roughly three hundred miles west sou'west of the Sandwich Group. I marked the spot with a pencil. 'She's working her way south. Eide says there's a good deal of ice about and the weather's thickening. We'll get their exact position tomorrow.' He turned and pushed through the door on to the bridge. 'Met the Chief yet?' he asked. 'He's a Scot.'

'Yes, I've just been talking to him.'

'Engines all right?'

'Yes,' I said.

He nodded. 'Our agents here have fixed everything. I've got all the necessary papers with me. You can get going as soon as you're ready. Do you need a tug?'

'I've never had to be towed out of port yet,' I said.

His big hand gripped my arm. 'You and I are going to get on fine,' he said, and levered his bulk down the ladder to the deck below.

I stood for a moment, looking out across the litter of cranes to the star-filled warmth of the night over Table Bay. The palms of my hands were sweating. I was nervous. A strange ship and a strange crew. And out there, way, way south, pack ice and a fleet of ships whose operations I didn't understand.

Footsteps sounded on the ladder to the bridge. I

turned. It was one of the crew. '*Kaptein* Craig?' He pronounced it Kreig. 'McPhee speaks me to come here.'

'Good,' I said. 'I want somebody to translate my orders for me.'

'*Ja.*' He nodded his big, bearded head. His eyes glinted below the greasy peak of his cap. 'I speak *Engelsk* good. I am two years on American ships. I speak okay.'

'All right,' I said. 'You stand by me and repeat my orders in Norwegian. What's your name?'

'Peer,' he said. 'Peer Solheim.'

I told him to get hold of the coxs'n and arrange for a man to take over the wheel. The coxs'n was short and broad. He rolled for'ard like a small, purposeful barrel. 'Okay, *Kaptein,*' he called up to me, and I saw that he had placed men at the warps and at the fenders. The gangway had already been brought on board. 'Let go for'ard,' I ordered. Solheim repeated the order. The heavy warp was hauled inboard. My mouth felt dry. It was a long, time since I'd done this. 'Slow ahead!' The engine-room telegraph rang before Solheim had repeated the order. The helmsman understood. 'Let go aft!' I watched the warp come in, heard their report of all clear in Norwegian as the gap between ship and quay widened. I ordered starboard helm and watched the bow come round. The stern didn't even graze the concrete of the wharf. The men with the fenders stood there watching the concrete slide by, and then they glanced up towards the bridge. I felt suddenly at home. 'Steady as she goes,' I ordered as the bow swung to the mouth of the basin. 'Half ahead!' The engine pulsed steadily. The bridge plates vibrated gently under my feet. The concrete arms of the basin mouth slid towards us out of the warm night. We passed through into Table Bay.

A voice at my elbow said, 'It's good to see the navy at work.'

I turned to find Judie standing behind me, muffled in her fur coat. She smiled. I thought of all the times I'd manoeuvred my old corvette in and out of harbours. I'd have traded a year's pay then for the compliment and the smile and the presence of a pretty girl on the bridge. Out of the corner of my eye I saw Bland's bulky figure turn abruptly on the deck aft of the bridge and make for his cabin. 'We were both a little scared you might have trouble getting out of the basin,' Judie said.

I grinned at her. 'You thought I might run into something?' I accused her.

'Well, we'd only your word for it that you could handle a corvette.' She smiled. 'But now I am requested to inform you that the company has the greatest confidence in your ability to sail the ship.'

'Thanks,' I said. 'Is this Bland speaking or you?'

She laughed then. 'I'm only a daughter of the company, so to speak. It's the chairman who has confidence in you. In a flash of inspiration he thought the message would be more appreciated if delivered by me.'

I glanced quickly down into her eyes. 'What about you?' I asked.

'A wise girl reserves judgment,' she said with a

little laugh. And then suddenly, as though she knew the thought that was in my mind, she turned and left the bridge with a quick, 'Good night.'

I stood for a moment, gazing at the stars, identifying the blazing constellation of the Southern Cross. Table Mountain was a dark shadow crouched above the lights of the city, a shadow that blocked out the night sky. I was suddenly conscious of the helmsman. 'Okay, *Kaptein*?' he asked, nodding towards the binnacle. He was steering S.50 W.

'Okay,' I said and clapped him on the shoulder. When I laid off the course I found the man was correct within 3 degrees.

All next day we steamed sou'west at a steady thirteen knots through blazing summer sun and a blue, windless sea. I wasn't a whaler and I couldn't adapt myself to their free and easy ways. I ran the ship the only way I knew, the way I'd learned in the Navy. I took the coxs'n with me in the morning on an inspection of the ship and was surprised to find that the decks had been hosed down, mess tables scrubbed, the galley shining and the men – practically springing to attention, all grins, whenever I spoke to them. When I reached the engine-room I said to McPhee, 'It's almost like being back in the Navy.'

He grinned and wiped a greasy hand across his freshly shaven jaw. 'Dinna fool yourself, sur,' he said. 'This is a whale towing ship, not a corvette. But they'll play your game for a day or two. The word got round you were a Navy officer and not a whaler. A lot of 'em were in the Navy during the war. They were tickled to death when they heard there was to be an inspection.'

I felt the blood mounting to my face. 'There'll be no more inspections then,' I said curtly.

'Och, dinna spoil their fun, sur. It'll be the talk of the fleet when we reach the *Southern Cross* – how they had a British Navy officer for the trip and stood to attention and were inspected.' He winked. 'Dinna spoil their bit o' fun,' he repeated. And then anxiously: 'Ye're no offended because Ah've put ye wise to it all being a wee bit of a game?'

'Of course not,' I said.

Looking over the list of the crew later in the day I found a name that didn't seem to fit in – Doctor Walter Howe. I was on the bridge at the time and I got McPhee on the blower. 'Who's this Doctor Howe and why haven't I seen him?' I asked. 'Presumably he messes with the officers?'

'Aye, but it's no verra often we see him for breakfast,' McPhee's voice replied up the pipe. 'He's the biggest soak in the whole whaling fleet. And that's saying something. He also kens more aboot what makes a whale tick than anyone else. He's a scientist. He's worked for the South Antarctic Company since the war. He's a wee bit o' a nuisance at times, but he's no a bad sort when ye get to know him.'

I got to know the doctor that night. I had had coffee and sandwiches up on the bridge and when the coxs'n relieved me, I went down to my cabin, put on a pair of slippers and relaxed with the assistance of a bottle of Scotch from Sudmann's locker. Then the door opened and Doctor Howe came in.

He didn't knock. He just came straight in. 'My name's Howe.' He stood, swaying slightly in the doorway, looking at me uncertainly out of rather bulging, bloodshot eyes as though he expected me to deny that that was his name. He was a tall lath of a man with a pronounced stoop and an oddly shaped head that was all forehead and no chin. He had a prominent Adam's apple which jerked up and down convulsively as though he were continually trying to swallow something. His eyes dropped to the whisky bottle. 'Do you mind pouring me a drink?' He moved forward into the cabin and I saw that the sole of his left shoe was built up. He wasn't lame, but that slight shortness of one leg gave him an awkward, rather crab-like way of walking and he swung his right arm out wide as though to balance himself.

He sat down on my bunk and fingered his frayed and dirty collar as though it were too tight for him. I poured him a drink and passed it too him. He absorbed it as the desert absorbs rain. 'Ah-ah, that's better,' he said and lit a cigarette. Then he saw I was looking at him and his thick rubbery lips twisted into a quick impish smile. 'I'm ugly, aren't I,' he said. And then as I turned quickly to my drink: 'Oh, you needn't be embarrassed. It amuses me – when I'm drunk.' He paused and then added, 'And mostly I'm drunk.'

He leaned forward, suddenly tense. 'Ugly duckling. That's what my sisters used to call me. God damn their eyes! That's a hell of a way to start a kid brother out in life. Fortunately my mother was sorry for me, and she had money of her own. I started drinking at the age of puberty.' He gave a harsh laugh and put his feet up on the bunk, lying back and closing his eyes. His clothes were dirty and looked as though he slept in them.

'What's your job with the company?' I asked.

'My job?' He opened his eyes, screwing them up as he stared at the ceiling. 'My job is to tell 'em where the whales go in the summer time. I'm biologist, oceanographist, meteorologist, all rolled into one. It's the same as fortune telling. Only I use *plankton* instead of a crystal and I'm called a scientist. Any of the old *skytters* manage just as well by intuition. Only don't tell Bland that. I've held this job ever since the war and it suits me.'

To stop him sneering at himself I said, 'I don't know anything about whaling, as you've probably gathered. What's *plankton* and who are the *skytters*?'

He laughed. It was a gobbling sound that jerked at his Adam's apple. The ungainly head slewed round and grinned at me like a gargoyle. '*Plankton* is sea food. The stuff the fin whales feed on. Oh God – now we're off.' He sat up and knocked back the rest of his drink, pushing the empty glass towards me in an unmistakable manner. I filled it up. 'There's two main types of cetacean,' he said, assuming a mock schoolmasterly voice. 'Those with teeth and those with finners. Whale, like the spermaceti, have teeth and live on large squids from the ocean bed. The fin whale has a mouthful of finners and lives on *plankton*, which is like a very tiny shrimp. He gulps twenty ton or so of water into his mouth and then forces it out through the fins, which act as a sieve. The water goes out, the *plankton* remains. It needs an awful lot of *plankton* to keep an eighty-ton whale alive,' he added. 'Mostly we catch fin whales. So if you know where their food is – well, that's what I try to do, forecast by water temperature, currents, weather and so on where the *plankton* is.'

'And *skytters*?' I asked as he paused.

'*Skytter* is the Danish origin of the English word shooter, and it's pronounced the same way. The *skytters* are the catcher skippers. It's always the skipper who operates the harpoon gun. Sometimes we call them gunners.'

He lay back as though exhausted by this brief dissemination of information. The silence must have lasted over a minute whilst I racked my brain for something in common that we could talk about. 'Queer about Nordahl,' he said suddenly. I only just caught what he said. He seemed to be talking to himself. 'He was a wonderful man.'

I could hear Judie's voice saying exactly the same. 'That's what his daughter thinks,' I said.

'To hell with his daughter,' he cried angrily, thrusting himself up on to one elbow. 'A little bitch that falls for a tyke like Erik Bland shouldn't be able to call Bernt Nordahl her father.'

'Don't shout,' I said. 'Bland might hear you.'

'Do Bland good to know what his son is really like,' he stormed angrily.

'What's wrong with him?' I asked.

He sat up, swinging his feet off the bunk. 'Nothing,' he said, 'except the way he's been brought up and the way his mind works.' His voice was bitter. 'Bland's a fool to think he can make his son fit to take over the business by sending him out for one season. All Bland thinks about is finance. It's Bernt Nordahl who handles the whaling side. He was the best *skytter* in Norway. Then after the war he and Bland floated the South Antarctic Company. Nordahl took over management of the factory ship. In some outfits it's the Master of the factory ship who's in charge of operations. In our case it's the Manager. And in the four seasons we've been operating, we've got more whale than any other outfit. Why? Because I know where the *plankton* is? Because the *skytters* have good intuition? No. Because old Bernt Nordahl can smell whale. And the whales went through the factory ship cheaper, faster and with less waste than on any other factory ship. And that's because the men would do anything Nordahl says – they worshipped him. Or rather the old crowd did – the Tönsberg men.' He gulped down the rest of his drink. 'And now he's dead. Lost overboard. Nobody knows how or why.' He shook his head. 'I don't know what to think. He'd been on ships all his life.' The very words Judie had used. 'He was as much at home in these frozen seas as we'd be in London. He couldn't just vanish like that. By Christ!' he added violently. 'I'll ferret out the truth of what happened if it takes me the rest of the voyage.'

I think it was then that I got the first premonition of trouble ahead. Howe had buried his head in his hands and was rocking gently to and fro. 'I'd like to know what was in his mind that night he died,' he murmured.

'What are you thinking of?' I asked. 'Suicide?'

'Suicide?' His head jerked up as though I'd hit him. 'No,' he said angrily. 'No, he'd never have done that.' He shook his head. 'You don't know him, of course. He was a small man, but he had great energy and a sense of humour. His eyes were always twinkling. He was a happy man. The thought of suicide would never enter his head. He enjoyed life.'

'But if Bland were planning to hand control of the company to his son – surely that might be grounds for suicide?' I suggested.

Howe gave a quick laugh – a jackal laugh, half bark. 'Bland pinched his girl once,' he said. 'Bernt Nordahl didn't commit suicide then. No, he went and consoled himself with a married woman.' He smiled as though at some secret joke. 'No. Whatever happened, he didn't commit suicide.' His fingers had tightened on his empty tumbler so that I thought he'd crush the glass. Then he leaned forward and picked up the bottle, automatically filling the tumbler to the brim with neat whisky.

'Why is Bland in such a hurry to hand over the business to his son?' I asked.

'Because every man dreams of a son to carry on where he leaves off,' he snarled. And I understood then why he needed to stay drunk.

'But why the hurry?' I asked.

'Why, why, why?' – his voice had risen again. 'You're as full of questions as a damned school kid. I was a schoolmaster once,' he added irrelevantly. 'Taught science.' He took another gulp at his drink. 'You want to know why Bland is in a hurry? All right, I'll tell you. He's in a hurry because he's going to die. And he knows it. He's had two strokes already. And as far as I'm concerned the sooner he's dead the better. He's a financial crook with about as much sense of – ' His voice jerked to a stop. His mouth stayed open, the jaw slack. He was gazing at the cabin door.

I twisted round in my seat. The door was open as it had been all along. And framed in it was Bland's heavy bulk. He came in and I saw that his face was mottled with the pressure of his anger. 'Get to your cabin, Howe,' he said in a terrible, controlled voice. 'And stay there. You're drunk.' Behind him, in the passage, I caught a glimpse of Judie's pale face.

Howe cringed away from him as though he expected to be struck. Then his long neck jerked out. 'I'm glad you heard,' he breathed. 'I wanted you to hear.' His voice steadied. It was unnaturally quiet as he said, 'I wish you were dead. I wish you'd died before you ever left South Africa and came to Norway and met Anna Halvorsen.' His hands clenched and he stared vacantly into space. 'I wish I'd never been born,' he whispered.

'Craig. Get him in his cabin.' Bland's voice shook.

I nodded. 'Come on,' I said to Howe.

The man staggered to his feet, swaying slightly. He

still had the vacant look, but he turned his head and focused slowly on Bland. His hands clenched again and he thrust out his head like a tortoise, peering into Bland's eyes. 'If you killed him,' he hissed, 'God help you.' His face was twisted with venom. Hate blazed in his eyes.

Bland's big hands caught hold of him. 'What do you mean by that?' He looked as though he was on the point of battering Howe's ugly face to pulp.

Howe seemed to relax slightly. His thick lips drew back from his teeth in a smile. It was as though he suddenly dominated Bland, as though the other were afraid of him and he knew it. 'If Uriah, the Hittite, had lived,' he said softly, 'what would have happened the next time?'

'Don't talk to me in riddles,' Bland snapped.

'Then have it in plain words,' Howe shouted. 'You tricked Bernt out of the woman he loved. And now you've been trying to trick him out of his interest in the company. For all I know you've done worse than that. But don't worry, Bland. I'll find out the truth about his death. And if you're the cause of it – ' he stooped his head down so that his eyes were looking straight into Bland's – 'I'll kill you,' he said.

He turned then, swaying slightly, and reached the door, his body inclined as though leaning against a strong wind. Bland found his voice again. 'As from to-day, you cease to be in the employ of the company,' he said abruptly.

Howe turned, smiling slyly. 'I shouldn't do that, Bland,' he said. 'Wouldn't look good – first Bernt, then me. Too much like making a clean sweep.' He was face to face with Judie now in the doorway. I saw her shrink back. Her eyes were very wide, her face a pale mask. Howe stopped and stared at her a moment. Then he laughed, and still laughing, staggered along the passage to his cabin.

Judie watched him go, her lips a tight-drawn gash of red against the white of her face. She didn't say anything. Bland turned to me. He gave an apologetic shrug of his shoulders. 'I'm sorry you should have been witness to such a melodramatic scene,' he said. 'The man's not right in the head, I'm afraid. I'd never have employed him but for Nordahl. But until this moment I didn't know he knew certain personal things. It gives his warped mind the sense of a grudge. I'd be glad if you'd keep the matter to yourself.'

'Of course,' I said.

The man looked terribly shaken. His face had a bluish tinge and his heavy cheeks quivered. 'Good night,' he muttered.

'Good night,' I replied.

He closed the door behind him. I poured another drink and sat there wondering what the hell I'd got myself into.

THREE

Next day the sun had gone. The sea was grey and flecked with whitecaps. A southerly wind drove ragged wisps of cloud across the sky. In a night's sailing we seemed to have left summer behind us. The wind was cold and I began to think of the miles of ice-infested seas that lay ahead. The deck heaved as *Tauer III* lurched over the waves like a drunkard. Things were different this morning. The crew stood about in little groups, talking furtively. There was a sullen, brooding air about the ship.

There were not friendly grins as I inspected the ship that morning. And later in the day an ugly fight broke out between two of the men. The coxs'n wouldn't let me interfere, so I got McPhee up on to the bridge and asked him what the trouble was.

'Weel.' He fingered his jaw the way he had. 'It's no exactly easy to explain. Ye see, this is a Nordahl boat. The men are all from Tönsberg. And noo that they know Nordahl is dead – '

'How did they find that out?'

'Ye canna have a row like there was between Bland and Howe last night wi'oot it getting aroond the ship. Ye'd be surprised, but the men are fond of Howe, the same way they were fond of Nordahl.'

'But they don't have to fight about it.'

'Och, that was just their way of blowing off steam. The coxs'n was quite right to stop ye from interfering. Ye see, there's no love lost between the Tönsberg and Sandefjord men, and it's a Sandefjord man got hurt.'

'Sandefjord's one of the whaling towns of Norway, isn't it?' I asked.

'Aye. The biggest. And Tönsberg another whaling toun.'

'But they don't have to fight, just because there's rivalry between the two towns.'

'Och, ye don't understand. It's this way. Nordahl was a Tönsberg man. When he and Colonel Bland started the company after the war, Nordahl had a free hand wi' the signing on of the crews. Naturally, he signed on Tönsberg men. But Mrs Bland – she's Norwegian ye ken – she comes from Sandefjord. Och, it's maybe joost gossip, but they say she fancies herself as a wee bittie queen of the place. Whatever the cause of it, Sandefjord men were included in the crews last season. An' this season the proportion's aboot fifty-fifty. Weel, it dinna make for smooth-running. There's a natural resentment amongst the Tönsberg men.'

'So they took it out of this poor devil from Sandefjord?'

'Aye, that's aboot it. They're in an angry and soospiscious mood – angry because they weren't told aboot Nordahl's death – soospiscious . . . Weel, there's one or two persons they would'na mind shoving overboard.'

'Meaning – who?' I asked.

But he shook his head. 'Ah'm no saying anither worrd.'

'Do you mean Bland and his son?' I asked him.

'A'm no saying anither worrd,' he repeated. But I saw by the glint in his eye that I'd hit the nail on the head.

'Well, I hope they don't do anything foolish,' I said. 'It's coming up dirty.'

He cocked his eye at the sky to windward and nodded.

'Aye, it'll be a dirrty nicht, Ah'm thinking. But

they'll sail the ship all reet. Ye dinna ha' to fash yerself aboot that.'

'And the Sandefjord man?'

'He'll be all reet noo.' He hesitated, shuffling his feet awkwardly. 'Ye'll no pass on what Ah said jist noo aboot they're wanting to get rid o' one or two persons?'

'Of course not.'

He suddenly grinned. 'It's the de'il when ye've got factions like this an' they're cooped oop togither in a God-forsaken place like the Antarctic for moonths on end. It's no so bad on the catchers and the towing ships. Each ship is either Tönsberg or Sandefjord, wi' a smattering of Scots in the engine-rooms. The Sandefjord laddie is only on board here because he was held in Capetown for hospital treatment. But I tell ye, it's no sa gude on the factory ship.'

'You mean they've a mixed crew on the *Southern Cross*?' I asked him.

'Aye. An' it isna only the crew that's mixed. It's the flensers and lemmers and labourers, that's mixed, too. And they're a violent bluidy bunch o' bastards.' He shook his head gloomily and turned to go.

'Perhaps you'd care to have a drink with me later,' I suggested.

His face relaxed into a dour smile. 'Aye, Ah would that.' And he slid down the ladder to the deck below, leaving me with a welter of half-digested thoughts in my head.

I paced up and down for a time, my mind saturated with conjecture. Perhaps Bland sensed this. It's the only explanation I can give for the sudden intimacy of his conversation. I hadn't seen him all day. He'd kept to his cabin. But about seven o'clock he pulled himself up on to the bridge. He was muffled up in coats and scarves and he looked even broader than usual. His face was blue and puffy, the blood-vessels showing through the skin in a mottled web. 'Has the *Southern Cross* given you her position yet?' he asked.

'Yes,' I said. 'I got a message from Captain Eide this morning.'

'Good.' He peered over the helmsman's shoulder at the compass and then stared out to windward, screwing his eyes up behind his thick-lensed glasses. 'Hear there was a fight,' he said.

'Yes. Sandefjord versus Tönsberg. Tönsberg won,' I added. I don't know quite why I put it like that. I suppose I wanted him to talk.

He gave me a quick glance and then leaned his heavy bulk against the windbreaker. 'Women are the devil,' he muttered. I think he was speaking to himself, but I was leeward of him and the wind flung the words at me. 'You married?' he asked, turning abruptly towards me.

'No,' I said.

He nodded slowly. It was as though he were saying – *You're lucky.* 'A man's no match for a woman,' he said, looking straight at me. 'A man's mind and interests range. A woman's narrow. They've a queer, distorted love of power – and they're fonder of their sons than they are of their husbands.' He turned his head away and stared down at the sea where it was beginning to break inboard over our plunging bow.

I didn't say anything. For a moment I thought the sudden intimacy had been broken. But then he said, 'Human relationships are queer. Have you ever thought what a thin veneer our civilization is? It's little more than a code of manners, concealing the primitive.'

'Human nature doesn't change,' I said.

He nodded. 'It becomes cribbed by the regulations and hoodoos of society. But I agree, it doesn't change. Once let slip the leash of organized society...' He didn't finish the sentence, but stood with his face to the wind as though to cool the inflamed blood-vessels that webbed it.

'What exactly are you trying to tell me?' I asked bluntly. He looked round at me then, peering up at me through his glasses. 'I don't know,' he said. 'But you're intelligent – and you're outside it all. A man must have somebody to talk to when things are getting too much for him.' He turned his head back to the sea again, hunching it into the fur collar of his topcoat. He was like a big bull-frog squatting there against the windbreaker. 'Howe told you I was dying?' It was a statement rather than a question.

'He said something about you having had a couple of strokes,' I told him.

'Well, I'm dying.' He said it matter-of-factly as though he were informing a group of shareholders that the company had traded at a deficit.

'We're all doing that,' I said.

He grunted. 'Of course. But we're not usually given

a time limit. The best man in Harley Street gives me a year at most.' His hand gripped the canvas of the windbreaker and jerked at it as though he wanted to tear it in little shreds. 'A year's not long,' he said hoarsely. 'It's twelve months – three hundred and sixty-five days. And at any moment I may get another stroke, and that'll finish me.' He suddenly laughed. It was a bitter, violent sound. 'When you're told that, it changes your approach to life. Things which seemed important before cease to be important. Others loom larger.' His hand relaxed on the windbreaker. 'When we reach the *Southern Cross*,' he said, 'get to know my son. I want your opinion of him.' He turned abruptly then and went ponderously down the ladder to the deck below. I watched him go, wishing I'd been able to hold him just a little longer. There were questions I'd like to have asked him.

In the middle of our meal that night, the radio operator brought Bland a message. His heavy brows dragged down as he read it. Then he got to his feet. 'A word with you, Craig,' he growled.

I followed him to his cabin. He closed the door and handed me the message. 'Read that,' he said.

I took the message to the light. It read: *Eide to Bland. Men demanding inquiry Nordahl's death. Erik Bland has rejected demand. Please confirm rejection. Mood of Tönsberg men dangerous. Whale very scarce. Position 57.98 S. 34.62 W. Pack ice heavy.*

I handed the message back to him. He crumpled it up in his big fist. 'The damned fool!' he growled. 'It'll be all over the ship that he's not happy about Erik's decision. And Erik's quite right to reject a demand like that. It's a matter for the officers to decide.' He paced up and down for a moment, tugging at the lobe of his ear. 'What worries me is that they should be demanding an inquiry at all. If the circumstances warranted an inquiry, then Erik should have ordered it right away instead of waiting for the men to demand it. And I don't like Eide's use of the word *dangerous*,' he added. 'He wouldn't use it unless the situation was bad.' He swung round on me. 'What's the earliest we can expect to reach the *Southern Cross*?'

'Eight days at least,' I answered.

He nodded gloomily. 'A lot can happen in eight days. The worst news in that message is that they're getting few whales. When men are busy they haven't the energy to brood. But when no whales are coming in – I've seen men change from smiles to hatred in the twinkling of an eye when the whales have been lost. And they'll link it in their minds with Nordahl's death, damn them. They're a superstitious lot, and Nordhal had a nose for whale.'

'What are you scared of?' I asked. 'You're not suggesting that the men would mutiny, are you? Presumably a factory ship comes under normal British maritime laws. It takes a lot to drive men to mutiny.'

'Of course I'm not suggesting they'd mutiny. But they can make things damned awkward without going as far as mutiny. There's three million pounds invested in that outfit. To make money on a capital outlay as big as that in a four-month season everything has got to move with clock-like precision.' He began tugging at the lobe of his ear again. 'Erik can't handle a thing like this. He hasn't the experience.'

'Then put somebody else in charge,' I suggested. 'Captain Eide, for instance.'

He looked up at me quickly. His small eyes were narrowed. I could see the battle going on inside him – pride against prudence. 'No,' he said. 'No. He must learn to handle things himself.'

He paced up and down. He didn't say anything. The silence in the cabin was the sort of silence that is audible. I could see the conflict working in the man. With sudden decision he went to the door. 'I'll have Eide report independently,' he threw over his shoulder.

I went up on to the bridge. The sea was a heaving mass in the dreary half light. I stood there for a moment, watching the heavy weight of water surging white across the bow every time the little ship plunged. An albatross wheeled over the mast. Its huge wings were still as it planed into the wind. The air was bitterly cold. A thin film of ice was spreading on the windbreaker so that the canvas was stiff and smooth to the touch. I went into the wheelhouse and looked at the barometer. 'No good,' said the bearded Norwegian at the wheel. He was right. The glass was very low and still falling. 'The sommer she did not kom, eh?' His bearded face opened in a grin. But there was no answering humour in his blue eyes.

The door flung back and Judie entered, the wind blowing her in with a swirl of sleet. She shut the door with difficulty. 'The weather looks bad,' she said. Her face was pinched and cold.

'We're getting into high latitudes,' I reminded her.

She nodded bleakly. I offered her a cigarette. She took it and as I struck a match to light it for her I saw that her hand was trembling slightly. She gulped in a lungful of smoke and then asked, 'Was that message from Eide?'

'Yes,' I said.

'What did it say?'

I told her.

She turned and stared out through the window. The sea was cold and grey, a tumbled mass of water, barely visible, yet seeming to crowd its menace right into the wheelhouse. She didn't speak for some time, and when she did she startled me by saying, 'I feel scared.'

'It's just the weather,' I said.

She dropped her cigarette and ground it out violently with her heel. 'No. It's not the weather. It – it's something I don't understand.' She turned and faced me. 'I should just be feeling wretched because he's dead. It should end there – with sorrow. But it doesn't.' And then she said again, 'I'm scared.'

I stepped forward and took her hand. It was cold as ice. 'It's rotten for you,' I said. 'But there's no need for you to worry. Things will sort themselves out when we reach the *Southern Cross*.'

'I don't know,' she said. 'I feel as though that's just the beginning.' She looked up at me. Her grey eyes were deeply troubled. 'Walter knows something – knows something that we don't.' Her voice trembled. She was overwrought.

'Why should Howe know anything we don't?' I said. 'You're imagining things.'

'I'm not imagining things,' she answered violently. 'I'm seeing things for the first time.'

I didn't say anything and we stood there for some time, quite silent. She didn't attempt to withdraw her hand from mine. But there was no contact between us. Then she suddenly jerked her hand away, pulled a packet of cigarettes out of her pocket and offered me one. 'Is this the farthest south you've ever been?' she asked, her voice controlled and a little abrupt.

'Yes,' I said and raised my other hand to show I was still smoking. 'But I'm not new to ice. When I was twenty I went on a university expedition to south-east Greenland.'

'So. You are an explorer?' She took one of her cigarettes and I lit it for her. 'But you'll find it very different down here. The land mass of the South Pole makes it much colder.'

She took a long pull at the cigarette and added, 'But it's unusual for the pack to be so far north at this time of the year. It's like it was in the summer of 1914 when Shackleton came down here in the *Endurance*.'

'I was in Oslo just after the war,' I said. 'I went over to Bygdoy and saw the *Fram*. I think that must be the best exhibition of Polar exploration in the world.'

'Yes. I like it, too. We are very proud of the *Fram*.'

The conversation languished there, so I said, 'I suppose this is your first trip into the Antarctic?'

'No,' she replied. 'Not my first. When I was eight years old my father brought me with him to South

Georgia. My mother had just died and we had no home. Bernt was one of the *skytters* at Grytviken. I was there about two months. Then he sent me to friends in New Zealand. He said it was time I learnt English. I learned my English in Auckland. I was there a year and then he took me back with him at the end of the next season.'

'Is Grytviken in South Georgia?' I asked.

'Yes. There are shore stations there. I made three or four trips with my father in his catcher.'

'Then you're quite an experienced whaler,' I kidded her.

'No,' she said. 'I'm not like Gerda Petersen.'

'Who's she?' I asked.

'Gerda is the daughter of Olaf Petersen,' she answered. 'Olaf was once mate on my father's catcher when he was at Grytviken. Gerda and I are the same age. We used to play together when we were at Grytviken. But she's tough. She's more like a man. This is her second season with our company. Her father says he'll make her the first woman *skytter* in Norway.'

'She must be tough,' I said.

She laughed. 'Poor Gerda. She's not very beautiful, you know. She ought to have been born a boy. She's passed all her exams. She could be master of a ship, like women are in Russia. But she prefers to come south as her father's mate. His men worship her. She may not be very beautiful, but I think she's very happy.'

A sudden gust of wind hit the wheelhouse. The ship heeled and dipped violently. I caught a glimpse of the white sheet of spray flung up by the bows as they crashed into a wave, felt the whole ship tremble. The door burst open and the coxs'n came in. Judie said, 'I think I'll go below now.'

'I'll come with you,' I said. 'I want to get some sleep before the storm breaks.' I told the coxs'n to wake me if it got worse and took Judie below. I saw her to her cabin. Below decks the movement of the ship seemed much more violent. I was very conscious that the worst was yet to come.

'I'll introduce you to Gerda,' Judie said as I held the door of her cabin open for her. 'She's very fat and very jolly – and you'll like her.' She gave me a quick smile. 'I hope you'll have enough clothing,' she said. 'It'll be cold up on the bridge when dawn comes.'

'Fortunately Sudmann and I are about the same size,' I said. I wished her good night and closed the door. Back in my own cabin, I took off my boots and climbed into my bunk with my clothes on.

For a long time I lay awake, listening to the straining of the ship, sensing the growing pressure of the wind and seas, and all the time wondering about the factory ship still two thousand miles sou'west of us.

The full force of the storm hit us just after four in the morning. I woke to sudden consciousness, feeling the weight of the water holding us down. The struggle of the ship against the fury of the elements was there in every sound of her – in the creaking of the cabin furniture, in the jerk and shudder of the engine, in the staggering movement of her as she plunged and climbed, plunged and climbed. I could feel the steel of the cabin walls bending under the strain. She was like a live thing fighting for breath.

I rolled out of my bunk and fumbled for my sea boots. The coxs'n came in as I was dragging on my oilskins. He didn't say anything. He just nodded and went out again. Outside the full force of the wind hit me, thrusting me against the rail, taking my breath away. Seas rolled green over the after deck. I hauled myself up to the bridge. The short night was over. But the dawn was a grey half darkness. The coxs'n had headed her into the wind. The waves seemed mountains high, their tops a hissing whirl of spindrift. And the sleet drove parallel with the wavetops, a wild, driven curtain of darkness.

I won't attempt to describe those next eight days. They were eight days of unrelieved hell for everyone on board. Sometimes it rained. More often it just blew. The weight of the wind varied, but I doubt whether it ever dropped below Force 6. It was from the southwest, varying about two points either side. The sea was like a mountain range on the move. There wasn't a dry place in the ship. Nearly everyone was seasick. In all those eight days we only saw the sun once, and that was a watery gleam that flashed out for a few minutes through a vent in the storm wrack. I ceased to think about the object of our journey, or about the *Southern Cross*; I ceased to think about anything but the ship. My mind was a blank of sleeplessness in which the safety of the ship was the only tangible idea.

I saw hardly anything of the others. I was up on the bridge most of the time. Bland came up twice, his heavy features blue with cold and the exhaustion of seasickness. Each time he asked for our position. The man had a driving purpose which was accentuated by the knowledge of his illness. His interest in life had narrowed down to an urgent desire to reach the *Southern Cross* as soon as possible. He was impatient at our slow progress, impotently angry at the elements. I remember him standing there on the bridge and shaking his fist at the sea and shouting, 'Damn you! Damn you!' as though curses could subdue the wind. Some ice had formed on the rungs of the bridge ladder. He slipped as he went down, and a wave, bursting against the side of the ship, nearly swept him overboard. He was wet through and badly shaken. He didn't come up to the bridge again.

Judie came up once and I was angry with her, telling her to keep to her cabin. I think I threw some bad language at her. I was too wrought up to know what I said. It had the desired effect and she didn't come up again. But after that every morning one of the crew brought up a flask of brandy.

'*Fra fru* Bland.' I was grateful to her for that.

Bonomi was the only one of the passengers who was a daily visitor on the bridge. He was suffering badly from seasickness, but he'd struggle up each day with his camera, regardless of the danger, and take pictures of the storm. His greeting was invariably the same: 'It is turn out nice again – yes?' And his monkey-like face, green under the olive tan, would crack in a wide grin. Once I asked him about Doctor Howe. 'Is he sick?' I asked.

'He is sick, of course,' he answered. 'But what is sickness to a man who drink two bottles of whisky a day? He is incredible, that man!'

In a way the storm was a good thing. There was no more trouble with the Sandefjord man. The crew were fully occupied with the weather. This, according to the old hands, was quite unprecedented. It was much colder than it should have been and the gale prolonged itself out of all expectation. But by the 14th we were in 54.42 S. 24.65 W. some 500 miles east of South Georgia. Daylight was now virtually continuous throughout the twenty-four hours. Visibility fortunately was not too bad for on the 15th we sighted our first iceberg. And shortly after the evening meal the masthead lookout reported land on the port beam. This was the first of the Sandwich Group. It was the only glimpse we got of it as the storm clouds closed in and heavy, icy rain reduced visibility to a few miles.

Our course was still S. 47° W. and we began to sight icebergs regularly, some of them big, towering masses of ice, pinnacled and ramparted like floating forts. One we passed must have been fully three miles long with a completely flat top except for one steep and sudden mass like the superstructure of a ship. It bore, in fact, a striking resemblance to a monstrous aircraft carrier coated in ice.

I was constantly up on the bridge now for we were closing the last position we had received from the *Southern Cross*. We should have been in radio telephone communication – the R/T set had a radius of 400 miles or more. But early in the storm our aerials

had been brought down and it had been impossible to
re-rig.

On the night of the 16th the gale got worse than
ever. Heavy, freezing rain brought visibility down to
almost zero and in the half light around midnight I
reduced speed. Shortly afterwards the lookout called
down, 'Isen.' I rang for slow ahead and a few moments
later caught the white glimmer of ice ahead. It wasn't
a berg. It was our first taste of loose pack. The floes
were small and broken – the thawing fringe broken
from the pack ice farther south and flung north-
eastward by the storm. The coxs'n shook his head
gloomily. 'Nefer haf I seen the ice up here in sommer.'

I turned the ship westward and remained at slow
ahead. Early that morning the wind suddenly veered
to the south and died away to a gentle breeze. The
clouds drifted away astern and we saw the sun clearly
for the first time in eight days. It was low on the
horizon and had little warmth. But it was wonderful
just to see it. The sky was blue and the world looked
suddenly cheerful. But the sea remained a mountainous, heaving mass and despite the blue of the sky it
had a peculiar, cold green colour. Away to the south a
glimmer of white showed the fringe of the loose pack
ice. Through bleary eyes I watched the sun climb
quickly up the sky. Soon everything was steaming.

Then gradually the sun's light paled. The warmth
died out of it and the blue gradually faded from the
sky. A damp cold gripped the ship. The horizon faded.
The distant line of white that marked the ice became
blurred and then vanished, merging into what looked

like a low strata of cloud at sea level. Then the sun vanished altogether. The colour drained out of everything. The scene became a flat black and white picture. It was cold, like an etching. Then the sharpness of it faded as the fog rolled over us, enveloping us in its chill, soundless blanket.

We kept at slow ahead with lookouts in the bow and at the masthead. I was taking no chances with icebergs, though in that brief glimpse of the ice-littered sea to the south I had seen no sign of any.

Shortly after ten Bland himself came up on to the bridge. Eight days of enforced idleness and little food had made a great difference to him. His face was leaner. The bluish tinge had gone and the mottled veining of his skin was not so noticeable. His movements were quicker too, and his eyes more alert. 'What's our position?' he asked. His tone was crisp. The personality that had driven the man to the top of his own world was there in his voice.

'Fifty-eight south, thirty-three west,' I told him. I took him into the wheelhouse and showed him the position on the chart – roughly 200 miles west of South Thule, the southernmost point of the Sandwich Group.

'We ought to be able to get the *Southern Cross* on the R/T,' he said.

'Sparks is rigging a new aerial now,' I told him. 'I'll let you know as soon as he makes contact.'

He nodded and went out on to the bridge. He stood for a while, staring out into the fog. He stood like that for several minutes, his big hands, encased in fur gloves, gripping the ice-stiff canvas of the wind-breaker. Suddenly he swung round on me. 'I've been mixed up in whaling for the last twenty-five years,' he said. 'I've never heard of summer conditions as bad as this.'

I made the same remark that Judie had made eight days before that it was the sort of conditions that Shackleton experienced in the *Endurance* in 1914. He gave a grunt. 'This isn't a damned polar expedition,' he growled. 'This is business. See any whale this morning?'

'None,' I said.

'Where's Howe?'

'I haven't seen him since the storm started,' I replied.

He turned and barked an order in Norwegian to one of the crew.

The man looked at him. It wasn't exactly insolence. But the man's manner was sullen as he said, '*Ja*,' and crossed the bridge to the ladder.

Bland spoke to him sharply. The man's face darkened. '*Ja – hr direktör*,' he muttered and slid down the ladder to the deck below. Bland said something violent under his breath and walked to the starboard wing of the bridge. He stood there alone, peering out over the side, until Howe appeared.

Howe looked thin as a wraith beside the squat bulk of the company's chairman. He had a weak growth of beard that looked untidy on his queer face and his eyes were bloodshot. But he was sober. Standing in front of Bland he seemed nervous as though, without liquor inside him, he found it difficult to face the man. 'For the last four years Nordahl has employed you as a scientist,' Bland rumbled, his small eyes looking the other up and down with marked distaste. 'Now it's up to you to justify that appointment. Conditions out here this summer are abnormal. The last report we had for the *Southern Cross* spoke of few whales. We've seen none. By tomorrow morning I want a report from you on the probable movement of whale in these conditions.'

'I understood you to say I was no longer employed by the company.' Howe's voice had developed a slight stutter. His Adam's apple jerked up and down under his scrubby beard.

'Forget it,' Bland said. 'You were drunk. I shall assume you didn't know what you were saying. Your continued employment will depend on your usefulness to the company. Now get to work. I want a full report first thing tomorrow morning.'

Bland turned on his heel. Howe hesitated. I knew what he wanted to say. He wanted to tell Bland that it was unfair to expect the impossible, that the very abnormality of the conditions made it so. He was being blackmailed and he knew it. Bland wanted whales. Howe was to produce them, like a conjurer, or be sacked. His Adam's apple jerked violently once or twice. His mouth opened and then suddenly closed. He turned and stumbled past me to the bridge ladder.

Shortly afterwards Bland went below. An hour later, Bonomi called up to me to say that the radio was working. I left the coxs'n on the bridge and stumbled

wearily down to the deck below. My eyes were bleary
with lack of sleep and the strain of staring into days
of wind and sleet and the morning's impenetrable blanket of fog. Bland and Judie were both in the wireless
room. Judie had dark circles of strain under her eyes.
But her smile of greeting was warm and friendly. 'You
must be dead,' she said.

'The daily flask of brandy was a great help,' I said.

She looked away quickly as though she hadn't
wanted to be thanked. Bland turned his big head
towards me. He had taken off the little fur cap with
the ear flaps that he'd been wearing and his mane of
white hair was rumpled. He looked like a rather surprised owl. 'Just trying to get the *Southern Cross* on
the R/T,' he said. 'We've been speaking to the *Haakon*
– one of the Sandefjord factory ships. She's got eight
whale in the last ten days. Now she's steaming south
towards the Weddell Sea. Hanssen, the master, says
he's never known conditions like this. He's about three
hundred miles west-sou'west of us.'

The radio crackled. Then clear and distinct came
a voice speaking in Norwegian. I guessed it must be
the *Southern Cross*, for Bland stiffened and his head
jerked round toward the receiver. The radio operator
leaned down towards the mike. '*Ullo-ullo-ullo – Syd
Korset. Tauer III anroper Syd Korset.*' There was a
quick exchange in Norwegian and then he turned to
Bland. 'I have Captain Eide for you,' he said, and
passed the microphone across to him. The chairman's
thick fingers closed round the bakelite grip.

'Bland here. Is that Captain Eide?'

'*Ja, hr direktör.* This is Eide.' The voice crackled in sing-song English faintly reminiscent of a Welsh accent.

'What's your position?' I nodded for Sparks to take it down. Fifty-eight point three four south, thirty-four point five six west. I made a swift mental calculation. Bland's eyebrows lifted in my direction. 'That's about forty miles west of us,' I said. He nodded, and resumed his conversation, this time in Norwegian. I didn't listen. I couldn't concentrate enough to pluck the sense out of it from the few words I'd managed to pick up. The warmth of the cabin was enveloping me. My eyelids became unbearably heavy. Sleep rolled my head against the wood panelling of the cabin wall.

Then suddenly I was awake again. A new voice was talking over the radio, talking in English. 'They're holding out for an inquiry. I've told them there isn't going to be any inquiry. It's a waste of time. There's nothing to inquire into. Nordahl's gone, and that's all there is to it.' It was an easy, cultured voice – smooth like an expensive car. But it was just a veneer. It revealed nothing of its owner. 'The real trouble is that the season's been terrible. Even the Sandefjord men are grumbling. As for the Tönsberg crowd – they're more nuisance than they're worth. If you hadn't been coming out I'd have sent the whole lot home.'

'We'll talk about that when I see you, Erik,' Bland cut in, his voice an angry rumble. 'How many whale have you caught so far?'

'Fin whale? A hundred and twenty-seven – that's

all. The fog's just beginning to lift now. Perhaps the luck will change. But there's pack ice to the south-east of us and the men don't like it. They say conditions are abnormal.'

'I know all about that,' said Bland. 'What are your plans?'

'We're cruising east now along the northern edge of the pack. We'll just have to hope for the best.'

'Hope for the best!' Bland's cheeks quivered. 'You get out and find whale – and find 'em damn quick, boy. Every day without whale is a disaster. Do you understand?'

'If you think you can find them when I can't – well, you're welcome to come and try.' The voice sounded sharp and resentful.

Bland gave an angry grunt. 'If Nordahl were alive –'

'Don't you start throwing Nordahl at me,' his son interrupted in a tone of sudden violence. 'I'm sick of hearing about him. He's dead, and the mere mention of his name, as though it were a sort of talisman, won't produce whale.'

'We'll be with you in a few hours now,' Bland said soothingly. 'We'll talk about it then. Put Eide back on.'

Eide's voice was comfortingly calm. He spoke in Norwegian and Bland was answering him in the same language. There was a pause. Then suddenly his voice was back in the cabin again, shouting. '*Hval! Hval! En av hval-baatene har sett hval!*' Bland's face relaxed. He was smiling. Everybody in the cabin was smiling.

I looked at Judie. She leaned towards me, and I

saw that even she was excited. 'They've sighted whale.' She turned her head to the radio again and then added, 'They have seen several *pods*. They are all going south – into the ice.'

'How many whales to a *pod*?' I asked.

She laughed. 'Depends on the sort of whale. Only one or two in the case of the blue whale. But three to five for the fin whale.' She shook her head. 'But it's bad for them to be going south.'

The skipper of the *Southern Cross* signed off and Bland turned to me. 'You got their position?' he asked.

I nodded and got stiffly to my feet. Sparks handed me a slip of paper on which he'd written the present position and course of the *Southern Cross*. I climbed up to the bridge and laid our course to meet up with the factory ship. *Tauer III* turned, heeling slightly as the helmsman swung her on to the new bearing. I told the coxs'n to wake me in four hours' time and went below for the first real sleep I'd had in eight days.

But I didn't get my full four hours. The messboy woke me just after midday and I dragged myself up to the bridge. The coxs'n was there, sniffing the air. 'You smell something, *ja*?' He was grinning. I smelt it at once – a queer, heavy smell like a coal by-product. 'Now you smell money,' he said. 'That is whale.'

'The *Southern Cross*?'

'*Ja.*'

'How far away?'

'Fifteen – maybe twenty mile.'

'Good God!' I said. I was imagining what the smell must be like close to. I ordered the helmsman to point the ship up into the light southerly wind. An hour later the fog began to lift and I ordered full speed. Slowly the fog cleared, revealing a bleak, ice green sea heaving morosely under a low layer of cloud. Away to the south-east I got my first sight of the ice blink. This was the light striking up from close pack ice, its surface mirrored in the cloud. The effect was one of brilliant whiteness, criss-crossed with dark seams. The dark seams were the water lanes cutting through between the floes, all faithfully mapped out in the cloud mirror above it.

Bonomi was up on the bridge with his camera. When I'd worked out our position and sent a lookout to the masthead, he came across to me. 'You feel good now, eh? Everything is fine.' He grinned. His cheerfulness added to the sense of depression that had been growing up inside me. I wasn't looking forward to closing with the *Southern Cross*. For one thing, it meant the end of my temporary command. For another – well, all I can say is that I had developed an uneasy feeling about the *Southern Cross*.

'Bland is saying we must go south into the Weddell Sea,' Bonomi babbled on. 'I 'ope so. He says that after Nordahl, Hanssen is the best whaler in Norway, and if he take the *Haakon* south, then we shall go too. In the Weddell Sea I think I get very good pictures. You will see.'

He was getting on my nerves and I was too dead with lack of sleep to have any hold over my tongue. 'Don't you think of anything else but your bloody pictures?' I said.

He looked up at me with a sort of shocked surprise. 'But what else should I think of?' He peered up at me as though gauging my temper. 'Do not worry about losing the ship. I find a nice job for you, oh – carrying my camera?'

We were both laughing at his little joke when there was a cry of Ship ahoy! from the masthead. Ten minutes later a thick blur of smoke, fine on the starboard bow, was visible from the bridge. Bland, Judie, Weiner – they all came up, gazing excitedly at that first glimpse of the factory ship. 'Trying out by the look of it,' Bland said. I glanced at him quickly. His small eyes gleamed behind their glasses. For him the smoke meant money. For Judie it meant something different and her gaze was clouded. Bonomi was excited. He positively bounced up and down and insisted on shaking everybody by the hand. Weiner looked at it with the apathy of a man to whom nothing has a sense of reality. Howe also came up on to the bridge and stood, a little removed from the rest, gazing out towards the smoke. I wished I could read his thoughts. I saw him glance covertly at Bland and then back again towards the smoke on the horizon. And in that instant I felt a tingle run up my spine.

Judie caught my eye. 'I hope the whales – ' She didn't finish the sentence, but stared at me, her mouth slightly open, caught in the utterance of the next word. I think she knew that Howe worried me.

Bland went aft to the wireless room then. The others followed. Howe was the last to go. He stood, gripping the windbreaker with his bony hands. Conscious of my gaze, he turned and looked at me. Then he swung away and stared for a moment south, towards the ice blink. I watched him, fascinated. His glance went once more to the factory ship, and then back to the mirrored brightness of the pack ice. He stared at it for a long time. Then he turned quickly. 'I must go and prepare my report,' he said and there was a curiously sly lift to the corners of his mouth as he said this.

Once I went down to the wireless room. It was a babel of sound. Norwegian voices boomed out of the R/T receiver: catchers to the factory ship, the factory ship to the buoy boats and towers – everyone was talking on the air at once. I gathered the whales were plentiful. Bland was smiling. And in intervals between communications he was discussing the new electrical equipment with Weiner, sometimes in English, sometimes in German.

It was a strange and rather wonderful sight as we closed the *Southern Cross*. It wasn't just a factory ship. It was a whole fleet of ships. I examined them through my glasses. There were five catchers strung out in a line behind the *Southern Cross*. They appeared to be idle. Another catcher was almost alongside. There were two towing ships. I recognized them by their corvette lines. There were also two old-type catchers that I was told were buoy boats – that is to say, they were towing vessels that could be used to supplement the catcher fleet if required. Behind these was an old whaling ship which ferried the meat to the refrigerator ship, a vessel of about 6,000 tons which was lying astern of the others. Near this was a large tanker and more catchers were scurrying about on the horizon. To see all those ships gathered together in these hostile southern seas fired the imagination. It was such a gigantic operation – a litter of masts that reminded me of D-Day.

Bonomi gripped my arm and pointed across the port bow. A spout of vapour rose not two cables' length away from us, and the water boiled as a smooth, sleek shape, like a submarine, dived. There was a snort almost alongside and another spout thrust ten or fifteen feet into the air, so close that the wind whipped some of the water on to our decks. It was our first sight of a whale. Bonomi dived for his camera. We were in the midst of a *pod*.

I brought the ship round in a wide circle to come up parallel with the *Southern Cross*. In doing so we passed right through the black, oily smoke that drifted to leeward of her. The thick, noisome smell closed down on us like a blanket. It was a heavy, oily, all-pervading smell. It seemed to weigh down on the senses, thick and cloying and penetrating.

As we emerged from it, I could hear the sound of voices on the factory ship and the clank of winches. The stern was open, like a dark cavern, and a whale was being hauled up through it to the after-plan. The ship was big – about twenty thousand tons. Her steel sides, already rusting, towered above us as we glided alongside. Up on the bridge a man in a fur cap held a megaphone to his lips and called down to us. It was Eide. I caught the name. That was all. The rest was in

Norwegian. Judie said, 'He's lowering a boat and coming over to us himself.' Her face looked puzzled. 'I wonder why?' she added.

I glanced across at Bland. He was standing in the port wing of the bridge, gazing aft to where the catchers were strung out in a line. His brows were dragged down and his face had a thunderous look.

We were all there on the bridge when Eide arrived. He was a gaunt, bony man with hatchet-like features and a trick of continually chewing on a matchstick which he slipped to the corner of his mouth when he spoke. He was wearing a thick polo-necked sweater and his gabardine trousers were secured by a wide leather belt with a silver buckle. 'Well?' Bland barked at him. 'What's the trouble? Why aren't all the catchers out?'

Eide looked quickly round. 'I will speak in English,' he said, noticing that the man at the helm was watching him. 'There is trouble. Half the men in the ship have struck. Also the men on five catchers and one towing ship.'

'The Tönsberg men?' Bland asked.

'*Ja.* They have threatened to stop the others working. But they have not yet made any trouble.'

'They're waiting to see what I do. Is that it?'

Eide nodded.

Bland's fist thudded on the bridge rail. 'You've not much more than a hundred whales to show for six weeks' work.' He was almost shouting. 'And now, when we are right in the midst of whale, they strike. Why? What's their complaint?'

'They want an inquiry into Nordahl's death.' Eide hesitated and then said, 'Also they wish your son to be removed from the position of acting manager.'

'Who's behind all this?'

'Kaptein Larvik, I think. He speaks for the others. As you know he was a great friend of Nordahl. It is he, I think, who start this idea of an inquiry. But they are all of them in it now – Larvik, Petersen, Korsvold, Schnelle, Strand and Jenssen.'

Bland's hand clenched into a fist. Then it relaxed. He took off his glasses and wiped them slowly. His heavy jaw was set, his small eyes steely. I watched his mouth spread into a tight-lipped smile. Then he put his glasses on again. 'Very well,' he said quietly. 'If that's the way they want it – ' He glanced quickly at Eide. 'Who do they want as factory manager instead of my son?'

'Kaptein Petersen,' Eide replied. 'He is a good leader and he manage one of the South Georgia stations for three seasons. He returns to catching because he likes the active life.'

'All right, Captain Eide. You will signal for the captains of those five catchers and the towing ship to come on board for a conference with me. I shall then give them an ultimatum – either they get on with the job or they are relieved of their commands.'

'Perhaps they will refuse to come.' Eide's voice sounded embarrassed.

'Good God!' Bland exploded. 'If things have been allowed to get as out of hand as that, then there are other methods of dealing with them. How will they get on in the Antarctic without oil and supplies from the factory ship? Come, pull yourself together, Eide. We can be just as tough. Get down to the wireless room and instruct them to come on board the *Southern Cross* right away.' His jaw thrust out suddenly. 'And if they try to make conditions, tell them they'd better not aggravate me further. Whilst you're doing that, we'll get our things into the boat. Craig,' he said, turning to me, 'you'll come with us. The coxs'n can take temporary command here. Before you know where you are you'll be in charge of a catcher.' He was almost grinning now. He was the sort of man who thrived on a fight. But I must say I didn't much fancy the role of strike-breaker amongst a lot of Norwegians whose feuds I didn't fully understand.

Eide was leaving the bridge now, but Bland stopped him. 'Why didn't Erik come to report this himself?' he demanded.

The skipper of the factory ship hesitated. Then he said, 'He is on the fore-plan. He could not come.'

Bland grunted. 'He's got assistants, hasn't he?' he growled. I must say that at that moment I felt some sympathy for Erik Bland. Whatever the man's nature, he'd certainly been handed a tough job, and I didn't blame him for staying up on the fore-plan. I looked at Judie to see whether she was feeling sympathy for her husband's position. But she was staring up at the towering ugly bulk of the *Southern Cross* and I realized that her thoughts were on her father.

FOUR

I wasn't present at the meeting between Bland and the skippers of the Tönsberg catchers. But I saw them leave and I got the impression that Bland had given them something to think about. There were five of them – tough, bearded men with fur caps on their heads, thick jerseys under their wind-breakers and feet encased in knee-length boots. They stopped at the head of the gangway, talking together in a little bunch. They were joined almost immediately by two other men. One was short and stout with a jolly, wrinkled face and the appearance of a seal. The other was a big man with a jagged scar on his cheek over which his beard refused to grow. They stood a little apart from the others for a moment, talking earnestly in low voices. As I passed them I heard the man with the scar say, '*Ja, Kaptein Larvik.*' Then he turned away and the other joined the group at the head of the gangway.

I was being conducted round the ship at the time. Captain Eide had allocated me a bunk in the second officer's cabin and had detailed one of his officers, a Scot from Leith, to show me round.

My guide had taken me first to the flensing decks. This is the centre of activity in a factory ship when the whales are coming in. There are two flensing decks – the fore-plan and the after-plan. And both looked the sort of charnel house you might dream up in a nightmare. Men waded knee-deep in the bulging intestines of the whales, their long-handled, curved-bladed flensing knives slashing at the bleeding hunks of meat

exposed by the removal of the blubber casing. The
winches clattered incessantly. The steam saws buzzed
as they ripped into the backbone, carving it into star-
shaped sections still festooned with ragged strands of
red meat. Men with huge iron hooks dragged blubber,
meat and bone to the chutes that took it to the boilers
to be tried out and the precious oil extracted. The
noise and the smell were indescribable. And the work
went on unceasingly as whale after whale was dragged
up the slipway, the men working like demons and the
decks slippery with blood and grease.

I followed one whale as it came up through the
cavity in the stern. It was eighty feet long and weighed
nearly a hundred tons. The men on the after-plan fell
on it when it was still being winched along the deck.
The flensers cut flaps of blubber from around its jaws,
hawser shackle was rigged in holes cut in these flaps
and in a moment the winches were ripping the blubber
off the huge carcase, the flensers cutting it clear of the
meat as it was rolled back. To clear the blubber from
the belly, they winched the whale over on to its back,
and as it thudded over on the deck urine poured out
of its stomach in a wave and the pink mass of the
tongue flopped over like a huge jelly. Stripped of its
blubber it was winched to the fore-plan. The meat was
cut away from the backbone and then the bone itself
was cut up and sent to the pots. In just over an hour
that hundred-ton monster had been worked up and
absorbed by the factory ship.

I want to give a clear impression of this ship,
because only then is it possible to appreciate the shock

of what happened later. She was a floating factory – a belching, stinking, muck-heap of activity two thousand miles from civilization. Her upper works were black with grease and filth from the cloud of smoke that rolled out of her trying out funnel. And over everything hung the awful smell of whale. It was like a pall. It was the smell of decaying flesh, mingled with oil and fish, and lying on the air, thick and cloying, like an inescapable fog. But though her decks might present the appearance of some gargantuan slaughter-house, below all was neat and ordered as in a factory. There were the long lines of boilers, hissing gently with the steam that was being injected into them and with gutters bubbling with the hot oil. There was the refrigeration plant and machinery for cutting and packing and dehydrating the meat. There were crushing machines for converting the bone to fertilizer. There were laboratories and workshops, sick bays, mess rooms, living quarters, store rooms, electric generating plant – everything. The *Southern Cross* was a well-stocked, well-populated factory town.

When we got up on deck again, the five catchers that had been lying idle astern of us had already scattered in search of whale. Four carcases were lying alongside, gashed to prevent decay through the internal heat of the mass of dead flesh, and horribly bloated through being inflated with air to keep them afloat. One of the towing ships was bringing in five more.

The whole fleet was in action now with whales spouting all round us. It was an incredible sight.

Standing there on the deck of the factory ship we could hear the dull double thud of the harpoon guns in action. I saw one catcher quite close. The *skytter* was running down the catwalk that connected the bridge with the gun platform perched precariously on the high bows. He seized the gun, his legs braced apart, waiting for the moment to strike. Twice the catcher drove the whale under. Then suddenly the spout was right under the catcher's bow. I saw the sharp-ended point of the harpoon dip as the gun was aimed. Then it flew out – a hundred and fifty pound javelin-like projectile with a light forerunner snaking after it. There was the sharp crack of the gun and then the duller boom of the warhead exploding inside the whale as it sounded. Next moment the line was taut, dragging at the masthead shackles and accumulator springs as the heavy line ran out and the winch brakes screamed. The whole thing took on the proportions of a naval operation.

But by this time my stomach was in open revolt. I thanked my guide hurriedly and staggered off to my cabin. Maybe if I hadn't been so tired, my stomach could have stood it. But the gale and sleepless days had weakened my resistance to that insidious, filthy smell. I gave up all I had to the cabin basin and, cold with sweat, fell into an exhausted sleep on my bunk. I didn't wake up until Kyrre, the second officer, came in. He grinned at me as I opened my eyes. 'You are ill, yes?' The corners of his eyes creased in a thousand wrinkles and he roared with laughter. He was a big, blond fellow with a beard and gold fillings to his teeth. 'Soon you are better,' he added. 'No more whale.'

'You mean you've finished catching for the day?' I struggled up on to my elbow. I felt weak, but my stomach was all right now.

'Finish for the day. *Ja.*' His eyes suddenly lost their laughter. 'Finish for altogether, I think,' he said. 'The whale go south. It is what you say the migration.' He shook his big head. 'I do not know,' he muttered. 'It is very funny, this season. I have been four times to the Antarctic. But it was never like this before.' He scratched at his beard with a great, dirty paw of a hand. 'Maybe we have to go south, too.'

'That means going through the pack ice, doesn't it?' I said, putting my feet over the side of the bunk.

'*Ja,*' he said and his eyes looked troubled. '*Ja* – through the pack ice. It is bad, this season. The *Haakon* she is going south already. We go also, I think.' Then suddenly he grinned and clapped me on the back. 'Come, my friend. We go to have some food, eh? But first, you try some *aquavit*. That is good for the stomach.' He produced a bottle and glasses. 'This is good stuff – real Line *aquavit*.' He thrust the bottle in front of me so that I could see through the colourless spirit the back of the label on which was printed the name of the ship in which the liquor had crossed the Line.

'*Skaal!*' he said when he'd filled the glasses. He knocked it straight back. I did the same. It was like a fire in my throat. 'God!' I said. 'Real firewater.'

'Firewater!' He roared with laughter. '*Ja.* That is good. Firewater! Now we eat, eh?'

The officers' mess was plain and well scrubbed, the

predominating note bleak cleanliness. Most of the men wore beards. They didn't talk. I don't imagine they ever talked much once the food was served. But a sense of tension brooded over the table. Covert glances were cast at Bland where he sat with Judie on one side of him and Eide on the other. Judie was toying with her soup. Her eyes were blank. She might have been alone. The man next to her made some remark. She ignored it.

'Which is Erik Bland?' I asked my companion.

It was as I had guessed. The man sitting next to Judie was her husband. He was taller and much slimmer than his father but he had the same round head and short, thick neck. Stripped of his beard, the features might have been those of Bland thirty or forty years ago. But there wasn't the same strength. There was no violent set of the jaw, no dragging down of the brows from a wide forehead. Instead there was a sort of arrogance.

I drank my soup and watched him as he talked to the secretary who was sitting on the other side of him. His manner suggested there was more of his mother than his father in his make-up. Nevertheless, with his fair hair and blue eyes, he looked a fair example of clean-limbed Norwegian youth.

The soup was followed by plates piled high with slabs of meat covered in a thick gravy. I was hungry and though it was a little too highly spiced, I was enjoying it until somebody said, 'Now you are eating whalemeat. It is good, eh?' My mind conjured up an immediate picture of the charnel house of the flensing decks and I pushed the plate away from me. This brought a roar of laughter. 'If you do not eat whale-meat,' Captain Eide said, 'I think you will starve on the *Southern Cross*.' Another gust of laughter shook the room and I realized that they were all glad of something to laugh at.

'Well, I'll stick to bread and cheese this evening,' I said. It was good rye bread, freshly baked.

The laughter evaporated. A gloomy silence invaded the room again. When the meal was over Eide asked me to have a drink with him. He took me to his cabin and we talked about the war. He had commanded a Norwegian destroyer and I found he'd been with several convoys that I had been attached to. At length I brought the conversation round to Nordahl's disappearance. But all he'd say was: 'It's a complete mystery. I don't understand it at all.'

'What's your opinion of Erik Bland?' I asked, purposely putting the question so bluntly that he couldn't evade answering it without appearing rude.

'How do you mean?' he asked guardedly.

'I gathered he'd been causing trouble with the Tönsberg men.'

Eide's brows lifted. 'On the contrary. He's done everything to smooth things over. He's young, of course, and inexperienced. But that's not his fault. He'll learn. And a lot of the men like him.'

'But he didn't get on with Nordahl, did he?'

Eide hesitated. 'You've seen the messages to Colonel Bland, eh?' I nodded. 'Well,' he said, 'Nordahl wasn't an easy man to get on with. I'm not saying he wasn't a good leader. He was. But he expected people to accept his views without question. He was impatient of opposition and wasn't open to suggestion. That suits the mentality of the *skytters* whose job it is to act and not to think. But it made the day-to-day management of the factory ship difficult.'

'There must have been more to it than that for Nordahl to send that ultimatum to Colonel Bland,' I suggested.

There was a short, embarrassed silence and then Eide said, 'If you do not mind I would prefer not discuss this matter with you. You understand – there are politics in every company and it is better not to talk about them.'

'Of course,' I said, 'I understand. You're not by any chance from Sandefjord, are you?'

He looked at me and his lips spread into a brief smile. 'My home is in Kristiansand,' he said. 'I am master of the *Southern Cross* this trip because Andersen, who was a Tönsberg man, has retired.'

After that I switched the conversation back to the war. About half an hour later I excused myself and went down to my cabin. I was still very tired and I slept as though I'd been drugged.

At breakfast the next morning there was soup and more whalemeat and a *koldtbord* of pressed whale beef, tinned fish and brown Norwegian goats' cheese. The pressed whale beef was good. Shortly after breakfast I was told that Bland wanted to see me in his cabin. I didn't know it then, but this was the morning of the fatal decision. I'd already been up on deck. The wind had sprung up again, a roaring blast of bitterly cold air out of the sou'west. The clouds were low and threatening. To the south the prevailing grey was turned to brilliant white by the ice blink. It was as though the moon were about to rise. The catchers were scattered, searching for a whale. Thick smoke continued to belch from the trying-out stack, but the clatter of winches had ceased and the smell of whale was less noticeable.

Eide and Erik Bland were in the cabin when I entered. Bland himself was seated in a swivel chair, his elbow resting on the desk. The man's face was pallid. He was wiping his glasses and I noticed that there were thick pouches under his eyes. 'Craig – I want you to meet my son,' he said. 'Erik. This is Commander Craig.'

Erik Bland came over and shook my hand. 'Glad to have you with us,' he said. His manner was friendly. 'My father thinks you're a fine sailor.'

'If I am,' I said, 'the credit's due to the British Navy.' My antagonism was already melting. His manner was easy and natural. He might not have the drive and pugnacity of his father, but his manners were better and he had confidence in himself. I suddenly began to wonder how much of Judie's reactions were due to a father complex.

Bland swung round in his chair so that he faced me. 'Sit down, Craig,' he said. 'I've got a job for you.' He put his glasses on and began fingering the lobe of his ear. 'For some reason that I don't understand the Tönsberg men have got the idea that Nordahl's death wasn't accidental. The man behind the whole thing is Larvik. But that's neither here nor there. I'm not interested in the logic of their suspicions. I'm interested only in the fact that they are suspicious and that until their suspicions are settled one way or the other it interferes with the working of the ship and the catchers. I've told them that an inquiry will be held. And since they seem to have an idea that in some way I or my son are involved, neither of us will be on the committee of inquiry. The committee will consist of three people. The two members will be Captain Eide here and my daughter-in-law.'

'Good God!' I said. 'You're not going to make her go through the agony of examining all of the men who had conversation with Nordahl just before he vanished? Surely you must understand her feelings in the –'

'I'm not interested in her feelings,' he growled at me. 'My problem is that a lot of damned suspicious nonsense has got into the heads of some of the men. With Judie on the committee they'll accept the findings, whatever they are. In fact, Larvik has already agreed.'

'Have you spoken to her about it?' I asked.

'Not yet.'

'But surely she has some –'

'I'm not prepared to argue.' His little eyes glared at me. 'Her husband agrees.'

'That's no answer,' I replied hotly.

'Do you think you have a better right to speak for her than her husband?' he asked. His voice was suddenly violent. I didn't say anything.

'Very well,' he said, relaxing. 'Now then – the reason I've asked you up here is this. I want you to act as chairman of this committee. You're entirely outside any company politics. With you, Eide and Judie on the committee, the men will be satisfied. Well?'

I hesitated. I didn't want to be drawn into it.

'I said I'd find you an interesting job,' he added. 'And this is it.'

The point he was making was obvious. I was being paid by the company and if I didn't know enough to operate one of the whaling ships, it was up to me to take on anything I was given. Whether it was this that decided me or the fact that Judie was on the committee and I wanted to lessen the pain of it for her, I don't know. But I heard myself say, 'All right. I'll act as chairman.'

'Good!' He shifted more easily in his chair. 'Get down to it right away. The sooner the job's completed the better.' There was a knock at the door. 'Come in,' he called.

It was Howe. He had a sheaf of papers in his hand. His face was slightly flushed and there was a queer excitement in his eyes. 'Ah, come in, Howe,' Bland said. 'Have you got that report for me?'

Howe nodded. He didn't seem able to trust himself to speak. He came across the cabin with that awkward, crab-like walk and handed Bland the papers. Bland didn't look at them. He looked at Howe instead. 'Well?' he said. 'What are your conclusions? Where's the best place to hunt for whale in a season like this?'

Howe swallowed nervously. 'Come on, man. You know very well not a catcher has reported whale all morning though conditions have been ideal. The *skytters* all say we just caught the tail end of a migratory movement. Where do you think we'll find whale? Do we go east or west? Back towards South Georgia or down into the Weddell Sea? Well?'

Howe's Adam's apple gave one final jerk. 'Through the pack,' he said. 'Through the pack into the Weddell Sea.' His mouth had a sly twist to it and his watery eyes gleamed. I suddenly had the feeling that the man's report was based on nothing more substantial than the fact that he wanted Bland to go south.

And the strange thing was that Bland himself seemed to want to go south, too. 'Good, good,' he said. 'Did you know Hanssen was taking the *Haakon* into the pack?'

'No.' The Adam's apple jerked again.

'Apparently he thinks the same. So do Petersen and Larvik and after Nordahl they're the most experienced men we have.' I glanced quickly at Erik Bland as his father mentioned the name Nordahl, but it produced no reaction.

Bland had got up and was staring out of the porthole. Suddenly he swung round. 'Very well, Captain Eide,' he said. His tone was abrupt, decisive. 'Recall the catchers. As soon as they have all come in, get the gunners aboard for a conference. My view is that we should go south right away. We've only just over two months left and to make up for lost time we need plenty of whale. Have we enough meat to give the refrigerator ship a full cargo?'

'No,' Eide replied and looked across at Erik Bland, who added, 'The *South* is only one-third full.'

'She must come with us then. Now go and recall the catchers.' He dismissed his son with a nod and turned to me. 'I want the findings of that inquiry completed whilst the catchers are assembling – before we start south. Captain Eide has agreed to release the second officer from all duties to assist you in deciding who you wish to come before you to give evidence. He's a Tönsberg man, he speaks English and he was on watch the night Nordahl vanished.' He nodded to us. 'That's all then, gentlemen. Tomorrow we will enter the pack ice.'

The imminence of our entry into the pack ice gave me little enough time to hold the inquiry. Immediately after the conference in Bland's cabin the ship turned its bow towards the ice blink. She was travelling at half speed. As soon as all the catchers were assembled, and they couldn't be more than a few hours' steaming away, all speed would be made to the south. Once in the pack I realized that it would be difficult to continue the inquiry. Captain Eide, for one, would not be available, nor would Kyrre. I was glad I'd had some experience of inquiries whilst in the Navy.

Kyrre had already received instructions and was waiting for me in our cabin. I got from him a brief account of Nordahl's movements on the night he'd disappeared and drew up a list of men to be interviewed. Bland sent down copies of a typewritten notice announcing the inquiry. The officers' smoke-room had been set aside for it and there was a blank against the time for me to fill in. It asked any man who thought he might have information relevant to the factory manager's disappearance to come before the committee. I found Eide on the bridge and fixed for the inquiry to begin at eleven. Then I went down to Judie's cabin. She was sitting on her bunk, very still, very scared looking.

'You've been told about this inquiry?' I asked. I made my voice sound as matter-of-fact as possible.

She nodded.

'I've fixed it for eleven,' I said. 'That's in just over half an hour. That all right for you?'

'Yes.' Her tone was almost harsh as though she were bracing herself for the ordeal.

I turned to go. The I stopped. 'It's a rotten job for you,' I said.

'I'll be all right.' She gave me a wan smile.

At eleven o'clock there were five men, besides the ones we'd called, scuffling their feet outside the door of the smoke-room. As I passed through them with Judie there was a muttered '*God dag.*' One man said, '*God dag, froken Nordahl.*' Not *fru Bland*, but *froken Nordahl.* Kyrre was already there. Eide came in as we were seating ourselves.

'Right,' I said. 'Let's have the men we've called first – in the order we agreed, Kyrre.'

It took us two hours to get the story of that night out of them. But it was quite straightforward. There was nothing in any of the evidence to prepare us for the labyrinth of ill feeling and suspicion we were to plough our way through later. On the evening of the 2nd January Nordahl had joined the other officers for the evening meal as usual. He hadn't talked much. But he wasn't any more silent that night than he had been since the ship left Capetown. He seemed to have had a premonition that the season was going to be a bad one. The secretary, who saw a lot of him, said that he was increasingly concerned about the absence of whale. Nordahl had a very considerable financial interest in the company. Judie couldn't say exactly what the figure was, but thought it might be as high as thirty or thirty-five per cent.

After the meal Nordahl had had a few drinks and then worked for half an hour in the office. A good deal of his time was spent in the office – not only was it necessary for him to supervise the checking of stores and the supply of fuel, stores and equipment to the catchers and towing ships, but also to keep an eye on the entry of whale brought in and handled, since all the men got a share, over and above their pay. The outfit was run on what amounted to a co-partnership basis. Young Bland wasn't much help to him here as he had insufficient knowledge. In fact, Nordahl bore the whole weight of management, both as regards policy and detail. The secretary said that he was very tired at the end of the day. He was sixty-two years old and the burden of decision and administrative detail must have been considerable.

After leaving the office, Nordahl went up on to the bridge. He stayed there for a short time, talking to the officer of the watch. The half light of the Antarctic summer night had fallen. But shortly after Nordahl left the bridge a bank of fog rolled up.

Leaving the bridge, Nordahl had gone as far as was known straight to Eide's cabin. There he'd had two drinks – that made about half a dozen he'd had during the evening, and he was a man with a big capacity for liquor.

Captain Eide, who then gave evidence, said that he had seemed perfectly normal. 'But he was tired, you know,' he added. 'There had been trouble between him and Erik Bland. I must say it – since it may have a bearing on his state of mind – Bland did not know enough about the job. On the other hand, the trouble was not by any means all Bland's fault. Nordahl did not like him and he took no trouble to conceal his dislike. Also he was impatient. He made no allowance for Bland's inexperience.'

'Was there open trouble between them?' I asked.

Captain Eide shook his head. 'I do not think so. Bland always treated the manager with the respect that was his due – even when he was provoked. But there were those messages to Colonel Bland. Things like that have a way of getting round a ship. The Tönsberg men supported Nordahl and most of the Sandefjord men sided with Bland. It did not make for smooth running.'

'And Nordahl took most of Bland's work on his own shoulders?' I suggested.

'*Ja*. That is so.'

'And you think this was too much for him? He was over-tired?'

Eide nodded.

After leaving Eide's cabin Nordahl had gone to the wireless room. He was there talking to the Chief Wireless Officer till shortly after midnight.

I then called Kyrre, who had been officer of the watch during the period Nordahl must have disappeared. He had come on watch at midnight. The ship was stationary and blanketed in fog. The navigation lights of the ships riding astern of her were not visible. Nothing unusual happened throughout his watch. After he had been on watch about half an hour the fog suddenly lifted and visibility increased to several miles. I asked him whether he had heard a cry or a splash. No, he had noticed nothing unusual. Had he seen Nordahl or anyone that might possibly have been Nordahl up on the deck? But he'd seen nothing. 'The fog, she was very thick. I could see nothing beyond the bridge.'

'And about twelve-thirty the fog lifted and visibility was good?'

'Ja.'

'If Nordahl had gone overboard then he would have been seen?'

'That is so. I was out on the bridge all watch, and there was the lookout.'

It was clear, therefore, that Nordahl must have gone overboard between the time he had left the wireless room and just after twelve-thirty when the fog lifted.

Finally I called Erik Bland. I nodded to a chair and he sat down. He was frowning slightly and his eyes were screwed up so that they were small, like his father's. I was conscious again of the similarity in appearance and the dissimilarity in character. He seemed nervous. 'There's only one question I want to ask you, Bland,' I said. 'Nordahl left Captain Eide's cabin shortly after ten-thirty on the night of 2nd January. Did he visit you at all?'

'No. I had a few words with him during the evening meal.' His eyes flicked towards Judie and he gave a slight shrug to his shoulders. 'I never saw him again.'

'Had you had a row with him?' It was Judie who put the question, and I remember the feeling of shock caused by the blunt way she put the question and the hardness of her voice.

Bland hesitated. 'Do I have to answer that question?' he asked me.

It was clear he was trying to save her unnecessary pain, but I had no alternative. 'I'm afraid so,' I said.

He looked at her then and said, 'Yes. You know as well as I do we couldn't get on together. It wasn't the first row we'd had.'

'What was it about?' Judie's voice was drained of any emotion.

'Nothing. Just a difference of opinion about the promotion of a certain man.'

'As assistant manager your duty surely was to assist my father, not to obstruct him?'

'I wasn't obstructing him.' His voice was pitched a shade higher. 'Listen, Judie – your father and I didn't get on. Leave it at that, can't you? I had nothing to do with his death.'

'Nobody is suggesting you had,' I said.

He looked at me quickly. His face was paler now and there were beads of sweat on his forehead. 'No? Then what is she driving at? And she's not the only one. Larvik and Petersen are spreading the idea through the ship – and the Tönsberg men will believe anything they say. Everyone on the ship knows Nordahl and I couldn't get on together. What they don't know is the reason.' He turned back to Judie. 'Your father did everything he could to make things difficult for me. I was new to the job, yet he couldn't have been more impatient with me over my mistakes if I'd been on as many expeditions as he had.'

'I don't believe it.' Judie's voice was sharp and uncompromising.

'Whether you believe it or not, it's true. He wanted to put me in a position where I'd be forced to ask my father to recall me.'

'Why?' I asked.

'Why? Because he wanted to control the company after my father's death. He wanted me out of the way.

'This is getting us nowhere,' I cut in. 'Have you any suggestions to make concerning Nordahl's death?'

'No,' he said. 'I've no more idea how it happened than you have. The only explanation I can think of is that he had financial troubles.'

'Financial troubles?' Eide repeated. 'What sort of financial troubles?'

'He was gambling – ' But Bland stopped short there. 'It's his affair,' he murmured.

'I don't believe that,' Judie said quietly. 'Father

never gambled. He couldn't possibly have had financial troubles. He was interested only in whale.'

'He would like to have controlled the company, though, wouldn't he?' There was a suggestion of spite in his tone. Then he gave a quick shrug to his shoulders. 'I'm sorry, gentlemen. I'd rather not say any more about it.'

'But he had financial worries,' I said, 'and you think this may have had some bearing on his death?'

'Perhaps.'

'And you saw nothing of him after he left the officers' mess?'

'I told you – no.'

'Very well,' I said. 'I think that's all.' I glanced at the others. Eide nodded to indicate that he was satisfied. Judie was sitting, very pale, staring at her husband. Her hands were clenched where they lay in her lap. She didn't say anything so I nodded to Bland. 'Thank you,' I said. He got up quickly. I could see he was relieved. I didn't know what to think. There was clearly something behind his statement that Nordahl had been in financial difficulties, but just what I didn't know and Judie either couldn't or wouldn't enlighten me.

The last witness I called was the officers' messboy who had brought tea to Nordahl's cabin as usual at six in the morning. He told how he'd found the cabin empty, the bunk not slept in. Finally Eide detailed the steps he had taken as captain to discover what had happened. His inquiries had told him no more than we'd discovered that morning. 'There are many men

on this ship who do not like Erik Bland,' he added.
'So much I discover. You will hear this after *middag*
when we see the men who wish to give evidence. There
will be talk of much bad feeling. But there will be
nothing definite.' He shrugged his shoulders. 'I think
there is no doubt what happens.'

'You're suggesting my father committed suicide,
aren't you?' Judie's voice trembled as she said this.
Neither Eide nor I said anything. I must admit it was
the conclusion that I had come to. Nordahl was clearly
over-worked. He may even have had personal worries
that we knew nothing of. Tired and worried, his mind
had become over-wrought. 'Captain Eide – you knew
him quite well,' she went on in a more controlled
voice. 'Was he, in your opinion, the sort of man to
take his own life?'

Eide hesitated, rubbing his beard with his fingers.
'No,' he said. 'Not in normal circumstances. But – '

'Please,' she interrupted. 'I knew him better than
anyone. He was my father. Please believe me when I
say – it would never occur to him to take his own life.'

I said, 'We'll adjourn now. After lunch we'll see
the men who want to give evidence.'

We broke up then. But all through *middag* Judie
sat silent and pale. She hardly ate anything. I saw Erik
Bland glance at her once or twice, and I thought there
was something half-pleading, half-scared, in the way
he looked at her. Bland himself only once referred to
the inquiry. He asked me when I'd be through. 'Some
time this afternoon,' I said. 'We only have to take

the evidence of those who have volunteered to make statements.'

'Hurry it,' he said. 'There are two more catchers to come in – that's all – and I want to start south as soon as I've had a talk with the gunners.'

But by the end of the afternoon we were still sitting. The men who had volunteered to give information were Tönsberg men, all of them, and their evidence put a different complexion on the whole business. Even allowing for exaggeration, it became clear that the trouble between Nordahl and Erik Bland was much more serious than we'd been led to believe.

The trouble, it appeared, had started a week after the ship had left Capetown. Certain rations essential for the prevention of scurvy had been withdrawn. When a deputation headed by one of the boiler-cleaners had raised the matter with Erik Bland, who had given the instructions to the chief cook, instead of admitting his mistake, he had enforced his decision. Nordahl had reversed it. A few days later a similar thing had happened over the issue of certain essential clothing. Bland had accused Nordahl in front of the slop-chest manager of toadying to the men. The first day they handled whale, a winch hawser had snapped and one of the lemmers had been seriously injured. Nordahl had found that the equipment had not been properly inspected. Bland had told Nordahl he wasn't going to be the scapegoat for everything that went wrong on the ship. He ignored the fact that he had been given the job of inspecting all equipment before use. They had a bitter row on the after-plan in front of the men. But the worst row appeared to have been over an error in the figures for whales brought in by *Hval 4*. Petersen, skipper of *Hval 4*, had queried the figures. The mistake was Bland's. He had reported these whales to the secretary as being brought in by *Hval 8*, one of the Sandefjord catchers. Petersen, who had come on board to right the matter called the plan foreman to substantiate his claim. It was this man who volunteered an account of what had happened in the office.

Bland had refused to admit his mistake. White-faced, he had accused Nordahl of concocting the whole thing between Petersen and the foreman. 'I know what it is,' he had shouted; 'you're trying to get rid of me. You're trying to get rid of my father too. You want to control the whole company.'

Nordahl had asked him what he meant by that, and he had answered, 'I know what you're up to. You crawl to me for financial advice. You thought you'd make enough out of it to buy control. Do you think I don't know what you were up to whilst you were in Capetown. Well, you wait till the crash comes. If I didn't know it was coming, I'd – I'd –' He hadn't finished, but had flung out of the office.

I recalled the secretary and asked him why he hadn't given us this piece of evidence. He replied that he hadn't thought it relevant. But I could see that his real reason was that he was scared of losing his job now that Bland was manager and his father was on board. Pressed by me, however, the secretary confirmed every word of the foreman's evidence.

There was another row in Nordahl's cabin, which was overheard by one of the winch-boys. All he heard as he passed was Bland saying, 'I refuse to sign. Fire me if you like. But see what my father has to say when he arrives.' And Nordahl had answered wearily, 'Your father can do what he likes. I'm not going to be saddled with a rat like you and I'll see that the company isn't either.'

There had been the sound of a blow then. And just as the boy, who had been listening outside, was slipping away, Bland had burst out of the cabin, his face white and his mouth working with anger. 'He looked as though he were about to burst into tears,' the boy added.

I looked at Eide, remembering his support of Bland. It was clear somebody had been pulling the wool over his eyes. And that could only have been Erik Bland himself. He'd almost fooled me too.

Next came the evidence that all this had gradually been working up to. The witness was a big man with a scar on his cheek over which his beard had refused to grow. I recognized him at once. It was the man who had accompanied Captain Larvik to the gangway that first afternoon just after I'd come aboard.

His evidence was that he'd been up on the deck shortly after midnight on the night of 2nd/3rd January. He had gone aft and had seen Nordahl smoking a cigar near one of the boats. The manager had been pacing up and down in a rather agitated manner. The man had seen his face in the glow of the cigar. When he went for'ard again, Nordahl was still there. A few paces farther on he met Erik Bland going towards Nordahl. He had stopped then, wondering whether there was any fresh trouble between them. He had heard the beginnings of an altercation. No, he couldn't say what was said. He was too far away. The men's voices grew angry. There was a sudden cry. Then silence. He saw Bland come back. His face was very white. Then he had gone aft to the point where Nordahl had been. Nordahl was no longer there.

'Did Bland see you?' I asked through Kyrre.

'No. I was beside one of the ventilators and there was the fog.'

I had been watching the man closely whilst he gave his evidence. He had a habit of nervously fingering the clean stretch of skin where the scar was. He kept his eyes fixed all the time on the table at which we were sitting. He spoke in a monotone. There was no feeling or interest behind his words. I got the idea that he didn't see the scene he was describing.

'And you say Bland's face was white?' I asked.

'Ja.'

'Yet it was so foggy he didn't see you standing beside a ventilator?'

'He was very much upset.'

Eide stirred. 'Why didn't you give me this information when I was inquiring into hr Nordahl's disappearance?' he asked.

The man hesitated. 'I was scared,' he said.

He didn't look the sort of man who was easily scared.

'What's your job on this ship?' I asked.

'Seaman,' he answered, frowning in puzzlement at the question.

'Ever crewed on one of the catchers?'

He nodded.

'On Captain Larvik's catcher?'

I saw the quick shift of his eyes as they glanced at me and then away again. He didn't answer.

I said, 'I don't believe a word of your evidence.' His eyes looked suddenly shifty. 'Who put you up to this? Was it Captain Larvik? Come on, man,' I shouted at him as though I were back on the bridge of my corvette. 'Let's have the truth now. It was Captain Larvik, wasn't it? Yesterday when he and the others came on board to see Colonel Bland. He told you to give this evidence.'

The man fidgeted awkwardly.

'All right,' I snapped. 'You can go.'

I looked across at Eide. There was no doubt in my mind. Captain Larvik had primed the fellow. 'Why?' I asked, voicing my own thoughts.

Eide was fingering his beard. 'I think we should call Kaptein Larvik.'

I turned to Judie for her agreement. She nodded. Her face was set, chin slightly thrust out where it rested on the knuckles of her two hands. 'I think he knows something,' she said quietly. 'Peer Larvik is a great friend of my father.'

We had a break then whilst Captain Eide sent for Larvik, whose catcher had just rejoined the *Southern Cross*. Up on the deck the air was cold. I took Judie down to my cabin and got one of the messboys to bring us tea. It was the first opportunity I'd had of talking to her alone since we had begun the inquiry. 'Look, Judie,' I said when the tea had arrived, 'is there anything you can tell us that would help to discover what really did happen?' Put like that it sounded ponderous. But I felt awkward. I knew what a strain the whole inquiry was on her.

She stirred her cup for a moment. Then she said, 'No. I don't think I can.' Her voice trembled slightly. 'All I know for certain, deep down in my heart, is that he did not commit suicide.'

'Do you believe the evidence of that man with the scar – Ulvik?'

'No,' she replied. 'No, you showed quite clearly that he was lying.'

'You agree that Captain Larvik put him up to it?'

'Yes.'

'But why?' I asked.

She looked up at me then. And there was something in her eyes that disturbed me. 'He had a reason,' she said. Her voice was suddenly beyond her control. It was harsh and violent. 'The man was saying what he'd been told to say. But it's what Peer Larvik believed happened.'

I hesitated. But I had to put it to her. 'Do you believe your husband murdered your father?' She didn't answer and I added, 'Is that what you believe?' My voice sounded peremptory.

Her grey eyes were wide as saucers as she looked up at me. Then suddenly something inside her snapped and she buried her head in her hands. 'I don't know what to think.' She was sobbing violently. 'It's horrible – horrible.' Her shoulders shook with the sudden pent-up force of her emotions breaking out.

I went over and put my hands on her arms. 'Stop crying,' I said. 'You're a member of a committee of inquiry, not a schoolgirl.' I shook her. It was the only thing to do. She was on the verge of hysterics. My violence and lack of sympathy checked her. 'Stop blubbering and try to reason it out,' I said, forcing her to meet my gaze. 'Either your father committed suicide, or your husband's a murderer.' She gasped. But I could see her mind was suddenly facing up to the facts that she had been trying to avoid.

There was a knock at the door. It was a message from Eide to say that Larvik was on board. 'I'm sorry, Judie,' I said. 'Don't think I don't realize how rotten this is for you. But we've got to find out what was in Larvik's mind. Will you question him?'

She nodded and reached for her handbag. When she had made up her face again we went down and joined Captain Eide. 'Mrs Bland will put the questions,' I said. I nodded to Kyrre to fetch in Captain Larvik.

At close quarters the whaling skipper looked even broader and even more like a seal. He sat down awkwardly on the edge of a chair. He was nervous. He didn't look at Eide or myself. His small, immensely blue eyes were fixed on Judie. Was it sympathy, or was there something else in the expression of his eyes? I had an uncanny feeling that those blue eyes were trying to tell her something. 'Kaptein Larvik,' she said. 'Yesterday, when you were on board the *Southern Cross*, you spoke with one of the crew – a man named Ulvik.' She spoke carefully in English.

'*Ja*. That is so,' Larvik replied in the same language. He was a Bergenske and he spoke English with a Germanic guttural accent, relic of the days when the Hanseatic League ruled the Bergen shipping trade.

'We have heard Ulvik's evidence,' she added, and outlined briefly what he had told us. 'Commander Craig here takes the view that that evidence is unreliable. In fact, he thinks you instructed the man to give false evidence.'

'And you, fru Bland – what do you think?'

She hesitated for a fraction of a second and then said, 'I think so too.'

Larvik shrugged his shoulders. He didn't say anything. He just sat there, staring at her.

'Why, Kaptein Larvik?' Judie asked him. 'Why did you tell him to say that Erik and my father had a row up there on the deck in the fog the night my father – disappeared.'

His big hands waved awkwardly like a pair of flippers. 'I do not wish to hurt you more than you have been hurt already,' he said. His voice was kindly, as though he were talking to a child or a dog of which he was fond. 'But it is what I believe happens.'

'You are accusing my husband of being a murderer,' she said, and Larvik winced at the bluntness of her tongue. 'Of murdering my father,' she added. 'Why didn't you come to us directly or to Captain Eide and make this statement yourself? To present your suspicions in this roundabout way, getting Ulvik to make a statement you and he knew to be false, is horrible. Erik didn't see my father at all that night – after the evening meal.'

'How do you know?' Larvik's voice was gruff. Sudden anger showed in his eyes.

'Erik made that statement in evidence before this inquiry.'

'Then he's lying,' Larvik growled.

Judie stared at him as though she'd been silenced with a blow. I could see she believed this fat, bearded whaler. I thought: *Larvik and her father are old friends. This man probably played with her as a child. She accepts him – everything he is and everything he says – in the same way that she would accept her father and anything he said.* I saw her lips tremble. Her body seemed to sag. 'Oh, God,' she breathed. She was shaking uncontrollably, her eyes quite blank. She wasn't crying. She was past that.

'How do you know Bland is lying?' I demanded angrily. If the man couldn't substantiate his statement, then why in God's name had he made it?

I saw Larvik steady himself. His eyes were full of sudden pity. His hands flapped awkwardly. But beneath the beard his lips clamped into a tight line. 'I have nothing more to say,' he growled. And then added, 'That is what I believe happened. I wished for the inquiry to know that and act on it.'

'But what makes you so sure that Erik Bland saw Nordahl later that night?' I demanded. 'You say Bland is lying?'

'*Ja.*'

'How do you know?'

'That is what I believe,' he answered stubbornly.

'But good God, man!' I shouted at him. 'You must have some reason for your suspicions?'

But all he replied was, 'Ask Bland.'

I looked at Eide. I could see that he thought the same as I did – that we should get no further with Larvik. It was no good asking Judie if she had any further questions to ask. She was staring at Larvik, dry-eyed, with a sort of dawning horror mirrored on her white face. 'All right,' I said to Larvik. 'We've no further questions to put to you. I would only like to add that I consider your conduct in this matter disgraceful. You have made a very dangerous accusation which you are not prepared to substantiate. I trust your attitude will be more helpful and less underhand when the police interview you.' I glanced at Eide, who nodded in support of my remarks.

But I could see that they had had no effect on Larvik. His eyes were fixed on Judie. They were full of pain. He was sharing the hell that she was going through. 'Please return to your ship, Captain Larvik,' I said.

He got up then, standing awkwardly in front of the table, still looking at Judie. Once he cleared his throat as though about to say something. Then he turned abruptly on his heel and left the room.

I looked at Eide. 'I think we should have Bland back again,' I whispered. He agreed. I turned to Judie. She hadn't moved. I put my hand on hers. 'Are you prepared to face your husband now,' I said, 'or shall we adjourn for a bit?'

She swallowed quickly. 'Please – now,' she said. She wanted to get it over.

'All right,' I said, and phoned the radio officer on duty to put out a call on the public address system for Erik Bland to attend the inquiry again. I did it that way to scare him. We waited in silence. Faintly we heard the amplifiers sounding Bland's name through the ship. The silence in the room seemed to cry out.

When Bland came in he was breathing heavily as though he'd been hurrying. And it was a different Bland to the disarmingly helpful young man who had faced us earlier in the day – or so it seemed to me. His face looked puffy. His eyes darted about the room, crossing, but not meeting, our gaze. I motioned him to a chair. He sat down quickly. The tension of the room was enveloping him. I let it work on him.

'Well?' he asked, unable to bear the silence any longer. 'What do you want to ask me now?' The abruptness of his tone was startlingly different to his previous ease of manner.

'We have just heard the evidence of one of the men,' I said. I let that sink in for a moment. If I handled it right, whatever he was scared of would come out. 'Do you still persist in your statement that you didn't see Nordahl after the evening meal on the night he disappeared?'

His eyes flicked up at me and back to the floor. 'Yes,' he said. 'Yes, I do.' Then his hands caught hold of the arms of the chair. 'You've had Larvik on board.

You've interviewed him, haven't you?' So that was what had got him worried. 'He's trying to fix it on me.' His voice was uncontrolled. Something was gnawing at his mind. Something he was scared of. 'It isn't one of the men who's been talking to you. It's Larvik. He's always hated me. He's a friend of Nordahl's. He's using Nordahl's death to get at me. He's lying. He's lying, I tell you.'

'He's says you're lying,' I said.

'It's my word against his.' Bland's voice was wild. 'He's guessing. That's all he's doing.'

I said, 'Wait a minute, Bland. We're not dealing with Larvik's evidence. We're dealing with the evidence of one of the men. He says that at about midnight Nordahl was standing by one of the boats.' I knew the man's statement was false. I had no right to use it to force Bland's hand. But I had to find out the truth. I justified myself on the grounds that if Bland were hiding anything it would force him into the open. 'Nordahl was smoking a cigar,' I went on. 'As the man passed him on his way for'ard again he met you. He says you were going towards where Nordahl was standing.' Bland's face was ashen. He seemed to be holding his breath. 'Well?' I said. 'Did you go towards Nordahl as he stood there by one of the boats, smoking a cigar?' I emphasized the details. I emphasized every point of the picture.

'No,' he cried. 'No.'

'The man said he then stopped by one of the ventilators,' I went on. 'He heard the beginnings of an altercation. There was a cry. And then silence.'

'No. It isn't true.'

'He said that a moment later you passed him going for'ard. Your face was very white. You didn't see him because of the fog and the fact that he was hidden behind the ventilator cowl. He then went back to the spot where he had seen Nordahl.' I hesitated. Bland was staring at me, fascinated. 'Nordahl wasn't there any more.'

Bland opened his mouth. But nothing came out. He seemed to be gasping for breath. Then he suddenly said, 'All right. I was up there. I did see Nordahl. We did have a row. But that was all. That was all, I tell you.'

'What was the row about?' I asked.

'What was the row – about?' He seemed dazed for the moment. His eyes shifted quickly round the room as though searching for some way of escape from the three of us sitting there behind the plain deal table. He moistened his lips with his tongue and then said, 'He accused my father of ruining him.'

'On what grounds?' I asked.

He looked at me then. And his eyes held my gaze as though he wanted to batter the information he had to give into my brain. 'Nordahl wanted control of the company,' he said. 'He wanted to run it his own way. He wanted all the men to be from Tönsberg. He liked to think of himself as an important figure in Tönsberg.'

'That's not true,' Judie said. The denial seemed to be torn out of her, it was so violent.

Bland ignored her. 'He didn't want me on the ship. He did everything he could to make it difficult for me. He even altered figures in the catchers' books so that the Tönsberg men should be able to bring complaints. He was afraid my father when he died would make me chairman over his head.'

'Come to the point,' I said, as he paused. 'Why did he accuse your father of ruining him?'

'He needed money,' Bland answered. 'He was making a desperate bid to get control of the company. He badgered my father until he let him in on a deal he was planning in South African mines. He put everything he'd got into it. The crash came two weeks after we left Capetown.'

'What was the name of the company he invested in?' I asked. 'Was it Wyks Odensdaal Rust Development?'

'Yes,' he said, and his voice sounded surprised.

The plan foreman in his evidence had suggested that it was from Erik Bland, not his father, that Nordahl had obtained financial advice. I hesitated. But there was no point in raising the matter. 'In your opinion Nordahl was broke then?'

'Yes. He'd mortgaged everything – all his holdings in the South Antarctic Company – in a desperate effort to cash in.'

'Then he was going to buy out the other people interested in the company?'

'Yes. That was his idea.'

'When he'd done that, would he have thrown your father out?'

Again Bland hesitated. 'I don't know,' he said.

'What you were really afraid of,' I said, 'was that he'd throw you out. Isn't that it?'

He ignored the point. 'The case didn't arise,' he said. 'My father was too smart to be caught like that. I tell you, Nordahl was broke – finished. And he knew it. He cursed me there on the deck.'

'Why did he cry out?' I asked quickly.

Again that momentary hesitation. 'He didn't cry out,' he answered. 'I think perhaps it was I who cried out. I don't know. All I know is that he hit me. I left him then. I didn't want to hit back at an older man, especially as he was wrought up over his losses.'

'Do you remember an altercation you had with Nordahl in his cabin?' I asked. 'One of the crew over heard it. Nordahl demanded your resignation. You refused it. You said – "See what my father does when he arrives." ' I looked down at my notes. 'Nordahl then said – "Your father can do what he likes. I'm not going to be saddled with a rat like you and I'll see that the company isn't either." ' I looked across at Bland's white face. 'You didn't baulk at striking an older man then,' I said. 'Are you sure it was Nordahl who struck you?'

'Yes,' he said. 'Nordahl struck me and I left him then.'

'The man whose evidence has produced all this,' I said slowly, 'went straight back to the spot where Nordahl had been standing. Nordahl wasn't there.'

'I tell you, he knew he was ruined.' Bland's face was tense. He was fighting to make us see it his way. 'He was finished. He could never face Tönsberg again. He took the only way out.'

'My father never took an easy way out in his life.' Judie's voice was clear-cut and distinct. It was like a douche of cold water on the heat of Erik Bland's argument.

'Well, he took it this time.' There was something almost truculent in the way he said it.

I looked at Eide. 'Any more questions?' I asked. He shook his head. I turned to Judie. Her lips were compressed. She was staring at Erik Bland with a sort of horror in her eyes. 'All right, Bland,' I said. 'That's all.'

He got up slowly as though he didn't want to be released like that. He started to say something, but then his eyes met Judie's and he turned quickly and went out. I realized then that whatever he had once meant to her it was finished now. And I was suddenly, unaccountably glad about that.

As the door closed behind him, I said: 'Well, do we need to call anybody else?' I was thinking: *It's a matter for the police now. Either Bland killed him, or Nordahl committed suicide. Those were the only two possible alternatives. Judie said he would never commit suicide. She ought to know if anyone did. She was his daughter. But who could possibly tell how a man would react when all he's lived for and worked for is shattered in the wreckage of a wild gamble? He'd played his hand and lost. He'd tried his hand at Bland's game – finance – and failed. How could she know what he would do in those circumstances?*

It was Judie who interrupted my thoughts. 'I would like to call Doctor Howe,' she said in a small, bleak voice. It was drained of all emotion – empty, toneless.

I looked at her in surprise. 'Doctor Howe? Why?' I asked. 'He wasn't even on the *Southern Cross*. He was in Capetown, waiting for us.'

'I think he might be able to tell us something,' was all she said.

'All right,' I agreed and nodded to Kyrre.

Howe was pale and nervous when he came in. It was as though he'd been nerving himself for this moment. Judie said, 'Walter, we want some information about father's affairs.' His Adam's apple gave a leap, but his hands were steady and his gaze was direct as he looked at Judie. 'Was he involved in Wyks Odensdaal Rust Development?' she asked him.

Howe nodded. 'Yes,' he said.

'And he'd mortgaged everything he had – all his holdings in the South Antarctic Company – for this gamble?'

'Yes.'

'I see,' she said quietly. 'And he acted on Colonel Bland's advice?'

'I don't know whose advice he was acting on.'

She nodded. 'Thank you. That perhaps explains it.' Her voice was barely audible.

I nodded for Howe to go. He hesitated, looking at Judie's bent head. He wanted to help her. I saw it in his eyes. His face didn't look ugly in that moment. Then he was gone and I heard myself saying in a matter-of-fact voice, 'Why is it that Howe knows so much about your father's affairs?'

'Bernt and Walter were very close,' she answered quietly.

'You're satisfied your father was gambling in South African mines?' I asked.

She nodded.

'You can call Colonel Bland himself if you like,' I said.

'It's not necessary. Walter wouldn't lie to me.'

I glanced at Eide. 'You satisfied, too, Captain?' I asked him.

'*Ja*. I am satisfied.'

'Very well then,' I said. 'It only remains to agree on our findings.' I glanced at Judie. Her thoughts were far away. 'Judie,' I said. 'Can I have your views?'

'I will agree to whatever you think,' she said. Her voice was vague. She sounded as though she were far away.

The telephone rang and I picked it up. It was Bland. He wanted to know whether we were through. 'In about five minutes,' I said. 'We're just deciding on our findings.'

'Good. As soon as you're through I want you and Eide to come up to the saloon. The gunners are all here.'

When I put the receiver back Judie had risen. 'You must wait until we have agreed on our findings,' I said gently.

'I don't want to wait,' she answered. 'I don't wish to talk about it any more. Please – I will agree with your verdict.' She went out then and I looked at Eide. He was massaging the side of his beard. 'Bland wants us both up in the saloon,' I said. 'Can I have your views?'

'*Ja*. I think it is a matter for the police. As far as we can discover it is Erik Bland who sees him last. It is either – murder, or suicide.'

'Fine,' I said. 'That's what I think. In the circumstances I think we should refuse to reach any conclusions. This committee of inquiry has no legal standing. We should merely file the evidence and hand it over to assist the police in their investigations.'

Eide nodded. His gaunt, hatchet face was set in the lines beaten into it by years of violent weather. 'Bland will not like it,' he said. 'It is bad for the men that we do not reach some conclusion. But we cannot. I agree. So.' He pulled himself to his feet. 'We had better go to the conference now.'

I gathered up the sheets of evidence I had so laboriously taken down, clipping them together and stuffing them into my pocket. Up on deck Eide paused, gazing south towards the ice blink. The white, mirrored on the undersurface of the low cloud, was streaked with wide, dark lines. 'See,' he said. 'There are many wide leads – and they all run south. That is good.' It was like looking at a map of the ice below.

The saloon was full of smoke when we entered. Bland was sitting in a big chair. The skippers of the catchers were grouped round him in a circle. Charts littered the floor. Erik Bland was also there. He was sitting close to his father. 'Well, Captain Eide,' Bland said as we sat down, 'the others agree with me – that we should go south through the pack. The *Haakon* has reached open sea 600 miles south of us. She reports plenty of whale.'

'Then we also must go south,' Eide said. 'There are good leads and the weather is fine.'

'Good. Then it's settled.' Bland rang for the messboy and ordered drinks. Then he got up and came over to me. 'A word with you, Craig,' he said. I followed him out of the saloon and along the corridor to his cabin. 'Now,' he said, as I closed the door. 'What are your findings?' His voice was hard and his small eyes had narrowed.

I pulled the sheets of evidence out of my pocket and handed them to him. He put them down on the desk. 'Your findings?' he repeated. 'Come on, man,' he added impatiently, as I hesitated. 'You must have reached some conclusion.'

'Yes,' I said. 'But I don't think you'll like it. In our opinion Nordahl's disappearance is a matter for police investigation.'

He blew his cheeks out like a grampus. It was as though he'd been holding his breath. 'Why?' he asked sharply.

'There are two possibilities,' I said. 'Either Nordahl committed suicide or he was – murdered.'

'Go on.'

'As the inquiry has no legal standing, we take the view that it would not be right for it to attempt to reach any conclusion. The evidence, which I have now passed on to you, should be handed over to the police on our return to port.'

'I see. You and Captain Eide and my daughter-in-law all take the view it is either suicide or murder.'

'That is my view and Captain Eide's. Mrs Bland was too upset to consider the findings.'

'And – is my son involved in any way?'

'Yes,' I said. 'He was the last person to see Nordahl at all after the evening meal. Later he admitted that he had had a row with him up on the deck. That was shortly after midnight. At twelve thirty-five the fog cleared. It was only possible for Nordahl to have gone overboard unobserved during the intervening twenty minutes.'

'I see.' Bland slowly sank into a chair. 'But it could be suicide.'

'His daughter doesn't think so. She says he wasn't a quitter, that suicide would never enter his head.'

'But you think it's a possibility. Why?'

'You should know,' I answered.

'What do you mean by that?'

'Weren't you in on the Wyks Odensdaal Rust Development racket?' I countered.

Bland turned on me with a quick oath. 'How do you know – ' He stopped then. 'Well?'

'Nordahl came to you and asked to be put on to something good in the financial world. He mortgaged all his holding in the South Antarctic Company and invested everything he had in Wyks Odensdaal Rust Development.'

'If he did, then it's the first I've heard of it,' Bland barked. 'He never asked me for financial advice in his life. And I wouldn't have given it to him if he had. He knew nothing about finance and I'm old enough to know that to give financial advice is the quickest way of making enemies.'

So it was Erik Bland who had advised Nordahl. 'Well,' I said, 'that's what your son says.'

'I see.' He stood by the porthole a moment, drumming with his fingers on the top of the toilet cabinet. At length he turned and faced me. He looked tired and somehow older. He didn't say anything, but sat down at the desk and began running through the sheets of evidence. Then for a long time he sat staring at one single page. At last he pushed the papers into a drawer and got to his feet. 'Very well, Craig,' he said heavily. 'I agree. It is a matter for the police. Some changes must be made now.' He went to the door and I followed him back to the saloon.

One of the *skytters* gave me a drink and I knocked it back. I needed it badly. Bland had sat down again. Something in his manner silenced the room. He watched them, his heavy brows dragged down, his face set in its solid, imperturbable rolls. 'I have some changes in command to announce,' he said. 'Nordahl's death has left us without an experienced leader. As I am here, and intend to stay out during the whole season, I shall direct operations personally. Petersen, you will take over from my son as manager of the *Southern Cross*.' There was a murmur of surprise and a quickening of interest at this announcement. 'Commander Craig, you are posted to command of *Hval 4* in Petersen's place.'

I saw the eldest of the whaling skippers stir in his seat and lean forward. 'Excuse me, sir,' I said quickly,

'I don't wish to query your orders. But I would like to remind you that I've no experience as a gunner.'

'I'm well aware of that, Craig,' he answered. 'But you will take command of *Hval 4*.' He rounded on Petersen before the old *skytter* could begin to argue. 'I know what you're going to say, Petersen. But I won't have a girl in charge of a catcher. Not down here. Craig will command the boat. Your daughter will remain in her present position as mate. But in addition she will act as gunner. Some adjustment will be made financially in her terms of employment. Does that satisfy you?'

The old *skytter* relaxed. '*Ja*, hr Bland. I am satisfied.'

'Good. Erik. You will take command of *Tauer III*. The ship is without deck officers at the moment. You can choose your own mates.' He turned to Petersen again. 'I shall rely on you to see that there is no more trouble between the Sandefjord and Tönsberg men. More than six weeks have passed and we've only just over a hundred whales. In the next two months the leeway has got to be – '

But I wasn't listening. I was staring at Erik Bland. His face seemed to have crumpled up on hearing his father's decision. But it wasn't his face so much as his eyes that held my gaze. There was something violent, almost vicious, about those small blue slits between the creases of fat.

I was brought back to the conference again with a jolt. It was Captain Larvik. 'Has the inquiry into

Nordahl's death been completed yet, hr Bland?' he asked.

'Yes,' replied the chairman, and glanced quickly at me.

'Can we have the findings of the committee then?'

'They have not been typed yet,' Bland answered. 'They will be published tomorrow.'

Again I was conscious of a quick glance in my direction and then he was hurrying on into details of organization for the journey through the pack. Finally he said, 'Well, gentlemen, I think that's all. We will start as soon as you have rejoined your ships.' He was as casual as if he were terminating a rather dull board meeting. The *skytters* got to their feet. There was no argument, no indication that only just over twenty-four hours before several of them had refused to operate. Bland sat, squat and solid in his chair, smiling genially, dominating them. There was something implacable in the calm assuredness of the man. I thought: *Money is power and he's had that all his life. He's had it because that's what he's fought for and in doing so he's learned to beat down all opposition. They know that. They know it's no good fighting him. So they do what he says.* I didn't like Bland. But I couldn't help admiring him. Out of chaos and a tricky situation, he had produced order – and obedience.

The whalers were leaving now. Bland motioned me over to him. His son was still hunched angrily in his chair, waiting to speak to his father. 'Craig,' Bland said quietly as I approached him, 'I want you to understand that the interests of the expedition must come first. I am referring to the committee of inquiry. Your attitude in the matter is quite correct. But the safety of the *Southern Cross* and the catcher fleet depend on the morale of the men. For the moment that must be my sole consideration. But privately I wish you to know that the whole matter of Nordahl's disappearance, together with the evidence you have taken, will be handed over to the police at the earliest opportunity. In the meantime, anything I may do in the matter will be done with Captain Eide's full knowledge. Do you understand?'

'Yes, sir,' I said.

As I turned to go his son rose from his seat. 'Does that include posting me to command of a towing ship?' His tone was pitched a shade high. I got the impression that he was scared of his father. But something stronger was driving him now.

Bland looked at him. 'It does,' he said.

'But Nordahl committed suicide. He must have done. It – it's the only logical explanation. He was finished. He'd ruined himself in that mad gamble. That's why he killed himself. I tried to make Craig understand that. He'd lost everything he had. He'd nothing to live for. Why didn't you tell the *skytters* the truth – that Nordahl was a ruined man?'

'I'm doing what I think best, boy.' Bland's voice was a deep, angry rumble.

'You're being weak.' Erik Bland was trembling, his eyes fever-bright and his mouth twitching. 'You're discarding me like you do everyone when it suits you.'

'Talk to me like that again, Erik, and I'll send

you back to the Cape in irons.' Bland took off his glasses and wiped them carefully. He was trembling with anger. He had calmed down a little by the time he'd put his glasses on again. He took out his wallet and extracted a piece of paper. 'Read that,' he said, passing it across to his son.

'*Cargo unloaded as per instructions*,' Erik Bland read aloud and his brow puckered.

'It's a copy of a radio message received by Nordahl on Christmas Eve. It was sent by Howe from Capetown.'

'What's it mean?'

'I'll leave you to think about what it means for a moment.' Bland turned to me. 'You'll please regard what has passed between Erik and myself here as confidential, Craig. You have my assurance that, whatever I put out for the benefit of the men in present circumstances, all the evidence you have taken at the committee of inquiry will be handed to the police immediately on our return to port. Now I suggest you join your ship.'

I nodded and turned to go. But he stopped me. 'I shall be sending Doctor Howe over to join you. I think it would be better if he didn't remain on the factory ship. He is excitable and when drunk he might – ' He shrugged his shoulders. 'Bernt Nordahl,' he began, and then hesitated. He seemed to have difficulty in finding the right words. 'Nordahl was his father,' he finished abruptly.

'His father?' I echoed in surprise. And I saw a shocked, almost dazed look on Erik Bland's face.

'Yes,' Bland said. 'He is Nordahl's natural son by a Mrs Howe of Newcastle. That is why I think it would be better if he were on one of the catchers.' He nodded for me to go and then added, 'You will find Gerda Petersen not very beautiful, but a good first mate.'

That he should be capable of this little flash of dry humour at that moment made me wonder whether Nordahl's death meant anything to him. I remember thinking that a man who was involved in the Wyks Odensdaal Rust business might not stop at other things. As I walked away from the saloon I heard the door opened and then closed. It was as though they had suspected me of listening in the corridor.

I went straight down to my cabin. Judie was there, sitting on my bunk. Howe was pacing up and down. They both turned to face me as I came in. 'Shut the door, Craig,' Howe said. He was agitated, almost excited. Judie sat very tense, her eyes dark shadows in the tightness of her face. She was beyond tears – near the breaking point.

I shut the door. 'Something happened?' I asked.

Judie nodded. 'Tell him, Walter.' Her voice was barely audible.

'All right.' Howe swung round on me. 'But understand this, Craig – not a word of what I'm going to tell you must be passed on to anyone. Understand?' I nodded. 'Promise?'

'I promise,' I said.

He peered at me quickly. 'I don't know you well enough to be certain you can be trusted.' He hesitated and then shrugged his shoulders. 'However, Judie wants me to tell you, so – ' He started pacing the cabin again without finishing his sentence. There was a sort of incredible violence about the man. I sat very still, watching him. It was like waiting for an animal to make up its mind whether it regards you as a friend.

At length he stopped his pacing and came and stood right in front of me. 'Erik Bland said Nordahl was ruined, didn't he?'

I nodded.

'That's the basis for thinking Nordahl's death might be suicide?'

Again I nodded.

'The only basis?'

'Yes,' I said.

'If Nordahl weren't ruined, it would mean that Erik Bland killed him?'

'On the evidence we have at the moment it would be reasonable to suppose that,' I said, cautiously, wondering what the hell he was driving at.

Howe nodded excitedly. 'That's what I told Judie. If Nordahl were a rich man then Erik Bland killed him, pushed him overboard in the fog.'

'What are you getting at?' I demanded.

'Why do you suppose I was left in Capetown?'

'I thought you'd been ill.'

'That was only an excuse. I stayed in Capetown to look after Nordahl's interests. Erik Bland was quite right – as far as he went. Nordahl invested everything he had in Wyks Odensdaal Rust Development, even to mortgaging his interest in the South Antarctic

Company. Erik Bland got the whole of his father's plan for the boosting of these shares from his mother. He passed it on to Nordahl as a straight tip, forgetting to mention that it was a racket, that the mine was to be salted and at a certain moment Bland was going to go on the bear tack. Nordahl had never dabbled much in finance. But he was an astute man. He saw through the reason for Erik Bland giving him the tip and he saw in it a chance to prevent Erik Bland from becoming head of the firm on his father's death. He got an introduction to one of the sharpest brokers in the business, and dealt through them. And when the *Southern Cross* sailed from Capetown I stayed behind with his power of attorney. On Christmas Eve I cabled the *Southern Cross* that I'd sold all the shares.'

'Cargo unloaded as per instructions,' I said. I was beginning to understand.

Howe looked at me sharply. 'How did you know the wording?'

I told him about Bland handing the copy of the cable to his son.

'So the old man knows, eh?' He chuckled to himself. 'It must have shaken him – reading the evidence and knowing that.' He caught hold of my arm. 'Nordahl was a rich man when he died. A very rich man.'

I stared at him. I don't think I made any comment. I only remember the shock of realizing what must have happened, that Erik Bland had killed him.

'Don't you see,' Howe rushed on. 'Up there on the boat deck, Erik Bland told Nordahl what had happened, told him he was a ruined man. You can imagine how sympathetically he broke the news. And then Nordahl told him the truth that he'd sold out, that he was rich. He probably told him that he'd see he never again set foot on one of the company's ships. And then Bland pushed him.'

'It could have been a accident,' Judie whispered. 'He may have struck Bernt without realizing – in the fog – ' Her voice trailed away.

Howe laughed. It was a derisive sound. 'You don't really believe that,' he said.

'Why didn't you tell this to the committee of inquiry?' I asked him.

'Why? Because it would have given my hand away. And don't forget your promise, Craig. Nothing I've told you must be repeated to anyone. I don't think the old man knew what his son was up to. But he knows now. And he's not the sort of man to regard justice as applicable to himself or his.' He stooped down suddenly. 'I hear he refused to give the findings of the inquiry to the *skytters* – said they weren't typed. Did he by any chance mention something to you about morale and the exigencies of the moment?'

I nodded. 'But he has assured me that all the evidence will be handed to the police on our return to port.'

Howe gave that derisive, barking laugh again. 'You wait. Vital witnesses will be sent home in another ship, Eide and the secretary will be persuaded that it's not in the interest of the company to incur unprofitable publicity, and the whole thing will quietly fizzle out.

That's why I wasn't coming out into the open. And I've still got something up my sleeve.'

But I wasn't listening to him any longer. I was staring at Judie. I remember thinking: *My God! She knows*. And realizing what hell it must be for her.

FIVE

Half an hour later I was up on deck with my things packed. The wind had freshened and ugly whitecaps were beginning to fleck the marching lines of cold grey water. Howe was waiting for me at the head of the gangway. 'Well, skipper,' he said, 'all the problem children being evacuated.'

'Bland's right all the same,' I said. 'There's two months of the season still to go.'

'I see you're one of the reasonable sort.' He smiled at me crookedly. 'You haven't much to do with the Blands of this world, have you?'

'How do you mean?'

'In your world, right is right and wrong is wrong. But there's another world where it's a free-for-all and devil take the hindermost. You're in that other world now – Bland's world.'

'Why not relax?' I said. Up there on the deck my sense of proportion had reasserted itself. We were going south into the Antarctic and I'd been given command of one of the catchers. That was quite enough without having Howe on board behaving like a maniac. 'There's nothing you can do about Nordahl's death now,' I added. 'Wait until we get back to – '

'You fool,' he hissed. 'Don't you understand Judie's a rich woman? She holds the key to the control of the company. When Erik Bland knows that – ' He paused and then added, 'A man who's prepared to commit murder to get what he wants won't stop at that. Just now he's probably scared. But sooner or later – ' He shrugged his shoulders. And then in a matter-of-fact voice he said, 'If we stand here talking all day we'll get wet going over to the catcher.'

I started down the gangway. But then I stopped. There were three boats at the bottom of the gangway and one of them was just pushing off. In the stern sat Judie. She was sitting next to Larvik and her face was tense.

'Why's she going over to Larvik's catcher?' I asked. 'Did Bland send her?'

'No,' Howe answered. 'She sent herself. Bland doesn't know she's gone yet.'

'But why?'

'Because I advised her to. She's safer there than on the *Southern Cross*.'

'But Good God!' I said. 'You don't think anything would happen – '

'This is the Antarctic,' he reminded me, 'not suburbia.' He went down the gangway then. As he dumped his kit aboard the boat I caught the chink of bottles. He grinned as he saw that I'd heard. 'Always believe in being self-sufficient,' he said. It was incredible how the man's mood could change. 'You've got to be if you want to drink. Officially all these ships are dry.' He sent the two seamen up to bring down his instruments whilst we held the boat to the ship's side. A few minutes later we had pushed off and were bobbing up and down past the yawning cavity of the *Southern Cross*'s stern. The clean, ice-fresh air blew the events of the past twenty-four hours from my brain. Ahead of me lay *Hval 4*, a battered little toy of a boat with a saucy rake to her up-tilted bows. The harpoon gun, loaded and with the tip of the harpoon pointed downwards, was a grim reminder of her job as a killer. The knowledge that this was my new command gradually took hold of me as we approached her through the rising anger of the sea and drove every other thought out of my head.

Olaf Petersen met us as we clambered aboard. He was a big, bluff man with sharp eyes and a queer way of looking around him with a swaying motion of the head, rather like a polar bear. 'I am happy to welcome you on my ship.' His English was heavy and solid, like the creaking of something little used. The grip of his hand was the clutch of a bear's paw. 'You haf not meet my daughter.' His head lunged round. 'Gerda. Here is Commander Craig.'

I shouldn't have known she was a girl but for the breadth of her hips, the bulkiness of her chest and the fact that she was clean shaven. She was dressed in a heavy seaman's jersey, blue serge trousers and wore a fur cap on her head. The only spot of colour was a rather dirty-looking yellow silk scarf half hidden under her jacket. Her hand was rough as it gripped mine. I glanced at her quickly. She had large, very brown eyes. Her face was tanned and smooth, a chubby, friendly face with a lot of fat flesh round the eyes and a nose that was almost flattened as though the Maker had forgotten about it until the last moment and then as an afterthought slapped on a little button of flesh without any bone. There was no resentment as she met my gaze, only amusement. Her eyes twinkled in the creases of fat as though at any moment they would burst out laughing. 'I do not expect you have women as officers in your Navy,' she said.

'Only ashore,' I said with a grin.

'Ah, yes. A woman's place is ashore.' The laughter gurgled up from her throat, warm and happy. 'And then you call them Wrens, eh – little birds!'

Her father's big paw slapped my shoulder so that I nearly lost my balance. 'You will haf to get used to Gerda,' he boomed. 'Always she make mock of people. Even me – her father – I am to be made mock of. Always since she was so high and learn to speak English she call me *landlubber*, me – *landlubber*.' His great laugh seemed to rattle round the ship, and he slapped me on the back again. But I was prepared for it this time and braced myself for the impact.

'Come,' Gerda Petersen said. 'I show you to your cabin. Walter, you come too. What's in that box – whisky?'

Howe grinned. He seemed relaxed for the first time since I'd met him. And when he grinned like that, it was strange, but he didn't look ugly any more. 'No,' he said. 'That's my instruments. The drink's in the bag here.' He kicked it and laughed when she scowled at the clinking sound of the bottles. 'That means you have not brought enough clothes and we must raid the slop-chest for you.' She glanced quickly at me and added, 'For you also, skipper. You look' – she hesitated, her eyes bubbling with laughter – 'you look as though you have borrow your clothes from all the crew of the *Southern Cross*.'

'Gerda!' Petersen's tone was half amused, half serious. 'You will not get in the good books of your new captain if you make fun of him. What must you think, Commander Craig? You will think I have brought up my daughter badly and there is no discipline on my ship. Well, by God, there is.'

His daughter laughed. 'Take no notice of him,' she whispered. 'He is a big bear and he think he is important now he is to be manager of the factory ship.'

Her father shrugged his shoulders in mock despair.

'I'll be only too glad to borrow from your slop-chest,' I said.

'Fine. Then come and take a look at your new command. I hear you are the devil for spit and polish.' She grinned at me slyly over her shoulders. 'Well, I can tell you, this ship needs some polishing. That dirty man has made a pigsty of her.' With this parting shot at her father she pulled herself up the ladder that led to the bridge accommodation.

The catcher was a good deal smaller than *Tauer III*. The captain's cabin was directly below the bridge, a part of the for'ard deckhouse. 'I am sorry,' Gerda said, 'but we have not the accommodation of a factory ship. You will have to share your cabin with Walter Howe. Do you mind?'

'That's all right,' I said. 'Provided he's willing to share his Scotch with me.'

She laughed. 'Do not worry. I will see that he is not dog-in-the-manger with his drink. I, too, get thirsty.' Her eyes twinkled. 'You must excuse me for my rotten English. It is vair rusty.' Howe staggered in then with his box of instruments. 'Walter, you will share the skipper's cabin and he is to share your whisky. Okay?'

Howe's eyebrows lifted. 'He'll have to drink fast,' he said, 'if he is to get the same share of my drink that I get of his cabin.'

They both laughed. They seemed to understand each other. 'This ought to be the wireless room,' Gerda said, leading me to the next cabin. 'But because I am Olaf Petersen's daughter, he make a little adjustment. This is my cabin and the wireless is aft in the second mate's berth. That is the only concession he make,' she added quickly.

She took me on a brief tour of the ship then, introducing me to the crew. 'Do not trouble to remember their names,' she said as she noticed my concentration. 'You will soon have sort them out.'

The ship was rather like a small Fleet sweeper in appearance with its high bow and high bridge and a long, low after-deck. She was narrow in the beam, built for speed and power. She was capable of about 13½ knots and looked a very seaworthy little ship, though I guessed she'd be extremely lively in heavy weather. Perched on a platform on the bow was the harpoon gun, a deadly-looking weapon with a three and a quarter inch breech and firing harpoon weighing around a hundredweight. The gun platform was connected to the bridge by a catwalk. Aft of the chain locker was a hold containing two 500-fathom coils of 2-inch manila. These whale lines ran up the winches on deck. Each winch had two drums and the line ran three times round each drum and thence up to masthead blocks and so out through a fairlead in the bow. The masthead blocks were connected to huge springs – accumulators – with a pressure of twenty tons. The springs performed the same function as the whip in a fishing-rod, allowing the whale to be played on the winches without the sudden movements of the vessel in a seaway parting the line.

Aft of the hold was the engine-room. Then came the crew's quarters – cabins with bunks for two or four – and finally the tiller flat. Below the captain's cabin in the bridge accommodation was the galley and the messroom.

By the time I had completed the round of the ship Captain Petersen was ready to leave. 'Well, I hope you will like *Hval 4*,' he said, gripping my hand as though trying to squeeze the flesh out between the bones. '*Ja*. I hope so. I hope also Gerda behave herself, no? There is one good thing about a woman as first mate – if she do not behave you can always put her across your knee. She has a vair big bottom. You cannot miss, even if you are drunk, eh?' And he went down the ladder to the deck below roaring with laughter.

'You have only the nerve to say that because you are leaving,' the girl answered, two angry little spots of colour showing on the dark tan of her cheeks.

'Because I am leaving, eh? *Ja*. That is good. When I am skipper here my life she is not worth living. It is Olaf this and Olaf that all day long. I tell you, Commander Craig, it is worse than being married to have a daughter on board.' He turned and looked up at us, his fat face creased in laughter. 'One thing I do not haf to worry about. My daughter is safe with any man. She is a nice girl – but ugly as a fat leetle pig, eh?'

Gerda made a face at him and put out her tongue. Still laughing, he climbed over the side into the boat that had been sent across from the factory ship. We watched it bobbing across the waves towards the *Southern Cross*. '*Mange hval*,' Petersen roared across at us and with a final wave of his big hand seated himself in the stern.

'I am afraid all this talk will have made you think this is a play-ship,' Gerda said, her voice suddenly serious. 'But that is just our fun.'

'I like it,' I said. 'I feel at home already. I think the ship must be a very happy one.'

'*Ja*, I think so too.' She wrinkled her nose. It was a habitual gesture, half serious, half humorous. 'You are nice,' she said. 'My father and I have been three seasons together out here. We are not bad whalers. We work well together. Last season we are second only to Peer Larvik in the number of whales we have caught. This time we lead all the fleet – though that is not much. We have twenty-two whale so far.'

'I hope we manage to hold the lead,' I said.

She patted me on the shoulder. It was a gesture

copied from her father, but I was glad to find it hadn't the same weight behind it. 'I think we get on fine, skipper. But I am not so good a *skytter* as Olaf. And you will have to learn how to control the ship for me.' She glanced at me quickly. 'I know what you are thinking. You are thinking the Antarctic is no place for a girl. But you must remember one thing. We can stand the cold well – I have much fat, eh?' And she tapped her bosom and laughed. I was thinking of the Eskimo women I had met on that Greenland expedition. They had stood the cold as well as the men. Looking at Gerda Petersen, I wondered if there wasn't some Eskimo or Lapland blood in her – she had the flattened face and narrow, fat-creased eyes of the northern Slav. Later I discovered her mother was a Finn from the Aaland Islands.

As we stood there on the deck a boat came across from *Tauer III*. It was McPhee. Bland had agreed to his transfer. I watched the Chief Engineer of *Hval 4* as he climbed down into the boat. It was clear that he didn't want to leave his own ship. But I'd had to have one officer that I knew. And McPhee was glad to come with me. I could see that in the dour way he said, 'Och, ye dinna ha' to fash yersel' aboot me leaving me ane engine-room. Ah'll soon have this ane as smart as the ither.'

At eight thirty-five there was a series of whoops on the factory ship's siren. The sea boiled under the ugly cavity of her stern. I ordered Half Ahead, and as the engine-room telegraph rang, the deck plates began to vibrate to the rising hum of the engine as we swung into position astern of the *Southern Cross*. The other ships took up station and the whole fleet, strung out in a long line behind the mother ship, headed south into the ice.

The sky cleared about eleven that night. The sun was almost due south, a flaming yellow ball, its lower edge just above the horizon. A towering iceberg loomed up to starboard, catching the sunlight and flashing fire like an enormous pink diamond. Fragments of ice began to drift past us – tiny 'growlers', almost completely submerged. And ahead of us the loose pack ice stretched like an unending, broken plain of pink straight into the sun. It was an incredible sight.

Gerda, who was standing between Howe and myself on the bridge, caught hold of my arm and said, 'It is beautiful, yes? I bet you do not ever see anything so beautiful as this. You are glad we go south?'

I nodded. But I was looking at Howe. I was thinking – *He doesn't see the beauty of it. But he's exultant. The ice means something else to him.* He was standing quite still, his long neck thrust out and his hand clenched on the canvas windbreaker. His face looked almost ferocious. Again I had that sense of being afraid of him – the feeling that I'd had on *Tauer III* when Bland had ordered him to prepare that report. It was as though the man were part of the destiny of things. After all he was Bernt Nordahl's son and I remembered Judie saying – *Bernt and Walter were very close.*

'Howe!' The unconscious peremptoriness of my tone jerked him away from his contemplation of the ice ahead. 'That report you did for Bland. Why did you come to the conclusion that we must go south into the Weddell Sea?'

He stared at me for a moment and the corners of his mouth lifted in that sly smile of his. He didn't attempt to justify his findings with a lot of technicalities. He just shrugged his shoulders and said, 'I wanted Bland to go south – that's all.'

'Why?'

Again the slight shrug. 'Why? God knows why. I just wanted him to go south – away from civilization.'

'But why?' I asked again.

He let go of the windbreaker then and caught hold of my arm in a grip that hurt, it was so violent. 'Because if he's given enough rope – ' He stopped there and gave a quick laugh. 'Just leave it at that.' And he turned away and went quickly down to the cabin.

'You find Walter a little queer perhaps?' Gerda said with a laugh that sounded unnatural. 'Poor man – he has not had an easy life. And he worshipped Bernt Nordahl.'

'And you' – I said – 'what did you think of Nordahl?'

'I think he is a big loss to the company – to all of us who work with him. He was a fine man.'

McPhee came up on to the bridge then to discuss a defect in one of the winches and the conversation was never resumed. By midnight, with the sun lipping the southern horizon, we had entered the ice, following a broad lead and steaming south at about ten knots. The lead was more than a mile wide and the water in it looked black by comparison with the shimmering iridescence of the ice on either side. On our port quarter was a large, flat-topped berg. Apart from this we were surrounded by loose pack – a flat expanse of ice tinged with pink and criss-crossed with innumerable black lines that marked the division between one floe and another. And as the sun climbed and circled northwards towards midday, the colours drained out of the scene and the ice became a blinding sheet of white, very painful to the eyes. Even with dark glasses I found it tiring.

There was nothing dangerous about the ice. The weather remained fair and we were able to observe a steady shipboard routine of watch and watch about. Sometimes the lead was so broad we might have been in the open sea but for the glare. At other times it narrowed down to a dark highway winding between occasional icebergs and surrounded by that unending plain of loose pack. Only once it petered out and then the *Southern Cross* thrust into the pack, parting the floes in great sheets that layered one on top of the other until we were in a new lead.

Occasionally we sighted whale. Once a big spermaceti came up to blow almost alongside. They were all headed south. There were plenty of the smaller killer whales hunting for seals among the icefloes. One morning a whole string of these ugly brutes passed across our bows. Their high triangular fins stood about five feet out of the water and the whole line of them rose and fell as they cut through the water, blowing steadily. Gerda and Howe were on the bridge with me at the time and she said, 'Ugh, those devils!'

'*Orca Gladiator*,' Howe said. 'That's the official terminology.'

'*Gladiators!*' Gerda's voice was almost angry. 'For once your official terminology, as you call it, is right. That's exactly what they are – gladiators. Have you ever seen one close to?' she asked me.

I shook my head. 'I've never seen them before.'

'Well, I do not advise it. Once I see one close to, and it is enough, I think. When he is full grown the killer is perhaps thirty feet long, his mouth is about four feet wide and he has ugly eyes and uglier teeth. I was hunting for seal with my father. It was near Grytviken and we had left our boat and were on a small icefloe. This killer whale, he start snorting and blowing all around us. Then suddenly he push his nose over the edge of the floe and look straight at us. Then he start to turn the floe over with his weight. Fortunately my father have his gun and he shoot. But it is a very near thing and it is long time before I go for the seal again.' Later I was to remember this story and wish she had never told it to me.

She was, in fact, a mine of information on the Antarctic and she would talk for hours about whales and ships and hunting expeditions on the ice in the same matter-of-fact way that most women would talk about a shopping expedition in Oxford Street. It was she who picked out a sea-leopard for me in the glasses so that I was able to watch the great spotted brute rushing across the ice with an undulating, snake-like movement as it charged a group of seals. She pointed out to me the small Adelie penguins clustered on an ice-ledge, where they bowed and chattered to each other with the distant dignity of foreign diplomats at an Embassy social.

On the morning of the fourth day in the ice the sky to the south became very black and louring. There was a lot of low cloud and at first I thought a storm was coming up. But Gerda shook her head. 'It is the open sea. It always look dark when you are in the ice blink.' She was right. The lead we were following gradually opened out. The floes became looser and more scattered, and early on the 23rd January we were in open sea in 66.01 S., 35.62 W. with the ice blink behind us.

Almost immediately *Hval 1* and *Hval 3* ahead of us peeled off. Gerda had ordered a lookout to the *tonne*, which is the barrel crow's-nest, and a few minutes later came the cry of '*Blaast! Blaast!*'

'*Hvor er den?*' Gerda called up.

'*Paa styrbord side.*'

We picked it up almost immediately. I ordered starboard helm and emergency full ahead and we were off on our first whale hunt. I've heard people say that there's no longer any excitement in whaling, that Sven Foynd's invention of the explosive harpoon took all the adventure out of it. Don't you believe it. Whaling is still the biggest of all big-game hunting and only the arm-chair whalers make statements like that.

I must admit that as we swung away at full speed on that cry of *Blaast* I was under the impression that the work of a catcher was just the shooting down of the whale. I hadn't realized the chase that was involved.

Almost immediately the whale sounded and Gerda suggested we reduce to half speed. All eyes were scanning the sea ahead, waiting for the next sight of the thin plume of vapour as the whale surfaced again to blow. I found myself nervous and excited as I stared into the heaving, slate-grey waste of water. Gerda plucked at my sleeve. 'You have not done this before, so perhaps if you take the wheel and I give directions –' She hesitated. 'It is very difficult to get so that we can shoot him. We must drive him under again and again until he is blown. You understand?'

'Of course,' I said. She didn't want to embarrass me, but at the same time she wanted our first whale hunt to be successful. I think we were both a little excited and a little awkward at sharing the command.

I took the wheel and almost immediately one of the hands gave a shout and Gerda ordered full speed. The whale was wallowing on the surface about two cables' length ahead of us. We were on top of him almost immediately and the sleek, grey back curved as it sounded.

Gerda ordered 'Stop!' and the vibration of the engine died as we drifted forward. When next he broke surface he was away on the port beam and we heeled over as I turned the catcher in pursuit. Five times we drove the whale under, and each time we were closer to him. Now we were driving him under almost before he had time to blow and all my nervousness was gone in the excitement of the chase. 'Now I think we have him,' Gerda shouted to me as it wallowed in the trough of a wave so close that we could hear the snort of the water being expelled from the huge body. Her eyes were alight with excitement. She thrust open the door of the bridge and ran down the catwalk to the gun platform. From there she directed me by hand signals which we had rehearsed beforehand.

We were steaming at slow ahead and turning to port. She had taken hold of the slender butt of the gun. She signalled for half speed and I saw the whale surface right ahead of us, not fifty feet away, as I jerked the engine-room telegraph. The catcher gathered speed. Gerda braced her legs apart and swung the harpoon gun. We were right on top of the whale now. I lost sight of it under the high bows and braced myself for the shock of our bows ripping into it. There was a flash, the sharp crack of an explosion and I saw the harpoon fly down into the water, the light forerunner snaking after it. There was another, duller explosion, a terrible flurry of spray and then the winch drums were screaming and the masthead block dragging down as the heavy two-inch whale line went roaring out through the fairlead in the bow.

Gerda came running back to the bridge. 'My shot is no good,' she said. 'I tell you I am not so good a *skytter* as Olaf. The harpoon, he explode outside. I do not hit the backbone. Slow now please.'

The whale had sounded and the line was still roaring out with the block dragged down to the danger mark. I watched one, two splices run through the block. Each splice meant 120 fathoms of line gone out. Altogether there were four lengths – three splices. Just when the third splice was reeling through the block we saw the whale surface half a mile ahead.

Gerda was gripping the windbreaker in a frenzy. This was her first whale independent of her father. It meant a lot to her. The last splice went through the fairlead. She ordered full speed. And just as I rang the engine-room telegraph, I saw the block start to rise up the mast. 'We win,' she cried. 'We win.' McPhee at the winch was braking now. I could hear the scream of the brake drums above the hum of the engines. Then suddenly the line was slack. Gerda ordered stop and the winch began to clatter as McPhee took in line. We drifted and the line continued to come in slack.

Then suddenly it was taut again, stretched so tight that from a diameter of two inches it was shrunk to half an inch. It was like a violin string. I thought it must break. The block was down the mast again and the whole ship was being dragged through the water at about 6 knots. McPhee paid out line on the winches. It lasted like that for perhaps a minute – maybe only thirty seconds. It seemed like years. Then it was over. It was the whale's last bid for freedom. We began to winch in. It was still lashing the water with its huge tail as we hauled up to it and Gerda ran down to the gun platform and fired another harpoon into it. There was a sudden spout of blood and then the great brute was motionless, lying alongside us like a half-submerged submarine.

'Next time I shoot better, I hope,' Gerda said and took me down to the bows to superintend the pumping of air into the whale. As one of the hands thrust the lance with the air pipe into it, there was a cry of

'*Blaast! Blaast!*' from the *tonne*. The air hissed as it went into the huge carcase. The harpoon holes were plugged, a long steel rod with a flag was thrust deep into the animal and a moment later we were back on the bridge and off after our next whale, two men working furiously to reload the harpoon gun and rig a new fore-runner as we went.

I have given this detailed account of our first whale hunt to show the degree of concentration the work entailed. It occupied all our waking thoughts and energies and when we fell into our bunks we were so tired we slept like the dead. For whale were plentiful and when we had killed one, another was sighted almost immediately. The cry of *Blaast! Blaast!* echoed almost unceasingly from the *tonne* and the crack of the harpoon gun slamming its deadly weight of metal into the whale sounded all day and on through the unending daylight of the night. When we'd flagged three or four whale we'd put through a call on the R/T for one of the towing vessels or a buoy boat and go on to the next kill whilst they picked up our catch and towed it back to the factory ship. All round us, through good weather and bad, the rest of the catcher fleet was working in the same frantic haste. The only occasions on which we returned to the *Southern Cross* were to refuel and take on provisions and a new supply of harpoons straightened out in the blacksmith's shop. I had neither the time nor the energy to think about Nordahl's disappearance and though I wondered sometimes how Judie was getting on in Larvik's catcher, my mind was so tired that the image it sketched of her was blurred as though she were a girl I'd met years ago.

Even the announcement over the R/T that the committee of inquiry over which I had presided had found that Nordahl had committed suicide whilst the balance of his mind was affected by financial worries made little impression in the fatigue induced by hard and constant work. Bland had said that he must consider the morale of the men in any announcement he made and I must say I agreed with him. Whatever Howe might say, I had no reason to suppose that he would not carry out his promise to hand over the evidence to the police on our return to Capetown. And if he failed in this I could always notify the police myself. Howe's reaction was, of course, very different. 'I told you what would happen,' he shouted at me. 'I told you they'd try to hush it up. But I can wait. I can wait. And sooner or later – ' But I was too tired to listen to his railing. Too many things demanded my attention for him to be able to corner me for more than a moment at a time. And when I wasn't on duty I was asleep and then not all the angels of wrath calling for vengeance could have got an answer out of me.

In two weeks we chased and killed forty-six whale. Most of these were shot by Gerda, for I felt it was unfair on the men to assume the role of gunner except at the end of a good day's hunting. They had a financial interest in the whale we caught. However, by the end of that fortnight I was becoming quite a fair *skytter* and the men, who were a good crowd, would ask me to go down and see if I could get one, laying small bets against each other as to whether I'd be successful or not with my first shot. They were very proud of their ship and I think they were unwilling to accept the idea of a skipper who wasn't also a *skytter*.

Towards the end of this period of intense activity an incident occurred which brought the whole question of Nordahl's disappearance back into my mind. We'd had a good day and after our fourth kill we radioed for a towing vessel to pick up the catch. As it happened it was *Tauer III* that answered our call. We were quartering the sea on the line of her approach and as she neared us she swung off her course and made straight for us, her sharp bows cleaving the water at a steady 14 knots. She came round in a wide circle and steamed up almost alongside. Erik Bland was on the bridge and he called to me on the loud-hailer, asking permission to come aboard and have a word with me.

Before I could reply, Howe came pell-mell up the ladder to the bridge. He was breathless and his face was working. He caught hold of my arm, forcing the megaphone away from my lips. 'Don't let him come on board.' His eyes looked wild and the grip of his fingers on my arm was like a vice.

'Why?' I asked.

'Why?' He shook me. 'You ask why?' His voice was trembling. 'If that bastard sets foot on board this ship, I'll kill him. That's why. I'll kill him. I swear it.'

I stared at him for a second in amazement. His violence had taken me by surprise. Yet the strange thing is, I never doubted that he meant it. We hadn't seen much of him during the last few days. He'd kept to the cabin mostly, working on what he'd told me was a treatise on whaling. He'd been drinking hardly anything. I realized suddenly that what he'd been doing was brooding. 'All right,' I said, and raised the megaphone to my lips. 'Ahoy there! I – will – come – over – to – you.'

The two vessels were steaming parallel only twenty feet or so apart. Bland waved his hand to signify he'd heard and I ordered the engine stopped and a boat swung out. As my men rowed me across the long swell to the waiting corvette I had time to wonder what it was Bland wanted to see me about. And in those few minutes I thought more about the antagonism between him and Nordahl that we'd unearthed at the inquiry than I'd had time to do in the past few days.

He met me at the head of the ladder they'd thrown over for me, and I was astonished at the change in the man. His face was almost haggard and there was a nervous twitch at the corner of his mouth. The small eyes seemed to have sunk farther into his head. He took me straight to his cabin without a word and poured me a drink with hands that shook. 'Skaal!'

I didn't say anything, but raised my glass and drank.

'Well,' he said. 'Don't you want to know why I asked to see you?'

'It would help,' I said. 'You're supposed to be picking up our catch and we're supposed to be searching for more whale.'

He toyed with his glass, running the yellow liquid

round the inside and watching it as though it were crystal. Suddenly he leaned forward, staring at me. 'You think I killed Nordahl, don't you?' And when I didn't say anything, he repeated – 'Don't you?' His voice was savage.

'I've no views on the matter,' I said. 'I took evidence at a committee of inquiry. The rest is for the police to decide.'

'What if there was a row?' he cried. 'What if it did come to blows and he fell overboard. That doesn't make me a murderer, does it?'

I didn't know what to say. The man seemed to me on the very edge of sanity and I wished I hadn't come on board. 'A court will have to decide that.'

He peered at me, measuring my mood, his hands clenching and unclenching. 'There's Judie,' he said quietly.

'What's Judie got to do with it?'

'She's Nordahl's daughter – and she's my wife.' He hesitated, and then said suddenly, 'You're in love with her, aren't you?'

I stared at him in shocked surprise. The unexpectedness of the question put everything else out of my mind. Put bluntly like that I realized that it was a question I'd been asking myself.

He sat back, suddenly relaxing. His face had a cunning look. 'You wouldn't want her dragged through an ordeal like that – her husband accused of murdering her father. Picture it in the English newspapers – the Sunday ones. And I'll swear that she was your mistress here on board *Tauer III*.'

I went for him then, I was so angry. But he caught my arm and flung me back into a chair. He was a big man and pretty powerful. 'Oh no,' he said. 'Oh no you don't. This isn't a matter to fight over. You just sit there and listen to me. I'm in a jam and I'm not having a rope put round my neck by you or anyone else, do you understand? Now listen. Only four people know the whole of the evidence taken by the committee of inquiry over which you presided. My father holds that evidence. He'll die soon, anyway. But I can handle him and I can handle Eide. Judie can't give evidence against me. She's my wife. There remains you.'

'There's also Howe,' I reminded him. After all, that cable must have shown him Howe's part in the business.

'Ah, yes. The illegitimate doctor.' The sneer in his voice made it clear that he didn't take Howe very seriously. 'I can look after him too. If you were to keep your mouth shut, then the whole thing could be hushed up. Will you do that?'

'The answer is No,' I said.

He nodded as though he'd expected that. 'All right then. I'll make a bargain with you. Keep your mouth shut and I'll let Judie divorce me.'

'You must be mad to think I'd do such a thing,' I answered hotly.

He shrugged his shoulders. 'Then I'd remind you again that Judie is my wife. If you go through with this I'll make her life hell. Whether I'm convicted or not, I'll see she curses the day she was born. I'll show her up as a common tart. I'll represent that the row with Nordahl was about her. Oh, you needn't worry. That sort of dirt sticks, and there's always enough evidence if used the right way to sway the minds of a jury. And when I'm acquitted, I'll still be her husband. And I'll see she lives with me. She'll get no grounds for divorce and if she tries to divorce me I'll oppose it and cite you for one as co-respondent.'

'You must be mad,' I said. I got to my feet. I didn't want to stay there another minute.

But he jumped between me and the door and said, 'Well, which is it? Do you keep your mouth shut or – ' He left the sentence unfinished. 'Look, Craig,' he said. 'You've no alternative. Nordahl's dead. Trying to hang me for what was no more than an accident won't bring him back to life again. You've a choice between Judie and revenge for something that happened to a man you didn't even know. Come on now. Be reasonable.' His manner was suddenly boyish as though he were asking me to keep quiet about some indiscreet prank.

I said, 'If you don't mind, I'll go to my ship now. You're lucky that you're a more powerful man than I am, or I'd thrash you within an inch of your life.'

He stood aside and his smile was almost friendly, as though I'd paid him a social call. 'All right,' he said. 'But think it over. And don't forget. I can break Judie mentally so that in two years you won't even recognize her.'

I stopped then. A wave of uncontrollable anger engulfed me. But there was nothing I could do. 'Watch out somebody doesn't kill you before we get back to

Capetown,' I said. And then I went quickly past him through the door. If I'd had a gun on me I swear I'd have shot him.

Outside on the deck the air was cold, the sea slate-grey and a mile away a flag stood out of the water marking a dead whale. The scene was just as it had been when I'd come on board. I could hardly believe the conversation in that cabin had really taken place. It seemed so horribly unreal. Yet when I glanced back there was Erik Bland watching me with that vicious little smile on his lips.

I climbed down into the boat and was rowed in silence back to my ship. Howe was there on the deck, waiting for me. 'Well, what did he say?' he asked. But I brushed by him and went straight to my cabin. There I paced up and down, my mind a bewildering turmoil of half-formed ideas. On only one thing was I really clear. It was there in my mind like a flash of light. Bland was right. I was in love with Judie. And in no circumstances could I let her go through the hell he'd planned for her.

At length there was a tap on the door and Gerda came in. 'We have sighted another whale,' she said. 'I think you should be on the bridge.' No questions. No desire to peer into my mind. Just – *I think you should be on the bridge.* I could have hugged her for that. It was something practical for my mind to grasp and cling to.

But with Howe it was different. When I came down that night to get some sleep, he was sitting at the desk, his papers spread out in front of him, waiting for me. I was tired out. All I wanted was to lie down on my bunk and sleep. But I'd hardly got my boots off when he said, 'Craig. Suppose you tell me what Erik Bland said to you.' His voice was tense.

'It's none of your business,' I told him and rolled over on to the bunk.

'Anything to do with Bernt Nordahl is my business,' he answered in a flat, obstinate voice. 'What did he say about Nordahl's disappearance?' He was leaning slightly forward now. 'That's what he wanted to talk to you about, wasn't it?'

'For God's sake,' I said wearily, 'get on with your damned book, can't you – or go to bed. I'm tired.'

'I'm going to sit here and ask you questions until I find out what happened,' he answered obstinately.

'The conversation was private. It was between Bland and myself.' I closed my eyes.

'But it was about Nordahl's disappearance, wasn't it?' He hesitated and then said, 'You know I've a right to know. You'll probably be surprised at this. But I'm related to Bernt Nordahl.'

'Yes, I know,' I answered. 'But my conversation – '

'You know?' he interrupted on a note of sudden anger. 'How do you know? Who told you?'

'Colonel Bland.'

'He would.' He sounded bitter. He was silent for a moment. Then he got up and began rummaging in one of his bags. 'And knowing I'm his son, you still won't tell me what Bland said?'

'No,' I answered. I was thinking that if I told him what Bland said, I would no longer be a free agent. I'd no longer be able to make a bargain with Bland if

I wanted to. And my mind stopped with a jolt on that thought. I realized suddenly that I was in fact seriously considering the proposition he'd made. My sense of justice wouldn't accept that. And yet there was Judie. I was no longer tired now. I was wide awake, my mind facing up to the problem, thinking of Judie and what the future would be for her if Bland was brought to trial.

'Perhaps this may help you to decide.' I looked up to find Howe standing over me. He had a gun in his hand. I sat up quickly and he laughed. 'It's all right, Craig. I'm not threatening you.' He sat down, turning the gleaming nickel of the pistol over and over in his hand. 'Life doesn't mean very much to me,' he said quietly, and the sudden steadiness of his voice compelled attention. 'I've nothing much to lose, you see. And this – ' he held up the pistol – 'this could be a way out. I know why Erik Bland wanted to see you. It's just as I said. They think they can hush the whole thing up provided they square you. What did he do – threaten you through Judie?'

'How did you guess?' I asked in surprise.

'Because I know the sort of bastard Erik Bland is.' The word *bastard* had a violence on his lips that I'd never noticed in it before. 'I suppose he offered to trade Judie for your silence?'

I didn't answer.

He laughed suddenly. 'If he knew the whole story nothing would induce him to part with Judie.'

'How do you mean?' I asked.

'Because Judie is the South Antarctic Whaling

Company. She controls it now – not Bland. My job in
Capetown wasn't only to sell Nordahl's South African
holdings on a certain day. With the profits I was to
buy out three of the larger shareholders in the South
Antarctic Company. Before we left Capetown, Nordahl held 57 per cent of the shares in the company.
They don't know that – yet.' And he chuckled quietly
to himself. Then suddenly he was silent, his eyes
searching my face. 'You like Judie, don't you?'

He didn't put it as bluntly as Bland had done, but
I knew what he meant. I think I hesitated. But I'd no
longer any doubts on the matter. 'Yes,' I said. 'I'm very
fond of her.'

I stared at him then, trying to read his mind. He
nodded slowly as though it confirmed something that
he was already satisfied about. 'If Erik Bland were
dead, would you marry her?'

'The situation doesn't arise,' I said, and my voice
sounded harsh.

'It could arise,' he said, tapping the gun against the
palm of his hand. 'Well. Would you?'

'I can't answer that,' I said.

'But you'd want to?'

'Yes,' I said.

He nodded. 'And that was the threat Bland held
over you, wasn't it?' His head had jerked forward and
he was gazing at me intently. 'Judie's happiness against
your silence?'

I didn't answer and he suddenly got up. 'All right,'
he said. 'I just wanted to know what the situation was.
Thank God I persuaded her to go across to *Hval 5*.'

He stood then, looking down at me for a moment, then he turned away, slipping the gun into his pocket. 'Bernt Nordahl's interest in life was the South Antarctic Whaling Company.' He walked slowly across to the door. 'He'd have liked you, Craig. Good night.' And he was gone, closing the door behind him.

I lit a cigarette and lay there in the half light that filtered in through the porthole, trying to understand the mind of the man. He wasn't mad. Of that I was certain. There was a cold, relentless sanity about him. And he wasn't entirely sane either.

In the next few days he worked steadily at his book. He no longer brooded. He worked all day and far into the night as though he had not too much time in which to complete it. And he was more natural, more cheerful than I'd seen him at any time since I'd known him. Occasionally he'd come up on to the bridge for a breath of air and stand there, cracking jokes with Gerda and watching everything with the excited interest of a small boy. Gerda reacted strangely, like a mother given an ugly duckling to rear. In a rough, good-natured way she fussed over him. I even found her mending a tear in one of his shirts on the day we had to put back to the factory ship to refuel. I made some crack about it being unusual for the mate of a catcher to take up darning in her spare time and she flew into a temper and told me to mind my own business. It was the only time I ever saw her put out. Afterwards she was sweetness itself to me, but I didn't make the same mistake again when I saw her mending a pair of socks that I knew weren't her own.

It was on the 6th February that we refuelled. Whale had suddenly become scarce. The catchers were out in a wide sweep, some of them as much as 200 miles away from the *Southern Cross*. *Hval 5* had just reported a *pod* 150 miles to the north-east and we were directed to steam in that direction. Early on the 7th we got two about 100 miles away from the factory ship and radioed for a towing ship. *Tauer III* answered our call. The clouds had come down very low. They were dirty, ragged wisps driving before a rising sou'wester. The glass was rapidly falling and visibility was reduced to little more than a mile.

Throughout the rest of the day we steamed slowly north-eastwards, searching. But a cold, stinging rain was driving across the ship, and this, combined with the spray driven from the breaking wavetops made it impossible for us to see the spout of a whale even if there were any about. The cry of *Isen* came more and more often from the wretched lookout, perched in the *tonne* at the bucking masthead. Sometimes it was an iceberg. More often it was a floe half hidden in the breaking waves. Gerda ordered a lookout in the bows as well and her foresight was justified when we narrowly missed a 'growler' – a large platform of ice almost submerged. 'I think we must find shelter,' she shouted to me. 'It is very bad.'

I nodded. The movement of the ship was becoming more and more violent as the wind rose to gale force. I realized the necessity of having a lookout in the bows. But I was getting concerned for the man's safety. He had lashed himself to the end of the catwalk, but the bows were buried at times so deep in the waves that he seemed to be up to his waist in water. I felt the catwalk itself might be torn out of the ship.

'*Isen.*' There it came again, that frightening cry from the *tonne*. We peered through the murk of a rain squall waiting. And then suddenly it emerged out of the storm wrack – a great wall of ice with breakers flinging water into the driven clouds. The helmsman swung the wheel before my order had even reached him. The catcher turned and we ran parallel to the ice wall, where it stood out of the raging sea on the edge of visibility. 'I think we find shelter here,' Gerda shrieked to me.

The berg was a huge one. We must have gone nearly two miles before we turned the edge of it. But it was quite narrow and in a few minutes we had turned north-westward and were cruising along in comparatively calm water. I ordered stop, and the sudden cessation of the engine was noticeable only in the absence of vibration. We drifted quietly, the wall of ice just visible to port, the little ship lifting and dropping away again as the long swell of the gale rolled under her. It was queer, there in the lee of the iceberg – an unnatural calm in the midst of chaos. There was hardly any wind, yet we could hear the gale screaming over our heads and in the intervals between rain squalls we saw the ragged clouds driving pell-mell towards the north-east. And over and above the howling fury of the wind we could hear a deep rumble like a heavy artillery barrage – giant waves battering at the farther side of the iceberg. 'I hope she do not capsize,' Gerda said to me. 'It has been known in a gale. If she is top heavy and the wind get hold of her – ' She didn't finish, but I could imagine the roaring tidal wave of water that would be set up by that huge mass, as large as Lundy Island, rolling over in the sea.

It was in these conditions, an hour later, that we received the SOS. I climbed out of deep sleep like a drowning man coming to the surface to find Gerda shaking me violently.

'You must get up please, Duncan. There is an SOS. One of the catchers is in difficulties.' Her face looked white and strained. 'I think we are the nearest ship.'

I swung myself off the bunk. 'What catcher is it?' I asked.

'*Hval 5.*'

'My God!' I said and pulled on my boots. 'Have they given their position?'

'*Ja.*'

'Get the chart then. Bring it to the wireless room. I'll be there. What's happened to her?' I asked.

'Damaged her rudder – possibly her propeller,' she answered as she hurried out.

I put on my oilskins and slid down the ladder to the afterdeck. I was thinking of Judie. A catcher with rudder and screw damaged would be at the mercy of the storm. When I reached the second mate's cabin, I found Raadal huddled over the radio. 'The operator on the *Southern Cross* tell all vessels east and north of the factory ship they must stand by their radios,' he said in his thick English. 'It is Gerda who hear the SOS. She is on watch and she listen as always at the hour.' I glanced at the clock above his bunk. It was five past one.

The door flung back and Gerda came in. Howe was close behind her. 'I have work him out,' she said, spreading the chart across Raadal's bunk. 'This is their position – 66.25 S., 33.48 W. And we are about here. We are not more than forty miles distant.'

'Have you given the *Southern Cross* our position?'

'*Ja*. They have the positions of all the ships in this area.'

I turned to the door, my mind suddenly made up. 'Raadal. When the *Southern Cross* comes on the air again, tell them that we are going to the assistance of *Hval 5*.'

He nodded. '*Ja, hr Kaptein*.' I was half out of the door when he called me back. The radio was crackling and a voice was saying – '*Ullo-ullo-ullo, Syd Korset. Hval Fem anroper Syd Korset*.'

I saw Howe stiffen and lean forward. Gerda, too, was straining forward, a set expression on her face.

'What is it?' I asked. 'What's happened?'

Howe silenced me with an impatient movement of his hand. A spate of Norwegian was pouring out of the radio. All of them – Raadal, too – were listening intently. Finally came three quick whistles and the radio went dead as the speaker signed off.

'What was he saying?' I demanded.

But no one seemed to hear me. Howe was staring at Gerda. She turned to Raadal. 'Send Kaptein Craig's message, Hans,' she ordered. 'We must go there immediately.'

I caught hold of her shoulder and spun her round. 'Do you mind telling me what's happened?' I demanded.

'They have been driven on to some ice. Kaptein Larvik is injured. They are afraid the ship will not last long.'

I seized the chart from the bunk. 'You stay by the radio, Raadal.' I slammed out of the cabin, leaving Gerda and Howe staring at each other, and ran on to the bridge. 'Half ahead,' I ordered the helmsman. 'Steer north-east.' I dived down the ladder to my cabin and worked out the course. Back on the bridge again I ordered N.55 E. and sent a lookout to the bow. Gerda joined me then. She still seemed dazed. She said something, but it was lost in the wind. We were moving out of the shelter of the iceberg now and sheets of stinging spray were lashing across the bridge as we ran before the full force of the gale.

Death seemed suddenly very close to us. As I stared out into the rain-driven murk, all I saw was Judie's face and *Hval 5* being hammered against a wall of ice. And I shouted ugly words into the wind because I didn't dare order more than half speed.

SIX

'*Isen! Isen!*' The cry was from the masthead. The lookout at the end of the catwalk signalled to starboard. The helmsman swung the wheel. The flat surface of a floe slid by, glimmering grey in the half light. Then the messboy came hurrying along the after-deck, clinging like a monkey to the life-line that had been rigged. He reported that *Hval 5* was still afloat but in danger of being trapped between two icefloes.

Shortly afterwards Howe came up. 'They're all right so far,' he shouted to me. 'I've been talking to Dahle, the first mate. He says they've been holed by the ice, but he thinks the pumps can handle it for a time at any rate. Eide has just been on the radio. He confirms your decision to go to *Hval 5*. We're the nearest boat. *Tauer III* has been ordered to stand by at her present position. But she hasn't acknowledged the order.'

'Do you think they're in trouble, too?' I asked.

He shrugged his shoulders.

'*Isen! Isen!*' Another change of course. Another floe. Gerda tugged at Howe's sleeve. 'Walter! Do you think we shall reach them in time?' She screamed the question at him, yet her voice barely reached me.

'Yes,' he shouted back. But I wasn't so sure. It depended on how much ice lay between them and us. I was feeling pretty scared. I'd never taken a ship into ice before. I cursed Bland for putting me in command on a catcher and in the same breath thanked God that I'd be the one to reach Judie first.

'*Isen! Isen!*' I reduced speed to slow ahead. The ice was all round us now. A sudden jar ran through the ship and there were a number of sharp, staccato cracks and then the grinding of ice along the sides. I stopped the engine, peering into the glimmer of white ahead. Then a squall came. It was sleet this time, not rain, and it blotted out everything. We lay there, drifting slowly forward, ice all round us. The sea was much less now. As though she read my thoughts Gerda said, 'There is much ice, I think. It is holding down the sea.'

Half an hour went by whilst we lay there, waiting for the sleet to pass. The water froze on our oilskins. It was bitterly cold and every now and then there was the horrible grating sound of ice against the steel sides of the catcher. But the weight of the wind was lessening. The sleet no longer drove horizonal with stinging violence. And with the passing of the sleet, an immense silence seemed to brood over us, as though we had drifted into a vacuum. 'It is getting lighter,' Gerda said, and her voice, raised against the wind that was no longer there, seemed unnaturally loud.

Visibility was increasing and we could see that we'd fallen foul of a small huddle of icefloes. We watched the black rearguard of the rain sweep north-eastward and as it went it showed us more and more ice. Behind us the low clouds were dark and louring as though heralding another storm. But ahead they were a dazzling white, their torn bellies mirroring the ice below, picking it up in a blinding light. I backed the catcher carefully out of the icefloes and headed her at half speed into the ice blink. A little group of Emperor penguins huddled on a floe watched us go, bowing sedately as though to hide the joy they felt at our departure in diplomatic etiquette.

The ice blink was criss-crossed by dark lines and we scanned it, reading it like a map, searching for the most suitable lead. As we approached the loose pack the ice blink mapped for us a narrow lead like a long tendril that ended at the broad line of a much wider lead running north-east, and we headed for this. The ice closed round us, a flat, broken plain of dazzling white that heaved to the swell like ground moving under the impact of an earthquake. In the distance a large berg towered like a small mountain. Another, smaller one, showed against the dark background of the clouds behind us. It looked like a sailing ship, hull down and driving under every stitch of canvas.

I didn't dare move from the bridge now. Gerda or Howe were constantly in Raadal's cabin and they kept me informed of all radio messages. *Hval 5* reported the propeller shaft cracked and rudder almost ripped from its seating. They were attempting to clear it and rig a jury rudder. With the passing of the storm they were no longer in imminent danger of being crushed. They reported a wide lead running sou'west and passing within half a mile of their position.

'I hope to God that's the lead we're making for,' I said to Howe, who had brought me this piece of information. The lead we were following was narrowing rapidly now. Another mile and it had petered out into a litter of small floes. I took the wheel myself and at slow ahead twisted and turned through the narrow channels. From the bridge we could no longer see the lead we were making for. I had to work on the instructions of the masthead lookout.

The channels were becoming narrower and narrower. Sometimes I had to stop the engine altogether, the ship's sides practically scraping the ice. Fortunately the edges of the floes were fairly smooth. The comparative warmth of the sea at that time of the year had smoothed off the sides except where they had been broken up in the storm. At times I had barely steerage way on the ship.

Soon we could see the broad lead from the bridge. But between us and it the pack seemed to huddle closer in a protective bank. I turned the edge of a floe into a narrow gap and jerked at the engine-room telegraph. I had turned into a cul-de-sac. The gap just petered out. And there, not two hundred yards ahead of us, was the dark water of the lead. As we drifted towards the flat sheet of ice that barred our progress, I went to the side of the bridge and leaned out, gazing aft along the length of the ship. The gap we had come up had almost closed behind us, the floes on either side having been sucked together by the movement of the ship. There was no question of going astern. We should have damaged our rudder, possibly sheered the blades off our propeller.

'Ram it,' Howe said. 'It's not thick. Only, for God's sake, shut your engine off before you hit, otherwise you'll damage it.'

I nodded. 'Send word round the ship – everyone to lie flat on the deck. Don't forget the engine-room.'

He clattered down the ladder and I stood there, waiting, my hands on the wheel, the engine-room telegraph at my elbow. I stared at the ice that barred our path, trying to gauge its thickness. It couldn't be more than a foot or two. The edge of it was scarcely above water. I wondered how strongly built the catcher's bows were. The sides, I knew, were like tin when it came to meeting ice, but surely they'd have given the bows some strength. Anyway, there was no alternative. *Hval 5* was holed. I didn't dare wait in the hopes that a gap would be opened out by the swell. It might just as easily start grinding the ice up against us. Also the glass was still very low, and I didn't want to be caught here in a resumption of the gale. It was a risk, but it had to be taken. I sent one of the crew to close the for'ard bulkheads and then, with a lookout aft, I rang for slow astern and backed down the cut until we reached the limit of clear water.

Howe came to the bridge and reported that everyone had been warned. I waited until the man I'd sent to close the bulkheads had returned to the bridge, then I stretched out my hand to the engine-room telegraph and rang for emergency full ahead. The ship shuddered as the screw lashed the water. Above the hum of the engine I heard the froth of the sea under our stern. I braced myself against the wheel. The catcher gathered speed. The heaving ice raced past, sometimes grazing our plates.

We had nearly a quarter of a mile of clear water and as my hand reached for the handle of the telegraph we must have been doing six or seven knots. The unbroken sheet of ice seemed to hurl itself towards us. I braced myself against the wheel and slammed the telegraph handle down. There was a sudden deathly silence as the sound of the engine dropped and the bridge became dead under my feet. There was an awful period of waiting – waiting in complete silence save

for the soft hum of engines running free and the sound
of water thrust back from our bows.

Then there was a crash. The ship seemed to stop
dead. I was flung against the wheel, all the breath
knocked out of me. The bridge swayed forward. A
sound like rifle fire crackled ahead of us and then was
lost in the grinding crunch of ice on steel. The whole
ship was staggering and the noise of the ice attacking
the steel plates was overwhelming.

Then we were driving slowly forward and a great
crack was opening up in front of us.

I rang for slow ahead and, with the ice still grinding
against our sides, we thrust like a wedge into the gap,
the swell that was running helping us to break through.
In a matter of moments it seemed we had thrust right
through the thin barrier of ice and were in the open
water of the lead.

I gave two whoops on the siren to tell the crew we
were through. Then Gerda came running along the
deck and up the ladder to the bridge. 'We're through,'
I told her.

'I know,' she said. 'Well done.'

'*Isen! Isen!*' Another half-submerged floe. I sent
Gerda to sound the well and make certain that we had
suffered no damage in ramming our way through the
ice.

Howe came and stood at my side. We stared sil-
ently into the frozen waste of black and white that lay
ahead.

'I wonder what Bland's up to?' he said suddenly.

'How do you mean?' I asked.

'*Tauer III* never acknowledged that order to stand by.'

'Perhaps she didn't get it,' I suggested. 'Maybe their radio's out of action.'

'Perhaps.' He was silent for a moment, and then he said, 'Craig. You realize you and I are the only people that have the evidence to convict him?'

'What are you getting at?' I demanded.

'I don't know. That's the hell of it – I don't know. But I've got a feeling. Here we are going into the pack and there's not another boat within a hundred miles except *Tauer III*.'

'You're crazy,' I said. Actually I thought he was getting scared. It was pretty frightening standing on the bridge there, driving into that world of ice. It gave one a horrible sense of loneliness.

'I don't think I'm crazy,' he said slowly. 'If Bland could get you and me out of the way at one blow he'd be safe.'

'What about Judie, Eide, Larvik, and there are probably others?'

'He doesn't think they're important, otherwise he wouldn't have tried to make a bargain with you.' He began stamping his feet. 'He can handle Eide. No man's going to risk a new command by trying to incriminate the chairman's son the first season he's out with the company. Judie can't give evidence anyway.'

'And Larvik?' I asked. 'He knows something. I'm certain.'

'Larvik knows nothing – nothing definite,' he

replied. 'I had a talk with him after you'd had him up for cross-examination.'

'Then how could he give such an accurate description of Bland's last meeting with Nordahl?' I asked. 'Bland himself confirmed it. It was correct in every detail, even to the cigar. He couldn't have made it up and got it so accurate.'

'He didn't make it up.' He stopped stamping his feet and turned to me. 'Apart from Erik Bland, Larvik was the last person to see Nordahl alive. He was with him up on the deck. He left him just after twelve. They decided the fog was going to lift and Larvik went to arrange for a boat to take him back to *Hval 5*. The fog lifted a quarter of an hour later.'

'Then why didn't he tell us he was one of the last people to see Nordahl alive?'

'Because he knew his evidence would be regarded as prejudiced,' Howe answered. 'He didn't see it happen. He only guessed at what happened. But he knew where Nordahl was at the time he disappeared. If you'd told Bland the information had come from Larvik you'd never have got him to admit he'd had a row with Nordahl up there by the boats. Peer Larvik never made any secret of the fact that he loathed Bland's guts.'

'I see.'

'Anyway,' Howe added, 'Judie and Larvik are on *Hval 5*. If we don't reach them for some reason, then Bland would be ordered to try. And if he said conditions were impossible. they might never be rescued.'

'What the devil are you suggesting then?' I demanded.

Howe slammed his fist against the windbreaker and a shower of ice tinkled on to the winches below. 'I'm not suggesting anything,' he said. 'I'm just wondering. Bland would never get an opportunity as good as this. That's all I know.' His voice was agitated and I felt as though he were wound up like a clock. 'Something's driving him. Something that's bigger than himself, bigger than life. And Judie, the little fool, hasn't made a will.'

He caught hold of my arm then. 'I know a good deal about psychology. It doesn't help me solve my own problems. But I can understand other people's. Erik Bland was brought up by his mother. He's always had money. Anything he wanted, it was there. He'd only got to ask for it – boats, parties, cars, girl-friends. But power – you can't buy that, can you? All his life he's been dwarfed by his father. I think that's what's driving him – a sense of impotence – an inferiority complex if you like. He's no real sense of values or morals. He's never given a thought for anyone but himself. That's what makes him dangerous. His sense of frustration is like a load of dynamite inside him.' Then, as though he'd revealed too much of himself, he added quickly, 'I'm just guessing. Forget it.' He turned towards the bridge ladder and then paused. 'Only for God's sake, make all the speed you can.' With that he left me and went below.

I thought of *Tauer III* somewhere astern of us. Suppose Howe were right? It was fantastic. But though

I tried to dismiss it, the idea kept coming back. If Erik Bland would commit a murder ... Well, a murderer doesn't always stop at one crime, and certainly Howe's diagnosis of the man's mental state seemed reasonable enough. It fitted his actions. But surely the man had shot his bolt. I remembered the scene in his cabin on board *Tauer III*. Fear had driven him then – fear of a rope round his neck. He'd been badly scared. Another squall enveloped us and the icy cascade of sleet washed all thought of Erik Bland out of my mind.

And with the squall came the wind. It seemed to materialize out of nowhere like a howling demon coming up out of the ice. This time it was from the north-east and it lashed the sleet in a stinging sheet against our faces. Visibility was cut in a moment to a few hundred yards. I didn't reduce speed. I just huddled my chin into my oilskins and kept on, peering into the watery murk, my face numb with the bite of wind and sleet.

We were in constant communication with *Hval 5* now. Gerda kept me in touch with the reports. Two miles south-west of the damaged ship there was a large iceberg with a flat top like Table Mountain except for a tall pinnacle of ice at its southern end. This was our mark.

We reached what I thought was the approximate position of *Hval 5* shortly after nine. That was on the morning of 8th February. Visibility was poor. There was no possibility of our sighting the ice mark and I hove to, waiting for the weather to clear. We were then in open water with no ice in sight. The wind was rising to gale force and there was a lumpy sea that caused us to pitch a lot. Above the howl of the wind we could hear the ugly sound of icefloes crashing against each other. Behind this was a deeper, more violent sound which Gerda told me was a pressure ridge building up amongst a solid area of pack.

That wait seemed endless. I had a horrible feeling of being trapped. I couldn't see it, but I knew there was ice all round us, and I felt as though it were closing in. We could hear it and in that twilight of driven sleet it grew like a barrier between us and safety. The only thing that gave me courage was the thought that Judie was somewhere quite close and that I was there to bring her out of the ice.

Then Gerda came up to say that we were no longer in radio contact with *Hval 5*. 'It was quite sudden – in the middle of a message.' Her face looked scared.

The loneliness of the Antarctic seemed to have moved a step nearer. 'What was the message?'

'He said, "The ice is very thick now. We are getting – " And that was all. I thought I heard someone shout. I am afraid – ' She didn't finish, but stared at me round-eyed.

'Get Raadal to call them,' I ordered.

'He is doing that.'

'Tell him to go on trying.'

She nodded and clattered quickly down the ladder.

Howe came up shortly afterwards. When I questioned him he shook his head. 'We keep calling, but there's no reply.' I listened to the grumbling of the ice out there beyond the grey curtain of the sleet, and the cold seemed to eat right into me.

'We must do something,' Howe shouted at me. 'Start the engine. We must find them.'

My hand reached for the telegraph. Anything rather than this enforced inactivity. But the rigid discipline of six years in the Navy stopped me. I shook my head. 'No good until visibility improves. We've the lives of our crew to consider.'

He opened his mouth to argue, then stopped and nodded. After that he paced up and down the bridge, with his awkward, crab-like shuffle, till every turn he made jarred on my nerves. And I just stood there, staring into the driving murk and praying for the sleet to lift.

Shortly after ten the weather began to show signs of improving. The sleet slackened and gradually visibility lengthened out and the atmosphere became full of light. Gerda came out on to the after-deck and sniffed at the wind. Then she hurried to the bridge. 'It is better, *ja*?' Her voice sounded thick and guttural.

I nodded, peering into the light that was beginning to hurt my eyes. 'Any news?' I asked.

'Nothing. They do not answer.'

A moment later the sleet lifted like a curtain and we could see the dark water of the lead with the ice all round it. It was like a black waterway in a dead, white plain. And as the rain rolled south-westward, a mercurial flash of sunlight showed an iceberg on our port quarter, flat like Table Mountain, with the pinnacle at its southern end like a spearhead.

I ordered half ahead and starboard helm. As the catcher swung round, the flash of sunlight vanished and the world was grey and cold, a frozen etching across which torn wisps of cloud scurried before the wind. 'There is more sleet to come – maybe snow,' Gerda said, gazing at the sky to windward, where the clouds were gradually darkening again.

I nodded. Every moment was important now. The break might last only a few minutes. I searched the area just north-east of the berg with my glasses. The ice looked a solid mass, torn like ground after an earthquake where the floes had been layered by the pressure ridge that had been built up against the massive bulk of the iceberg. Then suddenly I saw it. A black patch in the torn surface of the ice. Through the glasses it resolved itself into the upper works of a catcher. The masts and funnel slanted so sharply that it looked as though it were lying on its side. I gave several blasts on the siren. Then I called the lookout down and climbed to his place in the *tonne*.

From the masthead I could see it quite plainly. It was not more than a mile away and appeared to be in the grip of two floes which were layering under the pressure of the ice thrusting against the berg. I could see tiny figures moving about on the ice, and as far as I could tell, with the mast swaying and dipping, they were unloading stores on to the ice. I swept the area between the broad lead we were in and the ship. The shortest distance was about half a mile. Several leads thrust out towards the stricken ship like crooked lines drawn in charcoal. The sudden tingle of sleet on my face made me look at the sky. The weather was closing in again from the north-east. The clouds were black and heavy. The wind seemed to be driving the clouds on to the ice.

I turned my attention back to *Hval 5* and the lines of open water between the floes, trying to memorize them. The crew were up on deck, leaning over the rail, talking excitedly. I clambered down on to the bridge and took a bearing. I had barely finished before the sleet closed in on us.

Howe clutched my arm. 'Isn't that a ship coming up the lead towards us?' He was pointing away from *Hval 5*, straight over our bows. But even as I followed the line of his finger the atmosphere seemed to thicken and congeal into a solid wall of grey that blotted out sight.

'I didn't see anything,' I said. 'It couldn't have been.'

He hesitated as though about to argue. Then he shrugged his shoulders. 'I could have sworn I saw the outline of a ship steaming towards us.'

'The light plays tricks,' I said.

He nodded. 'Yes. I suppose that's it. I was thinking about *Hval 5*.'

I took over the wheel now and at slow ahead we felt our way down the northern edge of the lead until I saw what I thought was the opening we wanted. Cautiously I turned into the gap and we began to thrust our way between the floes on a general course of N. 55° W. Ahead of us we could hear the gunfire sounds of the pressure ridge building up towards the iceberg. Every 30 seconds I gave three blasts on the siren, hoping that *Hval 5* would still have steam up and be able to reply.

For perhaps ten minutes we forced our way deeper and deeper into the loose litter of icefloes, sounding our siren. We strained our ears, listening for the answering call. But there was no sound except the wind's howl in the rigging and the sizzle of the sleet as it lashed the decks. Beyond these sounds we could hear the sharp thunder-cracks of splitting ice. The floes gradually thickened, packing tighter until at last we could go no farther. I stopped the engine and we lay there heaving to the storm waves which were blanketed by miles of ice into a long, heavy swell. All we could do was keep sounding the siren and continue to listen. But there wasn't even an echo. Its moan went off in a wisp of steam at the funnel top and was instantly whipped away by the wind and lost in the grey void that surrounded us. It was like being buried alive. I thought of the *Flying Dutchman* and all the other mysteries of the sea. It was so easy to imagine ourselves lost for ever as we lay there in that waste of ice and storm with the floes grinding against our sides.

And it was at this moment that Howe gripped my arm and shouted, pointing over the port quarter. A vague shape drifted on the edge of visibility. I lost it and rubbed my eyes, thinking I must have imagined it. But a moment later it was there again. A ship! I could see the faint outline of funnel as well as bows. It was like a ghost ship – faint and indistinct, one moment visible, and the next, lost behind that curtain of sleet.

'Is it *Hval 5*?' Howe shouted to me.

I shook my head. I had lost it again. But I knew it wasn't *Hval 5*. It was bigger than a catcher and it was headed into the ice just as we were. It reminded me of a warship. Could a vessel have been lost down here in the ice during the war? But I could have sworn I'd seen smoke coming from its stack. I pulled myself together and ordered slow astern. There was a lead of clear water running towards the spot where we'd seen the ship and I decided to investigate.

I continued sounding our siren and with lookouts fore and aft began to manoeuvre into the lead. But I'd barely ordered slow ahead when there was a sudden shout from the lookout in the bows and Gerda screamed for full ahead. The telegraph jangled as the curtain of the mist to port seemed thrust aside by the knife-edged bows of a ship bearing straight down on us.

There was no time to do anything and yet the moment of waiting seemed like eternity. I seized the cord of the siren and kept it at full blast. But the ship that bore down on us seemed to gather speed. I could hear the hum of her engine and see the water creaming up in a cold green wave at her bow. Howe shouted something and jumped for the catwalk. It was only as he ran for the harpoon gun that I realized what he'd said; just one word – *Bland*. And immediately I recognized those warship lines, that sharp, deadly-looking bow. It was a corvette. And now I could see the name white against her black paint, *Tauer III*.

I awoke then to full realization of what was going to happen. 'All hands on deck,' I shouted. I rang for the engine to be stopped and seized hold of the engine-room communication pipe and ordered McPhee to get his men up as fast as he could. As I dropped the tube I saw Howe down on the gun platform, swinging the harpoon gun towards the oncoming ship.

One man stood alone on the corvette's bridge. Against the grey back-cloth of cloud he stood out clear like an etching. His oilskins were a dark gleam in the hissing sleet, his black Norwegian sou'wester framed his white face. His hands were braced on the wheel, his whole body hunched over it like a rider driving his horse at a jump. It was Erik Bland.

Then everything seemed to happen at once. There was the violent crack of an explosion from our bows as Howe fired. The harpoon rose in a wide arc, passing over Bland's shoulder and crashing down behind the bridge, the thin forerunner snaking after it. And in the same instant a man flung himself on to the bridge, swept Bland aside and swung the wheel over. The bows began to turn. The ship heeled. The engine-room telegraph clanged, loud and clear above the wind. But it was too late.

I can see it now as vividly as when it happened. It's like a strip of film running through my mind. Yet it all happened in a second or so. The bows were no longer driving straight at me. They were swinging away towards our stern. But they were right on top of us now. And as they drove through the last few yards of the gap, they seemed to grow bigger and sharper. I remember a patch of flaking paint just below the hawser-hole and a streak of rust that had almost obliterated the letter E of the name. I remember the way our bulwarks buckled in like tin sheet under the impact – the shriek of tortured metal.

She struck us just aft of the engine-room, smashing the port boat and ploughing up the deck plates. Men were coming out on to our after-deck as the bows broke into our thin sides. There was the heavy shock of impact and an awful grinding, tearing sound as metal was ripped and torn open. Men fell sprawling on the deck. And in the same instant I was flung sideways and fetched up against the wooden side of the bridge with a jolt that drove all the breath out of me. The grinding and ripping of the metal seemed to go on unendingly.

Then suddenly all was still. Nothing seemed to move. The wind howled and beyond its howl was the rumbling gunfire of the ice. I gulped air and caught my breath at the pain in my side. Slowly the scene round me came to life. Gerda picked herself up from the corner of the bridge where she'd been flung. Men were staggering to their feet on the after-deck. The bows of the corvette stood like a huge wedge in the twisted steel of the after-deck. Our funnel was bent over with the impact. A plume of steam was escaping from the engine-room.

Somebody moved on the bridge of *Tauer III*. It was the man who'd tried to take the wheel. Bland was cursing him, ordering him for'ard. His voice came to me on the wind as an angry scream. As the man left the bridge, Bland turned. His teeth were bared and he had a wild look about him. His hand reached out towards the engine-room telegraph. I yelled at him not to go astern. My wits were so dulled by the disaster that I don't think I'd really grasped that it had been intentional. I know he heard me yelling, for he raised his hand. It was a gesture of farewell. And then the engine-room telegraph rang.

I understood then and I gripped the canvas of the wind-breaker in a sort of dazed fascination. I'd never seen a man coolly murdering a ship's crew. I'd heard of U-boat commanders doing it during the war. But I'd never seen it happen.

The engine of the corvette began to hum. The black water at her stern was churned to an icy green and she began to back away from us. Our stern swung slowly with her. Then with a horrible tearing sound the bows wrenched free of us and she began to pull clear of the wreckage of our stern. Howe was screaming from the gun platform – screaming for them to stop. The forerunner of the harpoon lifted from the water in a slack loop, unwound slowly and as slowly tightened. And as it became taut there was a dull, muffled explosion from somewhere deep inside the corvette.

It's queer, but whilst I have that vivid mental picture of the actual ramming, I have only a confused recollection of what followed immediately after. I remember standing there for a second, watching the corvette draw away and stop, seeing Bland turn at the sound of the explosion, rage darkening his face, and hearing a confused medley of shouts and orders and the ugly roar of escaping steam from somewhere in the bowels of the ship. Then I was down from the bridge, running aft, shouting orders.

A quick examination of the damage made it clear we couldn't stay afloat for long. The after-bulkhead doors were damaged and water was pouring into the engine-room. The crew's quarters aft had borne the brunt of the collision. Raadal was dead – crushed beyond recognition. Another man had been pinned against the bunk by a jagged strip of metal. It had gone through his stomach. He was unconscious and there was nothing we could do for him. Two other men were injured – one with a broken arm, another with broken ribs. The radio had been completely wrecked. As for the gap in the little vessel's side, there was no question of patching it up. It was a great, ragged hole about eight feet wide and as many deep. It ran from deck to keel.

I sent McPhee down to the engine-room to see if he could get way on the ship and I ordered one of the men to the bridge with instructions that if the engine could be got going he was to steer the ship into the ice. Gerda I ordered to get the remaining boat swung out and to collect all the stores she could, in case we had to camp on the ice. Then I ran up to the bridge and hailed *Tauer III* through a megaphone. The ship was lying-to about twenty yards from us, her bows slightly crumpled and steam and smoke pouring out of her engine-room hatches. A man came running down to the bows. He looked scared. 'Can you come alongside and take us off?' I shouted to him.

But he shook his head. '*Nei, nei*. We have damage in the engine-room and fire.'

My stomach seemed suddenly empty. I looked back along the length of the catcher. Her stern was already badly down. 'You must take us off,' I shouted. 'We will help you fight the fire.'

The man hesitated uncertainly. He glanced behind him as though trying to decide whether his ship was in better case than ours. And as he did so a great tongue of flame leapt out from amidships. Almost instantly there was a heavy roar of steam and the whole ship was enveloped in a white cloud against which her battered bows stood out black and sharp. Then the white of the steam darkened, became black and turned to great billowing clouds of smoke. I knew what that meant. The oil was alight inside her. I turned to Howe, who was standing there beside me, staring with open mouth at the belching column of smoke. 'You bloody fool! You bloody, silly fool!' It wasn't any good cursing him. I knew that. His damned harpoon was fired now. But I went on cursing him. I went on cursing him because I was scared. *Tauer III* had been our one chance. I felt sure the men wouldn't have abandoned us even if that was what Bland had intended.

It was Gerda who pulled me out of my senseless mouthings. 'We must begin landing stores,' she called up. McPhee was standing beside her and the expression on his face told me that he'd failed to do anything with the engine. Fortunately the starboard boat was intact. 'Clear the boat and start loading,' I ordered.

I sent Gerda with the first boatload to choose a good stretch of ice. I remained on board, working to bring up the sort of stores we would need – food, clothing, canvas, petrol, oil, matches, instruments, charts, rifles and ammunition. My mind went back to that Greenland expedition, visualizing the things we'd needed then and on the basis of that trying to imagine our requirements now. Tobacco. I remembered that, and lighters. I could recall how short we had got of matches. The food stores I packed in wooden boxes. I got up every packing case we could lay our hands on. Wood was always useful. Two drums of oil. Blankets to make into sleeping-bags. Needles and thread. Cooking utensils. Nails. Tools. It was the little things that could so easily be overlooked. The after-deck was almost awash now. We hadn't much time. And once she went there would be no going back for anything that had been forgotten.

The boat returned, was loaded with stores and men, and was sent back to the ice, McPhee in charge. Gerda remained on board, her woman's mind quick to think of things I had forgotten: mending things, medical supplies, tins of fat, some personal stores of her father's including some brandy, leather ripped from chairs and seats, spare bootlaces. The boat came back again and this time we loaded the heavy stuff – frozen whale-meat, the two oil drums, coils of wire, steel

stanchions cut from the ship for tent supports, a roll
of canvas, packing cases filled with flour, axes, saws,
guns, a block and tackle with four 60-fathom lengths
of forerunner (my idea for hauling the boat if
necessary) and a whole pile of junk that had been flung
down by men acting on their own initiative as to what
would be necessary. We piled it all in and sent the boat
back.

It was a risk. There were still seven of us on the
ship and she was very low. But I was determined that
if we were forced to live on the ice then we should
have everything that was necessary. To occupy the men
I sent them to comb the ship – or what was left above
water – for anything else of use. Then I went over to
the port side and looked at *Tauer III*. I suppose in all
about half an hour had passed since I had last looked
at her. My whole effort had been concentrated in getting the stores together and ferrying them to the ice.
Now I was amazed at the sight that met my eyes. The
corvette was enveloped in a cloud of black smoke. Her
bows were still clear of it. But aft of the bridge she
was a roaring inferno with flames licking up to the
funnel height. A group of men were dragging stores
up on to a floe beyond the ship. They were just black
figures against the white of the ice that disappeared
into the grey curtain of the sleet. The boat was being
pulled back to the ship. I watched it come alongside.
More stores were being lowered. And then my eyes
went back to the corvette's bridge where something
had moved and I realized with a shock that Bland was
still standing there. I picked up my glasses, which were

lying on a pile of my own personal things, and focused them on him. He was no longer grinning. He seemed dazed, his face white and his lips moving as though he were muttering to himself.

And then Gerda tugged at my arm. 'I brought this down, Duncan,' she said. It was the radio from my cabin. 'It is a portable in case of emergencies. My father always say it is good to hear even if you cannot send.'

I cursed myself for having forgotten it and started to rack my brains in case there was anything else I had overlooked. 'I wonder if *Tauer III* managed to send a message?' I said.

She shrugged her shoulders. 'We shall know when we join up on the ice. I think they will have radioed the *Southern Cross*. You see their R/T is below the bridge and that is still clear of the fire.'

The catcher gave an ugly little wriggle then. I glanced quickly aft. We were very low now. The bows seemed higher. I dived for the rail. The boat was on its way back. 'Quick!' I shouted. The men bent to their oars. 'Just drop everything in,' I ordered the others. 'Then follow quickly. We haven't much time.'

The boat slid alongside. I felt another tremble run through the ship. I had a horrible feeling that the bows were rising higher and higher. The deck seemed to be slanting away to the stern like a water chute. And as the men tumbled over the side the water slid quietly over my ankles. The catcher was beginning to sink stern first. Gerda heaved herself over the rail. I dropped the radio into someone's lap and flung myself in after her. 'Row like the devil,' I shouted.

But they didn't need any urging. The oars bent under the thrust of the rowers. The heavily laden boat thrust away from the catcher. And as we pulled away *Hval 4* gave a violent shudder. Her tottering stack shook free of its mountings and fell with a crash. And as though that were the last straw, the little vessel slid quietly stern first into the sea, the sharp bows pointing higher and higher as she went and the harpoon gun swinging aimlessly. She disappeared with barely a ripple, mast tip and gun the last to go. And where she had been the icy water swirled in black whorls for a moment and then settled as though there had never been a vessel there.

It was the first time I'd lost a ship. I had no sense of personal loss. She hadn't been my ship in the way my corvette had been. But I felt an awful sense of emptiness, as though I had been suddenly disarmed in mortal combat. It took all the courage out of me. I glanced at Gerda and saw she was crying. Her brown eyes were staring almost unbelievingly at the spot where *Hval 4* had been and big tears rolled down her cheeks. For her it was different. The catcher had been her home. I leant forward to pat her hand. Then I saw that Howe was gripping her arm, staring into her face, his eyes looking hurt as though he felt the loss through her.

I looked about me, taking stock of my surroundings. From the deck of *Hval 4*, even though she had been sinking, I'd felt a sense of security as though the storm and the ice and the black, heaving sea were all slightly unreal – something apart. Now the ship had gone and from the slender free-board of an over-loaded boat the scene looked frighteningly real. I think in all that followed I never felt lower in spirits than at that moment. There was just the group of men huddled round the stores on the ice, another group farther away and the burning hulk of the corvette. And the icy sleet swept over everything – cold and wet and dismal. Behind it was the wind and beyond that still the staccato cracking of the ice.

The boat touched the ice, crunching into the thin edge of it, and we climbed out on to the floe. We were up to our ankles in a soft slush of half-melted ice. My first thought was for the stores, particularly the flour. Everything was just heaped there in the rotten ice with the sleet streaming off it. The floe was a big one, jammed in against other floes. It rocked gently to the swell that ran under it and its edges ground against the others. A little to the north of us one floe had layered on another so that the ice was higher and slightly sloping. I floundered through the slush towards it. Once I slipped and found myself up to my knees in water. For a moment I thought I was falling between two floes. But it was only a weak patch that had filled with a morass of half-melted ice. I reached the floe that had layered and climbed up on to it. The ice was hard here and clear of slush. I found a way back that avoided the hole I had stumbled into and ordered all the stores to be moved up to the new site. Tarpaulins were laid on the ice, and when all the stores were piled on to them, others were placed over the top. Then we set to work to construct tents and I ordered the steward to try and produce some sort of a stew.

There were fourteen of us on the ice and two of those were injured. As soon as there was any sort of shelter, Gerda and I went to work, first on Jacobsen's broken arm and then on Grieg's ribs. The arm we set in splints and we must have done a pretty fair job on it, for it mended fine. But though we didn't know it then, Grieg's ribs were not a simple fracture. Only an X-ray could have shown us the extent of the damage and it was to be a constant source of worry to us. It was whilst we were strapping him up that I became conscious again of the pain in my chest that I'd felt when I lay against the side of the bridge gasping for breath. Association of ideas, I suppose. Maybe I'd strained a muscle. Possibly I did have a slight fracture of one of the ribs. It went off in the end, but it gave me a lot of pain during the next few days, particularly when I was lifting anything.

We had just finished strapping Grieg up when McPhee called to me that a boat was coming alongside. We ducked out of the canvas shelter to find the sleet easing off and *Tauer III*'s boat running in towards our floe. Four men were rowing it and in the stern sat a big bearded man with a flattened nose and sharp, close set little eyes. 'Who's that?' I asked Gerda.

'It is Vaksdal,' she said. 'He is made first mate on *Tauer III*. He is a Sandefjord man. He is a good whaler, but I hear he have a bad temper.'

The man certainly looked an ugly customer. Howe

came up beside me as I watched the boat pull in to our floe. 'I wonder what sort of a story Bland has thought up,' he said, and his voice trembled slightly.

That was the first time any of us had commented on the cause of our predicament. We'd been too busy to think about it. We'd accepted the situation and concentrated wholly on endeavouring to cope with it. But seeing Vaksdal's set face and the purposeful way he came towards us, I knew why he'd come. I think Howe knew, too.

'You Kaptein Craig?' he asked. The gentle lilt of eastern Norway was entirely swallowed by the violence of his tone. The man was tense with anger.

'Yes,' I said. 'What do you want?'

'Did you order that harpoon to be fired?'

'No,' I said.

But he didn't wait for my reply. He went straight on: 'That harpoon explode in our engine-room. That is what cause the fire. That is what put us in this damn mess.' His little eyes fastened on Howe. 'You fire that harpoon.' He hunched forward slightly, his hands clenching as he moved in purposely on Howe.

'Just a moment,' I said.

But Gerda brushed past me and faced the man. 'What do you expect us to do, you fool?' she said, her eyes blazing. 'You wish us to sit still and be murdered? You go back to your Erik Bland and ask him why he ram us?'

The man had stopped. 'It was an accident,' he said. And his hand stretched out to push her aside.

'Don't you dare put your hands on me, Vaksdal,'

she said angrily. 'And you listen to what I tell you. That was no accident. Bland meant to ram us. There are people on this ship that he must kill if he is not to hang for the murder of Bernt Nordahl. Why do you think he bring *Tauer III* here when he is ordered to stand by at his earlier position?'

'Who say we are to remain in our old position?' Vaksdal demanded. 'And what is all this about murder? It is suicide.'

'It was murder,' Gerda snapped back at him. 'And it is Kaptein Eide who ordered you to stand by. Don't you listen to your radio?' The man hesitated and she added, 'Ask your radio operator.'

'He is injured by the fire when he send the SOS.'

'Well, somebody must have listen to the radio.'

'It was out of action for a little while.'

'So. Now you think. Was Bland near the radio when it go out of action?'

Vaksdal looked surprised. 'Yes, but –'

'And when did the radio work again?' she cut in. 'Not till Bland go down to the wireless room, I bet.' She suddenly stepped right up to him. 'Was Bland alone on the bridge when he rammed us?'

'When the accident happen –'

'Was he alone – just tell me that?'

'Yes.'

'Then you go back and ask him why he send the helmsman below at that moment. You go back and make a few inquiries before you bring your anger over to us. I think you find much to be angry about over there. Now go. And see you do not have trouble

210

with your men. It is bad to have trouble with men on the ice. They are from Tönsberg. And if you do not make inquiries, they will.'

He turned away then, a baffled look on his face. It was clear he resented being out-faced by a woman. But it was clearer still that he was puzzled about something. 'Just a minute, Vaksdal,' I said. 'Have you got your radio ashore?'

He half turned and shook his head. 'The fire has consume everything. But we have send a message to the *Syd Korset*.'

'With our position?'

'*Ja.*'

'And it was acknowledged?'

'*Ja.*'

'One more question,' I said as he turned again. 'Is Bland still on *Tauer III*?'

'*Nei*. The ship, she is on fire all over. Everyone is on the ice. Kaptein Bland is very sad man. He feel he is responsible for the accident.'

'Accident!' Howe screamed. 'It wasn't an accident. He rammed us. He rammed us deliberately.' He was moving forward impetuously, his skinny neck thrust out, his arms sawing the air in his excitement. 'Take me across to Bland. Take me to him. I said I'd kill him – and by God I will.'

'You have done enough, I think, already,' Vaksdal said.

'Enough? Do you realize what he's done? He's murdered us all. We'll never get out of this ice alive. Nor will Larvik or any of the people on *Hval 5*. He's killed us all as surely as if he'd mowed us down with a machine-gun.'

Howe's voice had risen to a high-pitched cry as he ran forward, flailing the air, mouthing threats about what he'd do to Bland. Vaksdal watched him come up. 'I think you *sinnsvak*,' he said.

'I'm not crazy,' Howe shrieked. 'Take me across to Bland. Take me over to him.'

Vaksdal flung him back and turned on his heel. 'You will hear some more about this,' he said over his shoulder.

Howe, sprawling in the slush of wet ice, watched the big mate step into the boat. He was trying to speak, but he couldn't. His whole body was shuddering in his effort to speak. The boat pushed off and the oar blades dipped into the ice green sea. Beyond it a great tongue of flame licked up from the bowels of the corvette, a red glare against the dark water sky to the west. Gerda ran forward and pulled Howe to his feet and they stood there, in silhouette against the flames, watching the boat row back to the dark huddle of men on the ice about a mile away.

SEVEN

That night the sleet turned to snow. It was bitterly cold now that we no longer had the protection of our ship. Out there on the ice we were exposed to the full force of the wind. It seemed to blow right through our makeshift tents. Our food was cold almost before we had time to swallow the first mouthful. Even with the whole party huddled together in two small tents the temperature inside was well below freezing. And a few hundred yards away the blazing wreck of *Tauer III* consumed as much stored-up heat in an hour as would have kept us warm for a whole year. We turned in about eight. Everyone was very tired and I wanted them to be fresh should the weather improve. The boat was moored to the floe by an anchor dug into the ice. Watches were of two hours' duration with two men on duty.

When I turned in the wind had backed to the sou'west and it was sleeting. Gerda and I had the radio between us and for a while we lay smoking and listening to the monotonous calling of the *Southern Cross*. Her operator would call *Hval 5*, then us, then finally *Tauer III*. There would be a five-minute pause. Then he'd start calling all over again. At length I switched off, not wishing to waste the battery. With my blankets wrapped tightly round me I tried to work up the warmth necessary to sleep. But the ground was wet and the wind blew under the canvas in an icy draught. The grinding of the floes seemed to run right through my body. Every tremor of the ice communicated itself to us as we lay in our tents.

When I did finally get to sleep I was roused almost instantly by loud shouts and the grinding clash of floes. I scrambled out of the tent to find myself in a grey-white world of driven snow in which men appeared like ghostly shadows leaning against the bitter wind. A voice shouted out of the void: '*Her! Kvikk! Til baaten.*' I staggered towards the voice. The grinding of the floes was very loud. The ice shook under my feet as though it were being battered by a huge steam hammer. And then in the half light I saw the reason for the lookout's cry. The open water where we'd anchored the boat was gone. There was only a narrow gap and this was fast closing as another floe swung in on us. I got out my whistle and blew on it till the men came stumbling towards me out of the murk of snow. We hauled on the painter and lifted the bows of the boat on to the ice. One man missed his footing and would have slithered into the sea but for Gerda, who caught hold of him by his collar. As it was he got wet to the waist. We dragged the boat clear of the water and right on up to our camp. When I went back to see that nothing had been left behind, I was just in time to see the gap close with a snap, the edges of the two floes grinding like a giant gnashing his teeth. I began to realize then how watchful we should have to be if we were to come alive out of this hell of ice.

As I turned back to the camp the snow slackened. The orange glow of the blazing ship showed for an instant in the weird light and was gone again. Before turning in I gave my whistle to one of the men on watch. It was a sharper and more penetrating warning than the human voice. I think the exertion in the middle of the night made us all very hungry. I know that I felt so ravenous that I could hardly sleep. But I also felt warm and I think I soon dozed off. I awoke stiff with cold, the shrill blast of the whistle sounding urgently in my ears and the floes clashing together like thunderclaps. When I went out the snow had stopped and the wind was dropping. For a moment I stood there, dazed, staring at the man blowing frantically on the whistle. The floe was covered in a white carpet of snow. But it had stopped falling. The camp with its tents and the men staggering sleepily out of them looked clear-cut and black against the snow. I saw no reason for the alarm. Then there was a splintering crash. The ice trembled under my feet and the man with the whistle pointed behind the tents. A dark line ran zigzagging through the snow. It broadened and then closed with the snap of a shark biting. Another crash, more trembling, and the line opened again. And this time it stayed open – a widening crevasse that wavered right across the floe.

There was no more rest for us that night. The boat was on one side of the crack, the camp on the other. We got the boat across the gap just in time. It widened out under the pressure of the other floes until we could see the sea. It became a sort of creek and widened till it was a river with sheer, ice-green banks. Tents and stores were right on the edge of it and everything had to be moved back to the middle of what was now quite a small floe. We were being battered by the ice from all sides. We huddled in the re-erected tents, drinking hot tea laced with rum, and waited for the floe to crack again.

Gerda said suddenly, 'I wonder what sort of a night it is for the men of *Tauer III*?'

'I'm more concerned about *Hval 5*,' I said. I was thinking of Judie.

She put her hand on my shoulder. 'I understand,'

she said. 'But you must not be angry with the men of *Tauer III*, Duncan. They are from Tönsberg. I know them all. They are good men. It is not their fault this happen.'

'What's more to the point,' Howe said, 'what is Bland up to?'

'Bland?' I remembered the dazed look on his face as he stood there alone on the bridge whilst the men worked at unloading. 'I don't think Bland will bother us any more. His men will have realized the truth by now. He's finished, whatever happens. Either he dies out here on the ice or he faces a charge of murder.'

'That's what makes him dangerous.'

'No,' I said. 'He's shot his bolt this time. You didn't see the dazed look on his face. I had a look at him through my glasses when he was alone on the bridge. He was numb with the shock of what had happened.'

'The numbness will wear off,' Howe said. 'And when it does he'll realize he's still got a chance. If he can get out alone – if he's the sole survivor and all the rest of us die, then he's achieved his purpose.'

'He still wouldn't control the company,' I reminded him.

'He doesn't know that,' Howe's voice replied out of the darkness. 'And anyway, if Bernt Nordahl's estate passes to Judie and Judie dies, the probability is he'll inherit it.'

'Anyway,' I said, 'the thing's impossible. He couldn't hope to get out on his own. That harpoon of yours finished him. He's hoist with his own petard and – '

'What is petard?' Gerda asked.

I spent some time trying to explain the quotation to Gerda and eventually we drowsed off.

The shuddering and grinding of the ice had gradually lessened. Sometime in the night it must have ceased altogether, for when I went out at five everything was quite still. The air was clear and frosty and the light from the new-fallen snow was blinding. There wasn't a cloud to be seen. The sun had huge circles of light round it with lines of gold radiating from the centre. At one part of the circle the light was intensified to produce a mock-sun of gold shot with prismatic colours. All about us the ice had a faint sheen of colour and towards the south and west columns of black smoke rose – frost-smoke caused by warm air from the sea lanes rising into the frozen atmosphere. It was breathtakingly beautiful and for a moment I just stood there, seeing the scene as a panorama without absorbing the detail. Then I saw the burnt-out hulk of *Tauer III* that had blazed at me so startlingly in the night. There were no flames now and only a thin column of smoke rose straight up into the incredible sky. Mast, funnel, bridge – everything except the hull were gone. She was completely gutted. Her crew were moving about on the ice, handling stores. Several floes had layered near them and it was clear that they, too, had experienced trouble from the movement of the ice during the night.

Our own situation might have been worse. The gap that had opened during the night had closed again. There were narrow sea lanes to the south and west of us, dividing us from the *Tauer III* camp. But to the north-east the ice seemed solid – a jagged, broken plain, with small, lumpy hills like rock outcrops, covered with snow, and broken edges where floes had been upended. The horizon was a trembling blur, constantly moving as though I were looking at it through water. There were some big icebergs there as far as I could see, but they were forever changing shape in the distorting mirror of the atmosphere.

On the face of it we looked secure. But the snow covered all the flaws and a thing that worried me was the grumbling thunder of ice movement to the east. It hadn't been there the previous day. And now I got the impression of a tremendous weight of ice thrusting towards us from the heart of the pack.

My main object was to link up with the survivors of *Hval 5*. Amongst the things Gerda had brought off the catcher were skis belonging to herself and her father. After breakfast I took Kalstad, one of the hands who was reckoned the best skier, and roped together with one of the harpoon fore-runners, we made for a floe-berg that stood up about a quarter of a mile to the north of us. The snow was crisp and the going quite good. We were glad of the rope, however, for in several places the ice was so honeycombed by the summer thaw as to be rotten and only our skis saved us from going right down into the water. It took us an hour to do that quarter of a mile, and with the sun getting stronger every minute it was warm work.

The floe-berg was perhaps twenty feet high. I imagined it was originally pack ice that had layered.

From the top of it we could look across to the black
bob of *Hval 5*. It was very difficult to see it clearly
through the glasses because of the shimmering of the
light off the snow. The vessel was lying almost on its
side, jammed up against a small floe-berg by a whole
series of layered floes. There were figures moving about
on the ice and some form of shelter or a dump of
stores had been set on a ledge of the berg. Between us
and the ship was nearly a mile of ice thrust up in
ridges and giant creases as though it had been compressed. Even as I stared at the scene through the
glasses I saw movement in the ice. At first I thought it
was a trick of the light that made the white mass
beyond the ship heave and writhe. Then I saw great
blocks of ice as big as houses being thrown into the
air as they were ejected between the jaws of grinding
floes. Faintly through the still air came the rumble and
crack of the pressure ridges building up towards the
table-topped iceberg beyond.

I got a mirror out of my pocket that I had bor-
rowed from Gerda, and after experimenting with Kalstad, managed to focus the sun glare roughly on the
ship. For about a quarter of an hour I endeavoured to
make contact by this primitive heliograph with no
result. I was just putting the mirror back in my pocket
when I caught the glint of an answering flash. It was
intermittent and I could make nothing of their morse.
Probably neither I nor they had succeeded in focusing
the flash accurately. For some time we tried ineffec-
tually to get a message across. In the end I gave it
up. Before turning back to our camp I made a close

examination of the ice between us and *Hval 5*. But without actually reconnoitring, it was impossible to decide whether we could link up.

The return journey took much longer and was much more hazardous. The snow was beginning to thaw and the going was sticky. More and more often our skis broke through the surface on rotten ice. We kept to the ridges as much as possible. When not actually on a ridge our field of vision was reduced to a few yards. It gave one the sensation of being hemmed in by a forest of ice. We made camp in the end, wet to the waist and actually sweating with heat. Gerda met me with a serious face. 'The pressure, she is increasing,' she said. 'Also there are several icebergs coming up from the south-west which I do not like.'

I stood by the camp, listening to the groaning and rumbling away to the east. It certainly seemed louder. And there was a faint and almost constant trembling of the ice, under us. Occasionally the low artillery rumble would be broken by a nearer and sharper sound like a signal gun where a section of the pack had suddenly split across. She took my arm and pointed to the sou'west. Clouds of white vapour lay along the horizon. They had no form, but were constantly changing like jets of steam in a gusty wind. They would flatten out into layers, then plume upwards, blossoming like atomic explosions. Once they looked like castles of ice upside down in the sky. 'Icebergs,' she said. 'I see them this morning. Now I think they are nearer.'

I nodded and cocked my ear again to the growl of the ice to the east. 'I don't like it,' I said.

'There is a storm there,' Gerda said. 'It is driving the ice down on us. But I think there is an eastward drift and that is what brings the icebergs up.'

'Suppose the two meet?' I asked.

She shrugged her shoulders and grinned with a slight down-dragging of the corners of her mouth. 'Then I think it is not ver nice. We must find stronger ice.'

I looked back to the floe-berg from which Karlstad and I had tried to signal to *Hval 5*. It looked solid enough. But then I thought of the way the ice had heaved and thrown up huge blocks over towards the table-topped iceberg. I felt suddenly as though there was no future in struggling against the giant forces that faced us. 'Any news from the *Southern Cross*?'

'*Ja*. She has dispatched *Tauer I* in answer to *Tauer III*'s SOS. Larsen, her *kaptein*, says he is approaching several icebergs about twenty miles from the position given by *Tauer III*.'

'Twenty miles!' I glanced back to the south-west. There was no open water visible at all. Perhaps there were leads and we couldn't see them. But the burnt-out hulk of *Tauer III* was entirely beset with floes and the ice ran uninterrupted to the horizon. A corvette wouldn't have a chance of breaking through. 'If only we had our R/T,' I murmured. 'It's useless sending one of the towing vessels.'

'Per'aps.' Gerda shrugged her shoulders again. 'But it is all we will get. They will not risk the *Southern Cross*.'

'Why not?' I asked.

'It is too much – too much value, too many lives – for the sake of even three of the catcher fleet. We must be content with a towing boat, or at best the tanker.'

'A corvette won't get through,' I said. 'And I doubt whether the tanker could.' I suddenly made up my mind. 'Better start trying to shift camp to that floe-berg. Divide the stores into two equal lots. We'll shift one lot today.'

We knocked up two makeshift sledges out of packing cases. Then we split into two watches – one made the journey to the floe-berg. I took the starboard watch out on the first run, blazing the trail ahead of them on skis. It was back-breaking work. Where I could travel on skis, the men very often sank to their waists in rotten ice. Several times the leading sledge broke through. The snow was wet, and the going was very heavy. It took three hours to reach our goal. We had a half-hour rest and then went back following almost the same route. The return journey took us an hour and a half. Gerda, who was in charge of the other watch, came out to meet us on skis. She was excited. I could see it in the reckless way she swooped towards us across the treacherous ice. She brought up in front of me with a jump Christi that sent the wet snow spattering over us. '*Southern Cross* is coming herself,' she cried.

'Coming into the ice?' I asked.

She shook her head. 'That I cannot say. But just after you have left Kaptein Larsen come on the radio. He say he is held up by the ice and can find no way through. Eide tell him to try again. But he fail. He say there is no way. Colonel Bland speak with him then. He tell him he damn well got to find a way. But an hour later he comes on again to say the pack is too close. He had patrolled it for ten miles, trying every lead, but it is no good. So then Bland say he come up with the *Southern Cross*. Maybe the *Southern Cross* try to break through, eh?' Her voice trailed away uncertainly.

'You said yourself they'd never risk the factory ship,' I reminded her. I wanted no false optimism.

She nodded. '*Ja*. I think perhaps they do not come, except to look.' She stood there fiddling with her ski-sticks, staring out across the ice.

I knew she had something on her mind, so I got the party moving again and slid alongside her on my skis. 'Well,' I said. 'What else did Colonel Bland say?'

She looked up at me quickly. 'It was not Bland. It was Larsen. He say there is a whole line of icebergs – five or six; some of them big ones – and they are drifting into the pack. He say already the ice is being built up into pressure ridges along a wide front. It is packing the ice in tight and he think it will get worse.'

'Are these the bergs we thought we saw this morning?' I asked her.

She nodded. 'Wait till you are at the camp and can stand on the boxes. You can see them quite distinctly now. You can also hear the ice. They are much nearer, I think.'

I didn't say anything, but pressed on into the camp. Gerda was quite right. The bergs were nearer. Standing on the packing cases I got a clear view to the west. I counted seven of them in a long line and I was no longer looking at their reflections in the atmosphere, but at the bergs themselves. Probably they had calved from the barrier ice somewhere along the Caird Coast or Luitpoed Land at roughly the same time and had been kept together by the current that had swept them down into our latitudes. They looked like a fleet of sailing ships in line ahead. 'I think there is a very big storm somewhere,' Gerda said. 'The pressure on the ice is increasing. The floes are being packed closer together all the time.'

'Well, there's nothing we can do about it,' I answered sharply, and sent her off with the second load of stores.

There was nothing to do but lie in our tents and smoke and listen to the radio. The men were excited, full of optimism. They talked and laughed. And when the *Southern Cross* ordered *Tauer I* to stand by and herself turned into the ice, I think they felt they were as good as rescued. One man produced a bottle of whisky, a smuggled piece of personal property, and offered drinks all round. Another produced a pack of cards and four of them settled down to a game of bridge as unconcerned as though we were waiting for a train. I sat sucking an empty pipe and wondering what had made Colonel Bland decide to risk the *Southern Cross* in the ice.

The factory ship was quite capable of crashing through the sort of ice we had come into the previous day. Her 22,000 tons and reinforced bows could smash a way through ice 12 feet thick. If conditions had been the same as yesterday she'd have had no difficulty in reaching us. But from where I sat at the entrance of the tent I could see across the smouldering hull of *Tauer III* to the icebergs on the horizon. I could feel the trembling of ice under me. It ran like a quiver up my spine. And I could hear the distant growl of the floes piling up under the eastward thrust of the distant storm. Bland knew nothing of this. I wished we were in radio contact so that we could warn him. But at least he could see the icebergs. He'd pass quite close to them, maybe through them. He was in a better position than we were to estimate the danger. And I began wondering again what it was that had decided him to risk the lives of over 400 men, quite apart from the ship, in an attempt to get through to us. Was it because of his son? Or was it because of Bernt Nordahl and what had happened? Or was it because he knew he was dying and didn't care anyway?

I tried to picture him, sitting there in his big cabin, making the decision. The man was quite ruthless. The lives of others wouldn't enter into his reckonings. Money, yes – but money was no longer important to him. Money couldn't buy him an extra minute of life now. He could afford to throw it away in some magnificent gesture. He'd always had to fight and now he was face to face with the elements. He'd risk the ship and every man in it if he decided to fight the ice. His decision might well be a queer mixture of quixotish bravado and a desire to purchase from his conscience an easy passage through the eye of a needle. It was tough on the men of the *Southern Cross*, that was all.

Shortly after eight the operator on the *Southern Cross* began calling us, first in Norwegian, then in English. He went on calling for half an hour. Then there was a pause. When he came on again it was with a message. '*At 21.00 hours we are going to make smoke. I repeat, at 21.00 hours we are going to make smoke. As soon as you sight our smoke make signals by whatever means possible. Southern Cross to catchers, Hval –*' And he went on repeating it. I had one of our barrels of oil tapped and arranged a drip on to a bundle of clothes. We piled packing cases on top of each other until we had a lookout post fully ten feet high. And just before nine I sent one of the younger hands up aloft as lookout. We were all pretty excited. None of us felt like staying in the tents and I had the radio brought out on to the ice.

At nine o'clock the *Southern Cross* operator came through with another message: '*We are now making smoke. We are three miles east of a line of icebergs, having passed between the second and third berg counting from the north. Signal to us if you can.*'

We were all watching the lookout now. His eyes were screwed up against the glare of the sun which was slanting down to the west and south. The man blinked and several times rubbed his hand across his eyes. I wished we had got sun goggles. Then suddenly he stiffened and pointed. '*Der er'n.*' The men cheered. Two of them began to dance, jigging from foot to foot. The ice trembled under us as a floe cracked under pressure with a noise like a thunderclap. If only *Tauer III* were still burning!

I gave the order to light oil-soaked clothes and then stopped the man just as he was about to strike the match. The lookout was rubbing his eyes and shaking his head. The two men stopped dancing. We all looked at him as he peered into the sun. Then he was pointing again. But the direction of his hand seemed farther to the south. I climbed up beside him, the packing cases wobbling under our combined weight. There was smoke there all right. But it was too near and in the wrong place. Even as I watched it broadened out into a great black streak. I couldn't see the icebergs now because of the glare. But I knew it was to the south of them. 'I think it's frost-smoke,' I said and the men were silent, staring westward. It was as though the cold hand of death had touched their spirits. I screwed up my eyes and tried to pierce the glare in the direction the *Southern Cross* must lie. But it was impossible to make anything out clearly. The whole atmosphere seemed constantly shifting. It was as though I were seeing everything through a film of water. A delicate, iridescent colour tinged the ice – prismatic and ephemeral. It was like a canvas full of beautiful pastel shades done by an impressionist portraying the coldness of beauty without the detail. Nothing had substance. As well try to see an object in a kaleidoscope as look for the smoke of the *Southern Cross* in that shot-silk curtain of blinding light.

The growl of the ice moved nearer, thundering at the floes and shaking our perch so violently that I jumped down on to the ice again. Somebody shouted and there, not a mile away, just beyond *Tauer III*, a floe turned on end, stood there for a moment and then slid back into the sea. A gap was opening out. We could see a stretch of water. It showed as a dark gash against the white of the surrounding ice. The air seemed to thicken and congeal like a gauze curtain. The gap widened. The air became solid and black. The frost-smoke rose like a fog, darkening everything, screening the sun. It wiped out the glare and drained the colour out of the ice. The world was suddenly white and cold. I felt a chill creep through me. I tried to buck the men up by telling them that the frost-smoke was a better marker than any smoke we could make. But it didn't comfort them. That cold, black curtain stood between them and sight of rescue. I ordered the steward to brew some coffee. The four who had been playing bridge returned to their game. I posted two lookouts and took the radio back to my tent. The ice shook under us. I began to wonder how long the thin layer on which we were camping would stand this battering from the east. I felt shut in and depressed. The growing pressure of ice and that black curtain of frost-smoke were overwhelming reminders of the forces we were up against. The chill of fear was in my stomach and not even the hot coffee warmed me.

'*We can see patches of frost-smoke, but no signals. You must try and signal to us. The ice is getting very thick. We do not know how long we can go on.*' For half an hour the *Southern Cross* went on imploring us to signal our position. One Olaf Petersen came on, speaking direct to Gerda, trying to encourage her and us. Colonel Bland, however, made no attempt to contact his son. The messages became more urgent. Finally the *Southern Cross* operator radioed: '*We are now making very slow progress. The icebergs are ploughing into the ice behind us. Unless we can pick up your signals soon, we may have to abandon the attempt to reach you.*' Previous messages had been in both English and Norwegian. But this was broadcast only in English, probably with the idea of not disheartening the crews. But even those that didn't understand English read the sense of the message in the faces of those that could. One of the men began cursing in Norwegian.

If only that frost-smoke hadn't appeared! If only we could see! At least we should then have been able to occupy ourselves with searching the glare for the factory ship's smoke.

There was a sudden shout from one of the lookouts and I dived out of the tent. 'Somebody is coming on skis,' he said.

'*Føken Petersen?*' I asked.

'*Nei, nei. Fra Tauer III.*' And he pointed toward the black curtain of frost-smoke.

I followed the direction of his arm. But I could see nothing except the cold, white shape of the ice. '*Der er'n. Der er'n.*' I caught a glimpse of something black moving on a ridge of ice and then it was hidden again. A moment later it reappeared not a hundred yards away. It was the figure of a man all right. He was covered in snow and ice. He waved a ski stick and called to us, then staggered and came on, thrusting himself forward with his sticks.

I don't know whom I expected – either Bland or Vaksdal, I think. I know I debated whether to go back to my tent for a rifle. I felt naked and helpless out there on the snow. And yet I didn't want to admit I was afraid by going back for my gun. So I stood my ground and waited, wondering whether I had to deal with a maniac or only a man with a violent temper. As the man approached I saw he was too short for Vaksdal. He suddenly got on to some hard ice and with a flip of his sticks he came towards me in a rush. He brought up with a quick Christi and a 'Salute, Capitano!' And I found myself shaking Bonomi by the hand. 'Oh, it is good to see you, Craig. You have no idea.'

'Why? What's the trouble?'

'Trouble? What is the trouble? My God!' His arms were waving so excitedly I was in danger of being hit by his ski sticks. 'You ask what is the trouble. It is that there is no order there. The men, they will do nothing for Bland, or the mates Vaksdal and Keller. They do not trust their officers and they are very bitter. At first Bland is very angry. He strike one of them. After that the men camp on their own. They are sullen and they go their own way. There is no order, no direction. I think there is danger, so I take the skis and come 'ere.'

'Have they got stores?'

'Si, si. When we abandon ship everything go fine. The trouble, she do not begin till later. Oh, but that journey across the ice. It is not more than per'aps a kilometre, but never have I made such a journey. And I am a vair good skier. Look, I show you. Come on to these cases. I will show how I come.'

'There is no time – '

But he cut me short and dragged me up to our lookout post. 'There. You can see the camp. First everything is fine. Then suddenly the ice is not there and I am to the waist in water. Look. I am very wet, am I not? Then there is much bad ice with many honeycombs. Also there is a gap filled with – how do you say – loose pieces of ice?'

'Brash?'

'*Si, si*. Brash. That is it, I ski across that.' His little chest was puffed out and his eyes glowed. 'You do not believe me, eh? But I am here – that is the proof, yes? Never am I so afeared. But I do it. I go very fast and I ski straight over this brash. Then – ' He spread his hands and laughed. 'But there so many bad places, I do not remember them all. Many times I think I give up and return. But then I remember that brash and I cannot face it and I go on. And so, here I am.'

'You shouldn't have done it on your own,' I said. 'Crossing brash is all very well, but you should have a companion, just in case.'

He was staring at me open-mouthed. 'Has – has anyone crossed this brash before? I thought that I would be the first to have dared this thing.'

I almost laughed. But instead I patted his arm. 'It has been done before, but not often. Only by experienced polar explorers who were desperate.'

'Ah, *si, si*. Of course, the polar explorers. That is

different.' His teeth showed white against the black stubble. 'Now tell me – what is the news? Have you a radio? Over there' – he nodded to the *Tauer III* – 'they have no radio.'

'We've a portable,' I said. 'We can receive, but we can't send.'

'Then you will know what is happening, yes?'

'The *Southern Cross* herself has entered the ice and is asking us to signal to her.'

'Ah. That is wonderful.' He beamed. 'Then I can have a bath. I am so dirty I think I must smell like a whale. I shall lie and wallow for an hour. Now I will rest a little.'

He was apparently not in the least interested in how we were going to signal to the *Southern Cross* through that black fog of frost-smoke. In fact, I doubt whether he even realized it presented any difficulty. The *Southern Cross* was coming into the ice to rescue us. He would get his bath. It was as easy as that. I almost envied him his sublime acceptance of the certainty of rescue.

I was beginning to be worried now about Gerda and her party. They had been away five hours. I waited half an hour and then got my skis out. But I'd hardly gone a hundred yards along the sledge trail when the lookout called to me that they were coming. I climbed an ice hillock and watched them winding like a black snake through the sunless white of our frozen world. Gerda saw me and waved and came on ahead on her skis. I told her the news. 'Then they must be quick,' was her comment. 'The ice is getting very bad. Over to *Hval 5* it is terrible. That table-top iceberg of theirs is nearer, you know. Whole floes are being tossed about under the pressure. The journey was bad, too. The ice round us is beginning to move.'

I nodded and told her how the gap from which the frost-smoke was rising had suddenly opened out.

'*Ja*. Soon we have double trouble, I think. But it is colder now. Perhaps the sea freeze in the gap. Then maybe we see the *Southern Cross* and can make a signal.'

When we got into the camp I stopped for a minute to look at the stores. A whole day's work and the pile still looked just as big. We'd shifted barely a quarter of it. Bonomi seized on Gerda as a fresh audience and throughout the evening meal, which the steward served as soon as the whole party were in, we had Bonomi's great trek across the ice. I'd barely finished the last mouthful and was just lighting my pipe when there was a shout from the lookout. The frost-smoke was going. By the time we'd tumbled out it was no more than a faint grey curtain. It was gone almost immediately. Colour came back to relieve the deadness of the eternal white. The sun was low to the south, slanting rays right across the sky and making the ice gleam with soft colour like the inside of an oyster shell. The scene was so soft and satiny that it was difficult not to believe that you could stretch out your hand and stroke it. But our eyes were on the lookout, standing on the packing cases and gazing westward. At length he shook his head. 'No *Southern Cross*,' he said to me. 'But the icebergs, they are nearer, I think.'

I climbed up beside him and the pair of us stared westward through screwed-up eyes. But there was nothing – not even a column of frost-smoke to mistake for the factory ship. The steward called me to the tent. His face was serious. 'It is the radio, Kaptein Craig. Listen! There is a message.' His voice was trembling slightly.

' . . . *repeat that in English. We have now ceased making smoke. If you are trying to signal us, do not continue. Do not waste your materials. We are temporarily held up by the ice which is much thicker here. I shall radio again at 22.30 hours.'*

There was a stunned silence when I broke the news to the men. 'It must be bad to hold the *Southern Cross* up,' one man said, and he cocked his ear, listening to the thunder of the pressure ridges. The others, too, were listening. It was as though they were suddenly awake to the fact that the sound might well be the forerunner of death for all of us.

'I do not understand,' Bonomi said suddenly. 'How can the *Southern Cross* be held up? She is a big ship and the ice is quite thin. We came through it yesterday. It is only of a thickness when it is an iceberg. But they do not have to go through the icebergs. They can go round them. Craig. What do you say? What is the trouble?'

I shrugged my shoulders. 'How the hell should I know?' I answered a little abruptly.

At ten-thirty the *Southern Cross* operator announced that they were still held up and that he would broadcast at half-hourly intervals. I set the watches and ordered the men to turn in. But I don't think anyone slept. At broadcasting times I turned the radio up so that they could hear it in the other tent even above the noise of the ice. The message was always the same – nothing further to report. I could feel despondency growing in our little camp. It wasn't only the broadcasts. The thunder of the ice movement to the east seemed to grow and grow. The floe trembled under us, sometimes so violently that it seemed as though we were being actually shaken. It was like trying to rest on top of an earthquake. But I was very tired and drowsed occasionally. I'd drowse a bit and then jerk awake, numb with cold, and look at my watch. At the hour and the half-hour I'd switch on the radio. It was comforting just to hear the voice of the operator. It gave us a false sense of security to be in touch with the outside world. The man's voice was so quiet and natural. I felt as though I had only to wait a little and he'd walk into the tent to tell us the *Southern Cross* had arrived to pick us up. I thought of the warmth of the cabin I'd shared and the good food and the sense of mastery over the elements that the huge ship had given.

I must have fallen asleep, for suddenly Gerda was shaking me. 'I think there is something wrong with the radio,' she whispered. 'It is past three and I can get nothing.'

I sat up and fumbled with the tuning knobs. There was a faint crackling, but I could pick up nothing on our R/T wavelength. I switched over to the next waveband and almost immediately picked up music from a shore station. 'Nothing wrong with the radio,' I said. 'Sure you didn't alter the tuning knob?'

'No. I switched on just before three. There was nothing. Then I look at the tuning. It is quite okay. I think they do not broadcast.' Her voice trembled slightly.

'But they must have done,' I told her. 'They know how anxiously we'll be following their broadcasts. They'd never just miss out one. I'll try again at three-thirty.'

I glanced at my watch. It was ten past three. I lit my pipe and sat there, waiting for the next broadcasting time. And as I sat there, listening to the thunder of the pressure ridges and the crunch of the man on watch pacing up and down outside, an awful thought crossed my mind. Suppose the operator were too busy to broadcast to us! I tried to put the thought out of my mind. But it persisted. It persisted and grew with the groaning and crashing of the ice and the sudden, deathly periods of silence. They'd never forget to broadcast, then there must have been a reason. And there could be only one reason – more important traffic. I glanced at my watch. It was fourteen minutes past three. I looked across at Gerda. She was lying down, breathing quietly. Twice in the hour, for three minutes, there is a period of radio silence. From 15 minutes to 18 minutes past the hour and from 45 minutes to 48 minutes past the hour every operator in every ship in the world listens on a Watch wave of 500 kc for emergency calls. I just had to set my mind at rest. I leaned quickly forward, switched the set on and tuned to the Watch wave. The radio crackled. I gazed at the luminous dial of my wrist-watch, and as the minute hand touched the quarter I was sweating despite the cold. The radio crackled. That was all. Relief flooded through me. I told myself I'd been a fool. And then, so faint that I could not catch the words, the voice of an operator crackled out of the set.

I leaned forward quickly and fingered the tuning knob. The name *Southern Cross* was repeated twice. Then I was on the wavelength and the operator's voice was echoing through the tent: '*We are beset by ice in 66.21 S. 34.06 W. Southern Cross calling all shipping. SOS. SOS. Can you hear me? We are beset by ice in 66.21 S. 34.06 W. Southern Cross calling all ships. SOS. SOS . . .*'

It went on like that unendingly. The operator's tone never varied. It was unemotional, ordinary. He might have been making a weather statement. But the monotonous repetition of the words drummed at my brain and I sat there, quite regardless of the cold, seeing nothing, hearing nothing beyond that voice, completely stunned.

There was a movement in the tent round me. Gerda caught at my arm. She was thinking of her father. Nobody spoke, but I knew they were all awake and listening. Sometimes the operator sent in English, sometimes in Norwegian. Always the message was the same. Then a new voice was on the air. '*Haakon to Southern Cross. Haakon to Southern Cross. Repeat your position. Over.*'

The position was repeated. There was silence for perhaps five minutes. Then the Norwegian factory ship was back on the air. '*Haakon to Southern Cross. Proceeding to your assistance. Our position is now 64 S. 44 W. We should be with you at about 20.00 hours. Report fully on your present circumstances.*' And the operator gave an R/T wavelength.

After I had tuned to him, Eide himself came on the air. '*We passed between two icebergs in a wide lead at 17.30 hours yesterday, going to the assistance of three of our catcher fleet damaged in the ice. At about 19.00 hours the lead came to an end and we entered the ice which was loose pack and not thick. At 21.45 hours we were held up by a mass of very heavy pack. We tried to back out of this, but the icebergs we had passed through were piling the pack up across our line of retreat. It appears that there is a strong eastward drift here. The icebergs are moving with the drift. But to the east there is a storm thrusting the ice westward. We are being caught between these two forces. When you reach the ice you will find there are seven icebergs in a row. Do not try to proceed beyond this line. I repeat, do not try to proceed beyond this line. We will keep you informed of all developments.*'

'*Haakon to Southern Cross. Thank you for your warning. We will do all we can.*'

'It is not believable,' Gerda whispered.

I didn't say anything. I felt utterly crushed. I think I prayed. I don't know. My mind was a sort of blank in which I could think of nothing but the fact that I needn't have been here. I wasn't a whaler. I wasn't a part of this Antarctic organization. If only I hadn't been so damned foolish about that fiver Bridewell had given us as a New Year present! Or if only I'd had the sense to confirm that Kramer could get me a job in Capetown! It was as though Fate had organized it all. I felt bitter and lonely.

'*Capitano*.' Bonomi's voice trembled in the dark corner of the tent where he lay. 'You will get us out of here, yes? You can navigate. You have been on a polar expedition. You can get us – '

'It wasn't a polar expedition,' I snapped at him. 'It was only to Greenland.'

'What is the difference? You understand how to travel on the ice. Tell me, please – is it possible to get out of the ice, eh?'

'In Greenland we had dogs.'

'Yes. But we have a boat.'

'Would you like to drag a boat through twenty miles of the conditions through which you ski'd this evening?'

'No. But I must get back. When I complete these whaling pictures, I am to go to the Rand to work for some gold-mining companies. Oh, you people, you do not understand. You are not artists. For me my work is everything. I must get back. I cannot be snuffed out here like any common photographer. I have much fine work yet to do.'

'Oh, shut up,' I said. But the way he'd talked made me realize that there were fifteen people right here on the ice with me who expected me to save them. The responsibility wrapped itself round me and lay like a heavy mantle on my shoulders. Gerda touched my hand. 'You must not worry, you know. God will help us.'

Bonomi heard her and said, 'God?' Though I couldn't see him, I could picture the down-droop of his mouth and the upward roll of his eyes. 'God has done too much for us already, I think. *Madonna mia!* We must do for ourselves now.'

The refrigerator ship, *South*, and the tanker, *Josephine*, were now on the air. They were ordered to close, but to stand off, clear of the ice.

All night the *Southern Cross* issued reports – to her own ships and to the *Haakon*. But they showed no improvement until shortly after six when our hopes were raised by the news that she had dynamited a patch large enough for her to be warped round. I felt then that there was a chance. She was facing out of the ice and a powerful ship of that size ought to be able to batter her way clear along the route by which she had entered. Everybody was cheerful at breakfast. But a broadcast shortly after eight-thirty shattered our hopes. The icebergs were charging into the pack and building it up into huge pressure ridges. The way out was blocked. Though we couldn't see the *Southern Cross* because of the glare, we could see the icebergs. And to do this we no longer had to climb to our lookout. They were much nearer and plainly visible from the tents.

Shortly after nine, Colonel Bland himself came on the air instructing the *Josephine* to refuel all catchers and towing vessels and escort them to South Georgia.

This, more than anything else, brought home to us the seriousness of the situation. To give such an order it was clear that the officers on board the *Southern Cross* considered there was no chance of their being able to resume operations that season.

There is no need for me to record here in detail what everyone knows. By ten o'clock the *Southern Cross* was reporting damage due to the pressure of the ice, though the pumps were still holding the water. But an hour later the whole starboard side of the factory ship was buckling under the constant attack from the ice. By eleven-thirty she was pierced in several places and the crew were off-loading stores and equipment. Oil was being pumped out to be ignited later as a guiding beacon.

Gerda took me aside then. 'Duncan. I think we must begin to carry more stores to the floe-berg. I am not happy here. If we get caught between those icebergs and the pack ice to the east we may lose everything.'

I nodded. 'You're right,' I said, and gave the order for my party to get ready. The men were reluctant. They didn't argue, but I could see it in their faces. The morbid fascination of listening to the reports from the *Southern Cross* had gripped them. The sky to the east of us changed as we began to load the sledges. The opaque iridescent light faded out of it till it was a dead, white glare. Wisps of cloud drifted across the sun and thickened like a fog. The last spark of comparative warmth vanished and the world was a cold etching in black and white. Then the first flurry of snow scattered like a handful of confetti through the camp. With the snow came the wind. At first it was just a cold breath of air out of the east. But in a moment a gust hit us, whipping at the end of one of the tarpaulins. It died away again and then suddenly it was blowing hard and the snow had thickened to a driving blanket. It was a thick cloud of black specks against the ice, but where it settled it produced a carpet of clean white. We secured the stores, pegging down the ends of the tarpaulins, and crawled into our tents.

From the clear sunlight of the morning, it had changed to a world of howling chaos. The wind moaned and screamed and the snow drove like a biting shroud across the ice. We sat and smoked. Nobody said anything. The only voice was the voice of the operator on the *Southern Cross*. The blizzard was making it difficult to unload their stores and they could no longer estimate the extent of their danger.

I shall always remember that morning. I think it was the longest I have ever spent. It was very dark in the tent. The other occupants were vague humps huddled under their blankets for warmth. The only thing that was unchanged was the steady voice coming out of the radio.

I think we all felt that the end was inevitable. Yet I remembered the profound shock the announcement caused. It was at seventeen minutes past two. Eide was speaking to the *Haakon*, which had now sighted the *Josephine* and the rest of the catchers. His voice was trembling as he announced: '*The ship is pierced in several places. The pumps are no longer holding the water. She is sinking and I have given the order to abandon ship.'* At 15.53 hours the operator on the *Southern Cross* announced: '*All the crew safely on the ice, together with a reasonable quantity of stores. The ship is very low. Owing to the blizzard our camp is not very satisfactory and the movement of the ice is threatening. We are right in the path of the icebergs and unless the westward thrust of the storm eases soon our position will be dangerous. Captain Eide is about to leave the ship and I shall now remove the radio equipment to the ice. I will radio again as soon as I have set up the equipment.'*

That was the last message we received from the *Southern Cross*. We sat there for hours in the semi-darkness of the tents, the crackle of radio barely audible above the sound of the storm, but no message came from the *Southern Cross* survivors. At six o'clock in the evening the *Haakon* began calling the *Southern Cross*. The voice of the *Haakon* operator went on and on, a monotonous drone that gradually got on our nerves. There was no reply and at length I switched the radio off. The voice was too much like someone trying to call the dead. We lay there in the shadowy gloom of our tents and wondered what had happened. And with each minute that passed the sound of the wind seemed to encroach upon our refuge till it dominated us all with its siren scream of warning. We were alone, without hope of rescue, and I think we felt our smallness and were afraid.

EIGHT

To wake up on an icefloe with a blizzard blowing and realize that you are responsible for the lives of thirteen men, a girl and young boy, is not pleasant. I knew I had to get them out, but in the moment of waking I was so dazed that I don't think I realized the full extent of the disaster that had occurred. I lay in the shadowed darkness of the tent listening to the blizzard and trying to measure our distance from the main centre of pressure by the trembling of the ice under me. And as I lay there it slowly came back to me – how the *Southern Cross* was gone and there was no prospect of help from the outside world and how a line of icebergs was driving towards us through the ice. At least the floe hadn't split up in the night. That was something. I climbed out of the tent into a screaming world of wind and stinging snow. The two men on watch were white ghosts against the dirty grey backcloth of the storm.

I got one of them to help me brew some tea and took it to the men myself. The only one of them who said anything was McPhee. 'Mon, ye'd make a bonnie waitress,' he grinned as I handed him his mug. 'Do you ken if they charge extra for tea in bed at this hotel?'

'The tea's free,' I said, 'and so's the weather.'

'Weel, thanks for the tea, anyway.'

Howe stirred at his side. 'And you can thank God for the weather.' He sounded bitter.

'Ye'll do no gude blaming the Almighty,' McPhee

admonished him. 'Better to get doon on your knees and pray to Him for guidance.'

Tempers were short and the hours passed slowly in that bitter cold. It was too dark to read or to play bridge. I found a notebook in my pocket, tore out all the used pages and started a log. The first entry is a queer scribble, written more or less blind: *11 Feb. The Southern Cross was abandoned yesterday. Still no message from the survivors. Blizzard blowing outside, but party all safe in the tents. No prospect of being rescued. Morale low. Movement of ice becoming violent. As soon as the storm ceases intend to move to nearby floe-berg.* I then listed the names of all the party, including Bonomi, and the names of the two men who were killed in the collision.

I was sitting there, wondering morbidly who would eventually read the log and whether it was worth entering the reasons for the collision, when the ice quivered violently under me. There was a shout and a report like a pistol shot. I felt the tent moving. I put out my hand to support myself and fell on my side. The floor of the tent was no longer there. In the dim light a dark gash was opening under us. The canvas of the tent began to rip. I flung myself towards the entrance, dragging Gerda with me. Bonomi gave a shout. Howe was slipping, but somebody had caught hold of his legs. Hans, the deckboy, was in the gap, clawing at the edge and screaming. He was all tied up in his blankets. McPhee pulled him out. We got to our feet and fought our way out of the tent, the men outside pulling the canvas clear of us.

The sight that met my gaze as I flung the last fold clear of my face was pretty frightening. A crack was opening right across the floe. Fortunately it missed the stores and the other tent. But it had cut our own sleeping quarters clean in half. Our sleeping positions were moulded in the ice by the warmth of our bodies. The shapes of our heads and shoulders were on the far side of the gap, our hips and legs on the near side. If the floe had split during the night, when we were asleep, nothing could have saved us. Even as I stared at it, the gap closed with an ugly snap. It did this several times – opening out to about three or four feet and then closing again with a clash of ice on ice. Finally it stayed closed and we could hear the broken edges grinding together under the pressure.

I knew we ought to move to the floe-berg. But it was impossible in that weather. We could not have made it and in any case we had no idea what was happening to the ice along the sledge route. We re-erected our tent as best we could and crawled inside. It was only then that we realized we hadn't got the radio. I went outside to look for it. The others joined me, searching anxiously in the snow. But it was gone. And then Hans said to me he saw it fall into the gap as he was being pulled out. Questioned by Gerda, he admitted that he had grabbed at it to hold himself and had pulled it in. After that we knew it had gone and we went disconsolately back to the tent.

You can't imagine what a difference the loss of the radio made. Whilst we'd had it we at least had the illusion of contact with the outside world. Now we were completely cut off. Its loss produced temporarily a mood of despair in all of us. But it also brought us face to face with reality. I don't think the men, or even I myself, had fully faced up to our position until then. As long as there was a voice on the radio telling us every move on the part of the rescue ships, bringing right into our tent the voices of men straining every nerve to do what they could to reach us, I think we felt unconsciously perhaps that we needn't exert ourselves, that we had but to stay put and everything would be all right. Now we were out of touch. We'd no means of knowing what the rescue ships were doing or what they planned to do. One thing we did know, however, and that was that our plight was now lost in the far greater disaster of the *Southern Cross*. There were over four hundred men out there on the ice somewhere, and their rescue would be the first objective.

McPhee put it into words when he said, 'Ah dinna think the radio is much o' a loss. There's nobody will save us noo except ourselves.'

All that day the snow continued and the wind blew like a raging monster out of the east. The cold was numbing and we lay huddled in our tents, waiting with fear in our hearts for the floe to open up again. Nobody spoke much and the cards lay forgotten, though it became just light enough to see. I cut watches to half an hour and that was quite long enough out there in that hell. Once one of the men on watch went a few yards from the camp to investigate a noise that sounded as though the floe were cracking again. We were shouting and blowing on my whistle for three-quarters of an hour before he stumbled into the camp again, utterly exhausted. You had only to go a few yards and the camp was lost to sight under its canopy of snow. It was only by luck that he'd found it again. After that I gave orders for the watch to remain close to the tents and within sight of each other.

At five the next morning the snow ceased. The wind remained, but we were no longer hemmed in by the blanket of the snow-storm. We could see, and the sight that met our eyes was truly terrifying. The icebergs were not six miles away and they were bearing down upon us, churning the ice up before them like giant bulldozers. I gave the order to load the sledges. I had biscuit tins broken up and the tin nailed to the outside of the boat round the bows. This was to save the woodwork from being pierced or damaged by sharp edges of ice, for I was determined to take the boat with me. The boat was our only hope of safety. Without the boat we were doomed.

Whilst these preparations were going on Gerda and I went on skis to reconnoitre the route to the floe-berg. The snow was deep and crisp. Our skis slid easily along the surface of it. It took us only a few minutes to reach the floe-berg – a journey that had taken Kalstad and I over an hour the day before. It was incredible. It seemed no distance at all. But though the snow was all right on skis, I wondered how it would be for the men on foot. The smooth carpet of white covered everything – all the flaws and honeycombs and areas of rotten ice. I was afraid the weight of the boat would soon find the bad patches.

When we got back the steward had breakfast ready. It was the best meal we had. I told him to use anything he liked from the stores we were leaving behind. We were ready to leave shortly after ten. Bonomi bustled about taking pictures. 'I must have pictures of everything,' he said. 'The camp of the disaster, the trek, the boat, everything. When we are back, everyone will say, "Bravo! Bravo! Aldo Bonomi, he has done it again." '

That was how we came to call the place Disaster Camp. The man was unbelievable. He had come across to us with a rucksack on his back and his camera slung round his neck. Do you think that rucksack contained so much as a change of socks? Not a bit of it. It was full of unused film for his camera.

Before we started he insisted on taking a group picture, all of us standing in front of the stores we were abandoning. It was just as he was taking this photograph that Howe seized my arm and pointed towards *Tauer III*. A line of figures was winding slowly through the broken contours of the ice. Somebody raised a cheer and in an instant the men were all shouting and waving excitedly. The fools thought it was a rescue party from the *Southern Cross*. I counted seventeen men – seventeen black dots moving against the dead white of the snow. I turned on my crew and shouted at them to be quiet. 'It is the crew of *Tauer III*.' The cheering wavered and died. I saw the light of hope leave their eyes. Their faces looked suddenly white and pinched under their beards. The deckboy, Hans, began to cry. The dry sobs that shook him were audible, even above the howl of the wind – it was as though the sudden fear in the men's hearts had been translated into sound. Gerda went to him and put her arms round him, comforting him. We waited like men frozen by the cold as the crew of *Tauer III* approached.

They were dragging improvised sledges piled with stores. But they had no boat with them. I searched the long, straggling line with my glasses. Vaksdal was leading. His big, Viking figure was unmistakable. With only one man to help him, he was pulling one of the sledges. I searched down along the line, peering at each man's face. Most of them I could recognize from the brief period I had been in command of them. But I was searching for one face and I did not find it. The full complement of a towing vessel was sixteen men and two deckboys. There were only seventeen. Erik Bland was not with them.

As they reached our camp, Vaksdal came towards me. His eyes avoided mine. 'The men wish to be under your command, Kaptein Craig,' he said harshly.

I ordered my steward to get the stove alight and prepare hot food for them. Then I turned to Vaksdal. 'Where's Bland?' I asked him.

'He remain with the stores,' he answered. He was shifting uneasily on his big feet.

'Why?' He did not answer me and I added, 'Why have you abandoned him?'

'Because the men wish it,' he answered. His voice was sullen and angry.

'The men wish to abandon their captain?'

'*Ja*. Also he do not wish to come with the men. He wish to stay. He ask Keller and me to stay, too.'

'Why didn't you?'

'Because the men wish to leave.'

'And you left Bland to die in the ice alone?'

The man's face was sullen. 'He would not come. He wish to be left.'

'You're the first mate, are you?' I asked him.

'*Ja.*'

'You assumed command?'

He nodded.

'Why?'

'Because the men refuse to do what Bland tell them. They say it is Bland's fault, that it is not an accident. They are angry and they do not obey orders. They are Tönsberg men.' He said it as though that explained everything.

'Did you take the view that Bland deliberately rammed my boat?'

'No. He would not do that, not here in the ice. No whaler would do a thing like that. It is true what Fröken Petersen say, that he send the helmsman below, but it is for some cocoa. It is also true that our radio is mysteriously out of order. These are things that will have to be cleared up at the inquiry when we get back to the *Southern Cross*. But I do not –'

'The *Southern Cross* is gone,' I interrupted him.

'Gone? I do not understand.'

'She got caught in the ice in an attempt to reach us. She is sunk.' I looked round at the ring of faces, listening open-mouthed. They looked scared and disheartened. 'Gerda,' I said. 'Get these men to work. I want all the sledges lashed together, nose to tail.' Then

I turned back to Vaksdal. 'So you are in command of these men?'

'*Ja*.'

'When did you assume command?'

'When it is clear to me that the men will not obey Kaptein Bland.'

'Then it was your decision to abandon Bland.'

'That is not true. The men wish to leave Bland, and also Bland wish to stay.'

'But you say you were in command?'

'*Ja*.' His voice was sullen and his tongue flicked across his lips.

'Who is your second mate?'

'Keller.' He nodded to a short, stout man with a woollen cap.

I called him over. 'Do you speak English?' I asked him.

'*Ja, hr Kaptein*.'

'Why did you abandon Bland?'

'The men demand that we –'

'Damn the men!' I shouted at him. 'The two of you were in command, yet you did exactly what the men wanted. You are forthwith relieved of your commands and revert to ordinary seamen, both of you.'

Vaksdal took a step towards me. 'You cannot do this,' he growled.

'I can and I will,' I answered him. 'You're neither of you fit to command.'

Vaksdal's eyes blazed. 'You dare to say that!' he shouted. 'You who have not served one season in the Antarctic. You know nothing and you tell us what we should and should not do. I have been eight voyages to the Antarctic. I know what is right.'

'You know what is right, do you?' I said. 'You assume command of a crew cut off in the ice, and you abandon your boats. How do you think you're going to get to safety without your boats?'

'I did not know the *Southern Cross* is sunk.' He was looking at the ground, shuffling his feet angrily in the snow.

'Did it never occur to you that the *Southern Cross* might not be able to reach us? Were you planning to just sit on your bottoms and wait to be rescued? Abandoning your captain when you believed him innocent of the men's charges is tantamount to mutiny. Abandoning your boats shows that you're not fit to command in these circumstances, either of you. You are now relieved of your commands. If you have anything to say, hold it for the inquiry when we get back.' I turned on my heels then and went over to Gerda. 'Get all the men together. I want to talk to them.'

'But, Duncan, it is too cold for talk now,' she said.

'They'll be colder if they die out here,' I answered. 'And that's what will happen if we don't scotch this trouble right at the start. I want another mate – one of the *Hval 4* men. Who do you suggest?'

'Kalstad.'

'Good.'

She paraded the men then and I spoke first to the men of *Tauer III*. I told them what they'd done was equivalent to mutiny. That unless they obeyed their officers they would never get out of the ice alive. I told them what had happened to the *Southern Cross*, that we were now entirely on our own. I then appointed Kalstad a mate, in command of the *Tauer III* crew, and announced that I had relieved Vaksdal and Keller of their commands.

One of the men interrupted me. He was the coxs'n of *Tauer III* and he started on a denunciation of Bland.

'That is no reason for abandoning him,' I answered. 'He will stand trial when we get back. You have no right to take the law into your own hands, which is what you have done in abandoning him. Moreover, you have abandoned your boats, too. And without them you have no chance of reaching safety.' I then asked for volunteers from the *Hval* 4 crew to go back and bring in Bland and the two boats.

Every man of them volunteered – even the two injured men and the boy, Hans. I was proud of them and I remember that my voice felt choky at this display of confidence in me. The coxs'n of *Tauer III* stepped forward a little shamefacedly then and asked if his men might not volunteer.

But I shook my head. 'You've done one trek today. My men are fresh.' I ordered Gerda to get the sledges moving as soon as the *Tauer III* men had fed. 'When you have set up the new camp. and the men are rested come back with a dozen volunteers to help us bring in the boats.'

Gerda nodded and began running out ropes from the sledges. I felt a tug at my sleeve. It was Howe. 'Bring back the boats, Craig,' he said. 'But for God's sake leave Bland there.'

'I can't do that,' I said.

'He's a murderer,' he said. 'You know that. Bring him back and you give him a second chance. Let him find his own way out – if he can without any boats.'

But I shook my head. 'I can't do that,' I repeated.

'My God!' Howe said. 'If you bring him back I'll have to kill him. I've sworn I will. I've sworn to avenge my father. But I don't want to do it – not now. You see, there's Gerda – ' He hesitated awkwardly and then said, 'Why not let the ice do it? Please. To bring him back will make so much unhappiness. Gerda is already frightened for her father. And if I kill Bland – '

'No,' I said. 'And you're not going to kill Bland either. When I've brought him back and if these icebergs don't finish us, I'll try him by a summary court here on the ice, and if he's convicted of deliberately ramming us, he'll be put to work as an ordinary seaman pending trial when we get back to civilization.'

Howe stared at me. 'You damned fool!' he said. He was almost crying, he was so worked up. 'You're not in the Navy now. This is the Antarctic. That man's killed my father. He's caused the loss of three ships and endangered the lives of over four hundred men. Can't you realize that he's better dead? If you bring him back he'll fight to kill us all and get out alone. You heard what Vaksdal said. He wanted to be left there. Well, if he wants to be left – '

'If he wants to be left,' I said, 'then I'll not force him to come. There, will that satisfy you?'

He opened his mouth to speak, but Gerda came up then. 'Everything is ready for us to go,' she said.

'Fine,' I replied. 'And don't forget to come back for us. It's going to be a hard trek with two boats.'

'I won't.'

'Good luck, then.'

'Thank you. And be careful, Duncan,' she added. 'You are a nice man and it would not be good if we lose you.' And with that she stretched up and kissed me.

I collected my volunteers, leaving only the two injured men and Hans and Howe of the *Hval 4* crew with Gerda, and we set out west along the sledge tracks that led towards the black hulk of *Tauer III*.

You may think it odd in that setting and amongst a bunch of tough men of whom she was in command, that Gerda should have kissed me. Perhaps the feminine element is out of place in the Antarctic. It certainly seems so as I write and I was tempted to leave it out. But I am setting down everything as it happened. Gerda was a mate in charge of men. But that did not mean that she hid the woman in her. Her method of handling men was quite different from a man's method. Yet all I can say is that if ever I am in as tough a position again, I'd give my right hand to have Gerda as my second-in-command. Her endurance was a constant spur to the rest. She'd shame them and coax them all in one and under her leadership they could achieve the impossible. As for the kiss – it was an open expression of her wish that we should return safely and accepted as such by the men. In fact, I not only had her kiss on my lips to encourage me but a cheer from the men of *Tauer III*. Only Vaksdal watched us sullenly as we left the camp and I hoped I had not made a permanent enemy of him, for he was a man I thought would prove useful.

We took with us three of the harpoon forerunners, our boat anchor and block and tackle. The snow had been packed down by the *Tauer III* sledges and the going was good, with the exception of one bad patch of honeycombed ice round which I managed to find a way. With the wind on our backs we made the trip in just over half an hour.

The camp itself was completely obliterated by snow. Only the sledge tracks running up to it and ceasing marked its position for us. As we neared the camp we could see the ice grinding at the wreck of *Tauer III*. The rusty sides of the ship stood up black and sheer above the floes, blotched here and there with white patches of snow. The ice was riding up on the farther side, and though we could not hear it, we could see that the steel plates were being broken under the stress. Beyond the ship the ice seemed in constant motion. It would lie dormant for a while, a lumpy plain of white, then suddenly a floe would heave up, showing jagged green teeth, or a great slab of ice would pop out of the snow as though ejected as indigestible by some giant sea monster.

From an ice hillock I looked beyond *Tauer III* to the line of icebergs. The nearest was not three miles away – a huge, wedge-shaped cliff of ice ploughing into the pack, turning it up on either side like the bow wave of a huge battleship held motionless in the still of a camera picture. But it was only motionless if you glanced at it quickly. I stood there for a moment, staring at it, and saw that it was moving all the time. Thick floes were being crushed and churned back. I thought of the survivors of the *Southern Cross*. The icebergs must have ploughed their way right across the position where the factory ship had foundered.

There was a chill in my stomach as I slid down into a trough of the ice on my skis, glad to have the sight blotted from my view. I felt there was no hope. Strive how we might, we were doomed to the same death as the men of the *Southern Cross*. The advance of the icebergs was slow but inevitable, like the Day of Judgment. I tried to grin cheerfully at the men, but my lips seemed frozen. I made some crack about the ice – I don't remember what, but it seemed a hollow mockery. The men laughed and I thought – *My God, they've got guts*. I found myself praying to God to give me strength. In that illimitable waste of storm-swept ice I felt the smallness of man and He seemed nearer to me then than ever before, nearer even than that time when I'd steamed away from the convoy in my corvette, one of a screen of tiny ships thrown out to halt the *Bismarck*.

As my skis slid along the sledge tracks into the *Tauer III* camp, Erik Bland emerged from a sail-cloth tent pitched in the lee of some packing cases. 'It's you, Craig, is it?' he said as I stopped just short of him. His voice was thick and he was swaying slightly. 'What do you want?'

I was well ahead of the men and for the moment

we were alone. 'I've come for you,' I said. 'I think you know why.'

'I suppose you think I rammed you deliberately?' His eyes had a glazed look and his face was white and mean under the dark stubble of his beard. He was very drunk. 'Well, what if I did? You can't prove it. You can't prove anything. If that bloody little bastard Howe hadn't fired that harpoon – '

'You'd be out of the ice by now, reporting that there was no way through. Is that it?'

'You think you're clever, don't you?' he sneered. 'Well, I'll beat you yet – all of you.'

'Better get your things together, Bland,' I said. 'You're coming back with me.'

'To have you rig another little court of inquiry?' He laughed. 'Oh, no. I'm staying here.'

'You're not taking the easy way out like that,' I told him. 'You're coming back with me to stand trial. If we ever get out of the ice I think you're going to find yourself responsible for a lot of deaths.'

'I'm not responsible for what the ice does,' he answered. 'You can't prove anything. It was an accident. And don't imagine I'm going to die. I'm not taking the easy way – ' He stopped then, peering out across the snow. He'd seen the men. 'So you're so damned scared of me you bring a dozen men with you.' His eyes were suddenly narrowed. He was fighting to sober himself up.

'I didn't bring the men in order to persuade you to come back with me,' I said. 'I brought them because

I've come for the boats Vaksdal was fool enough to leave behind.'

'The boats! You leave the boats alone!' He stared at me a second and then swung round and lunged into the tent. Like an idiot, it never occurred to me what he was after until he came out carrying a gun. 'You leave the boats alone!' he screamed at me. He was tugging at the bolt, which was jammed with frozen snow. 'As long as I have the boats, I've got a chance.'

I drove my sticks hard into the snow and charged him on my skis. I drove into him head first and we collapsed in a tangled heap. He was quicker on to his feet than I was, encumbered by my skis. But I had the gun and the bolt was free. I got up carefully, watching him all the time. I'd misjudged his motive in staying behind. I could see now that one of the boats had already been partly decked-in with pieces of packing cases. It was just as Howe had said. He wanted to be the only man out of the ice alive. Only his nerve had failed him when he was alone and he'd had to get drunk. 'How the hell do you think you'd get away in one of those boats without a crew?' I demanded angrily.

'I've sailed boats single-handed all my life,' he answered sullenly. 'If that berg missed the camp, I'd have got back to the *Southern Cross* somehow.'

'You damned fool!' I shouted at him. 'You don't realize the half of what you've done. The *Southern Cross* came into the ice after us. She was beset and smashed.'

He stared at me. His mouth hung slackly open. 'I

don't believe it,' he cried. 'It isn't true.' And then as I didn't say anything, he added, 'How do you know? Your radio went down with your ship.'

'We had a portable,' I said.

The men were coming into the camp now. I ordered them to start breaking the first boat out. Then I slipped the bolt out of the rifle and threw the weapon into the tent. 'Better get to work, Bland,' I said. 'You're going to help us run these boats back to the camp.'

He didn't say anything. He just stood there. It was as though he couldn't realize the truth of what I'd told him. I went over to help the men. They were hitching the ropes to the first boat and running them out to block and tackle fixed to the anchor bedded in the ice. Bland lumbered across to me and caught hold of my arm.

'Is she sunk?' he demanded hoarsely. The steam of his breath in the cold air smelt of whisky.

'Yes,' I answered.

'Any survivors?'

'We don't know yet. We've had no message since they abandoned ship.'

He suddenly laughed. It was an ugly sound, half drunken, half menacing. 'Nobody will dare come into the ice to rescue us now. We're alone. Alone, out here in the ice. An' it's a damn good thing, too. Damn good thing.'

'Doesn't the loss of that ship mean anything to you?' I demanded angrily.

'Why should it? The insurance people will pay.' He was grinning almost happily.

I fought down a sudden desire to strike him, knock him down and kick him till he understood what he'd done. 'Your father was on that ship,' I reminded him.

'Why should I care about my father? I hardly knew him.' His gaze wandered to the men straining on the rope to break the boat out. He lurched towards them and caught hold of the rope. 'Come on, damn you – pull!' He was like a man suddenly possessed of a devil. 'Come on, Craig,' he shouted. 'Don't stand there gaping. Lend a hand.'

He was like that for perhaps ten minutes whilst we broke both boats out from where they were frozen in. Then the drink died in him and he became morose and sullen. We ran the two boats out of the camp. There were eleven of us with Bland. But though we could shift them all right, it was exhausting work. With the aid of my skis I was able to put my full weight on the rope without breaking through the snow. But the others went through, sometimes up to the waist. It was hopeless. I spliced the forerunners together, ran them out to the anchor with block and tackle, and that's how we got the boats back to Disaster Camp. It was slow work. But it was the only way.

We reached the camp just before ten that night, utterly exhausted. The pain in my side was like the stab of a knife. Gerda had left one tent still standing. We cooked a meal and lay down. No watch was set, for I knew not one of us could stand even half an hour out here in the biting wind.

Three hours later I woke to find Gerda shaking me. 'You must come quickly, Duncan,' she said. Her voice was urgent. 'The icebergs are not more than two miles away and the ice is breaking up.'

I was so tired I did not care if an iceberg crushed the tent with us in it. It seemed easier to die than to go on. I was weak and numbed with the cold and pain. The ice was shuddering under me, yet my heavy eyelids closed and the movement of the ice merged into Gerda shaking me violently. Then my face was being slapped and I was dragged out into the freezing wind. I staggered to my feet then and stood swaying weakly, staring unbelievingly at the cold, ice-clad scene. *Tauer III* was gone. There was no sign of it. And along the trail we'd dragged the boats the ice was heaving like a frozen sea. An iceberg with a tall, jagged spire, like the Pillar Rock, was driving towards us, icy chaos running out ahead of it.

The others were being pulled out of the tent. 'Hurry! Hurry!' Gerda called to them. She had a dozen men with her. They began to move out of the camp, dragging the men from the tent with them.

'Wait!' I called. 'We must take the boats.'

'No,' Gerda shouted at me above the wind. 'We must go quickly or we shall be too late.'

I stared at the iceberg. There seemed little hope whether we stayed here or reached the floe-berg. I pulled myself together. 'Get your men on to the boats,' I ordered her.

She started to argue, but I stopped her. 'With the two crews there are over thirty of us. We need all three boats. If we do escape destruction and we lose these boats, then we are doomed anyway. Better to die with the boats.' I called the men together and there in the ice, with the wind driving right through us, we knelt down and I prayed that we might be delivered from the disaster that threatened. After that the men took up the ropes of the first boat without a word.

I shall never cease to marvel at man's determination to cheat death. It wasn't love of life that drove them out there on the ice. Life wasn't lovely to them then – it was days and days of cold and hunger and exertion stretching ahead of them unendingly. It was their determination not to die. Call it fear if you like. But whatever it was it gave them strength – incredible, fantastic strength – and courage.

With all twenty-two of us tugging on the ropes we'd take one boat in a rush a hundred yards, sometimes two hundred. Then we'd come back and do the same with the other boat. The ice was splitting all round us, the cracks opening like bursts of machine-gun firing. Yet they never hesitated to go back for the second boat and I never had to drive them. Twice men were only saved by the ropes from the opening jaws of the ice. Once we had to rush the second boat across a gap that was half a boat's length in width.

But we did it in the end. And as we dragged the second boat to the foot of the floe-berg, a whole crowd of men came down and took the boats with a rush to the top of the berg. I remember a vague impression of new faces, of soft hands, of another voice taking command in Norwegian, then I had slipped into oblivion.

My return to consciousness was like the slow drag

to the surface of a drowning man. I lay still, panting as though I'd run a race, and listened to the deathly stillness that seemed to surround me. I was stiff and numb. The cold struck through to the very core of me and the pain gripped me every time I breathed. There was a sudden grating roar. It rose till it filled all the place with sound, and terminated in one splitting crash. Was this death? Was this what Milton had tried to portray? The world-shaking sound did not roll on ponderously like thunder. It ceased abruptly. There was no echo. The stillness filled my ears, shutting me in upon my own thoughts. And yet I wasn't alone. There were others near me. I could hear their breathing, feel their faint stirrings. I could smell them, too – the sour odour of men's sweat. I opened my eyes. I was in a world of sepia glory with huddled shapes packed close beside me.

Then I suddenly wanted to laugh. The sepia glory was the sun slanting through brown sail canvas. The men around me were not dead. They were sleeping. I sat up and then I didn't want to laugh any more. I wanted to be sick.

I crawled out of the tent, staggered to my feet in the snow and stood there, retching. The wind was gone. The air was still and all the white, incredible snow-scape steamed in the sun so that the atmosphere was iridescent, impermanent – a water mirror in which nothing was real and every changing form of ice writhed and shimmered in mutability. The sweat broke cold on my forehead. I had nothing to bring up. The retching stopped. And in that moment the dragon's

roar of sound that had invaded the stillness of the tent
came again, terrifyingly loud, like a clarion call of
the Four Horsemen galloping through Hell's gates.
The crash that followed seemed like an atom split. I
straightened my aching side and searched the blinding,
gold-tinted ice for the source of the sound. And I stared
unbelievingly as a block of ice that seemed as big as
the Crystal Palace I'd known as a kid emerged out
of the ice. It opened up like a flower and then fell
crashing, shattered into a million fragments, each prismatic, each an enormous diamond throwing forth
sparks of eye-blinding light. The sound of its fall was
like the end of the world. But no mountain crags sent
the sound reverberating round the heavens. It was a
noise that split the ear-drums and then ceased – ceased
as though there had never been any noise. Stillness
shut down on the ice again and a hand touched my
arm.

'Feeling better?'

I swung round at the voice. The sound of it was
as loud as blasphemy in the stillness of a cathedral. It
was Howe who had spoken. His face was white and
his hand trembled as it held my arm. He was scared.
'Feeling better?' he repeated. And then as I nodded
dumbly he produced a flask. 'Take a swig at this,' he
said. 'It's brandy. Do you good.' I took a pull at the
flask. 'You were all pretty exhausted when you got in
last night.'

I didn't say anything. I was trying to remember
what had happened. Of course, we'd brought the boats
to the floe-berg. There they were, black against the

frozen snow. Four boats and a litter of stores, tents and makeshift sledges. Somebody had stuck a Norwegian flag on an up-ended oar outside one of the tents. The triangle of red with the blue cross hung dejectedly. A splintering shivered the frosty air and behind it sounded the deep, artillery rumble of ice pounded to rubble. Beyond the floe-berg the ice stretched westward in crumpled, jagged folds. And beyond that ploughed-up field of ice was a huge berg. It was a fairy crag, a gigantic, prismatic skyscraper citadel of ice, one pinnacle reaching like the torch of the Statue of Liberty into the gold-shot rainbow of the sky. At its base the ice was moving, turning back on itself, splintering and folding as the wedged cut-water ploughed into the floes. To the north of it was another, and to the south another and another – great masses of shimmering ice.

I shivered and handed Howe back his flask. 'Thanks,' I said. 'Not much future for us, is there?'

'I've worked it out that at its present rate of drift that one over there will be ploughing right through the camp at about midday tomorrow.' His voice was the voice of science, quite unemotional.

'There wasn't much point in shifting our camp, then,' I said wearily.

He shrugged his shoulders. 'If it were just one – ' he began and then again he shrugged his shoulders as though it wasn't any good talking about it. He didn't speak for a moment and when he did his voice was bitter. 'Why couldn't you leave well alone?'

'How do you mean?' I asked.

'Why couldn't you leave him to die in the *Tauer III* camp? I told you not to bring him back.'

'And I told you I'd only abandon him if that was what he wanted.' I felt very tired. 'He didn't want to be left – not when he knew I'd come for the boats.'

'What was he planning to do?'

'The fool thought he'd got a chance of getting away alone in one of the boats. He'd got one of them half decked-in before he started drinking.'

'What happened? Did he lose his nerve?'

'Maybe,' I said. 'Any man would lose his nerve on his own out here, watching those icebergs ploughing into the ice towards him.'

'Why the hell do you waste your sympathy on him?' Howe demanded.

'I'm not wasting my sympathy on him,' I replied wearily. 'I'm just explaining what happened. Where is he now?'

'Over there.' He nodded towards one of the tents. 'Talking to Vaksdal and Keller.' His gloved hand caught hold of my arm. 'Don't you realize what you've done?' His voice was hoarse. 'We're in a bad enough fix without having Bland here. He's a murderer. He knows it and he knows that we know it, too. It's not only Nordahl. There's Raadal and that other poor devil. And all these men here' – he waved his hand round the camp – 'they're all going to die. We're all as good as dead – you and me; Gerda and Judie, too. And why?' His voice was unsteady, almost out of control. 'Because of Bland. But for him we'd have got the crew of *Hval 5* out. Instead we're all locked in the ice and the men of the *Southern Cross* as well. Gerda's beside herself. She's scared for her father. She loved him. And you go and bring Bland back and Gerda has to be a party to his rescue. God, I could have throttled you to see you going out like a bloody little Sir Galahad to rescue a man who's responsible for the killing of nearly five hundred men.'

'I went for the boats,' I reminded him.

'What good are the boats to us?' He stared out across the ice, his hands clenching and unclenching. 'We're going to die and you've forced on me the choice of killing a man or dying with him without doing what I swore I would do.' He paused and then said, 'And if we do get clear of this iceberg, we're going to have trouble with Bland. He's lost his nerve for the moment. But if he can do something to get back his self-confidence, then he'll be dangerous. I'm going to have a word with Peer Larvik.'

'Larvik!' I swung round, not hearing what he replied, seeing four boats where there should only have been three and the Norwegian flag drooping from the up-ended oar. I seized hold of him, shaking him in my sudden excitement. 'Is Larvik here? Have the *Hval 5* crew joined up with us?'

He nodded and I hesitated, steadying myself, conscious of the pulse-beat in my body. 'Judie? Is she all right? Is she here, too?'

He stared at me, astonished. 'Good God! Don't you remember? You collapsed into her arms last night.'

I stood there for a moment, cursing the ice that

made our time so short, cursing myself for bringing her husband back.

'Where is she?' My voice sounded hoarse and unnatural.

'Over there – in Larvik's tent.'

I stood there without moving for quite a while. I was thinking that perhaps it was as well for both of us that we had only a few hours left of life. I bent down and scooped up a handful of snow, rubbing it over my face. I no longer felt weak. I felt strong – strong enough to cheat death and to fight my way out of the ice. And yet it was better this way. I knew that. I walked slowly over to the tent where the Norwegian flag hung and called to her.

In a moment she was out there in the glory of that iridescent sunshine, holding my hands, looking up into my face and smiling and laughing all in one, her eyes gleaming like frosted diamonds. We just stood and looked at each other and laughed with happiness. And then without a word we turned and walked through the powdery snow to the farther edge of the floe-berg and stood and watched the towering cliffs of ice tearing up the floes, not seeing them as death any more, but dominating their terror with our sense of life, so that they were just something exciting to watch. It was as though our love could exorcize the devil of fear. And that's a funny thing. We never had to ask each other about our love – the truth was there in our eyes.

But our moment alone together was very short. Kalstad came up. His round, rather Slavonic face looked worried. 'What's the trouble, Kalstad?' I asked, as he coughed awkwardly.

'It's Vaksdal and Keller,' he said. 'The men do not want them in their tents. They are Sandefjord men, both of them.'

'Good God!' I exclaimed. 'This is no time to worry about whether a man comes from Sandefjord or Tönsberg.'

'Also these two men will not do what I order,' Kalstad added woodenly.

'Then make them.'

'I have tried, but –' Kalstad shrugged his shoulders. 'Vaksdal is a big man and it is no time to fight, I think. Also he is very angry because he is no longer mate.'

'I see. What about Keller?'

'Keller will do what Vaksdal do.'

'All right, bring Vaksdal here.'

Vaksdal was in an ugly mood. I could see that by the morose way he slouched towards me. When he stood in front of me he was a good head taller. 'Kalstad informs me you refuse to obey his orders?' I said.

'*Ja*. It is not right he should give me orders.'

'Did you hear me appoint him mate yesterday?'

'*Ja*.'

'And I reduced you to ordinary seaman for abandoning your boats.'

'Kaptein Bland say you have not the authority to –'

'Damn Bland!' I shouted. 'Bland is –' I stopped then. I was seething with anger. 'You come and talk to Captain Larvik.'

'No.' Judie's hand was on my arm. 'You must not worry Peer Larvik with this, Duncan.'

'It's his responsibility,' I said. 'He's in charge now.'

But she shook her head. 'No. You're in command. Larvik is very ill. His ribs are crushed, and his legs. He got caught between the side of *Hval 5* and the ice. I was just going back to him. I don't think –' She hesitated and there were tears in her eyes. 'I don't think he'll live very long. You must handle this yourself.' She turned then and walked towards the tent where the Norwegian flag hung. I felt suddenly very tired again. So the responsibility was still on my shoulders. I looked up at Vaksdal. 'Have you ever thought what it's like to die?' I asked him.

He looked puzzled. 'No,' he said. 'I do not think about such things.'

'You've never looked death in the face.' I turned him round so that he faced the slow, inevitable advance of the iceberg. 'You are looking at death now,' I said. 'I don't think we have much hope. But so long as we're alive there's still a chance. So long as we're alive and working together. This is no time to cause trouble, is it?'

'I do not begin it,' he growled. 'It is the men who begin it. They are Tönsberg men. Me and Keller, we are from Sandefjord.'

'All right,' I said. 'I'll have a word with the men later. In the meantime have the sense to accept orders. If, when this iceberg has passed, there are any of us alive, then I'll discuss the question of my authority to act as I have done.'

He stared down at me for a moment and then I saw his eyes drawn to the towering bulk of the iceberg, as though it were a magnet. 'All right,' he growled, and turned quickly and went back to Keller who had been standing by the tents watching us.

I crossed the top of the floe-berg where the stores and boats were lashed down and reached the tent with the flag outside. The flap was drawn back and Judie was bent over a figure lying in a huddle of blankets. There was blood on the trodden snow and the man's head that showed in the sunlight over Judie's shoulder was unrecognizable. The blue eyes were sunk deep in their sockets and the lower lip showed red and bloody in the stubble of his beard where the bared teeth had bitten into the flesh with the pain.

Judie looked as my shadow fell across her. 'Is he conscious?' I asked.

She nodded. 'I was just coming to fetch you,' she said. 'He wants to speak to you.' She crawled out of the tent and stood up. 'Don't let him talk for long. He's very weak.'

I bent down and sat myself in the doorway of the tent. 'Judie says you want to see me,' I said.

'Craig?' The voice was very faint.

'Yes,' I said.

'Come nearer, please.' I slithered into the tent, and then I knew he was going to die. The tent smelt of rotting flesh, even with the tent flap pulled back and the cold air circulating. It was gangrene. 'You can smell my legs, eh?' There was no fear in his voice and his eyes were quite steady. 'Judie has done her best, but it will not be long now.' He said something else, but it was lost in a crash of splintering ice so loud that it seemed just outside the tent. His hand came out from under the blankets and fastened on my shoulder. It was grey and the veins and knotted muscles stood out like cords in the wasted flesh. 'You are in command now. You must get them out of the ice. There is not much hope, but – ' He gnawed at his lip, fighting the pain. 'What are you going to do?' he asked at length.

'We could start trekking,' I said. 'Now the wind has dropped, the westward thrust of the ice seems to be lessening. If we left now, we might be able to keep ahead of this iceberg.'

He shook his head slowly. 'No good,' he said. 'If you leave here, how do you live? How do you finally escape without the boats? I hear what you do yesterday. Gerda tell me. You know that there is only hope so long as you have the boats.' For a while he lay still without speaking, staring out through the open tent to the scintillating mass of the berg grinding its way towards us. 'If it is only one berg, per'aps south or north. But here it is a line. Also it is not good to retreat. It is not good for morale.' He turned his head towards me and I saw that his eyes were excited. 'I think you must advance, eh? That will have better appeal to the men, you know.'

I suppose my face must have shown that I was mystified, for his grip tightened on my shoulder. 'All morning I am lying here with nothing to do but look out of the tent. Look!' He nodded through the open tent flap. 'Do you not see something, on the berg to the south? There is a ledge there. It slope up like a ramp. I have look at him through the glasses. If you can transfer the camp to that ledge – '

'But it's impossible,' I said.

He shrugged his shoulders. 'It is difficult. But nothing is impossible. As you say, the rate of advance of the iceberg is becoming more slow. Already it is breaking the ice up more gently. Our camp here is a small berg. The icefloes round us will be broken up. We shall be thrown about, but perhaps we do not break entirely. Perhaps we are for a little while close to the ledge. With God's help we may get there. You are a sensible man. You think to bring forerunners and tackle. I also bring my forerunners. I think we have a chance. It is a very small chance, but it is the only one.' He looked at me quickly. 'You agree?'

I didn't say anything for a moment. I stared at the foot of the iceberg where it ploughed into the floes. It was less than a mile away now. I'd once seen lava engulfing a village – that was when my corvette was in the Bay of Naples and Vesuvius was in eruption. The iceberg was advancing at about the same speed and though it was as cold as the lava had been hot, it had the same slow, ponderous inevitability of destruction about it. It was advancing at the rate of about two hundred yards an hour directly towards us. For a mile or more to right and left of it the ice was in a state of chaos, the floes being splintered, broken up and layered. The outer fringe of this area of chaos was the worst, for there the chaos of one iceberg met the chaos of the next and all was a confusion of up-ended floes and great slabs of ice tossed in the air like snowballs. Nowhere could I see a floe-berg as substantial as the one we were on, and as the chaos was worse at the sides of the iceberg than in front of it, there seemed just the barest chance, for we were in the direct path of its advance. At least the idea of riding the source of the destruction appealed to me in its daring. I nodded. 'At any rate it gives us something to try for.'

'Something to try for.' Larvik nodded slowly. He looked drained of life and I realized that I'd let him exhaust himself. 'Something to try for,' he said again, his voice scarcely audible. Then he seemed to rally. He patted my arm. 'When you are on his back, he will be your horse and you can laugh when he charge the ice. Perhaps he – break a way out for you.' He closed his eyes. I stayed there beside him for a little longer, then as he still lay motionless with his eyes closed, I began to slide out of the tent. But his hand moved on my arm. 'Is Bland there?' he asked. His voice was thick as though his throat were clogged with blood.

'Yes,' I said. 'Do you want to speak to him?'

He didn't answer for a moment. Then he said, 'No. I do not think I am strong enough to say what I should wish.' He coughed and writhed in agony. I held his hand till he was quiet again. 'Whatever I may think of Old Bland, he is a man. This pup of his has gone wrong. He is dangerous, Craig. Judie is now the biggest shareholder in the company. Bernt Nordahl leave her everything. I know because I witness the will. Look after her, my friend. And see that Erik Bland does not get out of the ice alive. You understand?' His sunken eyes stared at me. 'Promise you – ' His voice was too faint for me to hear the rest. His eyes were gazing urgently into mine.

I knew what he wanted. But I couldn't promise that, so I slid quietly out of the tent. Judie was waiting for me. 'You've been a long time,' she said. 'Is he all right?'

'He's very weak,' I told her.

Her face looked small and unhappy. 'I am afraid he will not last the night.' She crawled into the tent then and I turned and stared at the giant iceberg, searching that ledge. It started right at the base of the berg and sloped gently up till it merged into the cliff of ice that formed the side about fifty feet above the surrounding pack. There was just a chance, I felt. Just the slightest chance. And I prayed that Larvik, who had given us this chance, would live to reach that ledge.

I got the men together then and told them the plan.

It appealed to them. Anything positive would have appealed to them and they threw themselves into the work of preparation with an enthusiasm that was derived as much from a desire to blot out the fear that was in them as from any sense of hope. Forerunners were thawed of ice and spliced together in long lines. Anchor stakes were prepared and sliding tackle rigged. Boat slings were fitted. Stores were packed and secured in bundles, for the idea was that boats and stores should be run out to the ledge on the iceberg on the life-line and bos'n's chair principle. But as the day wore on and the iceberg came nearer to our camp, I noticed the men glancing over their shoulders at it with a scared look in their faces.

By evening the work was done. Only the tents and immediate stores were left unpacked. After the evening meal there was nothing for the men to do. No one felt like sleep and they stood about on the ice in groups, gazing with awe at the towering mass of ice. It loomed over the camp like death in visible form. The noise of the floes being crushed and thrust aside as it advanced was incessant – a grinding rumble, penetrated by sharp, splintering cracks. Wonderful golden bars radiated from the sun's gleaming centre of light low to the south and from a fabulous mock sun much higher in the sky. The light glistened on crags of ice a hundred feet and more high. In the shadows, the naked ice, sheer in places like a glass wall, was a cold green or colder blue. But where the sun bars struck it, its surface gleamed like burnished metal, mirroring the prismatic and uncertain lights of the sky.

Our camp became as cold as death. The men's eyes shied at the blinding scintillation of the sunny side of the berg and turned more and more often to the green and blue of the shadows where glacial jaws gaped black and the spilling wave-crests of ice were cold and remote. They'd stand and gaze at the shadowed flank for a moment, their mouths agape and their faces awestruck. Then they'd turn with a shiver of cold and slink into the tents for warmth. But no one could sleep and soon they'd be out again to stare, fascinated by the inevitability of the end.

Bland kept mostly to his tent. Vaksdal and Keller

had erected one against some packing cases and he had moved in with them. I suppose I should have discouraged his association with his two mates, but there seemed no point. On the few occasions I saw him outside the tent, he was alone. He seemed to have withdrawn into a sullen, brooding mood so that he scarcely noticed anyone around him. I can't really recall how much the men knew or had been told about his part in the business. Our own men at any rate must have suspected that he'd rammed us deliberately. In other circumstances they might have killed him. As it was, the iceberg and the approach of death dominated everything. Only once did any incident occur.

It was in one of the rare moments when Judie wasn't looking after Larvik. We were sitting together on the edge of one of the boats. Gerda and Howe were standing at the edge of the floe-berg gazing towards the sun. They were holding each other's hands. As they turned back towards the camp, Bland came out of his tent. Howe stopped at the sight of him. His face was tense. Then he let go of Gerda's hand and went towards Bland.

He passed right by us. He was crying and there was a strange desperate look of longing on his face. Bland saw him coming and stopped, his eyes narrowing and his body stiffening. Judie's hand tightened on my arm. Howe looked so puny as he faced Bland. I got up. Howe might have a gun. He might have screwed up his courage to kill him. And if he hadn't, then I could see him being hurt. Bland could break him as easily as he could snap a twig.

But as I rose, Gerda ran past me. She caught Howe by the arm and dragged him away from Bland. As she brought him back, leading him by the hand, his face was horribly convulsed and there was an air of bitterness and frustration about him that was quite frightening.

Judie's hand slipped into mine. 'He is tearing himself apart,' she whispered. 'Oh, how I wish they could live!'

I glanced down at her. 'Do you think they would be happy?' I asked.

'Yes, I think perhaps they might,' she answered. She sighed and gave a little shrug. 'Poor Gerda – it's the maternal instinct with her. With Walter it's different. He's in love. I think he's found happiness for the first time in his life. That's what is tearing him apart. He wants to live – and kill.' She sighed again and added, 'I think it might have worked out very well.'

'Why the devil doesn't he enjoy the fact that he's alive and Gerda is with him?' I said.

She was silent for a moment. Then she said, 'If we ever reach that ledge, Duncan, you must have a trial at once. The men must know the truth. I wish you hadn't – ' She stopped short and I said: 'Hadn't what?'

'No,' she answered. 'I must not wish that. But he frightens me.'

I knew that what she was wishing was that I hadn't brought Bland back from the *Tauer III* camp. She wanted her husband dead and I could understand how she felt. I remember thinking: *Well, we'll all be dead soon. It doesn't matter.* I'd no real hope of our getting across that litter of broken ice on to the ledge. The mere sight of it appalled me, knowing that sooner or later I had got to attempt to cross it.

'But it doesn't matter now,' Judie said suddenly. 'Nothing matters now except that we are together – for a little.'

Judie had all the realism of her sex. She was not buoyed up by any preposterous illusion of hope. She saw the inevitable and accepted it. She made no attempt to bolster up her courage with the idea that we could cheat the death that stared us in the face from those glass-hard cliffs of ice. Her attitude affected me in a strange way. Instead of being scared, I, too, felt acceptance of the inevitable. And I almost welcomed it. To go like this – loving someone and loved by some-one; it was sublime. In that bitter cold there was no suggestion of passion. I can't explain it quite – but if we have souls then it was the merging of our two souls. In that twilight evening of death our love was out of this world. We were two people wanting to pass over into the beyond together.

I have often wondered since what Bland's feelings about Judie really were. The fact that he threatened me through her that time I went across to *Tauer III* is no indication. And anyway love and hate are never far apart. But I remember one occasion that evening when the man's feelings blazed through the sullen façade he'd erected as a barrier between himself and the people round him. It does not answer the question, but I think I should record it and the reaction it pro-duced in Judie.

It was towards midnight and she and I were watching the sun sweep low in the egg-shell pale sky to the south. Standing there I was suddenly conscious of being watched. Judie must have felt it, too, because she turned as I did. Bland was standing outside his tent. He was standing quite still about twenty yards from us. His face was heavy and brooding. There was something in his features, in the way he stood, that reminded me of his father. Our eyes met and I remember I was shocked to see such a violence of hatred. I have never, thank God, had a man look at me like that before or since. It was the look of the lone wolf – the rogue male – barred from the pack and bitter with the thought of what others enjoyed. It was bitterness and frustration turned to hate. But whether it indicated a depth of feeling for Judie that she was unaware of I do not know.

But I do know that she saw it and recognized it, for her fingers caught at my arm and as we turned back towards the sun her face looked white. 'You must be careful,' she said, and her voice trembled. She glanced quickly over her shoulder. Bland had gone back to his tent. 'Erik is dangerous,' she added. And then, 'I must go and see my patient.' She turned quickly away towards Larvik's tent.

The cold became intense that night. A very slight breath of air came out of the west and the thermometer fell as it brought into the camp the chill ice temperature of the berg. The hours passed vaguely as in a dream. The camp was restless and for the first time since we'd abandoned ship the men on watch had company.

There is a strange fascination about death. No one likes it to catch him unawares. And inside the tents the noise and the quaking of the ice seemed magnified so that one lay in a sort of tense expectancy of fear, the berg growing in one's imagination to undreamed-of heights and toppling down on the flimsy sepia curtain of canvas. It was a relief then to go out and see the real height of the berg and mark how slowly it ground its way towards us.

But though it might come slowly when we watched it, when we ignored it for a moment and looked again, we'd realize with horror how swift in terms of the future that advance was. The ledge on the south side gleamed clear and bright like a ramp leading to heaven in some super colossal colour-film monstrosity. But I don't think any of us had any hope of reaching it. Between us and that ledge was a slowly closing gap of moving ice. There were great crevasses that opened and closed with a snap, floes that stood on end, all jagged, and then sank slowly beneath the heaving mass, and huge blocks of ice that were spewed up and fell crashing on to the floes. And where the sheer prow of the iceberg crushed its way through the pack there was a moving wave of ice that looked like powdered glass, and along the flanks of the berg ran a black line in which water splashed, catching the sun on its green crests.

I wasn't scared. At least it didn't seem like fear to me then. The scene was so stupendous as to seem remote and unreal. I felt like a spectator. And I knew I should go on feeling like a spectator until the moment when I had to cross the gap and the ice overwhelmed me.

NINE

Most of you who read this will have faced death at one time or another. You'll know how it feels. The car coming at you on the wrong side of the road produces the same reaction as high explosive whistling down at you from the sky. There is the tensing of the nerves, the sudden photographic clarity of vision. But no fear. That comes later when nerves stretched beyond endurance relax, leaving you shivering with the reaction. It is the same, only more prolonged, with the man going into battle. He is tensed up, ready for it – and when it comes he conquers fear. And afterwards he is limp, exhausted. But when death comes slowly and inevitably, then the nervous tension cannot be sustained. That's when men crack. It's like battle exhaustion. Men can't go on facing death indefinitely. If the period is too sustained then the nervous reaction sets in before the moment of impact. Then comes fear – naked, uncontrolled fear.

That's what happened at our camp the morning the iceberg reached us.

Just after six Judie crawled into my tent. Her eyes were very large and dark-ringed. She looked exhausted. 'Duncan. Will you come, please. I think he's gone.'

I followed her to Larvik's tent. There was no sun that morning. A grey wrack of cloud drifted up and the wind was rising out of the sou'west. It was gloomy in the tent and I could hardly see Larvik's bearded face. His body was cold and when I became accustomed to the gloom I saw that his eyes were glazed. I pulled a blanket over him.

Outside the tent I saw that many of the men had come out of their tents. They were watching us furtively and there was an air of tension over the camp. It was as though they had sensed death. 'How shall we bury him?' Judie asked.

'Leave him where he is,' I said.

'But we must have a service for him.'

'No,' I answered harshly. She started to argue and I said, 'Look at the men. They're scared enough as it is without knowing that Larvik is dead.'

She turned and looked round the camp. I could see there were tears in her eyes. 'For God's sake don't cry,' I said sharply. 'They mustn't know. Do you understand?'

I saw her bite her lip. Then she looked at me and nodded. 'Yes, I understand. I think he will understand, too.'

I turned away then and shouted for the stewards to get a meal ready.

That meal was the best they could devise. But the men were silent and tense as they ate in their tents. And when it was finished they were out again in the open, staring at the crumbling ice.

It is frightful to think that you have had your last meal. The advance of the berg was as inevitable as the hangman's rope after the final breakfast. There was nothing I could give the men to do. They stood around in little groups staring at the berg, and occasionally their eyes wandered to Larvik's tent where the Norwegian flag still flew.

The prow of the iceberg was not three hundred yards from us now. And behind the prow the ice towered up and up in sheer crags of blue and green, cold and still, until it lost itself in the clouds. Losing its top like that in the clouds made it far more terrifying. It added to its stature.

The noise of the shattering ice was so loud that we had to shout if we wanted to make ourselves heard. The floe-berg was quivering. It was like being on a ship battered by giant seas. We could actually see the ice shaking. The boats rocked and the packing cases tied together rolled over. Our floe was like an island in the midst of chaos. All round us the ice was breaking up now. We were right in the thick of what we had been watching for so long. And in a little while I should be down in that maelstrom, fighting to get a rope across to the ledge. I felt fear gripping at me.

The moment of panic came when a floe between us and the berg split across with an earsplitting crackle. The half nearest us reared up, turning slowly on to its back. For a moment it seemed poised above us, forty or fifty feet high. Then it came crashing down. Its edge splintered on the forward ledge of our refuge. A piece of ice as large as a barn door knocked one of the *Hval 5* men flying. A great chunk was torn off our floe-berg. For a moment the sea boiled back. Then the gap closed, the floes rushing together, grinding and tearing at each other in their effort to get relief from the frightful pressure. It was a stampede of ice.

No one moved for a moment. We were stunned by the terrible power of the forces at work. Then Hans suddenly screamed. It was a high-pitched rabbit scream. The boy turned like a hunted hare and began to run. The men watched him for a second, immobile, fascinated. Then one of them also began to run, and in a second half the crews were following the boy.

I started forward to stop them, but Vaksdal was before me. He caught the first man and knocked him cold with one blow of his huge fist. And he got Hans – scooped the boy up with one hand and turned to face the break. The men stopped. They were breathing heavily. They stood watching him for a moment like cattle that have been headed. Then they turned and shuffled shamefacedly back towards the camp.

I met them as they came back. I realized that it was now or never. If I waited any longer their morale would be too low to make the effort. I couldn't talk to them because of the noise of the splintering ice. But I gathered them all round me and knelt down on the ice. They knelt down, all of them, and every man as he knelt turned so that he faced the advance of the berg. And as we knelt there I felt that comforting sense of oneness develop in us – oneness of purpose in adversity. I stared at the two-hundred-yard gap of jagged, surging ice that I'd have to cross, and then I looked at Judie. Her eyes met mine and smiled. And I felt sure of myself again. I could face it, whatever it was to be.

I got up from the ice and called out to the men that the moment for action had come, that now we were going to attack the berg itself. Judie was close beside me and I heard her say, 'Who makes the first attempt?'

'Vaksdal and I,' I answered.

I looked at her quickly. She nodded as though she had braced herself for that. I shouted to Kalstad and he brought the ropes. I don't know whether Bland knelt in prayer with the crews as they pressed round me. I remember his eyes were feverishly bright, a brightness that seemed a queer mixture of fear and excitement.

The ropes were coiled down on the ice at the side of the camp nearest the berg. I took the two ends and shouted for Vaksdal. He came forward sullenly. I handed him the end of one of the ropes. He hesitated. His eyes were angry. For a moment I thought he was going to refuse. 'Because of the boats,' I shouted at him. I don't know whether it was because he recognized the justice of my choice or because he was afraid of being regarded as a coward, but he took the rope and began to tie it round his body. I took the other rope and we went to the edge of the floe where the ice dropped in a steep slide to the quivering pack. Judie came up to me and kissed me. Then she took the rope and began to tie it round my body.

But as she started to tie it, there was a sudden surge in the crowd and she was swept aside. The rope was whipped away from me and Erik Bland slipped over the edge on to the pack ice below. He held the rope in his hand and I can see him now as he looked up at me with a sort of crazy grin, tying the rope round his waist and calling to Vaksdal to come. I seized hold of the rope to haul him back. Whatever relief I automatically might feel was swallowed in my instant realization of the danger of such an indisciplined action. But as I reached for the rope Howe gripped my arm. 'Let him go!' he shouted. 'Let him go, I tell you!' The scream of his voice was loud in a sudden, unnerving silence. As I hesitated, I saw relief and satisfaction in his eyes. He was convinced that whoever tried to make the crossing would die.

In that instant of hesitation I lost my one chance of stopping Bland, for as I reached for the rope again I saw it uncoiling steadily. Down on the ice Vaksdal and Bland were going forward together. And then I saw that Bland was wearing crampons. Where he'd got them from I don't know. But the fact that he was wearing them made it clear that his action wasn't done on the spur of the moment. This was what he'd planned to do. I looked round at the men. They were watching him intently and in some of their eyes I caught a glint of admiration. McPhee and Kalstad were paying out line. Bonomi was moving excitedly from one position to another taking photographs.

Down on the pack the two men were moving into the broken ice. Trailing the slender lines, they climbed out on to the edge of a floe that was slowly being tilted. They dropped from view. The floe rose almost vertical, hiding them. Then it broke across and subsided into the ice, showing us Vaksdal leaping in great bounds from one precarious foothold to another. Bland was lying flat, clinging to the edge of a floe which was slowly being ground to powder. I thought for a moment he was injured. But he pulled the rope into a coil beside him, gathered himself together and leapt for a block of ice no bigger than one of our boats. He was up and following Vaksdal now from one foothold to another.

They got within twenty feet or so of the ledge and there they paused, facing a gap full of powdered ice in which the sea sometimes showed. Vaksdal coiled his rope and leapt. For a moment I thought he'd made it. But the ice received his weight like a bog. In an instant he was up to his knees. Then he was floundering full length, with only the upper half of his body visible. He was within two yards of the ledge, but it might have been two miles for all the chance he had of reaching it. He was rolled over in the grey stream. His mouth was a dark gap in the blond of his beard as he cried out something or screamed with pain. We could hear nothing but the splitting and grinding of the ice.

Bland hesitated, staring at Vaksdal and coiling his rope. Then he backed away and started to run. Judie's fingers dug into my arm. Whatever she might think of him now, Erik Bland was after all a part of her life. Instead of jumping, he flung himself full length in a beautiful diving tackle. His impetus carried him half across the gap, his body sliding on the surface of the ice. Then he was clawing forward, his arms working like a swimmer doing the crawl. His body didn't sink, and foot by foot his arms dragged him across.

Then at last he was standing on the ledge itself and was hauling Vaksdal up after him. The men cheered wildly as the two men stood together on the ledge. They were symbols of renewed hope. They represented Life. Bland looked across at the cheering men. My eyes, weakened by the constant glare of the past few days, couldn't make out the expression of his face. But it looked as though he were grinning. Well, he'd a right to grin. And the men were right to cheer. He'd done a pretty brave thing. But Howe was screaming in my ear, 'He's laughing at us. He's on his own now. That's what he wanted.'

I brushed him aside, shouting to Dahle, first mate of *Hval 5*, whom I'd put in charge of loading, to get tools and anchors across. The men tied them to the rope and as they were hauled across the two-hundred-yard gap Howe was pulling at my sleeve and yelling, 'He'll abandon us, I tell you.'

'Don't be a fool,' I snapped. 'He can't do anything without boats and stores.'

'Well, get across yourself with the first batch of men.'

I shook my head angrily. The loading plan was all arranged – one boat, stores, then a dozen men. The process to be repeated until boats, stores and men had all been transported to the ledge. And now that Bland had done the job of getting the ropes across, as leader I was bound to be the last man to leave the camp.

Vaksdal and Bland were working like mad to fix the anchors firmly. As soon as this was done and the rope set up, the first boat was run across. Owing to the movement of the berg towards us, the rope sagged and we had to have men constantly swinging on it. About the middle the boat was bumping dangerously on the ice, and just before it reached the ledge one of the two anchors broke out. Fortunately the other anchor held and the boat was got safely to the ledge. But this and the constant slackening of the rope made me realize that more men were required on the ledge at once and that it was there that the major difficulties would be experienced. As the slings were hauled back I gave the order for the first batch of men to go, instead of stores, which were next on the loading table.

Gerda came across to me as the men were getting into the slings. 'I think you should be there, Duncan,' she shouted. 'It is important nothing go wrong at that end.'

I didn't like the idea of being one of the first across, but I had already reached the conclusion that I should be there. I ordered Dahle to assume command of the rear party and took the place of one of the men in the slings. We also hitched on the two remaining anchors.

It was a strange experience crossing that surging gap of ice supported only by a single sagging rope. The lines, as I have said, could not be kept sufficiently taut, and when we reached the centre the sag was so great that our feet were dancing on the moving surface of the ice. This would have been all right except that a floe split open as we were crossing it and rose on end so that for a moment it completely over-topped us and looked as though it would carry away the ropes and ourselves with it. However, it slid back under the ice and we made the ledge with nothing worse than sore buttocks where the rope slings had cut into our flesh.

With the extra personnel and anchors, we soon had both lines set up securely and began to ferry the stores across. I had arranged the order of transhipment very carefully, so that should the ice split the party at any time, each section would have its proper complement of boats and stores.

It was whilst we were hauling the second boat across that the movement of the old camp on the floe in relation to the iceberg first became really noticeable. We were using both ropes for the boats now, for greater safety. As we started to haul across, these ropes, instead of sagging, seemed to get tauter, till they were stretched like slender threads. We brought the boat over with a rush and slackened off. We were only just in time. Another minute and the lines would have carried away. What had happened was that the floe-berg had been caught in a sort of eddying out-thrust of ice and was moving steadily outwards, away from the berg.

With the arrival of the next party, I hacked a bollard out of a block of ice nearby and had the ends of the rope run through blocks and round this ice-bollard with men tagging on the ends. It meant a delay, but I was glad I had done it, for when we resumed operations it became clear at once that the floe-berg was beginning to show considerable movement. It was now no longer on the starboard bow of the iceberg, so to speak. It was abeam of the ledge and beginning to feel the bow-wave effect of the ice being thrown about by the berg's advance. One moment the men on the ropes would be right close to the bollard; the next they would be hauling back up the slope of the ledge. Then again, they'd be coming down and letting out rope. They acted like the accumulators in a catcher, moving back and forth along the slope according to the strain on the lines.

At length we were hauling in the last boat. As it came in to the ledge the men on the ropes came down with a run, paying out line as fast as they could let it through their hands. We swung the boat down on to the ledge. Somebody shouted to me. A rope-end went trailing over the edge. I glanced quickly across at the huddle of dark figures in the ice. They were standing, staring towards us, quite motionless. All the stores had been cleared. There was just the rearguard – Dahle and five of the *Hval 5* crew. The floe on which they stood was being whirled away from us, caught in a gigantic surge of ice. We flung our weight on the last remaining rope. But it was no good. It was dragged from our hands by forces that were far beyond our puny strength. The end of it trailed over on to the ice and we could do nothing but stand and watch that little group of figures alone in a heaving chaos.

I put my arm round Judie's shoulders. She was standing very tense, her face quite white and her whole body trembling. Her lips moved in agitated prayer. The floe-berg on which Dahle and his companions were marooned was turning slowly round and round, as though it were at the very centre of a revolving whirlpool in the ice. Then it seemed to rise up, caught between opposing forces. A moment later it split. The noise was like a battery of heavies firing and was clearly audible above the thunder of sound all round us. One or two of the men abandoned their shattered ice island and began floundering towards us across the churning ice. But their starting point in relation to the iceberg was very different to what it had been when Bland and Vaksdal had made the crossing. They were right in the broken ice now. They hadn't a chance.

Through my glasses I could see only three men standing near where our camp had been. One was Dahle. The remains of the floe-berg, now a block no bigger than a large house, began to roll. The three men scrambled and clawed their way across the ice, fighting to keep on the uppermost side.

It was horrible, standing there watching them go like that, especially as I should have been one of them. The *Hval 5* men had volunteered to be in the rear party. But I felt very upset, all the same. Judie must have understood my mood, for her hand gripped my arm as I stood staring out across the ice. 'It's not your fault,' she said.

'If we'd been quicker,' I answered. 'If we'd started on the job a few minutes earlier.' Three or four minutes more would have seen those six men with us on the ledge. I turned away angrily. No good brooding over it. There was work to be done and I set about the task of organizing the new camp.

I detailed a dozen men to cut a way through the jagged ice of the ledge and drag the boats up as far as possible. Then I turned to get the stores secured and the tents pitched. And as I turned Bland came towards me. I hadn't really noticed him since reaching the ledge. There had been too much to do. But now, as he approached me, he seemed to have an air of truculence, and there was something about his eyes – a queer sort of confidence, something like a sneer. He was somehow different. He'd lost the dazed look. He came right over to me and stopped in front of me. 'I want a word with you, Craig,' he said. There was a sudden authority in his tone that stopped me in my tracks. He had spoken loudly and I saw several of the men stop work to watch us.

'Well?' I asked.

'In future you'll keep away from my wife,' he said.

'That's for her to decide,' I answered, trying to keep the anger I felt out of my voice.

'It's an order,' he said.

I stared at him. 'The hell it is,' I said. 'Get to work on the boats, Bland.'

He shook his head, grinning. I saw the fever of excitement in his eyes. 'You don't give orders here.' And then in a moment of quiet he said, 'Mister Craig. Please understand that, now that Larvik is dead, I am in command.' He swung round on the men, who were all watching us now. 'In the absence of my father I shall, of course, take command here as his deputy. As commander I brought the ropes across. Craig, as second-in-command, should have remained with the rear party as I instructed, but –' He shrugged his shoulders. 'As a newcomer to the company,' he said

to me, 'you will realize that you are too inexperienced to have any sort of command in a situation like
this.' He turned abruptly and strode towards the men.
There was almost a swagger in the way he walked.

I just stood there for a moment without moving. I
was too amazed by the absurdity of the thing to make
a move. I remember thinking: *Howe was right. He's
got back his confidence. Nordahl's death, the ramming
– he's forgotten it all.* And I cursed myself for not
realizing he was dangerous.

He began shouting orders at the men. I saw the
amazement I felt written on their faces. But they were
overawed by the terror of their surroundings. They
would follow any leader, so long as he led. I started
forward, and as I came up to Bland I heard him
announce the reinstatement of Vaksdal and Keller as
mates. He gave an order. The men hesitated. Their
eyes shifted to me. Bland turned. The sneer was gone
now. But the truculence was still there. I ordered him
to pick up one of the packing cases. His eyes shifted
quickly from me to the men. Another instant and he'd
believe what he wanted to believe – that he was not
responsible for the predicament we were in. That mad
scramble across the ice had almost wiped any sense of
guilt from his mind. And as he didn't move when I
repeated the order, I knew there was only one thing to
do. 'McPhee. Kalstad.' The two *Hval 4* men moved
forward. 'Arrest that man,' I ordered. And then, turning quickly to Bland, I said, 'Erik Bland, you are
charged with the murder of Bernt Nordahl and also
with the deliberate ramming of *Hval 4*, an action

which caused the immediate death of two men and which may be responsible for all our deaths. You will be held and committed for trial when and if we ever reach civilization.'

I was watching his eyes all the time as I spoke. For a moment, they had a wild, almost hunted look. Then he laughed. 'You can't get away with this, Craig,' he shouted. 'First you try to steal my wife, now you try to get control of the company through her.'

I called to two or three of the *Hval 4* men and with Kalstad and McPhee moved in to get him. I knew just what he was capable of now and I was taking no more chances. I wanted him secured. He watched us approach and I thought for a moment he was going to fight. His face was very white under his brown beard and his eyes shifted uneasily from side to side.

Then suddenly he turned and slithered down the ice of the ledge. A man-hunt wasn't going to be good for morale, but I was determined to get him. I sent Kalstad and the rest after him. He had stopped at one of the packing cases that had apparently been burst open with a pick. I thought we'd mastered him without the sordid business of a fight. I had turned back to speak with the men, when Howe gave a shout of warning. As I swung round, Bland was lifting a rifle out of the broken packing case.

Kalstad started to run towards him. Then he and the men behind him checked suddenly. Bland had the gun cocked and levelled straight at them. He was laughing at them. A shot rang out close behind me. I turned to find Vaksdal struggling with Howe. Vaksdal had hold of his arm, and as he twisted it back the gloved fingers released the weapon. It fell to the ice. For a moment there was a glint of nickel-plating slithering down the ramp, then it disappeared over the edge.

Bland was coming up the ledge now, and he was driving the *Hval 4* men back at the point of his gun. He was immensely pleased with himself. You could see it by the gleam in his eyes and the way he walked. He bunched all the survivors together. None of us hesitated to obey. His eyes were narrowed and cold, and his manner and the way he held the rifle made it clear that he would not hesitate to use it.

He called Vaksdal and Keller over to him. They hesitated uncertainly. Bland as the son of the chairman of the company was one thing. Bland with a gun another. But they went down to him all the same. He spoke in Norwegian. They looked at me and then began muttering amongst themselves. 'He tell them it is safe to have only one leader,' Gerda translated for me. 'That he is in command and that it is mutiny if they do not obey him.'

The thing had got to be stopped at once. I called out to the men. And then Judie's hands were tugging at my arm. Bland was yelling at me to shut up. He had the gun to his shoulder and was aiming straight at me. 'Keep quiet, Duncan,' Judie pleaded. 'He will shoot. There is plenty of time.'

Howe, just behind me, said, 'We've got to get his gun.'

As we hesitated, one or two of the men moved

down the slope of the ledge towards Bland. In an instant they would all go. They needed a leader. Bland had a gun and the will to use it. It seems incredible now. But out there on that ledge in that chaotic wilderness of ice it didn't seem so incredible. The law of the wild holds good when it comes to pitting your puny strength against the violence of nature. If we could stop the men, isolate Bland and his two mates, then the sheer threat of our numbers would wear him down. I started forward. If I got killed – well, it was just too bad. In the moment of horror the men might rush him then.

But just as I moved out to stop what had begun to look like a general movement towards Bland, Gerda rushed past me. She stopped, facing the men with her back to Bland. Her small, bulky figure blocked their way down the ledge and she poured a flood of Norwegian at them, her eyes bright, her face flushed. The men stopped. She was telling them the truth now and the men growled angrily.

I glanced at Bland. He had lowered the gun. He was sane enough to realize that if he shot her the men would kill him. But he was coming up the slope, his face white and convulsed with rage. I called to Gerda to look out. But she kept on speaking. Bland struck her from behind, stunning her with one blow of his hand across the nape of her neck. Howe gave an inarticulate cry and ran forward. Judie clutched him, but too late. He flung himself shrieking on Bland, who met him with a jab of the rifle barrel to his stomach. And as Howe folded up, he brought his knee up sharply so that his head jerked back. Bland caught him as he slipped to the ice. I heard him shout something about wanting to do it for a long time, and he smashed his fist into the wretched man's face. Howe's face looked dazed and a gush of blood shone very crimson against the white of the snow. His knees gave and suddenly he was a crumpled bundle of clothing lying on the ice. Bland kicked him viciously, his gun ready, waiting for the first man to break and rush at him. He was grinning all the time.

I felt Judie stiffen beside me. This was the real Bland. This was the Bland she knew – the man who admired the Nazis and their methods. And seeing him kicking at Howe's senseless body, I knew that none of us would get out of the ice alive; not unless we killed Bland first. God! How I wished I'd never gone back to the *Tauer III* camp for the boats.

For a moment he was lost to everything but the pleasure of taking it out of Howe. We might have rushed him then. But I think we were all too astonished at the sudden display of violence. And by the time we had started to move in on him, the moment was gone. He checked us with the gun. And then he began talking to the men. And as he talked to them I realized how he had been able to pull the wool over Eide's eyes. It was impossible to believe that a moment before he'd been kicking a senseless man. With the gun in his hand and the memory of that dash across the ice to the ledge, he had complete confidence in himself. His manner was a queer mixture of the arrogance of the leader and the almost boyish excitement of the adventurer. 'He's trying to persuade the men to desert us,' Judie said.

I'd already realized that. 'You must do something,' she added: 'They may follow him if we don't do something to stop them.'

But it was no good my talking to them. The weakness of my position was that I was an outsider. And though I didn't understand what Bland was saying, I knew from the contemptuous way in which he mentioned my name that he was using that fact to sway the men. 'You talk to them,' I said. 'They're all of them Tönsberg men. Talk to them about your father.'

She stared at me in surprise. And then very reluctantly, as she saw I wouldn't move, she stepped forward. Her face was very white. It was hard for her. The man was her husband and she had to tell the men that he'd murdered her father. She began to speak, her voice clear even above the growl and thunder of the ice. For a moment she and Bland were talking at the same time. Then the attention of the men became riveted on her. Bland hesitated and then stopped speaking. The boyish arrogance gradually slipped from his manner. His eyes shifted uneasily from the men to Judie and back again to the men. His grip on his gun tightened as an angry murmur rose from them.

Then suddenly he shouted an order. His voice was crisp and hard. He was calling on the men to follow him. They talked uncertainly among themselves for a moment. Then they were silent. He called to them again. But no one moved. 'All right,' he shouted at them in English. 'Have it your own way then. Stay with Craig and see where it lands you.' He turned to me. 'They're your responsibility now, Craig.' He drew a line with the heel of his boot across the ice of the ledge. 'You'll camp above this line. Any mutineer that crosses this line will be shot. Understand? You'll be issued with tents and stores. Once a day, at midday, you'll send two men to collect rations. Bonomi.'

The little Italian started. '*Si, signore.*'

'Can you cook?'

'A leetle. But I am not –'

'You'll cook for the officers then. Go down and report to Vaksdal. The rest of you get back up the ledge. Go on. Get moving.' He made a threatening gesture with the gun. '*Go an. Go an.*' I could almost hear the Nazi *Raus! Raus!* echoing the violence of his voice.

'What about the boats?' I asked.

Bland looked at me. He was breathing heavily and his eyes were bright. He no longer looked in the least boyish. He had the mean look of something that's been cornered. 'The boats will remain with me. I'll look after them for you.' He turned to Judie and said, 'You'd better stay with your boyfriend.'

Judie turned without answering him. He watched her and there was a strange look in his eyes. It wasn't remorse. I think perhaps it was regret – a sudden sense of sadness for what might have been. Gerda had recovered consciousness and was staggering to her feet. I got two of the men and we picked Howe up. He was just beginning to come round. His upper lip was swollen and pulpy and his right arm was bruised, otherwise he seemed all right. The rest of the crews had already moved up the slope of the ice ledge. We followed.

Bland took no chances with the men. He got right on with the issuing of tents and stores. I imagine he picked the best of everything for himself and his companions, but there was still plenty for us. I set the men to levelling platforms for the tents and cutting into the ice wall at the back of the ledge to provide extra shelter, for when it began to blow again it would be terribly exposed up there on that ledge.

As the day wore on, Judie's attitude began to worry me. Only once did she speak to me and then it was to upbraid me for not doing something about Bland when he'd faced us with his gun. When I tried to explain to her that there was nothing I could have done, she turned away angrily. Her face was pale and tense. She seemed bitter and resentful. It was almost as though she were blaming me for what had happened.

She and Gerda were given a tent to themselves. As soon as it was erected, Judie crawled into it. And that was the last I saw of her that day. Once when I passed I heard the sound of sobbing. I hesitated, wondering whether to go in and try to comfort her. But someone called to me and I passed on. Setting up camp on that ledge was a job that occupied all my attention. I had no time to worry about her.

That night, after the evening meal, as I lay in my tent talking to Howe and McPhee and Kalstad who shared it, Gerda crawled in. 'What are you going to do, Duncan?' she asked.

'Nothing,' I said.

'But you must do something.'

'Not yet,' I answered. She was sitting close to Howe and I saw her hand was holding his. It made me think of Judie. I asked Gerda whether she were all right.

'*Ja*. I think so. But she is not very happy.' She peered at me uncertainly in the half light. 'It is not very nice her position, I think. Also she feel you must do something. You make her speak to the men. She have to bare her soul in front of them all, so that they will follow you and not Bland. Now she think you must – ' She stopped uncertainly.

'Must what?' I asked.

'Please do not be offended, Duncan. It is so difficult, not in my own language. But she feel – that you must justify the men's faith, that you must take control. It – it is not that she do not believe in you. I am sure of that. But – but you must try to understand. It is terrible for her, this position.'

'What does she expect me to do?' I asked harshly. I was very tired.

'I do not know. She is not clear in her mind, I think. You see, it is all a terrible muddle for her. Bland is her husband. She know he murder her father. She is in love with you, and Bland, whom you save from dying alone, now controls everything.'

'Gerda's right,' Howe said, his words blurred through his thickened lips. 'They're both right. We've got to do something.' That was what he had been saying before she came in.

'Yes, but what?' I demanded irritably. 'We've no weapons. Altogether Bland has three rifles and about a thousand rounds of ammunition. Also, he's not afraid to use them. There's no period of darkness in which we can surprise him. As for the men, they're well fed and for the first time for days they feel secure. When supplies get short and they get desperate, then we can rush Bland.'

'Perhaps it is too late then,' Gerda said. 'This berg may break out of the pack in the next storm. Then Bland will get away in one of the boats and stove in the rest. His one chance is to be the sole survivor.' It was almost as though Howe were speaking through her, but he remained huddled in his blankets, sucking at his swollen lips.

'We'll just have to wait,' I answered stubbornly. 'Don't worry. Time and the ice will wear him down. Anyway, I'm not risking anyone's life, my own included, in some premature attempt to regain control of the stores. I suggest you all get some sleep now.' And I rolled over in my blankets. Gerda stayed talking to Howe for some time. Then she left and there was silence in the tent, a silence that was dominated all the time by the grinding and crashing of the berg's advance through the pack, a violent pandemonium of sound that was paralleled by a constant quivering of the berg itself, a quivering that was felt through the whole body as one lay on the ice floor of the ledge. And then Howe produced an iron stanchion and with a file began working away at the tip of it. The rasp of the file and the grinding of the ice seemed to tear at my nerves as I fell asleep.

I won't attempt to give a day-to-day account of our sojourn on the iceberg. One day was very much like another, varying only in the intensity of cold and the strength and direction of the wind. For myself it was a period of loneliness and waiting. Technically I was in command. But it was not an easy command. The men of *Hval 4* were all right. I held them through Gerda. But with the others it was different. Even to the *Tauer III* men, whom I had commanded on the run out from Capetown, I was an outsider. Only the fact that they were Tönsberg men and believed what Judie had told them about her father's death kept them with us. Tempering every decision was the fear that some of these men might break away and join Bland. This became increasingly a source of worry as Bland's ration issue became less and the monotony of our existence grew. Bland had the boats and stores. They represented hope and a full belly. The men knew from Bonomi that in Bland's camp food and tobacco were plentiful. And once the men started to break away, it would become a stampede. Orders became little more than requests and all the time Judie kept to her tent and refused to speak to me.

I worried about Judie a lot. I worried about Howe, too. He took no interest in the work of the camp and made no effort to help. He hardly stirred from the tent. He was morose and silent, seemingly occupied with his own thoughts. And all the time he whittled away at the iron, working the end to a point with a double edge like a spear. The grating of the file seemed to rasp at my nerves till I could stand it no longer. 'For God's sake,' I snapped at him, 'stop it – do you hear?'

He stared at me sullenly and went on working at the tip of it. McPhee rolled over in his blankets, snatched the stanchion from him and flung it out of the tent. 'Noo, will ye let us get some sleep, ye crazy loon.'

Howe said nothing, but later that night I woke to the rasp of the file. I cursed him then, spending all my pent-up anger on him. He let me go on shouting at him and when I had finished he said quietly, 'What would you do if Bland had killed your father?' And then, as though he'd been bottling it all up inside him, he started to tell me about Nordahl, how he'd come to see him at Newcastle, how he'd bought him a boat when he was twenty-one, how he'd taken him out to Grytviken for a season. 'If I'd been his legitimate son he couldn't have done more for me. And then after the war he gave me this job. Do you think I don't know what I have to do? And I'd have done it, too. I'd have done it by now if it hadn't been for Vaksdal. I'd have shot him dead here on this ledge. But Vaksdal had to interfere, damn his bloody hide. Why did he have to stop me? Why didn't he let me do it then?' His voice had risen now. 'I had him. I'd only to pull the trigger. Bland would have been dead by now if it hadn't been for Vaksdal. Vaksdal deserves to die. If I can't kill Bland without Vaksdal, then I'll – '

There was a muttered curse and McPhee sat up. 'Will ye shut up, for Christ's sake.'

'I tell you, I'll kill them both if I have to. I'll kill them all if they –'

'Shut up, do ye hear!'

But Howe's voice went on and on, talking about killing, eternally talking about killing. I fell asleep to the drone of his voice and woke in the morning to the rasp of the file. It was enough to drive a man crazy.

I told Gerda what he was up to, but whenever she came into the tent he hid the stanchion under his blankets. When she asked about it, his face puckered up like a kid about to cry. He hadn't wanted her to know. I saw that at once, saw the struggle going on inside him between his love of her and the need to justify his existence by avenging the one man he'd loved. He wasn't really sane. Every flicker of emotion was mirrored instantly in his features. And when Gerda took the wretched thing away from him, he behaved like a kid whose favourite toy has been confiscated. He had it back by evening and was filing at it with desperate energy, till the rasp of it drove us nearly crazy and McPhee tore the iron out of his hands and flung it out over the ledge on to the ice below. Howe burst into tears then. But by next day he was at work on another stanchion. By then we were too tired to care and the rasp of the file seemed to merge with the grinding of the ice as we fell asleep in a coma of exhaustion.

It was on the 17th February that we established ourselves on the iceberg. A period of fairly good weather followed and to keep the men constructively occupied and to give them some constant glimmer of hope, however slight, I set them to work cutting steps in the side of the berg.

We maintained a constant watch, and each day this lookout was posted higher and higher as we laboriously cut our way upwards, until at last our lookout post was on the flat top of the berg. This was at about 120 feet above the pack. We did not attempt to climb the pinnacle, which rose another fifty feet. It would have been of little use to us had we done so, for we experienced almost constant low cloud and more often than not the pinnacle was lost in a swirling mist.

On 23rd February shortly before midday I was dragged from my tent by an excited lookout. 'There is smoke, *hr Kaptein*,' he said.

'Where?' I asked.

'*Vestover*,' was his reply.

I climbed the hundred and forty-seven steps to the lookout and there, just to the south of west, was a great column of smoke. It could have been frost-smoke. But the sea was freezing over now wherever it was exposed to the atmosphere for any length of time and all day the column of smoke continued to rise from the same spot. And that night, when the sun dipped just below the horizon, we could see a red glow under the smoke. The whole camp was in an uproar of excitement. The sudden thought of rescue was in everyone's mind. It was a hard thing for me to have to tell them that the only thing it could possibly be was the crew of the *Southern Cross* igniting the oil they had pumped out of the ship as a guiding beacon to the rescue ships. But even that didn't damp their spirits. If the survivors of the *Southern Cross* had decided to make a signal, then it must surely mean that there were rescue ships in the vicinity.

For two days everyone was cheerful and the talk was all of rescue. Then the gale hit us. It came up out of the south-west and flung itself on us with a banshee howl that drowned the constant thunder of the breaking ice, seeming to pin us by its very weight to the ice walls of the berg.

When the storm broke, our ledge was facing straight into it. Our situation would have been bad enough down on the ice. But up there, on an exposed ledge, we got the full force of the wind. And with the wind came sleet and snow. It was terrifying – the bitter cold and the constant noise, the inability to breathe outside our tents and the lack of hot food. It sapped our strength and damped our spirits.

No one spoke of rescue any more. In fact we hardly spoke at all. We were glued to the face of the berg, by the weight of the wind, like flies on a flypaper, and the snow piled up round us and froze, so that there was no longer a ledge. Drawing rations from Bland each day became a major expedition.

We lost a man during this storm. He went out with two others and never returned. They were *Tauer III* men, all of them, and though I questioned them later, I never really got to the bottom of it. They admitted to going down to the lower camp to scrounge extra rations from Bland, but they wouldn't say any more.

I think what really happened was that they went down there with the intention of deserting our camp for Bland's only to find that Bland didn't want them. That one of them disappeared over the edge was, I believe, an accident. It was easy enough to slip over in those conditions and whenever a party went down to draw rations I insisted on them being roped. At any rate, the two who came back suddenly became violently anti-Bland and infected their whole tent.

For six days we lay in a coma of cold and hunger, hardly daring to go out, the tents overcrowded, insanitary and wholly covered by a mixture of snow and ice. On the sixth day all was suddenly quiet. The wind had gone. And on that day, the men, led by the two survivors of that trip to the lower camp, complained to me about the amount of rations Bland had issued. They were getting desperate. Bonomi had told them that food was still plentiful in the lower camp. I said I'd go down and talk to Bland himself. Howe dragged me aside then. 'This is what we've been waiting for,' he said.

But I knew what that would mean. 'If we led them amok like that,' I said, 'they'd pillage the stores. Three men eating well doesn't make much of a hole in rations being doled out for over forty.'

'It's the chance we've been waiting for,' he insisted. His eyes were sunk deep in their sockets and feverishly bright.

'No,' I said.

I went down the ledge before he could argue further. Bonomi was standing by the barricade of frozen snow that marked the boundary between the two camps. I called to him. 'I want to speak to Bland,' I said.

He put his finger to his lips. 'I wish to speak with you.'

'Well, what is it?' I asked. I didn't want to talk to him. I felt he was a toady and he looked sleek and well fed by comparison with the wraith-like figures who had crowded round me a moment ago demanding more food.

'I wish you to know that Bland is becoming frightened,' he said. 'All the time I am telling him the men are getting desperate and how they believe he killed Nordahl and rammed your ship. At first he would tell me to shut up. Once he strike me in anger. Now he sits morose and uneasy and all the time I am telling him how desperate the men are become. I do not think he sleep well any more.'

'Is this true, Bonomi?' I demanded.

'*Madonna mia!* Do I trouble to tell it to you if it is not true? I tell you, he is becoming desperate. He is hoping all the time that the iceberg break out of the pack. The storm makes him hopeful. But now he no longer have any hope of that. I think he abandon the camp soon. There is only twenty-five more days of food left and he does not dare to reduce the rations any more.'

'Go and tell him I want a word with him,' I ordered.

He hesitated, looking a little crestfallen. I think he

had expected me to congratulate him on his Machia-
vellian campaign.

Perhaps I should have, for when Bland came up
the slope towards me I saw his confidence was broken.
He looked well fed, but his eyes were sunk into their
sockets and his body seemed slack. His gaze did not
easily meet mine. 'Well?' he said, with an attempt at
self-assurance.

'The men are complaining about the rations,' I
said.

'Let them complain,' he said.

'There's no rationing, I believe, down in your
camp,' I accused him angrily.

'Why should there be?' he answered. 'They made
the choice.'

'They're getting desperate,' I told him. 'If you're
not careful they'll rush the stores. You know what that
means, don't you, Bland?'

He passed his tongue quickly over his chapped lips.
'I'll shoot anyone who attempts to rush us. Tell them
that, Craig. And tell them also that it's not my fault
we're short of food.'

'They'll believe that when they know that you're
on the same scale of rations as they are,' I answered.
'How many days' supply is left? Bonomi says only
twenty-five.'

'Damn that little bastard,' he muttered. 'He talks
too much.'

'Is that correct, Bland?'

'Yes. They'll get the present scale of rations for
twenty-five more days. That's all. Tell them that.'

I made a quick mental calculation of the quantity of food four men, unrationed, would consume in that period. 'I want thirty days' rations for my men, three boats together with our full share of stores and navigating equipment by nightfall,' I said.

He stared at me and I saw he was scared at my tone. 'If you're not careful, Craig, I'll cut off rations completely.'

'If what I've asked for isn't ready at this barrier by 18.00 hours tonight, I won't answer for the consequences. That's an ultimatum,' I added, and left him to think over what I'd said. If Bonomi had told the truth, and it certainly looked like it from Bland's manner, then he'd do as I'd demanded.

I told the men what I'd done. For the first time in days I saw them grinning. 'But it doesn't mean the end of rationing,' I warned them. 'It just means that we shall control our own rationing.'

The men gathered in hungry groups at the snow barrier. I saw Bland watching them uneasily. Just after midday the men cheered. Down in the lower camp Bland's two mates and Bonomi had started humping stores. Bland himself kept guard with his rifle. We broke down the snow barrier and boats and stores were run into the upper camp. I put McPhee in charge of stores and Gerda in charge of food. Without Gerda, I think the men would have broken into the food in one glorious orgy. We were all desperately hungry.

The end of the month came and went with only the entries in my log to mark the passage of time. There was a period of darkness at night now, and each day this period lengthened with amazing rapidity. But though the weather was calmer, in ten days I only managed to shoot the sun once. My calculations gave me a position of 63.31 S. 31.06 W., just about 230 miles nor'nor'east of the position at which we had abandoned *Hval 4*. It gives some idea of the rate of drift.

All this time Howe had been working away at his stanchion, working secretly for fear that McPhee would send it flying over the edge after the other one. Every time either of us or Gerda came into the tent, he hid it from us and lay there, feeling it with his hand, watching us with a guilty smile on his face.

Apart from this and our general situation, Judie was a source of worry. Her attitude was an additional weight on my mind, so that I found it very hard to shake off the increasing periods of depression. She hadn't spoken to me since the day we had reached the ledge. She seemed to have withdrawn into herself, into a state of more or less blank misery. Gerda told me that she sometimes woke up in the night to find her crying and murmuring her father's name.

'You must do something,' Gerda said to me one day. 'If you do not. I think she will just fade away.' That was on 8th March. I went to Judie's tent and tried to speak to her. She looked very pale and thin and her eyes were huge in their sunken sockets. She stared at me without a word as though she didn't recognize me. I told Gerda to feed her some of the precious meat extract that had been included amongst the rations Bland had handed over to us. I left the tent in a mood of utter despair.

That was the day the aircraft flew over us. It was an American plane, the star markings plainly visible as it passed over at about 500 feet. We had nothing to signal with and half blanketed in snow on the sheer flank of the iceberg it was hardly surprising that they did not see us. We piled inflammable stores together and kept constant watch in a fever of excitement and renewed hope. Two days later we saw another plane, away to the south. I picked it up in the glasses, but it was too far for our smoke to be visible and I would not give the order to ignite our precious reserves of fuel.

Sleet and snow followed and we never saw another glimpse of the search planes. The monotony of hunger, cold, and dying hope settled on the camp.

Once in the middle of the night I was woken by one of the lookouts who told me Howe had passed him without a word making for the lower camp. We found him halfway down the ledge, standing quite still, the spear-sharp stanchion gripped in his hand. He didn't move as I came up to him. He seemed lost in his own thoughts and in the cold light of the stars I saw the conflict inside him written on his face. He must have been standing there for some time, for he was so stiff with cold that he could hardly move. He let me take the weapon from him and as I led him back he was crying. He would have done no good anyway, for I saw a movement down in the lower camp and knew that a guard was posted. I called Gerda and left him with her.

There were no storms now. Just the everlasting glare of low cloud and the nights lengthening with the increasing cold. The steadily falling temperature was magnified by lack of food and our decreasing resistance. Life became a monotony of waiting for the end, without hope. The men no longer looked hungrily at the lower camp, for through Bonomi we knew that their ration scale was as low as ours. Daily I checked the stores and watched our meagre reserves of food dwindle. The lookout no longer searched the sky for planes, but peered at the ice through eyes inflamed by the constant glare, searching for some sign of life – seal or penguin, anything that would do for food. The movement of the berg through the ice gradually slowed. Everything was much quieter; the silence of death seemed to be settling over us. No pressure ridges sent their roaring battle challenge thundering over our precarious perch. All round us stretched a silent, lifeless waste. Our fuel was almost finished. Soon we should have nothing hot. Without any hot drinks, life would quickly desert us.

The 19th March carries the following entry in my log: *Reduced rations still further. Greig dead. Broken rib probably pierced lung. Has been weakening for a long time. Slipped his body over the edge as though burying at sea, none of us having the strength to cut a grave in the snow, which is hard like ice. Very cold. Wind has dropped and iceberg now stationary in pack. No hope now of breaking out to open sea.*

I knew it was time for the last desperate effort I had been planning. Gerda apparently had the same thought. She came to my tent next morning. As she sat there in the dim light I was surprised to see how much weight she had lost. She was almost slim. Howe was with her, thin as a wraith under the bulk of his clothes, his ugliness lost in the aesthetic sunken appearance of his features. He reminded me somehow of a modern artist's impression of Christ on the cross.

'Duncan. It is time we do something,' Gerda said. 'We cannot just stay here, waiting for death.'

I nodded. 'I've been thinking the same thing,' I said.

'Anything is better than to die without effort. I think soon I go to join my father.' She paused and then said, 'It is quiet now. We can go down on to the ice. The *Southern Cross* was per'aps fifteen, not more than twenty miles from us when she sink. Per'aps my father is alive. I do not know. But I must go and see.'

'You realize we've drifted nearly 250 miles from the place where the *Southern Cross* went down?'

'*Ja, ja.* But they also will have drifted. I think perhaps we do not find them. But I must try.'

'Don't forget we've been on this iceberg,' I said. 'We've been moving steadily through the pack for days. Suppose there are some survivors, they'll be a lot more than twenty miles away. You'd never make it. You're too weak.'

She shrugged her shoulders. 'I also think they will be a long way away. Also, we cannot be sure in what direction they now are. But I must go. Per'aps I am

too weak as you say. But it is the spirit that is important. My spirit is strong. I shall go to search for my
father.'

There was no point in arguing. I could see she had
made up her mind. 'And Howe?' I asked.

Her face betrayed no emotion. She knew it meant
his death. He would die first and she would have to
watch him die. But she never flinched. She just said,
'Walter comes with me.'

I could see they had been over this together. Their
minds were made up. In their faces was a sort of glow
of exaltation. I almost loved Howe's ugliness in that
moment, for he wasn't ugly – he was beautiful. His
spirit, purged of all bitterness and cynicism by Gerda's
love, shone through his features and transformed
them.

I lay back, not saying anything, but going over in
my mind something that had been there for a long
time. At length I sat up. I was looking at Howe, wondering how he'd take it, hating myself for having to
do it. 'Walter,' I said, using his Christian name for the
first time. 'You're not strong – physically. Whatever
your strength of will, you know you will die before you
reach the position where the *Southern Cross* survivors
might be. You know that, don't you?'

His eyes clouded. The glow died out of him. He
knew the drift of my words. He nodded slowly, and
there was a queer resignation in his face. It was as
though I'd killed his spirit. 'You think I should say
good-bye to Gerda here?'

'Are you prepared to if it would give her a chance

of reaching her father – and give us all just a chance of preserving life a little longer?'

'Yes,' he said, his voice scarcely audible.

I got up then and crawled out of the tent, Gerda clutching frantically at me, pleading to know what I intended to do. I think she was a little scared at the thought of making the journey without Howe. He was now the source of her strength. I said, 'Wait,' and called the men together, those that could still crawl out of the tents. The air was cold and still as they assembled round me.

'You know there is food for only a few days more?' I said.

They nodded.

'I checked the stores this morning,' I went on. 'On your present rations there is food for seventeen more days. That is all. After that there is nothing. We have seen no sign of any living thing in all this time. Unless we get food and fuel we shall die.' They stood there, dumb – stunned by having what they all knew put bluntly to them in words.

'Gerda Petersen wishes to try and reach the position of the *Southern Cross*,' I went on. 'She wishes to know whether her father is alive. She has the right to go, if anyone does.' They growled agreement, waiting for me to continue.

I then told them what I planned to do. 'The *Southern Cross* unloaded stores on the ice before she went down,' I said. 'She had a big cargo of whale-meat. This and blubber would have been transferred to the ice. If there are any survivors, then they will have meat and fuel. I intend to try and reach them. It is a desperate chance, and you must decide whether you agree to my going. We have no hope of reaching them in our present condition. The party, which should consist of three, must be properly fed for at least two days. That and the rations they will have to take with them will cut your own food supplies by about three days. It is up to you to decide whether you wish to take this chance.'

The men nodded and began to talk amongst themselves. Gerda stepped forward and said, 'Whatever you decide I must go. I do not need your food.'

The men stared at her. Then one old man from her father's ship said, 'We will not let you go without food. *Hval 4* will give you part of their rations.'

The men of her own crew nodded agreement, their eyes kindled – not by hope, but by their sacrifice for something they thought right and good.

McPhee stepped forward and said, 'Will ye tell us, sir, who ye'll be taking with ye?'

'Yes,' I said. 'Kalstad, if he agrees to come.' And then I added, 'Before you decide, let me warn you that there is little hope in this and we shall almost certainly die on the way. But it is a chance, and we should take that chance, however slight, before we are too weak to attempt it.'

'I will kom,' said Kalstad.

'Good,' I said, and asked the men for their decision. They didn't say anything, but I saw one of the stewards had gone to prepare a meal. They were all grinning excitedly like children. They made of their sacrifice a sort of festival. They crowded round the cook-pot, advising, offering more food. Gerda was crying, her eyes starry, and she went amongst them, thanking them, kissing them in her excitement and her sense of their innate kindness. She thought that they were doing it for her, and not for any desperate hope of relief – and I'm not at all sure she wasn't right. Rough men have a way of showing their love with inordinate sacrifice, and there wasn't a man who hadn't gained strength and courage from her indomitable cheerfulness.

So it was arranged and for two days the three of us fed like fighting cocks. I could literally feel the strength flowing back into me. It coursed with the blood through my veins. Depression was thrown off. I even had some hope. And the cold receded. Kalstad grew taller and more cheerful. And as we were fed up, the rest of the men seemed to shrink into sunken-eyed ghosts by comparison. The air of cheerfulness was kept up at a forced and artificial level as the men crowded round us to watch us eat, trying desperately to hide the hunger fever in their eyes and the saliva that drooled from their lips at the sight of so much food.

On the evening of the first day on full rations, something happened which should have warned me what Bland was planning. Bonomi came into our camp and asked to speak to me. He looked shrunken and cold and very frightened. He pleaded to come and join our camp. 'They eat everything,' he cried wildly. He was almost in tears of self-pity. 'They will give me nothing, and they eat and eat. Soon there is nothing left. I am 'ungry and I do not wish to be cook to them no more.'

'That's a matter for you to sort out with Bland,' I said. 'You've done pretty well out of being their cook so far.'

'*Si, si.* But now they will give me nothing. Nothing, I tell you.'

'Better go and talk to Bland. He holds your rations.'

'But he will give me nothing.'

'It's a matter between you and Bland,' I repeated. 'Go and sort it out with him.'

I am afraid I was rather brusque. My mind was on more vital things than Bonomi's rations. That morning we completed the building of a really good light sledge. We turned in at midday and the evening meal was served to us in our blanket sleeping-bags. One more day at Iceberg Camp then we should be out on our own, trekking across inimitable wastes of ice searching for the *Southern Cross* Camp. We didn't know where it was. We didn't even know whether it existed. We should just have to go on and on until the end came. It was a frightening thought – more frightening now that our bellies were full and we had the energy to hope. The three of us were together now in my tent and we talked interminably of the best possible route, little knowing that the route would be chosen for us.

I was wakened very early the following morning by somebody shaking me and calling my name. For a moment I thought it was time for us to leave. But then I realized that it was not until the next day, the 22nd, that we were starting out. I opened my eyes to find Bonomi bending over me. '*Capitano. Capitano.* They 'ave gone. They 'ave gone and they 'ave leave me nothing. Nothing at all.' He was excited and scared.

I sat up. 'Who's gone? What are you talking about?' I demanded.

'Bland,' he cried. 'Bland is gone and he take all the rations, everything. He is down on the ice – he and Vaksdal and Keller. Come and see if you do not believe.'

I crawled out of my tent and stood in the cold stillness of the ledge, shielding my eyes from the glare and trying to see what Bonomi was pointing to. It was an incredible morning. The sun was a blood-red orange away to the north-east, the sky a sort of greeny blue and all the ice was tinged with silken pink, like a damask quilt. 'There. Do you see?'

I followed Bonomi's pointing finger and saw three figures moving across the ice – three tiny figures dragging a sledge. They had their back to the sun and they were headed towards the position where the *Southern Cross* might be expected to be. I ought to have realized what it had meant when Bonomi had said that Bland and the two mates were eating full rations. Bland had finally despaired of the iceberg breaking through to the sea and had started westward in search of the *Southern Cross* Camp or the rescue ships which might still be searching on the edge of the pack.

Bonomi's excitement had roused the camp. One by one the men stumbled out into the satin-pink morning and stared at the three figures moving slowly across the ice below. I remember one man said, 'I think perhaps you do not go now, *Kaptein*. They have more food, those three. If anyone reach the *Southern Cross* Camp they will. There is good hope now.'

Howe heard him and he said, 'If Bland reaches the *Southern Cross* Camp, no rescue party will come here. He's gambling on being a sole survivor. That's the only way he can save himself from being hanged for murder.' He turned to me. 'Craig,' he said, 'you've just got to get there. Don't let him beat you on the last stretch. You and Gerda have got to reach the *Southern Cross* Camp.'

It meant that we should have to follow Bland's tracks. I had no illusions about the man. Somewhere along the route he would abandon Vaksdal and Keller. And if he did reach the *Southern Cross* Camp and we didn't, then there'd be no rescue party for the survivors on the iceberg.

The three of us remained in the tent all day, conserving our energies and eating enormously. We'd talk over our prospects, possible routes, what would happen if we caught up with Bland; then we'd drowse, only to start talking about the same things as soon as we woke. Lying there, warm and well fed, the iceberg assumed the friendliness of a home. In contrast, the trek that was to begin next day seemed more and more frightening.

That night, shortly after our evening meal, the flap of the tent was pulled back and Judie's voice, very low, almost scared, said, 'Can I come in a moment, Duncan?'

She crawled in, caught hold of my hand and fell, sobbing, into my arms, her cold cheek against mine, her body trembling. At length she said, 'I have been so stupid. All this time – I have wasted it, lying in my tent being miserable. And now – ' She kissed me and lay close against me, quietly crying. It was as though Bland's departure had freed her from the thing that had lain so heavy on her mind.

At length she said, 'You must sleep now. I shan't watch you leave tomorrow. I'll say good-bye here.' She kissed me, her fingers caressing my beard. Then she said, 'I don't think we shall meet again, Duncan – not in this world. Will you please remember that I – love you – always. And I'll be with you out there – if it helps.' She stretched her hand across to Gerda. 'Good-bye, Gerda,' she said. 'I wish I were coming with you to find *my* father.' She kissed Gerda. Then she kissed me again. The flap of the tent dropped back. She was gone and I'd only the salt of her tears on my face to remind me she had been in the tent.

Gerda touched my hand. 'You must get through, Duncan, for her. You must go on, whatever happens. You understand?'

I didn't say anything. I understood what she meant. Decisions like that couldn't be taken in the comfort of a full stomach and a warm tent. That was for the next day and the days and days of weary ice that lay ahead.

TEN

Next morning, as soon as it was light, we started out. We carried food for six days, a little tobacco, a pair of skis, one length of rope, a small primus with a little fuel, tent, blanket sleeping-bags and a change of clothes. All this was piled on one sledge. The morning was very still and our breath hung round us like a cloud of steam. The sun came up as we went down the ledge and the world turned gold with an orange band along the horizon. Most of the men turned out to see us off. They came with us as far as the bottom of the ledge and a ragged cheer went up as we lowered ourselves on to the broken surface of the pack ice. Our sledge was lowered after us and then McPhee, who had climbed down with us to help get the sledge on to the ice, gripped my hand. 'Good luck, sir,' he said.

'We'll be back with whale-meat within a fortnight,' I said. I spoke loudly and with confidence I did not feel in order to encourage the men. 'If we're not back by then,' I said to him privately, 'do the best you can.' Poor devil, it was a rotten job I'd given him. Gerda said I should have put Mueller, the second mate of *Hval 5*, in charge. But I didn't know Mueller. I did know McPhee. He was an engineer, not a whaler, but he had all the tenacity of the Scot and I knew he could be relied on to the bitter end.

'Och, ye'll find 'em,' he said. 'Dinna worry aboot us. Maybe the berg will break out into the open sea yet.'

I clapped him on the shoulder and picked up the sledge ropes. Gerda was saying a last farewell to Howe, who'd scrambled down beside us. Kalstad and I started out with the sledge along the track that Bland and his party had blazed. Howe called after me: 'Craig, you've got to get through. If Bland gets through alone . . .' He didn't finish, but I knew what was in his mind.

I waved my hand in acknowledgement and Kalstad and I began to wind our way through the hummocks of snow-covered ice. Gerda caught us up, and in a moment the three of us were swallowed into a strange world of ice – an iridescent fairyland of golden silence.

As we wound our way through the great humps of ice we caught occasional glimpses of the iceberg with dark figures moving back up to the ledge to the tents that showed black against the green of the ice as yet untouched by the sun. Once I saw a figure I thought was Judie waving to me. I waved back and then turned my face resolutely to the west. It was surprising how quickly the iceberg was lost to view in that broken plain.

I am familiar, as I've no doubt you are, with the great ice treks of Polar exploration: Peary's sledge run to the North Pole, Scott and Shackleton's desperate struggles and Amundsen's great dash to the South. In execution and design our trek across the ice was in no way comparable. I realize that. But in fairness to my companions – both of whom are dead – I must make it clear that what we suffered was little short of what the great explorers suffered in the most desperate of their journeys. We had no dogs, no special equipment, no finely designed sledges or proper clothing – not even real tents. And we were weakened by exposure and starvation before we started. We weren't explorers and therefore we had no great goal to lift our morale and keep us struggling forward. We were shipwrecked sailors with shipboard clothes, and sledges made out of bits of packing cases, an old piece of canvas for a tent and short rations. Our only goal was to save our own lives and those of the men we'd left behind on the iceberg. We were going to try and find the survivors of a ship. We weren't sure whether there were any survivors and we weren't sure of the position in which it had gone down. In fact we were on a forlorn hope – a last desperate bid for life in which I don't think any of us really believed.

Finally, there were none of the smooth miles of snow to be found on the Ross Barrier or the high land in towards the South Pole. True it was not so cold and the blizzards not so severe, but winter was coming on and it was cold enough in our weakened condition. And the area across which we were trekking was the area through which our own iceberg had smashed its way, leaving chaos in its wake – an area of jumbled, broken, jagged ice in which every step forward was a struggle. The skis were useless. We trekked on foot, one of the party pathfinding, the two others following, dragging the sledge.

But though we had soon lost sight of the iceberg owing to the broken nature of the pack, I remember the bitter disappointment I felt when on pitching camp that night I climbed to the top of an ice hummock and saw berg and ledge picked out clearly in the pink of the setting sun. It was like a fairy castle and seemed so near that I had only to stretch out my hand to touch it. I could even see the camp and figures moving about it. Gerda had some sort of a hot stew ready by the time I returned to my tent. We ate it hurriedly and turned in, taking our boots into our sleeping-bags with us to prevent them from becoming frozen.

In four days, trekking fourteen hours a day, we made about thirty miles. It doesn't sound much, but though the weather was good, the going was incredibly bad. We were trekking back over the pack through which the icebergs had ploughed their way. It was as though an earthquake had thrown the floes in all directions. In addition, the snow which half covered this fantastic litter of ice was partly thawed, particularly at midday, and time and again the pathfinder was only saved by the rope. Also, of course, we were weak after our long period of malnutrition, exposure and inactivity. I doubt whether we would have made thirty miles in four days if we hadn't been following the tracks of Bland's sledge.

It was strange, those sledge tracks. At first, we had regarded Bland as the enemy, something to be beaten in addition to the ice. We followed the sledge tracks for convenience, knowing we could leave them when it suited us or when our planned route lay away from his. But as we trekked on and on, those tracks gradually ceased to be hostile. We'd no gun. If we caught up with Bland he could kill us if he wanted to – and if there was any chance of reaching the *Southern Cross* survivors or being rescued by the search ships, I knew that that was what he would do, just as he would have to get rid of his two companions. And yet, though we never actually mentioned it, I'm certain none of us, after the first few days, would have thought of turning aside from the tracks and striking out on our own. With hard frosts and clear skies the tracks remained as sharp and clear as when they were made. And as exhaustion gripped us, they became our only friends in that white wilderness. Those two lines ran out endlessly ahead of us, our only contact with other human beings. Soon we were following them blindly, not caring where they led, buoyed up by the constant hope that somewhere ahead of us, round the next ice hillock, over the next limit of our horizon, they would connect us with the outside world.

On the fourth day Gerda began to show signs of weakening. Kalstad was limping from a swollen ankle and I was beginning to feel the stabbing pain in my chest again. We made little more than two miles that day, the snow having softened with the result that we sank through the honey-combed ice. We nearly lost the sledge in a crevasse. In a strange land of cold green caverns draped with almost golden icicles we pitched camp. Up to that time, I think we had been going faster than Bland, for early that morning we had passed his fourth camp site. It makes a lot of difference in the conditions we were experiencing if someone has blazed the trail for you. But we were pretty depressed that night. The only thing that encouraged us was that from the top of an upturned floe we had seen a dark line along the western horizon that looked as though it might be a water-sky, indicating open sea ahead. But how far ahead? It might be forty miles, and we knew we could not do very much more.

Next day Gerda was weaker. She showed signs of dysentery. Kalstad and I were also suffering from diarrhoea and beginning to weaken. Also the constant glare without sun goggles was inflaming our eyes, so that it was difficult to see. The snow held crisp that day and we pressed on fast, using up in savage effort the last reserves of energy. It was the first day of good going and we had to take advantage of it.

By midday I think we had made as much as ten or eleven miles. I know that when I climbed to the top of a hillock of snow-covered ice and looked back I could only just see the tips of the icebergs on the horizon to the east of us. They were all ships sailing in a line on the horizon's glare, insubstantial mirages that came and went, now expanding, now contracting. Only by taking a bearing could I decide which was our own berg.

After eating a biscuit and two pieces of sugar each we pushed on. The sun became a pale disc shining wanly through a curtain of mist. The air became colder and the world we moved through lost its colour. It was less painful to the eyes, but it was also less friendly. I think we must have gone on to the limit of endurance. And then suddenly we knew we could go no farther and we pitched camp.

In the stillness of early evening I thought I heard

voices. Imagination plays hellish tricks. That night as we lay in the tent Gerda whispered, 'Duncan. It is no good. You must leave me behind.'

I remember experiencing a terrible sense of shock. I hadn't realized how near the limit of endurance the day's trek had brought her. I remember I shook my head angrily. 'We'll go on together,' I said.

She caught hold of my arm. 'Please,' she whispered. Her voice, though weak, was urgent. 'It was selfish of me to come. I should have known I have not a man's strength. It is your duty to go on without me. I shall hinder you and always you must think of all those peoples on the iceberg.'

'We'll talk about it in the morning,' I said. And I got close against her, so that if she moved I should know. I was afraid she might walk out into the snow.

For a long time I lay half awake, thinking over what she had said, arguing against what I knew was inevitable. And at length I shifted my body away from hers and went to sleep. It was horrible. But I knew she was right. Too many lives depended on us. The fittest must always push on until the very end.

Some time in the night the wind rose and by morning it was blowing a blizzard. I looked out of a corner of the tent into a grey swirling void. Then I turned quickly to see if Gerda were still there. She was, thank God, for we could not move, and the enforced rest might enable her to make another day's march.

For three days the blizzard continued, and in those three days we finished all our food with the exception of five biscuits and fifteen lumps of sugar. The tent as in perpetual darkness. It was like being buried alive. We used an old biscuit tin as a bed-pan and just lay listlessly in our sleeping-bags, never stirring except to turn over to relieve the aching stiffness of our limbs.

The night it stopped we smoked our last cigarette. In the grey light of morning I wrote in my log: *There is now no hope and no reason to go on. The others, I think, realize this now. I shall not abandon Gerda. There is no point.*

We made an early start, wishing to take full advantage of what little energy we had been able to store up by lying still. For the first time there were no sledge tracks running out ahead of us. The snow was feet deep. I made Gerda put on the skis. The snow was crisp and fairly firm and we moved off with a feeling almost of cheerfulness. And round the first snow hillock we came upon the trampled snow of a camp. It had been evacuated that morning, for beyond the camp, sledge and ski tracks marked the new snow, stretching out ahead of us again and disappearing round the cornice of blue, snow-free ice. 'Bland?' Gerda asked as she stopped beside me.

I nodded. So I really had heard voices that night the blizzard started. It was incredible. For three days we'd been camped within a hundred yards of Bland and his party and not known it. 'They're probably not more than an hour ahead of us,' I said.

'What will happen when we catch them up?'

'I don't know,' I answered her. 'I don't think it matters much.' I didn't think there was much chance of our catching up with them. There were three of them to pull the sledge and both Bland and Vaksdal were big men.

'Perhaps we should strike away from their tracks,' she suggested.

But I shook my head. 'They're travelling roughly in the direction we decided on. The going is easier for us if we follow their tracks.'

So we went on, following the sledge marks through the fresh snow. Kalstad and I pulled the sledge and Gerda kept up with us easily on the skis. For two or three hours we made good progress. But about midday the sun came through. The glare was frightful and soon the snow began to soften and the going became harder as our boots broke through the surface crust. In some of the drifts we struggled forward through sifting snow that was well over our knees and had the consistency of rice grain. It took too much of our small reserve of energy and I made camp.

When darkness fell the stars came out in a clear, frozen night. It was terribly cold and none of us slept very well. The cold seemed to eat our under-nourished bodies. Gerda suffered agonies of pain in her stomach and Kalstad complained of frost-bite due to the fact that his boots, worn by the ice, were no longer water-tight.

The next morning was cold and cheerless with low cloud and a biting wind out of the south. We were late in starting. Gerda had no energy, no desire to move. Also, she had left her boots outside her sleeping-bag and they were frozen stiff, so that she could not put them on until we had softened the leather over the primus. When we did start we made good progress, for the cold wind had frozen the thawed snow of the previous day into an ice-hard crust. Ahead of us Bland's sledge tracks unwound steadily like a snaking line meandering through the snow hills of the churned-up pack.

'Soon we kom to their camp I think, *ja?*'

Kalstad was right. The snow hills gradually flattened out until finally we emerged into an almost flat desert of white where the pack had had time to settle before becoming frozen solid. And in this dead plain we saw the sledge tracks running straight, like parallel lines drawn by a ruler to a black patch. 'That is their camp,' Kalstad shouted to me. 'And they are still there. I see some peoples moving.'

I screwed up my eyes, trying to concentrate sufficiently on my vision to produce a clear picture. But the throbbing pain at the back of my eyeballs obscured my sight. All I could see was a dark patch in the virgin white of the snow, a patch that danced and wavered. I don't know why we pressed on so hard then. We didn't really want to join up with Bland. It wouldn't help us. And yet the mere thought of contact with other human beings in that grim waste of frozen snow spurred us forward. 'Your eyes are better than mine, Kalstad,' I said. 'Are they striking camp?'

'I think so,' he replied. '*Ja*. There is no tent.' And a moment later, he said in a puzzled tone, 'I do not see more than two people.'

'Only two?' I screwed up my eyes in an agony of concentration. The dark patch in the snow wavered and separated into two figures. There seemed to be nothing else but those two men. We threw ourselves on the sledge ropes. I think we were both in a panic that it would prove to be a mirage, that the two dots that looked so like human beings would vanish and the snow demons would laugh at us in the howl of the wind. And then faint across the frozen waste came a hail in Norwegian. We could see the two figures waving to us now. We shouted back and ran, slithering on the ice-hard snow towards them. Kalstad was limping badly, yet for a brief spell we must have been going forward at a good three miles an hour.

'It is Vaksdal and Keller,' Kalstad gasped.

'No sign of Bland?' I asked him.

'*Nei, nei*. Only Vaksdal and Keller.'

They came out to meet us, shouting and cheering and waving their arms. But when they were about a hundred yards from us, they stopped and were suddenly silent. We dragged the sledge up to them, exhausted, gasping for breath. They made no move to help us. They just stood and stared at us dumbly. Vaksdal looked thinner and gaunter and he had no boots on. Keller also had no boots. He had a knife and a piece of leather in his hand. 'Where's Bland?' I gasped, dropping the sledge rope and staggering slightly now that the impetus of moving forward no longer held me in a straight line.

'Bland?' Vaksdal's eyes suddenly blazed from their deep sockets. 'He is gone on. We thought you were a rescue party who have found our sledge tracks. How much food do you have?'

'None,' I said. 'A few pieces of sugar and a biscuit or two.' I sat down on the sledge. Now that I'd stopped exhaustion was taking hold of me. I just wanted to lie down and sleep. God, how sleepy I was! And the cold drove right through me. 'What did you say about Bland?' I asked, trying to concentrate my mind.

'He's gone.' Vaksdal's voice was angry. 'You are right, *hr Kaptein*. You are all right and Keller and I are fools. He is left us. This morning we wake to find the wind blowing on us and Bland pulling the sledge out of the camp with the tent thrown on top of it. We shout to him and he just laugh at us. We start to follow. But he has take our boots. My gun is gone, but Keller has his inside his blankets. He try to shoot then. But Bland is too far. We have nothing; no tent, no food, no boots, nothing. The bastard have left us to die.'

So it had happened, just as Howe said it would. He'd used them as pack mules, and when they were nearly fifty miles from the iceberg and there was a chance of reaching open water and rescue, he'd abandoned them. He'd chosen a lone death just as he had when he'd stayed behind at the *Tauer III* Camp in order to have the faint chance of coming out alive as the sole survivor. 'How much food had he?' I asked Vaksdal.

'For one man – perhaps three or four days. But very little, you understand.'

'And he's weak?'

'*Ja*. Too weak to pull the sledge alone for very far.'

'All right,' I said. 'Start pitching camp, Kalstad.'

The skis; that was the answer. I turned to speak to Gerda. But she wasn't there. I looked back along the line of the sledge track. Gerda was lying in the snow several hundred yards behind us. I unstrapped our gear and cleared it from the sledge. Then Kalstad and I started back. I don't think I knew how exhausted we were until I turned back for Gerda. It was only about three hundred yards, but it seemed miles that we dragged this empty sledge before we reached her crumpled figure lying face down in the snow.

She was alive. I could see that by the way her breath had thawed the snow around her nostrils. But she was quite unconscious. It was as much as the two of us could manage to lift her body on to the sledge. Her weight made a vast difference and I thought we'd never reach the spot where I'd off-loaded our gear. I don't think we'd have got her there, but for the fact that Vaksdal and Keller came out to help us.

We set up camp then and got some water boiling and made some beef tea. Gerda's return to consciousness was slow. The beef tea she retched up. But I managed to get a little of our precious brandy down her throat. And when she could speak, she kept on saying, 'You must leave me now, Duncan. You must go on.' Her voice was so urgent that she exhausted herself. To keep her quiet I told her how Bland had abandoned his two companions and gone on alone with all their stores. She didn't say anything when I'd finished, but just lay with her eyes closed, her face grey and puffy. I thought she hadn't heard. Then her hand touched my arm. 'One of you must go on,' she whispered faintly. 'Take the skis and go on. He must not get out alone. There are all those men on the iceberg.'

I said, 'Don't worry. One of us will go on.'

She seemed to relax then and I think she went to sleep. Kalstad pulled at my arm. 'Her spirit has outrun her body – I think,' he said. 'She is like a horse who is too willing.'

He was telling me she was going to die. I felt the tears at the back of my eyes. I should have known how terribly driven she had been to keep up with us and not be a burden. And still she had had energy to think of us and of those others back on that ledge. I crawled out of the tent. One of us must go after Bland. I thought immediately of Vaksdal. He was the strongest. And he could be trusted, now that he knew the sort of man Bland was. Anger at being abandoned to die like that would spur him on. But when I began to organize the thing, I soon discovered that in removing their boots, Bland had as effectually stopped them following him as if he'd shot them down as they lay in the snow. Whoever went after Bland must go on skis, and that meant well-fitting boots. Kalstad's feet and mine were much smaller than Vaksdal's or Keller's. To loan them our boots was, therefore, out of the question. The choice lay then between Kalstad and myself and Kalstad was suffering from frost-bite.

There was nothing for it. I should have to take what little rations remained and go on myself. 'Get your rifle, Keller,' I said, 'and some ammunition.' I packed a rucksack, and when I was all ready to go I crawled into the tent. I don't know whether Gerda was asleep or unconscious. She was quite still and her eyes were closed. I bent and kissed her. She moved slightly. Perhaps she knew I'd kissed her. At any rate, I'm glad I did and I hope she knew – knew that I was saluting a very brave woman.

I went out into the biting cold of the wind then. Kalstad helped me to fix the skis. I slung Keller's rifle over my shoulder. Then Kalstad lifted the rucksack on to my shoulders, the rucksack that contained for him all that was left of life. I was leaving them nothing but the remains of the beef extract and the primus with the last of the fuel. He clapped me on the back and said, 'Good luck, *hr Kaptein*.' I gripped his hand. Vaksdal and Keller looked on, sullen and morose. Since the discovery that we were not a rescue party and had virtually no food they had been in a state of miserable despair. Not even the fact that I was going out after Bland had stirred them.

'You are in command now, Kalstad,' I said. 'Look after Gerda Petersen.'

I turned then and set out along the track of Bland's sledge. I didn't look back. I didn't want to be reminded of the pathetic loneliness of that last camp. Gerda and the rest would die there. And somewhere out along the sledge track I was following, I, too, should die. I kept my eyes on those ruler-straight tracks and concentrated on the thought of vengeance.

Christian teaching would say it is a bad thing to go out to your death with only the thought of vengeance in your mind. I can only say this, that it was through that thought of vengeance that I achieved the strength to go on. It gave me a purpose. I no longer had any hope of finding the *Southern Cross* Camp, or even any hope that there was such a camp. I was going out to kill the man who had brought about all our deaths, who had killed Judie's father, rammed my ship and abandoned his two companions. I didn't stop to think that if there was no chance of him being rescued, then the ice and snow would do the job for me. I just knew I had to kill Bland with my own hands. That alone in my mind would justify my existence in that moment. And that alone gave me strength.

It was surprising how much easier and quicker I found it travelling on skis. The surface of the snow was crisp and firm. The skis slid forward with a crunching hiss, and only the constant driving of arms on sticks was tiring. And the going was over flat, snow-covered ice. In places it was ridged like the sea and here I had difficulty until I learnt to control my legs, for it's extraordinary how, in the unending white of limitless snow, it is impossible for the eyes to differentiate between an undulating and a flat surface.

Bland had, I reckoned, a three-hour start on me. I had left the others shortly after midday. Presuming that I could travel twice as fast as a man dragging a sledge, I should be up with him about three in the afternoon. I had, therefore, only a few hours' margin of daylight. If I wasn't in possession of Bland's tent by nightfall, then I should never see another day. A night in the open would kill me. I don't think I really thought about this. But it was there at the back of my mind, a spur to my body, for I knew that if I were to achieve my purpose, it must be done before nightfall.

Ahead of me the sky was dark, like the beginning of night. In contrast the low cloud behind me seemed dazzlingly white. The world was flat – flat like the Western Desert, but white; blindingly, eye-searingly white. And as I slid through this unending world of snow, the surface began to change. There were crevasses, under the surface. Without the skis I could not have gone a mile. The snow bridged innumerable gaps and I heard it crumble as I slid across. Then I was in an area of open fissures, gaps too wide for the snow to bridge. The sledge tracks began to wind between these crevasses and in one place I saw Bland had had trouble getting his sledge across where the snow had crumbled into a gap.

It was shortly after two that I saw the first open water in weeks. It was like a black lake and clotted thick with brash ice. I pressed on faster now, drawing on my last reserves of energy. Darkness was not far off and the patches of open water that were beginning to appear suggested we were nearing the edge of the pack. Bland had food for four days. There was still just a chance. And this ray of hope seemed to revitalize me.

I wasn't far out in my reckonings, for it was just after three when I sighted a small, black dot moving ahead of me. For some time the sledge tracks had been winding amongst black pools of half-frozen brash towards a small berg caught in the pack, and it was against the sheer green slope of this berg that the figure showed like a small dot dancing in the white void. It was painful to try and keep my eyes on it, and dangerous because it tended to make me lose my balance. After I'd had one fall through not watching my skis and had got up again with great difficulty, I ceased to worry about the mark ahead and concentrated on skiing as fast as possible.

When I looked again the berg was much nearer, but there was no sign of Bland. Presumably he'd passed behind it. Or had he seen me? Was he lying in wait? I left his tracks and circled away to the north of the berg. I soon caught sight of him then, not half a mile away and moving along the flank of the berg, which was a long one. Between us the snow lay flat, like a sheet of white. I drove my sticks into it, thrusting forward on a line that would converge with Bland.

He had almost reached the end of the berg when he saw me. He stopped and then his voice reached me on the cold wind. He was shouting to me and waving his sticks. Just as his companions had done, he thought I was part of a rescue party.

I unslung my rifle then, cocked it and slithered forward with the ski sticks looped over one wrist. Now that the moment had come I found my heart hammering wildly. I fought to steady myself as I went forward.

Something in the way I moved towards him must have warned him, for he suddenly stopped shouting and stood quite still, staring at me as I advanced on him. I was getting close now, and though the snow-glare made it difficult for me to see, he was outlined against the final shoulder of the berg and a good target.

But I was taking no chances. I closed him steadily, just as I would have done an enemy ship.

'Who are you?' His hail came to me quite clearly and I realized I was getting into the shelter of the berg.

'Craig,' I yelled back, and there was an exultant feeling inside me and I saw him stare at me for a moment and then dive for the sledge and his gun. But he didn't get up again and a moment later the thin crack of a shot sounded across the snow. He was firing from the shelter of the sledge. I turned then and circled to the west of him, cutting off his line of advance and reaching the shelter of the western end of the berg. He fired at me several times before I was out of sight, but I was a moving target and his bullets vanished into space.

The snow was heaped in fantastic shapes round the berg and I moved steadily through the sheltering hummocks towards the final shoulder. And here, round the corner of a hollowed cliff that gaped with green jaws filled with the white teeth of icicles, I saw Bland's sledge deserted in the snow. He was in the cover of the broken ice close in to the berg's flank. I crept slowly forward. There was the crack of a shot and a puff of ice in my face. I felt blood flowing from a cut. I brushed it away and raised my gun. I could see him now, peering from behind a fluted column of ice, his gun raised. I was just about to fire when I saw something moving behind him. It was travelling fast across the snow with a strange undulating movement like a well-sprung sleigh. It was a big, ungainly animal, tawny-coloured with brown spots, and although I'd

never seen one before, I knew what it was. It was a
sea-leopard, after the killer whale the most dangerous
inhabitant of the Antarctic.

Bland must have seen it at the same time, for his
gun swung away from me, and I heard the sharp crack-
crack as he fired. The huge beast did not check. He
fired once more, at point-blank range, and then it was
on him. He staggered as he was borne back and then
he fell with the beast on top of him.

I went towards him as quickly as I could over the
uneven surface. Blood was staining the snow crimson
at his side. I saw the beast move, jerking as though
injured. From a range of a few yards I pumped a whole
magazine into it. I went forward then. The beast was
quite still, lying across Bland's legs. I saw Bland move,
trying to free himself. He still had his rifle gripped in
his hands and he was trying to work the bolt. I tore it
from his grasp and threw it clear of us. Then I saw
that the huge brute's jaws were dripping blood and
there was a terrible wound in Bland's side. He started
to say something. Then he lost consciousness.

Looking down at him, with the big carcase of the
sea-leopard stretched across his legs, I suddenly
realized what this meant. It was the end of Bland, and
for us new hope. Here, stretched dead at my feet, was
thousands of pounds of fresh meat and blubber. Here
was life for Gerda – and hope for the future. Somehow
I'd got to go back, go back along those weary miles
loaded with meat and fat.

I got Bland's sledge and dragged it up close to his
body. As soon as I had erected the tent, I dug Bland's

legs out from under the sea-leopard and got him onto it. Then, when I had bandaged him as best I could, I got to work with my knife and soon I had a blubber stove warming the tent and big steaks of juicy meat grilling in the smoke. Bland couldn't eat, but I managed to feed him some of the hot blood. Meantime I ate more in a few minutes than I'd eaten in as many days. The blood seemed to give Bland strength for once he shifted his position and asked who had left the iceberg with me. When I told him, he grinned and said, 'Now we can all die in the snow together.' He seemed to relapse into unconsciousness then and I lay wrapped in a blanket, unable to sleep for the gripping pains in my stomach caused by unaccustomed food.

In the darkness of the night I awoke suddenly with a feeling of being choked. I sat up, gasping for breath and racked by violent coughing. I didn't know what had happened for a moment. Then I realized that the tent was filled with smoke. I turned towards Bland and found he wasn't there. Through streaming eyes I saw an orange glow against the canvas of the tent. I crawled out. Flames were leaping up out of the snow, licking over the body of the sea-leopard, reaching out with wind-fanned fingers towards the fabric of the tent which was already blackened and charred at one side. Bland lay in the middle of the flames, his face buried in the smouldering carcase, the snow steaming and beginning to form in crimson pools.

I pulled Bland clear and scooped up armfuls of snow, throwing it over the flames till they were completely smothered under a white drift. At first I thought

Bland had tried to stop the fire. But as I was smothering it, I saw an empty kerosene container and the primus with the stopper of its tank unscrewed lying in the snow. I knew then that he'd started the fire, started it in order to burn the carcase, burn the tent with me in it. Both pairs of skis had been thrust well into the blaze and had been badly charred.

When the fire was out at last I crawled exhausted back into the tent. To this day I don't know whether Bland was dead when I dragged him clear of the fire he'd made. All I know is that he was dead and frozen stiff when I went outside the tent in the morning. For all I know I killed him by leaving him out there. But I don't care. I only know I was glad to find him dead.

Fortunately I'd saved the skis in time. They were charred, but they were still usable. I cooked myself a meal. Then I covered Bland with some snow, and leaving the tent all standing, set out on the journey back, carrying Bland's skis and enough meat and blubber to give the rest of the party a good meal.

The wind had swung round to the west and was blowing hard. And as I started out I was conscious of a slight movement of the ice under me. However, the going remained good, and though a fine drift of snow had sifted across the sledge tracks, they were still visible and I reached the other camp without mishap just after midday.

It was then that I received the most bitter blow of all that ghastly period. Gerda was dead. She had died in the night never having regained consciousness since my departure. Kalstad showed me the mound of snow where they had buried her, and I stood there in the wind and cried like a child. Lying there, three hours' journey away, was the means of giving her strength. Her death seemed so unnecessary. Why is it always the nicest people that go? 'She look very happy when we burry her,' Kalstad said. 'I think per'aps she find her father. If he is also dead, then it is per'aps best. She love her father very much.'

Kalstad had trekked out along the sledge route the previous day and found where Bland had buried his companions' boots in the snow. We were able, therefore, to start out for the new camp as soon as we had had a meal. We all suffered from terrible pains at the unaccustomed food. Kalstad was sick and weakened rapidly. We were trekking straight into the wind, which was rising to gale force and gradually obliterating the tracks. It was a nightmare journey. The ice was heaving under us, breaking into fissures and growling as the broken edges of floes ground together under their covering of snow.

But for the iceberg I don't think we should ever have found the sea-leopard again, for by three o'clock we were struggling across a plain of virgin white, all traces of my ski tracks made only that morning having vanished. I saw the iceberg black against the pale circle of the westering sun and within an hour we were snug in two tents with a blubber stove going and meat cooking.

At the time I blamed Fate for what happened. But it was really my own fault. I should have remembered that there had been stretches of open water the previous day and realized how thin the ice was. We should have camped on the berg. But I don't know that any of us had the strength to drag tent and stores and sledges up on to the higher ground.

All that night the wind howled with demoniac force. I slept fitfully, racked with pain and conscious all the time of the increasing movement of the ice and the rising sound of the grinding floes. Towards morning I must have fallen into a heavy sleep, for I was woken by the ice splitting with the crackle of rifle fire. I crawled to the entrance of the tent, but it was dark and I could see nothing. I lay back and dozed off again to the sound of lapping water.

In the grey light of early dawn I was horrified to see water slopping in at the tent entrance. My feet were numb and the bottom of my sleeping-bag was frozen stiff. It was as though I were lying with my feet in a block of ice. I put my head out of the tent. The scene had changed completely. In place of the flat white expanse of snow-covered ice, I found myself looking across a black expanse of brash-filled water. All round us the ice had broken up into separate floes which drove against each other under the lash of the wind. As I leaned forward on my hands and knees the ice tipped slowly under me. I gazed with fascination as the water lapped the edge and slopped over my hands. When I drew back into the tent the water receded. I fought down a feeling of panic and pulled back the canvas at the other end of the tent.

I knew why the water had lapped over the edge as I'd leaned forward, of course, but it wasn't nice to have that knowledge confirmed. The two tents were floating on a raft of ice not more than forty feet across and we were in the middle of the open channel of water. The jagged edge of our floe fitted like a piece of a jig-saw puzzle to the main floe from which it had calved. The spot was marked by our sledge and the carcase of the sea-leopard. It was hard to see us drifting slowly away from all that meat. We had three or four pounds of the meat in the tent which we were keeping thawed. But it wouldn't last long. We were drifting away from the only source of life and strength we had.

I was just putting back the canvas to exclude the cold when I saw something – a fin moving slowly through the water, slipping along like a black dhow sail, making scarcely a ripple. It was a killer whale. As though attracted by my gaze it turned quickly and came straight towards our floe. The high dorsal fin passed out of my view and a moment later I heard the great beast snorting on the other side of the canvas. It was an ugly, pig-like sound and deadly sinister. I waited, scarcely daring to breathe. The floe trembled as the monster skimmed beneath it. More snorting. I put back the canvas and lay down, rigid and trembling, waiting, tense, for the moment when the whale would see us and tip the floe over.

That was what Gerda had said they did – peered over the edge of a floe and then tipped it up with their weight. How long ago that seemed now! I remembered how she'd teased her father that day I had come aboard *Hval 4*. I remembered other things she'd done and said – her indomitable cheerfulness, her guts, the way she handled the men. And I was comforted by the thought that at least she'd been spared an end like this.

The snorting was close beside me now. I lay still, not waking the others. Better that they should not know till it happened. It would be over quicker for them that way.

The snorting went on for what seemed eternity. Once the floe tilted, rocked violently, and I tensed, waiting for the sudden flurry of water, the cold and the snapping jaws. But the snorting died away. The floe rocked gently to the movement of the water. I relaxed slowly and with relaxation came sleep, a queer half coma of things remembered and things imagined.

I woke suddenly to the soft grinding of ice on ice and a knocking, juddering under the floe. For a moment I thought it was the killer whale back again. Then the soft grinding of the ice told its tale and I peered out, praying that we'd fetched up the same side of the channel as our meat.

But fortune was against us. About a quarter of a mile of water separated us from the sledge and the sea-leopard. Still, at least we had fetched up against a big, solid-looking floe. I woke the others and got them onto firm ice. Then we re-pitched the tents and cooked a meal. And whilst we ate I racked my brains for a means of getting across the water to the sea-leopard meat.

But it was impossible. The wind had swung to the south and the gap between us and our old camp was widening all the time. I didn't know whether to push on or wait in the hope that the gap would freeze over or the wind change. The break-up of the ice might mean we were nearing the edge of the pack. But when I mentioned this to the others, Vaksdal shook his head gloomily and pointed to the west. 'The ice-blink,' he said. 'I think there are many miles of pack yet.' It was true. There was no longer a water-sky to the west of us. Ice and cloud were merged together in a void of blinding white. Anyway, Kalstad was delirious and seemed too weak to move, and I decided to remain in the hope of being able to reach the carcase of the sea-leopard the following morning.

At some point during that timeless day, Kalstad woke me. His eyes were very big and his face was quite white. He wasn't delirious any more, but he was shaking slightly and seemed possessed of some sort of a fever. 'You must go on, *hr Kaptein*,' he said. His voice was very faint.

I shook my head. I knew what he meant. His voice was merged with the memory of Gerda's. 'There is no point,' I said.

'The others,' he whispered. 'I shall die here. You must leave me and go on.'

'You're not going to die,' I told him. But I didn't believe it. I knew we were all going to die.

As night came on we made a blubber fire, and though we practically choked ourselves with the acrid fumes, we managed to cook the rest of the meat. Kalstad refused to have any. Shortly after that I went to sleep. For the first time for days I slept like a log without dreams or any disturbance. It was more a coma than sleep, for I was numb all over with no feeling at all in my feet.

When I woke it was clear and sunny. A channel two miles wide separated us from the iceberg where the sea-leopard lay. To the north and west the pack seemed to have closed again in a solid mass. When I crawled back into the tent again I saw that Kalstad was dead. The skin of his forehead was waxen under the dirt. His mouth was slightly open in the stiff mat of his beard and his eyes stared at me sightlessly. I felt his hands. They were rigid and quite cold.

I roused the others, and we buried him there in the snow. For him the struggle was over. 'Now we go on, *ja*?' Vaksdal had seen the wide channel of water. He accepted the loss of the sea-leopard and the inevitability of going forward until we dropped. His eyes were running and horribly inflamed, so that they seemed rimmed by raw flesh. His long beard looked dirty against the transparent pallor of his gaunt face. Both he and Keller were suffering from the beginnings of frost-bite due to walking in the snow after Bland had taken their boots. Yet they were willing to go on. They were tougher than I was. I just wanted to crawl into my tent and die as Kalstad had died.

But somewhere there is always a last flicker of energy. We took one tent, our sleeping-bags and the rifle. Everything had to be carried. Before leaving, we ate the blubber off the stove over which we'd cooked the last of the meat the night before. Then I got out the compass, set our course and we started off, leaving

Kalstad to his lonely vigil in the ice, just as we had left Gerda.

We were all very weak. We took it in turns to use the skis. But soon we had to discard them, for we hadn't the strength to hold our balance, and the extra weight on our legs when we had to lift them over broken outcrops of clear ice was too much. The food we'd had caused us great pain. So did our feet. We were all suffering from frost-bite now. Keller weakened rapidly and only the fact that I refused to give in until the two Norwegians were beaten kept me going.

Our progress was painfully slow. Constant detours had to be made round patches of open water. But the ice was fairly flat. By midday we had made something like two miles, but by then Keller had to be supported between the two of us. The glare was like a red-hot needle against my eyeballs. I began to see things that weren't there. At times the landscape vanished into a blur of blinding white. It was the beginning of snow blindness.

If we'd only had some definite goal it would have given an impetus to our struggle. But there was no goal, only a vague hope that none of us believed in. There was no point in going on. I found myself dogged by an overwhelming desire to drop in the snow and let the relief of death steal over me. The longing for death became an obsession that completely replaced any hope of finding survivors from the *Southern Cross* or the store of whale-meat the crew had landed. It was a thing that had to be fought together with exhaustion, the griping pains of hunger and the aching stab of my eyes.

That night Keller wanted to be left behind. He said he was too weak to go on. But we couldn't leave him. There was only the one tent. We had to go on together or stop and die together. Vaksdal told him he was a coward. He didn't deserve to be called that, but it had its effect and he came on with us. There is an entry in my log made that morning which reads: *14th Day. We are going on. But this is the last day we can hope to move. Those on the iceberg will run out of food today. God help them.*

Barely able to stand up for weakness, we made about a mile that morning. My eyes had become so bad that I could hardly see to lay a course. Keller was barely conscious as he stumbled on with his arms about our necks. At times he was actually delirious as he walked, babbling incoherently in Norwegian. Vaksdal and I were in little better case.

Shortly after midday we pitched our tent for the last time. It was whilst we were doing this that Vaksdal seized my arm and pointed into the snow-glare. '*Pingvin*,' he croaked. Penguins? That meant food. I followed the line of his arm, screwing up my eyes against the glare. Several dark dots hovered in the mirage of ice, waving their flippers. I picked up the rifle. God give me strength to shoot straight. The gun was incredibly heavy. The barrel wavered. I could not get the sights to stay for a second on the target. I told Vaksdal to kneel in the snow and I rested the barrel on his shoulder. The penguins were waving their flippers over their heads and vaguely, like sounds in a dream, I heard shouts. The trigger was heavy. I couldn't see the sights properly and the shouts kept ringing in my ears.

Then suddenly I knew they weren't penguins. Penguins didn't wave their flippers over their heads. Those shouts were real. I dropped the gun and started forward. The figures melted, lost in a mirage of light that wavered uncontrollably. It was all a dream. There was no substance in those dark dots against the snow. I was delirious and imagining things. I knew this was the end even as I stumbled forward at a ridiculous, wobbly run. I heard hoarse raven croaks coming from my throat. Then I stumbled and pitched forward. The snow was soft. A wonderful lethargy stole through me. I knew I must struggle to my feet. But I hadn't the strength. And I didn't want to. I didn't want to struggle any more. I remember I thought for a moment of Judie, dying of starvation up there on the ledge of the iceberg. But there was nothing I could do about it – nothing. I was finished. And slowly – luxuriously – unconsciousness came like a blanket to cover me.

I woke to the warmth and the smell of food. A spoon was pushed between my cracked lips. My gorge rose as I tried to swallow the hot liquid. I opened my eyes. Pain flamed at the back of my eyeballs. Captain Eide was bending over me. I couldn't believe it at first. I was convinced that I was dead. But then he was forcing hot liquid between my teeth again and I knew that I was alive and that I'd linked up with the survivors of the *Southern Cross*. His face came and went in front of me and I heard a croaking sound that was my own voice. There were things I had to tell him. But I kept losing the drift of what I wanted to say as I slipped back into unconsciousness.

I'm told I slept for sixteen hours. When I finally got my eyes open I found Kyrre, the second officer of the *Southern Cross*, in the tent beside me. The things I'd been trying to tell them rushed to the forefront of my mind. 'They have no food,' I croaked.

Kyrre put out his hand to steady me. The violent urgency of my voice must have shaken him. 'It is all right, Craig,' he soothed me. 'Lie down and rest. Kaptein Eide left yesterday, you know, with nine men. We are to follow.'

'But he doesn't realize the urgency,' I cried excitedly. 'He's doesn't know they are –'

He smiled and patted my arm as though I were a child. 'He knows everything. You have been delirious. For hours you say nothing else but they have no food and will die soon if no one reaches them. You are still telling us that long after Eide has left. He has two sledges and a week's meat for them and he is making forced marches. He tell me to say – do not worry. He will get there.'

'But the gap,' I cried. 'He does not know there is a channel of water a quarter of a mile wide only a few miles to the east of us.'

'You tell us that also – many times.' Kyrre's hand pressed me back. 'You must rest, for soon we must start. We have sledges piled with whale meat and soon we must start.'

I thought of the long trek back over that frightful road to the iceberg. I knew I couldn't make it. 'Give us one man as guide and some food. We will go on to the *Southern Cross* camp. We shall only hinder you.'

But he shook his head. 'You did not hear what Eide tell you last night. The *Southern Cross* camp is abandoned. You see, though we have an enormous quantity of meat and blubber, we have no boats. They were destroyed. So we go where the boats are. Each day we make a journey with half the sledges and then return for the other half. When we are too weak for this we make a dump of half the sledges and go on with the others.'

'How many men have you?' I asked as I lay back.

'Forty-six, including those who have gone forward with Kaptein Eide.'

'The boats will not hold them,' I said. And added, 'Even supposing we ever find open water to launch them in.'

'That is so. But we are agreed that everyone must be together. While the ice holds we shall continue to make journeys until all the meat is with the boats. So we may perhaps survive the winter, if we must. Sometime the iceberg must drift out of the pack. Then the fittest will try to reach South Georgia, as Shackleton did, and bring relief. It is our only hope.'

'Is Colonel Bland with him?' I asked.

But he shook his head. 'Colonel Bland is dead. It was his heart. He died soon after Dahle reach us.'

'Dahle?' I stared at him. 'Do you mean the mate of *Hval 5*?'

He nodded. 'He is gone on with Eide now to the iceberg. He and two other men reach us early last month.'

'But – how?'

'It seems they were swept away from you in the ice. They are on a floe-berg. When it is quiet they find the *Tauer III* Camp. Then –'

'You mean the *Tauer III* Camp was still there?' I interrupted him.

He nodded.

So Erik Bland had been right. The icebergs would have missed him there. If he'd stayed he'd have had a chance of getting out alone. 'Go on,' I said.

'There is not much to tell. They get food and shelter there and survive the storm. Then, when the weather clear, they see the oil smoke with which we try to signal to aircraft and they join us. They are five days without food and the journey is terrible, I think. But they are all right.'

'What about you? What happened after the *Southern Cross* went down?'

'We lose our radio so we cannot talk with the rescue ships. Then we were caught by one of the icebergs, as you were. Only a few survive. Olaf Petersen and the others are dead. Then Dahle tell us how you are on a ledge on an iceberg with four boats, and Eide start out with volunteers to reach you. But they are caught in a blizzard and have to turn back. We were beginning a second attempt with all the men when we are lucky enough to find you.'

I was beginning to feel tired again. Behind Kyrre I

could just make out the grotesque, emaciated features of Weiner. As I went off to sleep again I remember thinking: *He's just like all D.P.s. You can't kill them. They're indestructible. It's always someone else that saves them, always someone else that dies.* And I thought how Gerda had gone and Peer Larvik and Olaf Petersen. The good ones, the fighters – they're always the ones that are sacrificed. I thought of Dunkirk and Salerno and Anzio and the ships that had gone down in convoys I'd escorted. It was always the fighters.

Next morning, after an early meal, all the tents but the one in which Vaksdal, Keller and I lay were struck and Kyrre set out with his men and the first convoy of sledges loaded with whale-meat. One man was left behind to help us. We were to lie in for a bit and then come on in our own time. We should have nothing to carry and only a single journey to make to the new camp, whilst the rest made three journeys over the same ground.

The trek east, back along the trail we had come, was painfully slow. For the first three days we just made the single journey from camp to camp. We carried nothing and could take our time, for Kyrre's men, when they'd pitched the next camp, had to go back for the second lot of sledges. The open water where we'd been parted from the sea-leopard couldn't have been very extensive. We made a slight detour to the south and saw no sign of it. For all I know the ice may have closed up again, or perhaps it had frozen over, for the air was very still and there would have been little movement of the water to break up new ice. On the fourth day Vaksdal and I were sufficiently recovered to pull our weight on the single journey. Keller was still weak. But next day he, too, was pulling the single journey, whilst we had progressed to the full three trips between camps. With an abundance of regular food my strength quickly returned, only the deadness in my feet and the pain in my side remained.

Slowly the line of icebergs came up over the horizon. I began to dread their approach, for when we reached them I should have to tell Howe about Gerda's death. And I didn't want to do that. Eide would have broken it to him. But he would still want to hear how it happened from my own lips. The thought of that meeting weighed on my spirits like the depression one gets after flu. It was going to knock him for six. I remembered how embittered he'd been as he soaked up the liquor like a sponge on the trip out from Cape-town. And then the change that had come over him whilst he was with Gerda. What could I possibly say to him? I remembered that scene on the ledge when he'd renounced his right to accompany Gerda. He'd committed her to my charge. I was responsible for her – not only to him, but to myself. The fact that we were without hope, certain we were going to die, did not help now. Only one thing consoled me; that was that she died without knowing that her father had been killed. But that wouldn't help me with Howe.

I could see his features quite distinctly as I trudged through the ice, leaning my weight on the sledge ropes. I could see the bitter look coming back into his face.

And when we got back – if we got back – he'd start drinking again. Drink was all that was left to him. It would kill him in the end, and somehow I didn't want him to go like that.

At last we could see the whole of our own iceberg. The sky was black behind it – a water-sky – and against the backcloth the berg stood out white like a giant pillar of salt. The pinnacle of ice on the top stood up free of cloud with all the sublime upthrust of hope that belongs to a church spire in a flat plain. With my inflamed eyes I looked through Kyrre's glasses and saw the ledge on which our camp should be. Perhaps we were too far away, but my heart sank as I saw no sign of life, no dark smudge that could be the boats and stores.

But at midday the following day – that is, on 9th April – we saw figures coming towards us across the snow. I thought: *My God! It's Eide coming back. They're all dead.* I wasn't worrying about Howe then. I was thinking of Judie and there was an awful ache in my heart. Then the figures were waving to us and shouting. My stabbing eyeballs couldn't recognize them. I dropped the sledge ropes and broke into a stumbling run towards them.

There were about half a dozen of them and the first one I recognized was Eide. I was sure then that the others were dead. He caught hold of my arm, grinning and slapping me on the shoulder. Then he pulled one of the others forward and the next instant Judie was sobbing and laughing in my arms.

And when I looked at her, she was no longer thin

and emaciated. She looked well fed and fit, except for the tears that ran down her cheeks. 'I thought you were dead,' she said through sobs of laughter. 'Then Captain Eide came and told us you were all right. Oh, Duncan – I didn't want to go on without you. I couldn't have faced it without you.'

I had my arms tight round her. She was trembling. The cold air seemed suddenly warmer and I no longer felt tired. 'The others?' I asked. 'Are they all right?'

'Yes,' she said. 'Yes, everyone's fine. Except Walter.'

'Except Walter?' I stared at her. 'What do you mean?'

'Two days after you left,' she said. 'Only two days – and thousands of penguins appeared on the ice round the berg. Migrating, or something. We killed over two hundred in one day and more the next. We were rolling in food. We tried to make signals. But you didn't see. Then Walter went after you. He went in the night without telling anyone. In the morning we could see him going out along the trail of your sledge. Eide says he didn't find you?'

'No,' I said. A great weight seemed to have been taken off my mind. Howe was dead. He was safe from the bitterness of life. He was dead and I didn't have to tell him about Gerda.

'There's open sea within five miles of us.'

I was thinking about Howe and I didn't take that in until she repeated it. 'We're drifting north and the ice is breaking up. If there's a gale the iceberg may break though the pack in a matter of days.'

I turned to Eide. 'Is this true?' I asked incredulously. 'Is there a chance of the iceberg breaking out?'

'Not only a chance,' Eide answered. 'It's a certainty. We'll be able to launch the boats inside a week.'

'And then?' I said, glancing round at the *Southern Cross* survivors.

He caught the drift of my thoughts. 'And then we split up. We have four boats. Four chances of getting help. The rest must camp on the iceberg. One of the boats will surely get through.'

I turned and stared at the iceberg. It looked solid enough, but the open sea was different to the pack. It wasn't going to be pleasant marooned on an island of ice swept by gales and the piled up waves of the South Atlantic. And those tiny boats! Winter was closing in. There'd be gale after gale. This area was noted for them. An almost constant holocaust of wind. What chance had they? The thought made me shudder. I thought again of the trip I'd just made – the futility of it. We had gone in the wild hope of bringing back meat, and two days after we'd left they'd had meat in abundance. Gerda and Howe need never have died, and Eide would have joined up with us anyway. But we hadn't known that. Just as now, we didn't know whether or not a rescue boat would sight us on the iceberg if we stayed there. And because we didn't know, we'd have to attempt the impossible and sail those flimsy lifeboats to South Georgia.

I put my arm round Judie's shoulders and pressed her to me. It was worth it for her sake. But – 'I hope to God Fate doesn't play us any more dirty tricks.'

She looked up at me quickly and I realized I'd

spoken aloud. Then she said, 'You're thinking of Gerda, aren't you?'

I nodded.

'She was a lovely person. But, you know, she wouldn't have been happy without her father. Walter couldn't fill his place in her life.' And then she looked up and smiled. 'I think we are all right now. Everything is going to work out.'

The sledges were moving forward again and we turned our faces towards the great castle of ice ahead of us – and the future. Behind the ice was the black cloud-scape that marked the open sea. And beyond was South Georgia. One of the men began to sing. It was a Norwegian song I'd heard them singing on board ship, something about going home. In an instant it was taken up by the rest of the men and the sledges slid forward to the swelling of men's voices, breaking the eternal silence of the ice with their challenge of hope and longing. The sound was thin in the limitless plain of pack ice, but it was indomitable and it sent a thrill of pride and courage through me. Judie was singing, too – singing for me, with her grey eyes laughing and her young body flung forward, straining on the ropes. And her words echoed in my ears – *I think we are all right now. Everything is going to work out.*

CHAPTER THREE

THE SURVIVORS

On the 21st April a radio message from South
Georgia put the name of the *Southern Cross* back
in the headlines of the world's newspapers. It was
from Jan Eriksen, manager of the whaling station at
Grytviken, to the offices of his company in Oslo, and
read: *Two boats containing survivors of the* Southern
Cross *arrived Grytviken.*

Two hours later a further message was received
containing the first news that there were survivors
marooned on an iceberg in the Antarctic. This read:
*Two boats each carried six survivors. Commanders:
Hans Eide, Einar Vaksdal. List of crews to follow.
Two further boats (Kyrre and Dahle) not yet arrived.
Sixty-seven persons, including Mrs Judie Bland,
marooned on iceberg in open water, position 62.58 S.
30.46 W. Four catchers dispatched to search for missing boats. On arrival station relief ship, Pingvin, I will
attempt to rescue survivors marooned on iceberg.*

Winter was closing in on the ice-capped island of

South Georgia. In two days the whaling station would have been closed and the place deserted. Eide had made it with just two days to spare. It was an incredible story.

The iceberg had broken out of the pack in a gale on 10th April. The ledge on which their camp was situated then faced straight into the wind. Swept by icy spray from the waves that thundered against the berg, they clung precariously to life for twenty-four hours. Then the berg swung round so that their ledge was sheltered from the wind. They had already decked-in the boats with pieces of packing cases and canvas. They now re-cut the ledge, and on the afternoon of the 11th when the gale had begun to subside they ran the boats down the ice slipway with the crews in them, letting them take the water like lifeboats being launched from a shore station.

In the mountainous waves and the almost continual gloom, the four boats were soon swept apart and separated. For ten days they drove northwards towards South Georgia, their scraps of sail driving them pell-mell through the water on the crests of the waves and hanging slack for lack of wind in the troughs.

Eide, in his radioed report of the boat journey, said: 'I have never experienced such hardship during my thirty-two years at sea. There was a crew of six to each boat. There was no place to sleep. We were constantly bailing for our lives and chipping away the ice that coated the boat and threatened to sink her. Only once was I able to shoot the sun and check my navigation. It was so cold that men froze stiff as boards at the tiller and could not move their limbs until they had been well rubbed to restore the circulation. By the fifth day we were suffering badly from exposure and there were cases of frost-bite. The fear that I should make an error in navigation, miss South Georgia and drive on into the Atlantic was constantly with me.'

They experienced one bad gale. And then late on the tenth day they sighted the south-eastern tip of South Georgia, and in the morning as they sailed up the northern side of the island, they saw Vaksdal's boat following about a mile behind them.

These were, in fact, the only two boats to get through. What happened to the others we shall never know. Maybe they missed South Georgia and drove on into the Atlantic. Maybe they were swamped or the men became too weakened to chip the ice off and they just capsized. The catchers sent out from Grytviken to search for them reported nothing, not even wreckage.

Meanwhile messages were pouring in to the *Nord Hvalstasjon*. The attention of the whole world had suddenly become focused on this lonely whaling outpost. Eide found himself with offers of assistance from a dozen different countries. But they were all useless. Within a few weeks the pack ice would have moved north with the winter and the iceberg would be beset again. There would be no hope of rescue then until next summer, and he knew that those on the iceberg could not survive the winter. His only hope was the *Pingvin*.

This little vessel arrived at Grytviken on the 22nd and began refuelling at once. It left in the early hours of the 23rd with Eide and Eriksen on board. Before he left, Eide had radioed a full account of the disaster and the names of the survivors marooned on the iceberg. This was the first intimation we had that a Scot, Duncan Craig, was in command of the survivors.

There followed an anxious period of waiting. The catchers searching for the two missing boats were forced by heavy storms to return to Grytviken. No messages were received from the *Pingvin*. The ship was held up by loose pack and heavy seas, and though we didn't know it at the time, Jacobsen, the captain, insisted on turning back early on the 26th. Only the pleading of Eide and Eriksen persuaded him to risk his ship and his men a few more hours in those terrible seas.

On the evening of that same day came the first piece of good news. A radio message from Grytviken reported: *Pingvin has sighted iceberg. Pack ice heavy and weather conditions bad*.

After that – nothing. For over twenty-four hours Grytviken had nothing to report. Newspapers began running gloomy accounts of conditions in the Antarctic in late April, and as the hours of waiting passed and still there was no news, fears grew that the rescue attempt would fail.

Then, just after midday on the 28th, the teleprinters began clacking out the news for which the public had been waiting.

ICEBERG SURVIVORS RESCUED. OSLO APRIL 28 REUTER: MESSAGE RECEIVED FROM STATION RELIEF SHIP PINGVIN STATES ALL SURVIVORS OF SOUTHERN CROSS MAROONED ON ICEBERG NOW SAFE. PACK ICE AND HEAVY SEAS DELAYED RESCUE OPERATIONS. SURVIVORS SAY CONDITIONS VERY BAD ON ICEBERG IN OPEN WATER OWING TO HEAVY SEAS BREAKING OVER LEDGE CAMP AND FREEZING. REUTER 1317

Well, that is the end of the story of the *Southern Cross* disaster. There is little more to add, except that now, just over a year after it all happened, a new *Southern Cross* is building at Belfast. It is to cost over £2,500,000 and is expected to be ready for next season. The South Antarctic Whaling Company still has its offices in Fenchurch Street. Only the list of directors has changed. Sir Frederick Sands, well-known financier, is the new chairman, and Duncan Craig is on the board.

Judie Bland is now Judie Craig. They were married in Capetown on their way back from South Georgia, and according to Craig most of South Africa turned out for the wedding. Besides being a director of the company, Duncan Craig sails as master of *Southern Cross II* when the South Antarctic's next expedition leaves in October. Eide, who was cleared of all blame for the disaster, is already in the Antarctic as master of another factory ship.

It is unlikely that Judie Craig will make another

trip to the White South. Already she is a mother and they have a charming house looking out over the Falmouth estuary, where they spend the summer months sailing. There is nothing to remind them of the terrible hardships they suffered except for a series of beautiful ice studies presented to them by Aldo Bonomi. And – most treasured of all – a picture of Gerda Petersen taken just before the start of the trek across the ice. It faces you in the wide entrance hall as you go in, so that no one can enter their house without meeting her.

All Pan Books are available at your local bookshop or newsagent, or can be ordered direct from the publisher. Indicate the number of copies required and fill in the form below.

Send to: Macmillan General Books C.S.
          Book Service By Post
          PO Box 29, Douglas I-O-M
          IM99 1BQ

or phone: 01624 675137, quoting title, author and credit card number.

or fax: 01624 670923, quoting title, author, and credit card number.

or Internet: http://www.bookpost.co.uk

Please enclose a remittance* to the value of the cover price plus 75 pence per book for post and packing. Overseas customers please allow £1.00 per copy for post and packing.

*Payment may be made in sterling by UK personal cheque, Eurocheque, postal order, sterling draft or international money order, made payable to Book Service By Post.

Alternatively by Access/Visa/MasterCard

Card No.

Expiry Date

Signature _____

Applicable only in the UK and BFPO addresses.

While every effort is made to keep prices low, it is sometimes necessary to increase prices at short notice. Pan Books reserve the right to show on covers and charge new retail prices which may differ from those advertised in the text or elsewhere.

NAME AND ADDRESS IN BLOCK CAPITAL LETTERS PLEASE

Name _____

Address _____

_____

_____

_____

8/95

Please allow 28 days for delivery.
Please tick box if you do not wish to receive any additional information. ☐